BLOOD RELATIONS

By

Edward Cohen & Kathy Cohen

For information contact :
Kathy Cohen at k.cohen@mac.com

Cover design by Allison East Moore

Publishing Consultant Jacque Hillman
The HillHelen Group
Jackson, Tennessee USA

Praise for BLOOD RELATIONS

“A well-constructed mystery with a knockout surprise ending.”

Kirkus Reviews

“BLOOD RELATIONS is brilliantly crafted all the way through—and the ending! NEVER saw it coming! Bring on the movie!”

Jill Connor Browne, multiple #1 NYT Bestselling Author of the SWEET POTATO QUEENS series

“Great read! You nailed the Southern dysfunctional family!”

Margaret Robbins, Executive Secretary, Mississippi Institute of Arts and Letters

“BLOOD RELATIONS offers a complex, but not unrealistic plot that grips readers from beginning to end, and just when readers think they know who actually killed the beautiful Laura ... surprise, surprise! But as engaging as the plot [is] and trying to figure out who did the deed are the personalities of the key characters.

“If BLOOD RELATIONS sounds like your kind of reading, don’t hesitate to pick up this novel: you won’t be able to put it down.”

READERS’ FAVORITE REVIEW. Five-stars.
By Viga Boland

“A twisted legal thriller which satisfies with as much grit as intrigue, BLOOD RELATIONS by co-authors Kathy

Cohen and Edward Cohen keeps you rapt and wound tight till its shocking ending."

BESTSELLERSWORLD REVIEW.
By Lisa Brown-Gilbert.

"A suspenseful novel with detailed settings and complex relationships."

MISSISSIPPI LIBRARY ASSOCIATION SUMMER NEWS 2019
By Justin Easterday

"BLOOD RELATIONS is a love letter to New Orleans disguised as a legal thriller.... A stellar whodunnnit. The pages flip like mad as the Cohens blend in a parade of twists and turns. The big reveal will shock you. Please turn this novel into a movie!"

THE MISSISSIPPI CLARION-LEDGER USA TODAY NETWORK
By JC Patterson

"The authors have created that rare intelligent and intricate thriller complete with masterful turns of phrase and sly humor and characters that breathe in your ear as you follow the dark pathways they tread. This novel is as good as it gets."

Mel Layton, Former Sr. VP of Acquisitions and Productions, Republic Pictures Corp.

ONE

THAT SUMMER IN NEW ORLEANS WAS the hottest in memory. Rain steamed off the sidewalk and people shimmered surreally through the haze. Except for tourists and criminals, no one voluntarily went outside. I stood in the dark in Laura Niles' bedroom, only my second time there.

All was silent except the air conditioning, which hummed relentlessly. Though my shirt was soaked with sweat, I began to shiver. My breathing was fast, and I fought to control my thoughts. Don't panic, don't run, don't touch anything. Breathe slowly! My life would depend on what I did next.

I stared at Laura, who lay naked in bed, her hands entwined above her head. A rivulet of blood dripped from her long auburn hair. A jagged scrape marred her right cheek. On the floor lay her blood-soaked gown. Blood spatters climbed from the white dust ruffle of her four-poster bed all the way up to the canopy.

A clot of terror gathered in my throat. My fingerprints could be on doorknobs and—where else? The phone? No, it was safe. What else? The bathroom! I went in and, with my shirttail, wiped off the doorknob and sink handles. Hurrying out, I grabbed the knob and then had to wipe it off again.

I opened Laura's top dresser drawer and retrieved a photo, then took an engraved pendant from her jewelry box. I wiped the drawer knobs clean. Moving back to the bed, I looked to see if she was wearing jewelry. None. Beside her bed, her answerphone message light blinked insistently. One! one! one! one! I pressed "erase" with the tip of my key to her front door.

Careful to avoid stepping in her blood, careful to wipe the remaining doorknobs clear of fingerprints, I hurried outside and, forcing myself to leave the shadows, crossed the lawn. Laura's fragile crepe myrtle blossoms, downed by the first September storm, still were vivid. I crushed them underfoot.

I drove down Saint Charles like a madman, unaccustomed to my new Jeep. My headlights caught movement. A large dog darted into my path, and I careened off the street to miss him before I broke down in gulping sobs.

A sharp knock on my window jolted me. I looked out at a young, wary cop staring in, one hand resting on his gun. Fear froze my breath and tears.

"What's going on here? Have you been drinking?"

"No."

"What's your car doing up on the curb?"

"Dog ran out in front of me."

The cop peered around the front of the Jeep. No corpse. No blood.

"You missed him?" he asked, waiting for an explanation as to why I was crying over a dog that lived. I tried but couldn't form an answer.

He'd had enough. "Would you step out of the car, please."

In two seconds he'd be asking for my I.D. I was only ten blocks from Laura's house. It wouldn't take the cops long to piece together enough circumstantial evidence to charge me with her murder.

"It's my girlfriend," I said, keeping my seat. "She's sleeping with my best friend." Tears flooded my eyes again, and they were real.

"Tough luck," he said, glad not to be me. His hand on the gun relaxed. "You think you're able to drive home in that shape, Big Guy? I'll be glad to follow you."

"I'll be okay." I was able to control my shaking until he walked away.

My Jeep took me to Audubon Park, my feet led me to the bench where I'd first seen Laura, my knees folded and dropped me onto the hard planks. With my sanity slipping away, my only thought was that I had to talk to Alison, my former girlfriend, former fiancée, former everything.

I drove to her house. It was late, just after 2:00, when I knocked. She got up and came to the door, her sleepy eyes pained by the light.

"What do you want?" Her voice was hard.

"I have to talk to you."

"After all this time? I've got a life now, Kyle. And you're not in it."

"I need you, Alison."

"See how it feels."

Sitting on the balcony of my French Quarter apartment, I rode that night to its death. Just past daybreak I went outside my apartment to wait in front of my garage. Cameron & Munger's van was to pick me up for our annual three-day retreat. The purpose—fellowship—had always been a joke and now was a macabre one. Munger would complain that Laura wasn't waiting out front. Who would be sent in to get her? God, not me.

The Quarter was deserted, as if chastening itself after a night of excess. A homeless man crept past me, a familiar figure I'd seen many times as I came home after a hard night of revels. We had a relationship, of sorts, bought with ten-dollar bills I stuffed in his styrofoam cup. My form of prayer. As he passed, dragging his bad leg, he looked up at me and I gave him everything in my wallet. It could've been a thousand.

Finally the van, with "Cameron & Munger, Criminal Law" in small, tasteful lettering on the side, swung into view and bore down on me. For a second I thought it might not stop.

My father, Jake, was driving. I could feel him watching me as I opened the door, his eyes flat and hard, the way I'd seen him stare down a thousand poor bastards on the stand. I climbed in back without a word. He began driving off before I even sat down.

All the firm, except Laura, were inside, grumpy and groggy. Tommy Munger sat with Jake up front, his long legs cramped even in the oversized van. He was silently studying a spreadsheet, one of his computer projections on how the firm would prosper upon adding new lawyers.

Behind him sat Ginger Allred, at thirty-eight still Tennessee-Williams sexy. She opened a box of doughnuts and picked over the pastries, finally settling on chocolate coconut, which would soon thereafter settle on her hips. Against all evidence, she seemed to sense some infinitesimal promise in me.

"What's up, loverboy?" she asked, out of Jake's earshot. She found my amatory life amusing.

I just shook my head.

"Jeez, Kyle, you look like death boiled over." Jeb Turnage winked. "Rough night, huh?" Turnage was thirty-one, not Supreme Court material but blessed with a ready smile. He agonized daily over his mutinous red hair and what he called his "goddam pink matching skin." He had lusted ceaselessly after Laura.

I stared out the window, the way I would on an airplane if seated next to an overcaffeinated Jehovah's Witness.

"I couldn't sleep either," Ginger announced. "I kept having nightmares we were going on a goddam firm retreat."

Turnage looked up, baffled. "We are going on a firm retreat."

Ginger fought a smile. Finally the brow lines on Turnage's forehead unfurled. "I get it," he muttered.

"That's everybody except the ice queen," Ginger said. From what I understood from Turnage, Ginger and Laura had surveyed each other the first time they met, and neither liked what she saw.

We neared Laura's and a thrill of terror sang through me. Her porch light was still on, her copper-gold Saab in the drive.

"Everybody was supposed to be waiting out front," Munger complained.

"She's exempt from the rules of normal human behavior," Ginger said. "Honk, Jake."

"Too early," said Jake. "Go get her, Ginger."

"Why me? Just because we have the same plumbing?"

"Just get her, okay?"

Much put upon, Ginger walked to Laura's door. Jake and I watched her ring the doorbell, then knock and call out, "Laura? We're late, dammit." She tried the door, walked inside. I knew her scream was coming but wasn't ready for it. Jake tore out of the van, followed by Munger, Turnage and finally me. I couldn't run; it was all I could do to stay on my feet.

Laura lay on the bed as I'd left her, except the blood had dried. I forced myself to step into the room.

"Good God. Laura." Jake stared at her in horror.

"Well, fuck me runnin'," Turnage said.

Jake moved closer, appearing stunned, and felt her neck for a pulse. "Call an ambulance, Ginger," he instructed. All she could do was sob.

Munger felt Laura's wrist. "She's dead, Jake. No one touch anything. I'll call the police from the van."

Turnage stepped closer, pruriently. "God, what a body that woman had."

I took a quilt from the chair and walked toward her.

"What in the hell are you doing?" Jake demanded, pushing me away.

"I'm going to cover her up."

"Put it back. You're destroying evidence. Come on, everybody, out."

I followed after the rest. As I closed the door, I couldn't stop myself from looking back.

I would see Laura again only in her coffin and every night in my dreams and nightmares.

* * *

Just two months and a day before, on the first of many hellish days in July when the humidity topped 95 and the thermometer 100, I had stopped for a chilled beer after work at the F & M Patio Bar, the best party-till-dawn spot in New Orleans. With a trial coming up in less than fifteen hours, I vowed to leave the F & M by dark or, failing that, shortly thereafter.

As I stood in the doorway of the F & M, I saw no one I knew and actually was considering leaving, going home, doing my duty, when Turnage made his way over, dual saucers of sweat penetrating the sides of his suit coat.

"Thought you had trial tomorrow, Cameron."

"Ready to roll," I said. Everything except me. I had a briefcase full of potential, questions for witnesses and a serviceable opening argument, but until I rehearsed it all a few dozen more times, it would remain merely that, potential. And somewhere in my office, I had a few exhibits, which I'd have to locate when I stopped by the next morning.

"Then you've got time for me to whip your ass at pool," Turnage challenged. "Or will your daddy be checking up on you?" In fact, he would be, and more than once.

"Rack 'em," I said. Turnage rewarded me with a moist back slap. He had an ingratiating manner that stood him in good stead not only with his drug-pushing gangbanger clients, whose egos required unrelenting respect, but, amazingly, even with my father, who was not known in the legal community for being tolerant of incompetence. That I knew, as Jake Cameron's only child, his only hope for posterity, and his only serious disappointment.

"Your daddy's been on roll lately," he noted.

"So they tell me."

"Eight straight wins."

"Seven."

"He's good," Turnage pronounced, ill advisedly attempting a combination shot. "Nobody could argue that."

He waited for my assent. Instead, I ordered another beer. Dark came late to New Orleans in summer. Who knew, I might play till nine. As to the trial prep, I was a quick study. Even Jake said that.

At eleven, I was running the table, taking Turnage's last twenty bucks and congratulating myself for deciding to leave before midnight. Even that late, it was the kind of night when sweat seeps through the back of your pima cotton, when mosquitoes sing their pleasure at your loud enticing fragrance, and when corpses decompose more rapidly than the coroner and undertaker prefer. Although I didn't know it at the time, Cameron & Munger's most notorious client had just begun doing exactly that.

The F & M was becoming crowded, its arctic-strength air conditioning troubled. My hair clung to my forehead. Everybody in the room looked pretty ripe. Turnage was pinker than usual, sweat beading on his upper lip.

"Damn, it's hotter'n a lit fart," he said, drunkenly unaware of the volume of his speech. "I wouldn't want to be downwind of me."

"I am downwind of you," said a tall blonde he'd been silently lusting for all night. Moving away, she added, "I thought it was the oysters gone bad."

"Fuck the horse you rode in on," he lashed out.

"I'd rather," she replied.

I ran the rest of the table, each shot accompanied by Turnage's regular whacks of frustration on his pool cue. As soon as I sank the last ball—another whack! from Turnage--a Tulane grad student raised her drink and her eyebrows, a non-verbal for "Join me?" She had lovely legs and, more important, the light of intelligence in her appraising eyes.

I didn't want to make myself say no, but I had to. I had a client and a girlfriend—fiancée actually--who deserved better and a father who demanded it. I had to say no. And I would, soon.

• • •

Just then I noticed a prosperous-looking businessman, an older guy—old enough to be fatcatting at the Petroleum Club--signaling the bartender to give the girl a drink. She glanced over at me, a question in her lifted eyebrows.

I hesitated, resisting, but then the older guy leaned in and put his arm on her chair back. At the last possible moment, I gave the girl a smile and an almost imperceptible nod. A yes. She held my eyes. Another yes.

"How do you do it, Cameron?" Turnage asked.

"Years of practice," I answered, pretending I thought he was asking about the shot I'd just made.

"Not pool, shithead. Women. Every damn time. It's not fuckin' fair."

There was nothing I could advise him; women could detect desperation clinging to him like the odor of three-day-old pompano. Care too much, and you are lost. Hadn't I learned the dangers from being around my father?

"Pay up, Turnage."

"Triple or nothing, Cameron."

Damn him, he knew I had that trial. Moreover, he knew the girl was waiting.

"Can't, Turnage."

"Triple or nothing, and I'll throw in dinner for two at Antoine's if you win."

A quick and dirty calculation told me I'd be clearing $300 in ten minutes, an astonishing hourly rate, far better than even Jake made. I gestured to the girl, "Mind if I play one more?" She smiled her easy permission.

I sank the first ball and lined up another.

"No way will you be ready for trial," Turnage said, poking my briefcase with his cue in an attempt at child psychology.

I sank the shot.

"Some of us haven't turned thirty yet, old man," I responded. Unmarried with no prospects, Turnage was sensitive about his age. "Some of us can still pull an all-nighter."

"Don't you mean pull it out of your ass, Cameron? That's what Jake calls it."

My shoulders tensed slightly. "I believe the expression is 'flying by the seat of your pants'." I cleared my mind and took a long breath as I measured a tricky bank shot. The girl's eyes were on me. Made it.

"He says eventually you'll try pulling it out one too many times. You'll reach up there to yank and come out empty-handed. Or worse."

Had Jake actually said that? Talking about me to that jackass Turnage?

"Kyle Cameron, shit out of luck," Turnage bellowed, as befit his beefy frame. He was laughing, and everyone on our end of the bar turned our way.

"I can hear you just fine, Turnage." I closed my eyes to clear my mind and found myself thinking how satisfying it would feel to strangle him permanently silent.

"Take your shot, Kyle. Put me away." I had a long, easy shot for the five-ball. "Like your daddy always says, go for the throat."

"The gospel of Jake."

"He's some kind of lawyer," Turnage offered, smiling, as I aimed.

"And I'm the other kind." I stabbed at the cue ball, missing the five-ball entirely and damn near ripping the felt.

The girl smiled over encouragingly. Was that pity in her eyes? Was I that transparent? What else had Jake said about me?

I went on to lose the game, down in flames, unable to pull anything whatsoever from my ass or anywhere else.

Six months later, when I was in the thick of my first murder trial, in way over my head and sinking fast, it occurred to me that Turnage hadn't been drinking much that night, hadn't been drunk, indeed, was far from being the idiot I'd always thought him, and that Jake had always seen through his facade and secretly admired his dumb-blonde strategy. And then, as I appreciated my father anew for his perception and caginess, I wondered for the thousand millionth time if maybe he hadn't also been right in thinking me, not Turnage, the fool.

I woke up in the girl's bed at seven—a miracle considering we'd been at it till four. I remembered, first, that it was my mother's birthday, and, second, that my trial was two hours off. My mind coursed over my to-do list and determined that I'd have just enough time, forty-five minutes, to review the papers in my briefcase and recollect my trial strategy. My bedmate moved one leg between mine.

"Sunny side up."

"I have to go," I said. Her hand replaced her leg, and I was compelled to revise my initial, overly optimistic estimate down to fifteen minutes.

It was 8:00 a.m. when I threw on the previous day's wrinkled navy linen suit, grabbed my briefcase, and ran outside to my Alfa Romeo. Driving maniacally, I shaved in the car, an old hand at both. I sped past the elegant gray-blue Victorian that housed Cameron & Munger Criminal Law, unable to do more than glance up wistfully toward my office, where my exhibits slumbered. There Jake would find them.

I made it into court just as the judge did. My client was holding her hands to her face as if praying. Up from the projects,

Nadine Jackson had seen more at age twenty than I ever would—or so I then thought. She'd snagged a waitressing job at a four-star restaurant by emulating the upper middle-class accents she'd heard on public television.

Nadine looked up. "Where the hell you been, Kyle?" she reproached, her accent understandably slipping. "I been scared I was gonna have to try this case my own self."

Commensurate with my trial preparation, I initially made no progress cross-examining the landlord, whose neckless head protruded from his shoulders like a hairy turnip. According to him, Nadine had bashed his face with a Conair 2000 metal blow dryer when he came to evict her. According to Nadine, he had appeared, unannounced, uninvited, and undressed, in her shower.

"You testified you rang Miss Jackson's doorbell," I challenged.

"Rang it twice."

"No, you didn't."

"My rule is I never enter a tenant's place unless I ring twice."

"No, you let yourself in with your master key."

"Rang it twice. Ring, ring," he imitated and a couple of jurors laughed.

I had to interpose another question, anything to try to regain control, but I saw my father enter the courtroom and take a seat in back. All thoughts vacated my mind. Stalling, I fumbled through my notes. I prayed for inspiration to save my client, and myself, undeserving as I was.

Picking up some trial papers, I held them out threateningly, as if they were official. And one question later, Nadine's landlord was rendered into an apologetic puddle. I turned to see Jake's reaction but his chair was empty.

I drove back to the firm, taking Saint Charles Avenue. Even on a bad day, I loved Saint Charles, with the old greenish brown streetcars rumbling along their tracks in the median, the ancient oaks so immense they shaded the entire street, the grand antebellum and Victorian mansions (more than a few of which belonged to the firm's criminal clients), and the smell of the trees and rich alluvial dirt after one of our frequent thunderstorms, as if a forest stood right in the heart of the city.

On its corner lot, the law firm dominated the block. Jake's car wasn't in the parking lot, as if he were avoiding the necessity of congratulating me. I stepped inside and felt dwarfed, as always, by Cameron & Munger's vast marble entryway, with its twenty-foot high ceilings. It reminded me of a giant's tomb.

Sitting beneath a massive antique chandelier, certain to perish if New Orleans were ever to have an earthquake during business hours, was Wendy, our cute little receptionist, barely of age.

"How was your trial, Kyle?" she asked. "You won again, I bet."

"Pulled it out."

"I like that suit."

The navy linen I'd worn two days in a row. "Thanks."

"Have you heard about Richard Flowers?" she asked with import. He was Munger's client, a quiet, likable family man who had a love of fine things and a strong desire to please others, an unfortunate alloy in a man with fiduciary duties. As Chief Financial Officer of Trust Life Insurance Company, he'd been under escalating pressure from the Louisiana Attorney General for over a year to explain his suspicious entries in Trust Life's books, as well as the company's astronomical executive salaries and perks.

"What about him?"

"Carbon-monoxide poisoning in his garage," Wendy confided, her cornflower blue eyes wide. "His blood alcohol was 2.2. They found him this morning in his car with a glass of Scotch in his hand."

And there it was on her desk, the banner headline blazing across the front page of the *Times-Picayune* : KEY TRUST LIFE OFFICIAL DIES 36 HOURS BEFORE TESTIFYING. I barely knew Flowers; his death would affect me far more than his life.

"How'd Munger take it?" Flowers was his key witness. If I knew Munger, the prospect of losing his case troubled him significantly more than the death of his friend and longtime client. He had a horror of defeat, stronger even than his will to win.

"I can't ever tell what Mr. Munger's thinking," Wendy said. Could anyone? He had the expressiveness of an eel, not to mention warmth.

Upstairs, on my office doorknob hung a rubber chicken, the coveted firm symbol for trial victory.

"Didn't surprise me one bit," Myrt, my secretary, declared with a fair measure of credibility. "Born lawyer."

Myrt was a streetwise Cajun older than my mother (handpicked for me by Jake), and if her feminine charms were not of the physical variety, they were every bit as indispensable to me.

"How'd word get back here already?"

"My galfriend in the courthouse called."

"Clarisse?"

Myrt nodded. "Don't you be getting you any ideas about Clarisse. She's a nice gal."

"Yes, ma'am."

Clarisse, who was sixty if a day, wore three-inch spike heels and a red Dolly Parton wig whenever she stepped foot outside the house. Every Friday night Myrt drank wine and played gin at Clarisse's little shotgun duplex so Clarisse could wear a housecoat, her own hair, and bobby socks.

"Is Jake coming back?"

"Gone for the day. Said not to be late tonight."

I didn't need to be reminded. My mother's last year had been her hardest. But now she was fifty, a birthday I never thought she'd reach, and I hoped the celebration would mark a turning point for her. I'd made sure the restaurant had soft-shell crab, her favorite, though these days she ate almost nothing, and I'd reserved a table in one of the small upstairs rooms where she wouldn't feel overwhelmed by the glittering crowd.

I went into my office—the dunghole, as Jake referred to it—closed my eyes, and once again savored the image of the landlord's face when I took him down on the stand.

That evening, as I drove Alison to my mother's birthday dinner, she was happy to let me speed along with the Alfa top down, even though her fine blonde hair was flying everywhere. Over our many years together, she'd put up with quite a lot from me. Exuberant over my trial win, I executed a tricky pass around a lumbering SUV.

"God, slow down, Kyle, do you want to kill us both?"

I obediently slowed and allowed myself to be pumped for the minutest of details about my epochal victory.

"Did your client tell you how brilliant you are?" Alison asked.

"Something like that." After the verdict came in, Nadine had given me a lingering kiss on the lips, then rushed out to her evening shift at the restaurant, which I now intended to try.

We were a mile from Commander's Palace when Alison announced, "I know what let's do, Kyle. Let's not wait any longer to tell your parents we're engaged. We can make it a double celebration. A triple one, counting your trial. Your mother would be so excited. Your father too," she added diplomatically. We both knew the last time he'd been excited over anything I'd done was the day I'd managed to find my way out of the womb.

"I'd rather keep it between us for awhile... wait a little longer till things at work settle down."

"When will that be, retirement? We've been together nine years! We've been supposedly engaged for three months." At that she held up her naked ring finger. "I thought you'd be happy. It's apparent I'm the only one who's happy. Do you not love me?"

"I do."

"Do what? Love me or not love me?"

"Do." And I did, like a best friend, like a wife of twenty or thirty years.

"Which?" she insisted. She hadn't noticed I'd been slowing until the Alfa was at a crawl. The car behind us blasted its horn. "What are you doing? We'll be late for Nola's birthday."

"You said slow down."

She gave up and shook her head. "Why do I love you anyway?"

Alison was literally the girl-next-door. She'd noticed me first, when she was in the sixth grade and I in the eighth. That entire spring she watched me climb down at midnight from my upstairs bedroom to make out with an experienced tenth-grade girl under the low limbs of our magnolia tree. Not low enough, apparently, because Alison recalled observing that I got the hang of things very quickly. All Jake knew was that my grades inexplicably plummeted that spring, never to rise again. Instantly jealous of the tenth-grade girl, Alison determined early on that I was hers. By high school I was.

Although she knew not to trust me with other girls, she passed up college with me at Tulane to study art history at Harvard. That gave me a new respect for her, knowing she had the strength to leave me. After graduation she came home to work at the New Orleans Museum of Art, slipping back into my life as if four years and fifty-odd women hadn't intervened. I was in law school then, quite the unprepossessing legal scholar, already setting the precedent for my performance at the firm.

I glanced over at her profile, delicate but resolute, and knew she was turning the subject of our engagement around in her mind. With six blocks to go to the restaurant, I sped up and took a challenging back route, zooming into Commander's Palace five minutes early.

"You're insane," Alison protested, hand gripping the armrest.

"You said speed up." I kissed her, left the keys with a familiar valet, and marched her into the restaurant so bustling that intimate conversation would of necessity be foregone.

I spotted my father the instant we entered Commanders' bar, standing up in the midst of the crowd, dominating the pack. He was fifty, looked forty, and, as a result of eight strenuous hours a week at the gym, moved like he was thirty. He was nicknamed Tiger, for more than one reason, not the least of which was temperament. When I was a child, he'd seemed like a mythological god, towering, powerful, arbitrary. At my age he'd been unusually handsome; now he was merely striking, a man whom women of all ages invariably turned to watch, regretful, as he walked gracefully on by. Though two inches shorter than I—five foot ten to my six feet—he was heavier set and stronger, yet lighter in his step, like a dancer or an athlete. We had the same dark eyes and hair (his was streaked with silver), but Jake, unlike me, didn't have his ear pierced to hold a small gold loop.

"So you made it," he announced, waving us over to seats he'd managed to save next to my mother. After twenty-eight years of marriage, they still held hands, and though I didn't care to emulate Jake as a husband, much less as a father, I did want my marriage—whenever it finally transpired—to be as happy as theirs.

"Of course, I made it," I replied. "Eight sharp, as specified. In fact we're early."

"Not by my watch," he said, not even bothering to check it.

Mom took an anxious sip of her vodka martini. She was blonde and small—not short in high heels but extremely fine-boned, apt to be crushed in a crowd of merrymakers. Her steady gestures told me the martini was only her first; if our table came up soon, I could butter her some French bread and she'd last a few more hours.

"I'm here and I'm on time," I insisted. "I told you ten times I would be."

"You've told me lots of things." No mention of my trial win.

"Just what does that--"

I felt a gentle pressure on my upper arm and looked over to see Alison, smiling, signaling me to relax. My fists, I noticed, were clenched, as if to deck Jake right there amidst the gin fizzes and Sazerac cocktails.

My father was a stubborn man, and in that, at least, I was his son. When I was a teenager—admittedly, a difficult teenager—our adamantine heads butted with such force and frequency that we had to eat our meals in separate rooms.

Commander's Palace was his favorite spot, a five-star Creole restaurant whose second floor during Prohibition had housed a high-priced bordello. The upstairs now consisted of a large main dining area and several smaller, more intimate rooms, all furnished with the crystal chandeliers and burnished mahogany of antebellum New Orleans reborn. On the nearest grand buffet stood a silver candelabrum massive enough, were it to topple, to dent a hardwood floor or shatter a skull.

"Happy birthday, Nola," Alison said and hugged my mother warmly. She gave Mom a small wrapped box containing hand-sewn lace, an interest they shared, and my mother kissed her cheek. I felt enormously grateful for the many hours they spent together, particularly during Mom's precarious last year.

"Doesn't Alison look pretty tonight?" Mom asked, in that uniquely southern way of delivering and eliciting a compliment at the same time. Jake and I concurred that Alison looked lovely, which she did. She reminded me of the Breck girls in the old magazines, so scrubbed and fair-haired that just being around her seemed to purify any dark thought or deed. Alison liked projects. Maybe she'd talk to my mother about the drinking.

"This is going to be a great year for you, Mom," I said, determined that it would be. I hugged her, holding back a little because she seemed so fragile, the kind of delicate beauty some men give up everything to protect. If she'd waited to marry, she certainly would've had proposals other than my father's.

She unwrapped my gift, an antique cloisonné vase she'd briefly admired six weeks before when we'd passed by a pricey shop on Magazine Street. It was the first flutter of interest in months that she'd shown in much of anything, and I raced back to the shop to buy it. No flowers would ever grace it though; she couldn't stand to cut them.

"How could you have known I craved this very vase?" she asked in her soft accent, passed down unchanged from ancestors who'd been in New Orleans under God knew how many flags. If it would've worked, I'd have bought a thousand vases and parceled them out to get her through the days.

Jake handed Mom a small wrapped box, a gift, I knew, she'd save to open with him alone.

"Gorgeous as the day we met," he said, softly, and kissed her.

Now she was beaming. "I may not deserve to be this happy," she said, her voice catching. Suddenly her mood threatened to shift. Tears came to her eyes. I glanced at her drink. Nearly below sea level. Where the hell was our table?

"Of course you deserve it," I insisted. "You deserve it more often, that's all."

Jake's law practice was built now, had been for years, would hardly suffer if he took a week's—hell, a month's—vacation. No reason he couldn't trim a few hours off his overwhelming workload, hire new lawyers, give her more attention.

Just then the hostess appeared, tan, sleek, stunning. She glanced at me and would've smiled but saw Alison observing her. Instead she turned her gaze, now businesslike, to Jake.

"Armand is serving in the Garden Room this evening, Mr. Cameron."

"Garden Room all right with you, Baby Doll?" Jake asked my mother. She loved being called Baby Doll.

"She likes the smaller rooms, Dad. You know that."

"The Garden Room is perfect, Jake," Mom interceded. "Whatever you want."

We followed the hostess upstairs. Aware that my eyes would track her hips, she exaggerated just slightly their hypnotic sway. She led us on toward the main dining room, past women in high fashion laughing and flirting with other women's men. At one dim candlelit table, a saucepan of Bananas Foster erupted in a blue rum fire. Mom's eyes were getting a slightly panicked look.

"You know the Garden Room's too big a scene for her. It hasn't been all that long," I told Jake as the hostess led us into the trendy, crowded arena.

"She said, quote, it's perfect. You heard her. Did you not?" he demanded. Everything with him was an adversarial proceeding.

"You know she said that to please you."

Alison squeezed my hand, hard. "Shut up," she was signaling. Semaphores would be next.

"Taking up psychology, Son? In lieu of law?"

A reference to my trial, for which he still hadn't congratulated me.

"Let him have the last word," Alison hissed.

That was the best way to handle him, of course, but I could never stop myself. Then the retorts would fly back at me, tougher, faster, truer. I willed myself mute.

Our hostess deposited us at the table of Armand, Jake's favorite waiter. As Jake escorted Mom to a chair, I stepped ahead of him. He stiffened.

"Here, Mom," I urged, seating her so she could overlook the massive oak tree in the courtyard instead of the sea of chattering faces. "This chair has the best view." I could feel the black wave of Jake's irritation wash over me.

"I'm Holly Lefoldt, Mr. Cameron, if you need anything," the hostess said to Jake, loud enough for me to hear, slow enough for me to recall. I felt pretty sure that Holly Lefoldt would be in the book. If not, she could be reached at Commander's. To Alison's immense pleasure, she departed.

"Your mother's a grown woman," Jake cranked up again, not caring if my mother or the entire Garden Room heard. "She can take care of herself. You're the only one who doesn't seem to recognize that fact."

"Is that right? And what if I hadn't looked out for her? Nobody else was."

He looked up and I knew I'd drawn blood. He always said go for the throat, didn't he?

"And what if I hadn't looked out for you, Son?" Unsaid, unnecessary to be said, was the fact that all my life he'd gotten me into places I wanted to go and out of places I didn't. He damn well knew where my throat was.

"Funny you haven't said one word about my trial today." I'd managed that on my own without one bit of help from him.

"Exactly the mention it deserves."

Puzzled, Alison looked over, wondering if she'd misunderstood my account of the trial.

"I won, goddammit." I hated the way I sounded, exactly the defensive tone I'd had when I was a teenager.

"Watch your language, Son."

"I won, dammit."

"Technically."

"Technically? Is there some new standard for lawyers now? Winning isn't good enough?" For once, I would have my due, induce, at the very least the same respect he accorded his pea-brain hire, Jeb Turnage.

"No, it's not good enough," Jake rammed back in a measured cadence. "And what's more, you know it." "I cracked the witness," I told him, unable to keep my voice down. "On the stand. Don't see that very often."

"That's true," Mom said, smiling her nervous smile.

"I hope to God I don't. It was a flimsy, amateurish ploy. A juvenile stunt."

But it had worked, hadn't it? I'd thrust out my sheaf of scribbled notes at Nadine's landlord, as if they were official, and asked him, "What if a New Orleans Housing Authority report stated that the defendant's doorbell had been nonfunctioning for four months, in spite of her repeated requests to repair it? Would that change your recollection about ringing the doorbell twice? 'Ring, ring,'" I'd imitated.

"What if the landlord hadn't been an idiot?" Jake demanded. "What if he hadn't panicked?"

"There's no way that doorbell was working. At that slum of his?"

"The only reason you won that case is blind luck. The law's a jealous mistress, Son, and you're about as faithful as a damn alley cat."

Armand approached to take our orders, then took in our strained faces and thought better of it. Now Alison mirrored Mom's nervous smile. They exchanged looks that said, "What is wrong with these men of ours, that they won't behave?"

"Isn't that Judge Caravello at that back table?" my mother proffered. My fine intentions to keep her afloat had long since been jettisoned, and Jake was right there with me.

"How in God's name do you expect to make partner if you don't even try?" he kept on. "I'm only one vote."

"Lucky for me."

"Stop it," Alison whispered to me.

She'd had enough. But I hadn't. Especially when my eyes caught something on the floor.

"Look at that, would you," I raged in disbelief, pointing at an all too familiar black object near Jake's chair. "You brought your briefcase to Mom's birthday party."

"I've got the Vickers hearing tomorrow, since you inquired. Renee's coming in early to type up my notes, so I'm dropping them by the office. Your mother already said she didn't mind. Isn't that right, Baby Doll?"

"That's right," she replied, her lips carving a brittle smile.

Just then Armand approached, undeterred. He held out a telephone, his manner urgent.

"Oh no," my mother whispered when she saw the phone.

And, to Jake's credit, I thought, he held up his hand and said, "No phones tonight, Armand. It's Nola's birthday."

"It's Mr. Vickers, sir. He said it's an emergency." Armand waited, ready to obey either whim, as Jake made up his mind.

Finally Jake relented. "Dammit to hell."

Annoyed, he took the phone, talking about Vickers' upcoming grand jury testimony, trying to bully him into waiting until the next day. "We've rehearsed you plenty. You're not a virgin, Vickers. Why do I have to hold your hand through this?"

My mother watched, not even breathing, as if the sun had vacated her solar system. Long before Jake had hung up, she could tell that her fiftieth birthday party was over. She raised a smile so that Jake, her Mr. Wonderful, wouldn't feel guilty about leaving. I could hardly stand to watch. Alison and I might chat with her entertainingly, offer her tastes of turtle soup and sauté of crawfish and chocolate bread pudding, but the one who would hold hands with her and call her Baby Doll would be gone, tending to a wealthy gangster who on her birthday night would take precedence.

Jake had pulled this kind of crap for years. My twelfth birthday, Mom's fortieth, my tenth-grade play, two Thanksgivings, one high school graduation. And for what? More money? More ego? How much more would it take?

Jake sighed, displeased, looking around at all of us. "Day before Grand Jury, and Vickers is bouncing off the wall. He wants to change his testimony. I've got to meet him at the office and either talk him out of it or rehearse him from scratch. I'm sorry, Nola."

As he stood to reach for his billfold, I pulled him aside. "Can't you tell Vickers no? We're all together for once. She's having a good time for once." A major exaggeration we both let pass.

"I wish I could," Jake said. "Criminals are fuck-ups. This kind of emergency comes with the territory. I just need you to take her home for me." He thrust a wad of cash toward me, his solution for all human problems.

Six one hundred-dollar bills to pay for a four-hundred-dollar meal. A reminder of who was in control.

I waved his money away. "I'll get the check. I've got money."

"What's the difference? It's all coming from me anyway."

The throat, he never missed.

"Bye, Miss Alison, take care of Kyle now," he said, as if I needed a keeper.

He kissed my mother. "Bye bye, Baby Doll. I'll try not to be late."

I wished her eyes wouldn't follow him out of the room, but then mine did too. A genial man with great personal charm, Jake stopped and shook hands and clapped backs as he went. I watched as, with genuine warmth, he tousled the hair of a friend's ten-year-old son.

"Could they have switched fathers at birth somehow?" I asked, trying to joke it off.

Alison touched my arm. "Kyle, your mother said when you were little, your daddy would take you to the merry-go-round at Audubon Park every Sunday. He'd ride with you till you quit asking."

"Really?" I tried to conjure the memory but couldn't.

"Every last Sunday," my mother answered. "Hot ones, cold ones, even the rainy ones. Proudest father in New Orleans."

"How things change," I thought but managed not to say.

"Kyle, look," Alison said, pointing toward the floor. "Your daddy forgot his briefcase."

I smiled, taking my pleasure where I could find it. "So he did." An uncharacteristic show of human fallibility.

"Take it to him," my mother said. "He needs it."

"He's already gone. Why do you even care?"

"Kyle, honey, do it, please. For me." When she got that tone of voice, it wasn't a request. I grabbed up the hateful symbol and hurried after Jake.

Outside, he was just pulling away in his vintage black Jag. I ran after him through the still steamy night air but he didn't see me, in too big a damn hurry to appease Vickers.

I dialed his cell phone. Moments later, it rang inside his briefcase at my feet.

"Ten-dollar tip if my car comes out in a shake," I said to the valet, and he ran for the Alfa.

In another shake I was speeding after Jake, along Saint Charles Avenue toward Cameron & Munger, his briefcase propped up beside me in the passenger's seat like a pampered pet. If I could catch him at a red light, I could avoid having to make the forty-block round trip.

Traffic, heavy for that time of night, was surely slowing him as much as it was slowing me. I saw the reason for the delay: a wreck, a bad one with the driver's door caved in, somebody dead on a stretcher, cops everywhere. I edged past a child, bloody, clinging to his mother. She stared into space, eyes crazy with grief.

Finally I caught sight of Jake's Jag ahead and worked my way into the right lane to prepare to turn at Cameron & Munger. But he stayed left, leaving me baffled at his slowness. Tiger was not a hesitant driver. When I saw his left blinker flash, I slalomed across the lanes and followed as he made an incomprehensible left turn. The heavy twisted oaks along the boulevard arched over me, blotting out the night sky.

Jake made another puzzling turn, onto Prytania, a narrower tree-lined street of Creole cottages. Several blocks down, he parked and walked up to a frame house, its porch light dark. Crepe myrtle trees, at their July peak, bloomed a violent magenta.

Would a multi-millionaire like Vickers live in a simple bungalow? And hadn't Jake said they were meeting at the firm? Watching from my idling car, I saw Jake knock, then the porch light come on and the door swing open. Someone stepped out.

Lovely even under the harsh incandescent bulb was Laura Niles. Fragmented thoughts—idiotic in retrospect—shot through my brain. Was she assisting Jake on the Vickers case? Was Vickers in there? Then I saw her reach for my father and coil her leg around his.

When Jake leaned down and kissed her, I jerked my head as if someone had flung acid in my eyes. She drew him inside and shut the door. A lamp in her next room—the bedroom, I was sure—came on. What held me back from tearing across the lawn and banging on the door? Instead, I slammed the Alfa in gear, shooting down Prytania Street, trying to outrun the image of Jake Cameron, father of me, husband of Baby Doll, embracing Laura Niles and not my mother.

I'd met her my first day at work—if the briefest coolest handshake could be said to be an introduction. Haughty—no, icy—she worshipped at the altar of her own image, or at least I assumed she did. For Laura Niles was uncommonly beautiful, lithe yet softly curved, with hazel eyes a trace more golden than green.

We were the same age, but, humiliatingly, Laura was above me on the letterhead and had been handling bigger cases for some time. Although she'd graduated from LSU Law the same semester I'd finished at Tulane, she had seniority at the firm because, unlike me, she hadn't failed the bar exam once, much less twice. No, she'd gone straight to work earning her keep, while I stayed on Jake's dole for another year until I finally passed.

I'd seen her once before, though she never acknowledged it. She was sitting on a bench at Audubon Park, sobbing into her hands. It was the day my bar exam scores were coming—third round—and I was jogging the track at Audubon Park, trying to keep myself from calling the Admissions Board yet again. When I approached to make sure she was all right, she turned and shook her head no to signal me to stay away. Unable to obey, I took another step. She held up her hand, another no, more definite, warning me off, and I turned back.

The entire time that I circled the track, I cursed my stupidity for leaving. I raced around it like an Olympian, bar results forgotten, only to find her gone when I returned. Since then, she'd spoken only a few words to me at work, but I kept jogging there hoping to see her again on that bench.

She'd been crying over Jake, I now felt sure. And that knowledge, coupled with the fact that he'd abandoned my mother on her birthday, convinced me their affair was serious.

I hesitated outside the Garden Room, watching my mother, her world still in its orbit. One thing I was certain of, the only thing, was that she could never know. Armand, the traitor, was serving our entrees. "Tough business, the law," I said as I sat, giving him a piercing stare. "Client must come first."

"Yes, sir." The look he returned was one of opaque servility, the same I'd seen since I was a child.

On my mother's plate lay a whole sautéed soft-shell crab. Imprudently, like its compatriots, it had molted its shell for a few vulnerable weeks. Soft-shell crab was her favorite dish, in season only during her birthday month and again in early fall. Though every part, supposedly, was not only edible but a delicacy, it had never looked particularly appetizing to me. Now, smelling it, seeing its long legs bent at right angles like a mosquito's, thinking of Jake—where he was at that moment, what he was doing—I became perilously queasy.

"Did you have to go all the way to the firm?" Mom asked me.

"You know how Jake drives," I said with determined casualness.

Dinner was interminable. Alison and I attempted a three-way conversation with Mom, but she was far away, wondering, I knew, if it were somehow possible that Jake might finish early and return. We finally subsided into silence.

"Remember that time your father surprised us by leaving his trial for Mama and Daddy's anniversary?" she suddenly injected with baseless hope and inaccurate memory. It had been a directed verdict and he had arrived, not in time to toast his in-laws but to awaken Mom from her Champagne slumber with a Prince Charming kiss.

"Remember, Kyle?" she insisted.

"I remember, Mom." Seeing the hope in her eyes, I wanted to smash my fist on the table. I fought down an impulse to tell her. I might as well have leapt across the table and stabbed her in the heart with my long-tined fork.

To protract the evening so Jake might yet appear, Mom and Alison split a chocolate fudge Sheba, their favorite dessert. In the waning birthday spirit, I ordered crème brulee but then lost my appetite completely. Finally, the last Cafe Diablo was cold and the evening was dead. Curtly, I motioned for Armand.

"My father appreciates the exceptional service," I said, then presented him with all six of Jake's hundreds, again taking my pleasure where I could find it.

My Alfa only held two, so I paid for Alison's cab and drove my mother to her exquisite empty home.

"Can't you make Dad stay home more?" I asked her just to fill the asphyxiating silence.

"Have you ever tried to make Jake Cameron do anything?"

"Only all my life."

She fell silent again. Little was left of the college actress I'd heard about as a child. Now she stowed her feelings away until they became too heavy to carry.

"I'm coming in," I said as I turned up the long driveway. I couldn't abide her sitting alone, on her birthday, while Jake.... I killed the image that formed in my mind.

"No need," she said. "You go have fun."

"I'm coming in," I repeated.

To my surprise, she nodded and said, so softly I could barely hear it, "Thank you."

When I was young, it had started off the other way around, with Mom as my protector, taking my side, right or wrong. She was home every day when I came in from school, listening always to whatever indignities I'd endured. Even then she was an almost ethereal presence, and as a very young child I'd confused her with an angel.

Then in fourth grade I hurried home one day from school, late and fuming because Mrs. Robicheaux had made me stay in. Yes, I'd been in a fight, but I hadn't started it, only finished it, and the other boy hadn't been punished. My father always automatically sided with my teachers, so I would mention it only to Mom.

Uncharacteristically, she was gone and the house was empty. Where was Eunice, our maid, who was always there? Mom's car was in the garage so she couldn't be far, but when I checked next door, Alison's mother hadn't seen her. It was a hot New Orleans spring day so I didn't really expect her to be outside, but I inspected our brick courtyard in back anyway, searching through the lush semi-tropical foliage. After I spotted one of her gardening gloves, abandoned palm up under an azalea in brash red bloom, it occurred to me to worry.

I ran back in. My grievance with Mrs. Robicheaux forgotten, I raced through the house, calling my mother.

Our house, like most Victorian behemoths, had many cubbyholes—a wine closet, an under-stairs closet, an attic, a greenhouse. As I ran to the wine closet, the hope of finding my mother expanded in me like a breath, straining at my chest. I opened the closet door. Empty. I tore to the next cubbyhole. And the next, and the next, and then the last. All empty. Something awful had happened to her. A new sensation seized my body, flushing out the hope. Only recently have I come to recognize that feeling as terror.

The final room that I tried, her stark white bathroom, was off-limits, and I almost didn't go in. When I did, knocking first, tentative, then peering in as I cracked the door, my mother lay... what, sleeping?... in a tub of red water. Her breasts—large for her delicate body—were visible, half-submerged, and I jerked my head away, afraid I'd get in trouble for seeing them. But she didn't correct me, so I raised my eyes to the footed tub. Her left arm, inert, lay draped over its side, and a drop of blood from her wrist spattered into a startlingly red pool on the white tile floor. What was wrong with her? She looked so tired.

"Mama, wake up!" I yelled. She didn't move.

I ran to the phone and dialed "9-1-1." When the paramedics found me, I was kneeling in her blood, my hand clamped around her wrist like a tourniquet, my eyes averted from her body, as I whispered over and over, "It'll be okay, it'll be okay."

One of the paramedics said, "Kid, you did great. You saved her life. We can take over now." Still in shock, I wouldn't let go until he popped his hand across my cheek.

After she came back home, I always felt uneasy--when I left for school, when I was playing ball, actually any time I was gone over an hour if my father was away. Hadn't I saved her life before? With my father so busy at work, wouldn't it always be up to me?

Though just in elementary school, I became a barometer of her moods. My favorite days were the ones when she went shopping for clothes. One spring she bought a winter coat, and that old feeling of hope rose up in my chest. She planned to be alive for six more months!

In high school I called home between classes, from parties, from dates, needing the reassurance I'd get—if but for an instant—from hearing her living voice.

Even during my first year as a lawyer doing menial assignments in Jake's firm, I still checked on her regularly, but, lulled into complacency, not as consistently as before.

One day, only six months back, I called during a break at trial and didn't get an answer. I was sitting second chair to Jake, which meant I was silently taking up space, but when he impatiently motioned me to get back into the courtroom, I obeyed, curbing my desire to drive over and check on her. Alison, though, had stopped by her parents' house to pick up a lamp and, on impulse, went next door to visit. She found Mom upstairs, lying across the bed, perfectly attired, her face slack, her pill bottle empty. Another hour would've been too late. She would've died because I was afraid of Jake. I could never relax my vigilance.

Nor would I this night. I turned on the lights inside the house as if that would dispel the solitude. My mother settled onto the sofa with her lacquered embroidery box. Above her, a life-sized portrait of her father, a former Louisiana Supreme Court justice. I sat down on the edge of Jake's easy chair and watched her work on her latest project, an intricately designed lace tablecloth.

She saw me watching. "Embroidery is a jealous mistress." I wasn't used to irony from my mother.

"Are you doing okay?" I asked, taking care that only my usual concern for her was in my voice. She was extraordinarily sensitive to shifts in moods. "Alison and I could stop by more."

"Don't you worry about your mama," she said, shaking her small bottle of tranquilizers like a maraca. "As we said in my day, she's got mother's little helpers." She shook two pills into her hand. Her mask of gaiety cracked, and she averted her face. "You go on home now. I'll be fine."

"I'm staying till Dad gets here."

No response. Stitch stitch. The bottle of pills, near full, reposed on the table.

"Where are you going to put your new vase?" Get her thinking about the future.

"You pick a spot."

I put it on the sideboard in the dining room, my best guess as to where she'd want it. Also where Jake would have to see it every time he sat down to eat.

"Perfect," she said but didn't really look. I noticed her gift from Jake, unopened on the table, awaiting the moment he returned.

"More jewelry," I surmised, breaking the unspoken rule against criticizing Jake. Mom wore very little jewelry, but Jake kept giving it.

"It'll be lovely," she said, and I knew it was a gentle chastisement. She squeezed my hand to show she wasn't mad and picked up her needles. She wanted to be left alone, to wait.

I went upstairs to my old bedroom to do my own waiting. It was unchanged, a fixed point in my universe, as I'd thought my parents were. I sat down on my bed, the old single bed where I'd first had sex with Alison, while our parents had gone to dinner together at—where else?--Commander's Palace. Ordinarily I felt comforted there, surrounded by mementos of my childhood. Instead, in the space of one evening, all were tainted.

In the closet I spotted the basketball from the one-on-one games Jake delighted in winning, slamming into me for what he liked to call his kill shot. I no longer had the brace from when he broke three of my ribs. On a shelf, my sixth-grade insect collection, lacking a Monarch butterfly because I couldn't kill anything that beautiful, still wore the "C+" he'd berated me for. "You're too soft, Son," he'd said. "It's a hard world. You can't hold back your whole life long." Behind were my old, banged-up water skis. I'd gotten up my first try, shaky but so proud. Jake had gunned the boat until we were practically flat out (a lesson, he said later, for when the going gets tough), and I had no choice but to hang on as we roared across choppy Lake Ponchartrain.

I picked up a photo of my parents from when I was fifteen. They looked happy, but—who could tell?--maybe he was pretending even then. Maybe my grandfather's money, or his family connections, had been irresistible to a poor but ambitious law student.

If the unnamed sorrows of everyday life had twice driven Mom to try to kill herself, then my father's outright betrayal would destroy her. I was her son, but Jake was her life. That was the way it was; I accepted that. I also knew it would be up to me to save her.

Several options, none good, presented themselves. I could confront my father—the prospect terrified me—and demand he stop. Make him see—what? The error of his ways?

I wasn't much of a moral authority. And if he didn't stop—what then? My mother unconscious on her bed? In the bathtub with her blood on the white tile floor?

Another choice: confront Laura Niles. I pictured her listening to my demands, my threats, then turning wordlessly and going straight to Jake. Or maybe not even telling Jake, just working secretly to get whatever she wanted, as she no doubt always had. Or laughing at me.

Or I could prevail on someone to straighten him out. Who? He had few close friends, the law being his mistress, along with of course Laura Niles. His partner, Munger? An even more dubious moral authority than I.

Most of all I wanted to talk to Alison but I couldn't risk the chance she'd tell my mother. Whatever I did I'd have to do alone.

By 1:30 a.m., when I heard Jake's Jag turn into the driveway below, I had a plan. It was simple enough, and feasible. And it seemed sound, as plans at first glimmer often do. But had I not concocted it, all involved would be alive and only one a murderer.

It was almost 2:00 when I pulled up at the firm. The moon shone through the tall windows of Cameron & Munger, making the old house, familiar since childhood, easily navigable without lights. With Trust Life sure to be continued, I couldn't think of any trials in progress that might require the other lawyers to be working all night. Turnage, I knew, had a habit of coming to the office whenever he had insomnia. If he showed up, I'd have no excuse for being there. Work? He knew me too well.

Using a tiny flashlight, a party favor from one of Jake's Mardi Gras balls, I entered the business office with a master key Jake was unaware I knew about. In the antique oak file cabinet, I found Laura's personnel file with her home phone number and her birthday, which I noted was the 17th of July, less than two weeks away. She'd left "next of kin" blank. Interests were sailing, food, horseback riding and travel. I saw no need for her Social Security number but copied it anyway.

I went up to the second floor, where Laura and Munger had adjacent offices down the hall from me. Munger, I remembered now, also occasionally came down to the firm in the middle of the night to work.

Using the master key, I entered Laura's office. Quickly scanning the walls, I saw LSU diplomas in English Lit and in law, but no family photos. She had several expensive oil paintings, one small Persian rug. Gifts from my father? And she had an antique mahogany desk—exactly the kind he would've selected for her—with all the drawers locked. On its leather top, her files were neatly stacked alongside a calendar. I shined the flashlight on it.

Everything looked very businesslike. Client interviews, hearing dates, deadline reminders. But, I noticed, in the upper right corner of many blocks were lightly penciled numbers: 12:00, 6:00, 8:30. I did a quick cross-referencing of these hours with what I remembered of my father's schedule and felt reasonably sure that these times denoted their assignations. Checking Mom's birthday, I saw that Laura had penciled in "9:15 p.m." He'd even managed to see her New Year's Day—though Alison and I'd been invited over to watch the game. I recalled his curious disappearance for the entire third quarter.

Jake never made fewer than three visits a week, I saw, even during his heaviest trial schedule, and occasionally as many as five. On some weekdays he stopped by at 5:30 a.m. before work. No question, it was serious.

I turned on Laura's computer and discovered she was using a private e-mail server in addition to the firm's. I copied down her address and that of Sam Ireland, which I gathered was Jake's cover. Her e-mail had been erased except for Sam's incoming message: "I love you, Baby Girl." I trashed it.

Even though I was certain I was alone at the firm—it was approaching 3:00 a.m. by then—I was suddenly gripped by the sensation that I was going to be caught. Perhaps, at some level below consciousness, I'd heard a car door slam in the back lot. I turned off Laura's computer, walked into the hall, and re-locked her door behind me.

My flashlight, where the hell was my flashlight? Burning away on Laura's desk. I fumbled to reopen the door but put the damn key in upside down in the dark. I heard a chime—the elevator! The key slipped in just then, I grabbed the flashlight, stuffed it in my pocket, then relocked the door and distanced myself from it as twenty feet away the elevator opened.

Tommy Munger stepped out. His thin face was unreadable as always, but he seemed as uncomfortable at being seen as I was. Though he was two years younger than my father, he seemed much older—withered, wintry, bloodless. His every word and movement seemed premeditated. When I was a child, he'd reminded me of a praying mantis.

"Kyle? I didn't see any lights on from the lot. What exactly are you doing up here?"

"I remembered an appeal deadline tomorrow. It almost slipped past me." It was at least half-believable, the part about my missing the deadline if not my remembering it.

"What case?"

I cast my mind over my scant docket for something feasible. Nothing.

"Dupree," I mumbled.

"Dupree," he said slowly, wrinkling his expanse of forehead. Though his hair was starting to recede, it was swept back magisterially. "I don't recall that case."

"Too small. You wouldn't." So small, in fact, it didn't exist.

"Your car's not in the lot," he noted.

"Parked on the street. Didn't remember to stop until I'd missed the turn." I noticed that my little flashlight, still on, was shining through the fine weave of my linen pants.

"I didn't expect to see you either," I added idiotically.

"But you did," Munger said.

I made my way past him to the stairs—escape—clicking off the flashlight as soon as my back was turned.

"How was your mother's birthday celebration?" he called, as if my answer might reveal something useful.

"A grand affair," I replied, as impenetrable as he, and took the stairs, resisting the urge to bolt down them two at a time.

As I walked down the street to my car, I looked back at the blue-gray Victorian. Munger's office was lit, and one slat of his blinds was cockeyed, positioned so he could watch me leave.

Blood Relations

Every house on Saint Charles was dark as I drove to see Evan Jacobs, my best friend since childhood. It wasn't the first time I'd come over uninvited with bad news, though never of this magnitude. As I figured, he still had on the light in his rundown Uptown duplex. He kept the hours of a vampire, working as a waiter to support his non-income-producing writing career, then coming straight home to work the rest of the night on his comic novel. Nothing had ever seen print except in little magazines with a readership of twenty-three.

In high school we both thought we'd be writers, having been inspired by our tenth-grade English teach, Ms. Lanier, who wore her blonde hair long and her skirts not.

After she'd given him an "A" on some short story, Evan had taunted, "Talent rewarded, Cameron." My darkly atmospheric, if plotless, piece about dogs devouring the last man on earth, had garnered a bare "B-."

"You can jack off with your "A," Jacobs, while I'm slow-dancing with Amy."

"You asked Ms. Lanier out?"

I wasn't that precocious. She'd asked me.

Even after Ms. Lanier married a Delta planter, Evan persevered. After Jake appraised my efforts, I did not.

I climbed the metal stairs to his ramshackle balcony on the second floor. Below on the street, his car: a self-painted 1973 BMW with an unrepaired bash in the side, courtesy of a motorist as uninsured as he.

Inside, Evan still wore his waiter's black pants, bow tie, and starched white shirt as he typed furiously on his computer keyboard. Lining the walls were bookshelves and paintings, some of them his own. He was tall—taller than I--and lean, good-looking, I suppose, if a woman favored the arty type.

"You look like deep-fried shit," he said, letting me in. "Alison?" He'd dated her briefly in high school before I started seeing her.

"She's fine."

"But you're not." Straddling his chair, he stared at me with a mixture of concern and his never-absent bemusement.

I told him, everything from the briefcase to the kiss to my mother's state of mind. Evan's face lost its bemusement.

"That's the girl you've mentioned a few times? More than a few actually."

"Only in the context of being a cold bitch. Not as the instrument of my mother's death."

Evan, the wordsmith, was unable for once to decoct some irony that would numb life's little wounds. "Want a drink?" Without waiting for my answer, he poured us both glasses of a $200 Bordeaux that somebody with money to burn had left half full at dinner. I took a swallow. It tasted rank and I knew it wasn't the wine.

Evan regarded me with his authorial eye. "What's your plan?"

"What makes you think I have a plan?" Already I sensed the need for secrecy.

"Unlike Tiger, I know you."

"Is that right? Then why am I such a fuck-up?"

"I always thought that was your plan."

I finished my wine, still rank, and poured another. "What would you do if you were me?"

"Irrelevant. You know my philosophy. Besides," he continued, with a penetrating gaze, "like I said, I have the TWO feeling you've already made up your mind."

I had. Everyone has one special talent, even I, and at twenty-seven I had never been rejected by any woman I'd seriously pursued. I'd inherited Jake's looks, if little else, I loved women, they sensed it, and some said I had a touch, slow or fast or rough or withheld, whatever suited, whatever brought pleasure. I had focus, imagination and duration. My father, soon to be fifty-one, couldn't compete with me in this arena. I couldn't know then that the gods would, as usual, use their gift to destroy.

If I were successful in seducing Laura away, Jake would have no choice but to return to my mother, who would live to celebrate her next birthday and her next. I'd return to Alison, who would never have to know. Jake—if he found out—would have no just cause for anger; I'd never admit knowing about their affair, much less that I'd intended to terminate it.

My plan had the geometrical symmetry of either genius or insanity, I didn't know which. It was just beginning to terrify me.

* * *

As the surviving members of Cameron & Munger waited for the police outside Laura's house, I stared down at the crepe myrtle blossoms I'd trampled the night before. Insanely, I wondered if they might contain some clue that would lead the police to me. Could they somehow connect the crushing of the blossoms to the time Laura died? Could they reconstruct my footprints? Who knew what they could do? I tried to smooth out my breathing, keep my hands still, deaden my eyes, but I couldn't. I'd lost all control. Better to run, just bolt down Prytania Street.

A hand roughly grasped my shoulder. "Get a grip on yourself, Son. Now." Jake clutched harder, and the pain shocked me back like a well-delivered slap.

Inconspicuously, he steered me away from the rest of the firm. "She'd been helping you on a case," he stated. I understood.

That was to be my story for the police. So he considered me a suspect.

"What if her neighbors saw you?" I asked him.

"Business. All of it. Business." He looked at me hard, making sure I grasped it.

"Mom can't find out. It would kill her."

"Laura wasn't seeing anyone at the firm," he instructed.

"Okay," I agreed shakily. Only then did he release the grip on my arm. I didn't know what surprised me more, his utter calm or his helping me. He stared off into the distance, maybe getting his own story straight, maybe feeling the first sharp stabs of grief about Laura. Some of both, if father was like son.

Two squad cars pulled up, followed by an ambulance. Neighbors started peering out. Prytania Street would soon draw a maggot-swarm of thrill-seekers. I watched the uniformed cops encircle the house with their yellow no-cross tape, trampling the liriope that ringed Laura's flower beds, dead now at the end of a merciless summer.

Jake softly muttered, "Damn," and I knew why when I saw two homicide detectives get out of an unmarked police car. I recognized them both from watching Jake's trials, required viewing as I was growing up.

Ott Balthazar nodded genially at Jake. He was a grave, methodical Cajun, a large, sleepy-looking man who reminded me of an old, tenacious retriever that never stops going after the stick. Over the years, he'd put away more than a few of the firm's clients.

The other detective, Mel Rimers, didn't speak. Rimers belonged to three gyms and always seemed to be looking for a place he could use all those ornamental muscles. He was handsome, or had been before he started losing his hair, one more injury life had dealt him, and he looked like he kept count.

In a murder case a few years earlier, Jake had skillfully gotten Rimers enraged, then caught him in an inconsistency about his handling of crime scene evidence. After Rimers testified he'd logged it in at 2 p.m., Jake established that he'd stopped off to see his first wife for two hours, then fudged the figure on the log to cover his absence. Aided immeasurably by Rimers' temper, Jake had managed to blow up this relatively insignificant inconsistency into reasonable-doubt proportions, getting his client off and leaving a blot on Rimers' record, not to mention his second marriage.

Jake left me and joined Munger by the van. Ginger and Turnage stood together, an uncomfortable pairing. Ginger thought Turnage was a frat-boy buffoon, and he thought the ambit of her entire gender should consist of a barefoot path from the kitchen to the bedroom. But when Ginger walked over to me, Turnage, who never liked being alone, followed.

"Poor Laura," Ginger offered.

"I didn't know you were friends." I looked at her sharply. Laura would've hated being pitied, especially by Ginger.

"She could be a total bitch. That doesn't mean I wanted her to die."

"She ever talk to you any, Kyle?" Turnage asked.

"Business. If I had a question about a case."

Ginger looked at me; Laura's unwillingness to help anyone was legendary.

"She never said one word to me. Not one single word," Turnage reflected.

"News probably got around about your little dick," Ginger jibed.

Turnage made a mirthless noise. "So who do you think did it, Ginger?"

The question caught her off-balance, and her answer was almost a non sequitur. "Surely the cops wouldn't think it was one of us."

They stood up taller, more nervous, their instinct for self-preservation kicking in. They examined each other, and me, suddenly suspicious.

"Well, you know who's usually the guilty one," Turnage offered. He studied Ginger with the piggish shrewdness that had first signaled me he wasn't as stupid as he appeared.

"Who's that?" she asked.

"The one who finds the body."

I tensed. But Turnage kept his eyes on Ginger, waiting for her reaction, and as he dissolved in nervous laughter, she hit him in exasperation. They saw the police watching their uneasy antics and sank into silence.

I could see Munger's lean profile, utterly composed, as Balthazar interrogated him in the law firm van. Nearby, inside his police car, Rimers hammered Jake, enjoying his work.

When my turn came, I drew Balthazar. I'd read transcripts of Bal's interviews with suspects. He'd start out slowly, like a crocodile easing into the mud. Careful, I had to be careful.

"Son, I guess you saw the same thing as the rest, but let me hear it from your eyes."

I told him—her upraised hands, her naked body, the blood. What I didn't mention was my earlier visit.

"You friends with the girl, Kyle?"

"Not really."

Bal turned off the air conditioner, the act of an insane or very determined man. The van quickly turned into a steam bath, yet not a drop of sweat appeared on Bal's placid face, like those mystics who can stop their heart from beating, or, like Laura Niles, from feeling. Bal smiled as the sweat beaded on my forehead. He looked at me with his sleepy eyes. I knew then he'd figured out an angle the second he saw Laura.

"Sure you weren't close to the girl, boy? I ask again only because your reputation precedes you."

"Bal, I was engaged."

He smiled at that.

"Can't say I never tried," I added for credibility. "I asked her for advice on a case one time. That's all I got."

"How about anybody else at the firm? That boy with the freckles?"

"Jake's got a rule about company ink."

"How's Jake and your Mama doing? Hadn't seen her in a while."

"When I get married, I hope it's good as theirs."

Bal looked at me and just blinked once, a slow blink. "Decedent ever work on that Trust Life case? Where the gentleman drunk him a garage-full of carbon monoxide couple of months back?"

"You'd have to ask Tommy Munger."

"Course I would. Guess Tommy was pleased to win that case. Not to mention surprised."

"We all were. Pleased."

After Richard Flowers' death, no one, including Munger, thought he had a chance of saving the case. But CEO Randall Chaney insisted that Flowers had been a rogue employee, expertly doctoring the books; and the only one who could testify otherwise now occupied a one-quart urn.

"You said 'was engaged'?" Bal asked, circling back. Another long blink.

"Work. Law's a jealous mistress. Like Jake says."

"Unforgiving, the way I heard it."

When Balthazar was through with me, I stepped outside, soaked in sweat, the September day for a moment seeming almost cool. Jake was out there staring into nowhere.

"Dad?"

He didn't answer. Now that he no longer needed to coach me, his priority had changed, to Laura. I could see it in the coldness of his eyes.

"I'm your lawyer, got it?" he said, finally.

"What?"

"Got it?" he repeated, his voice hardening.

"I got it."

That's when he turned to look me full in the face. "Did you do it?"

That was why he was, for this moment at least, my lawyer. Any admission would be covered by privilege.

"No," I swore. "Did you?"

He studied my face and found something wanting. "I can't be around you for awhile."

* * *

Evan always used to say that character is fate and outcomes can't be averted. If I believed that, which I never would, then my father was who he was and I was who I was, and if events hadn't happened exactly the way they did, eventually they would've happened another. Though I can't imagine a worse one.

The morning after I discovered my father with Laura, I arrived at the firm early, wanting to hear Jake's outright lie, and at the same time hoping I wouldn't. Little Wendy again congratulated me for my glorious trial victory, which now felt as distant and meaningless as some preschool sandbox tussle. It seemed strange no one knew about the all-eclipsing image I'd seen on Laura's porch not twelve hours previous.

I walked upstairs to Jake's aerie, which encompassed the entire third floor. It was a spacious room, nine hundred square feet, larger than his family's entire house in New Orleans' Irish Channel when he was growing up. He hated being confined—I suspected he had a touch of claustrophobia—but since law, that jealous mistress, required him to work indoors, he insisted that his office have windows on four sides. Unlike when he was young, he'd be certain of having an escape route.

Puzzled at my rare appearance in his office, he squinted, expecting bad news. I certainly could've given him some. At his feet I heard a familiar jingling: I.D. tags belonging to Gumbo, his faithful chocolate Lab and surrogate son—Gumbo, who never once had failed to live up to his potential and who accompanied Jake everywhere, excepting presumably on his liaisons with Laura.

"What happened with Vickers?" I asked him. Jake's phantom client. I deposited Jake's briefcase on his desk without comment. "Is he changing his testimony?"

"Managed to talk him out of it."

And that was the moment, before the lie turned rank and rotten between us, that I should've blurted out what I knew, not as a threat (which never worked) nor a plea (of which I was not capable) but just as a fact that by the sheer force oits utterance might've changed our course. Instead, I nodded. That was all I could do. So deep was my need to believe all was right between my parents that I walked out wondering if somehow I'd misinterpreted what I'd seen on Laura's porch. Then I recalled his e-mail to Laura: "I love you, Baby Girl."

"Firm meeting in ten minutes," he reminded me.

"I'll be there."

• • •

I made it on time, a first, as Jake took care to note in front of the others. Laura hadn't arrived. I claimed my usual corner chair away from the table. We wouldn't begin for another two minutes; Jake believed meetings should start on time and end the same way, with nothing but essentials in between.

Ginger leaned over. "I guess you were out runnin' 'em last night as usual." She meant running women.

"I'm through with all that."

She looked at me shrewdly. "Getting some sense in your old age?"

"There's Alison, you know."

Ginger smiled and, for a second, she looked like she was eighteen instead of thirty-eight. Ginger, for all her street smarts, was in love with love and believed in it like a fairy tale.

Twenty seconds before the hour, Laura made her appearance and walked to her seat next to Jake. Her off-the-rack Neimans clung and hung like designer originals, and she moved with the offhand eroticism of a runway model. All very businesslike, of course.

She and Jake were good at concealment. If I hadn't known, I wouldn't have. But since I did, I could detect the infinitesimal movements that gave them away. Breathing in rhythm. A swallow. A repressed smile. I'd underestimated the effect seeing them together again would have on me.

Jake began, and his presence was such that all conversations ceased mid-syllable. "About Richard Flowers," he said without preamble. "You'll be receiving inquiries from the press. Refer them to Tommy or me."

"What if friends ask?" Ginger posed.

"It was a tragedy," Jake answered and all understood that what he'd said was a quote and not to be expanded. "If the police question you," he added, to his credit, "tell them what you know about it."

"Within reason," Munger amended .

"Do you expect a continuance?" Jake wanted to know.

Munger shook his head. "Trial's postponed until after the funeral. I won't request any further delay, and I doubt if the Attorney General will either. We're halfway through, and he's as sick of it as I am."

Jake nodded, pleased. Ordinarily, Munger liked to exhaust every convoluted procedural possibility. Jake despised delays, and, unless they were essential to strategy, he always sought to win cases with a brisk efficiency, freeing his clients, then moving on to the next challenge. They differed in almost every way, Munger, with his austere coolness, and my father, with his fire. Jake had started the firm, bringing in the high-profile criminals. Munger had supplied the old New Orleans pedigree needed to attract wealthy white-collar ones, better known as corporate officers.

"Who's got new cases?" Jake asked, his routine check for conflicts of interest with existing clients. His eyes swept the room, not lingering on Laura but, more revealingly, avoiding her.

Munger, to whom the rest of us deferred so as not to attract his cold eye, spoke first. "I have two, Jake. The Wittenhurst boy—"

"Rape by the rich," Ginger pronounced. Munger gave her a hard look, but she was unfazed. --and Myron Jones."

"Good work, Tommy," Jake said, impressed. This news would keep him in high spirits for the next week, assuming I didn't piss him off.

"Roger's father was my fraternity big brother at LSU," Munger noted to emphasize the sacral importance of the case.

The accused, Roger Wittenhurst, was a sophomore at Tulane, son of old-moneyed restaurateur Joshua Wittenhurst. I'd never met Joshua, but if he and Munger were friends, he and I wouldn't be. Not surprisingly, in his frequent photographs in the *Times-Picayune*, Joshua looked aloof, with a healthy sense of entitlement. Also well fed. He resided inside New Orleans' most exclusive gated community, Audubon Place, a few doors from Bob Dylan's former residence, an incongruous juxtaposition typical of New Orleans.

Myron Jones was also a noted local figure, though his money was brand new. He too resided behind a gate, one of his own making, to discourage drive-by attempts by some enemy druglord's vassal. Both Roger and Myron could afford our high fees, both had been in the news, and both would attract more business, particularly if their cases were won.

"And Myron Jones is accused of ordering the murder of one Tyrone Cleets," Munger said. "Any conflicts there?" Again, we shook our heads no.

"Jeb Turnage has asked to handle the Jones case," Munger continued. "He'll need someone sitting second chair. I know Laura is due for a murder trial."

"I'd like one of my own," she responded. "First chair. It doesn't have to be the hottest one going. So thanks for thinking of me, Mr. Munger, but I pass. I prefer the Wittenhurst case. Maybe Ginger would like to work on Myron Jones."

"Oh, I wouldn't dream of taking a case from Laura," Ginger said, caustic as dry ice. Though Ginger would've walked naked through Jackson Square on Mardi Gras Day for the Myron Jones case, first or second chair, she wasn't about to let Laura throw her a bone. "I'll take the Wittenhurst case if you don't mind," Ginger said firmly. "Laura got assigned the last three we both asked for, and I'm higher on the letterhead. Ten years higher but who's counting?"

Ginger was edging for a showdown. Roger Wittenhurst in all his entitlement was not her kind of client. She'd put Jake in a squeeze. I wanted to see how he'd extricate himself.

"Let's see if there's any more interest. Tommy, do you want the Wittenhurst case?"

Munger shook his head no. "Busy with Trust Life."

"Turnage?"

"I don't need some little rich prick to coddle. Besides, my plate's full with Myron Jones."

So Jake would have to split the baby in two, and it appeared he'd have to do it publicly. "Ginger, I'd like you to handle the Jones murder with Turnage."

She nodded, trying to hide her pleasure at getting the case without losing her dignity, but her hands gave her away, the way she grasped them and brought them to her chest.

"You've got the experience to do a great job. Frankly, that's where I need you most. Turnage, would you mind sitting second chair on this one and letting Ginger run it?"

Better than Ginger could've dreamed.

"Sure thing, Jake." Turnage's smile wasn't beaming its usual full wattage.

"Appreciate it. I'll keep in mind that you get first choice next time."

"Thanks, Jake. I'll hold you to it." Back to the big smile.

I noticed Turnage and Munger briefly exchange a glance.

"So, Laura, Wittenhurst is yours."

No surprise, Jake hadn't even considered me.

"Anyone have a conflict with Earl Hutchison?" Jake asked.

"Who's that?" Turnage wanted to know.

"Porn producer and distributor. Out of Houston, connected on both coasts. He and two of his guys are up on thirty-seven counts of obscenity, plus extortion, bribing state officials, filming minors, drugs."

"I could get into that," Turnage said without irony.

"Sheep alert," Ginger called out. "Turnage erectus."

"I have a conflict," Laura said. "One of my clients has a civil action against Hutchison."

"Jeez, so we lose this super scuzz client."

"Mooo," Ginger moaned, broadening Turnage's oeuvre.

"I have an issue I'd like to bring up for discussion," Munger interrupted, his much-exercised prerogative. "It affects us all, not just our case loads but our income."
"Is this what I think it is?" Jake asked.

"Hear me out on this, Jake. We invested in this building with the intention of expanding the firm from the five lawyers we had then to eight and, once we'd absorbed them, to ten."

"I like the size we are," Jake said. He'd been stonewalling Munger on this for a year, incongruent behavior for someone who'd taken risks all his life. My theory was that he feared that new lawyers might side with Munger and overwhelm the delicately crafted voting formula that gave Jake, as firm founder, his power. Currently he could win with a tie; Munger required a majority. With the existing lineup, ties were numerically impossible, and Jake always got the majority.

Munger persisted. "We're only up to six and we wouldn't even be there if Kyle hadn't been up for hire."

Politic as always, he was reminding Jake that, by agreeing to hire me, he'd done Jake a big favor and was owed for it commensurately. At the same time he'd skirted my humiliating bar failures, thus keeping me a possible ally against Jake.

"We have room for four more," Munger continued. "I propose taking on two new associates a year. We're all turning away profitable cases as it is. I've done a five-year plan with conservative projections on income--"

"I've got enough money," Jake cut in. "I believe everybody here is amply paid."

"Turnage agrees with me, don't you, Turnage?"

"Well, Jake," Turnage began slowly. He knew who to address, who buttered his beignet. "Seems to me we could try taking on one, see how that worked...." His voice trailed off. He'd clearly promised Munger to support him, but he sure wasn't ready to die in the ditch.

"So you're backing Tommy on this?" Jake incised, laying Turnage's insides open. If you're not with me, you're against me was Jake's strategy, his usual.

"Well..." Turnage temporized.

"Well?"

"Gee, Jake, I don't know."

"Who would, if not you?"

Turnage hesitated, then, feeling Munger's eyes direct themselves his way, backpedaled. "Okay, well uh, I say try taking one on."

Jake nodded abruptly, noting Turnage's treason, then turned away. "How about you, Ginger?" he asked.

"Hell, I'd like to make more money and work less too, but I say give it another year as is." She was backing Jake all the way but without being obvious.

"Laura?"

"I prefer to remain exclusive. One reason we're in such demand is the perception that we're hard to get. Sometimes the little restaurants with the long lines don't do as well when they expand and just anyone can get in."

Ginger rolled her eyes out of everyone's sight but mine. Jake nodded, playing it out as if he hadn't known whether or not Laura would choose his side.

"Kyle? Like to hear from you."

I was surprised to be consulted. Ordinarily I might've sided with Munger and Turnage—not that Jake with his tie-wins voting would lose the hand—but I could at least raise his adrenaline. Instead I replied, "I think Laura made a good point. I prefer not to expand." I wanted to see her reaction. She never took her eyes away from Jake.

Alison's house was just a mile from the firm. With its large rooms and high ceilings, it was a refuge that soothed me whenever I stepped inside. She'd decorated the walls with some of her largest paintings—she was good enough to be a professional but preferred regular paychecks—and her favorite was a full-length of me standing, unsmiling, no earring. I'd never cared for the stern set of my jaw.

"How's the Grim Reaper?" I inquired that night when Alison let me in. That was her title for my portrait.

"I'd say he had a bad day," she answered, assessing not the painting but me. "Jake?"

I nodded. I'd spent the drive over gnawing on Jake's hypocrisy—he'd criticized me for being a womanizer, and I was single. Engaged, yes, but he didn't know that.

After all these years Alison didn't even bother inquiring into the details. "What's happening with Richard Flowers?" she diverted. I shrugged, his death inconsequential against my grievance.

"So much for inside information," she said. She turned on the six-o'clock news, selecting the channel. The anchor, Charlie Dumaine, wearing her trademark red, swam into view. Perfect ivory skin, graceful hands, black bangs that pulled you right to her Gulf blue eyes. Charlie and I had a history at Tulane. In its death throes it became a tortured history.

"—the curious death of Richard Flowers." Charlie was saying, "Flowers was to testify for Cameron & Munger Criminal Law in their defense of Trust Life Company, whose actions many policy owners consider indefensible—"

"Can she say that?" Alison asked. "Right in the middle of the trial?"

"She just did."

"While beneficiaries, predominantly below the poverty line, were consistently denied benefits, Trust Life CEO Randall Chaney received, according to reliable sources, unrecorded bonuses in excess of ten million dollars."

"How can she know that?" Alison injected.

"She just can."

I could feel Alison looking at me. Years had passed and still Charlie Dumaine was a sensitive spot in our relationship. My junior year, when Alison was away at Harvard and we'd agreed to date other people, I invited Charlie—a drama major, like my mother had been—to my fraternity Christmas dance, The Black and White Ball. It was a night for uniformity, when the entire fraternity would be photographed for the yearbook with our dates, who were to wear floor-length black or white formals.

When I picked up Charlie, she came to the door in a short, cherry red strapless sheath. Wow! I thought. This girl is an outlaw. As we entered the ballroom, every head in the vast room turned as if she'd pranced in naked. Couples stopped dancing.

Smiling, unflustered, oblivious to everyone's dismay, she walked with me onto the dance floor.

"How can you do it?" I asked her.

"Acting." She smiled, like a gleeful kid. "I wanted to see if I had it in me."

"You're an amazing girl."

"I love it."

"Why?"

"The risk."

That night we had sex outside, across the street from the college in Audubon Park, not far from the bench where I later found Laura crying over Jake, the bench where I would later cry over her.

During my three-month run with Charlie Dumaine, I cut many—most—classes to be at her side. I waited in the wings while she rehearsed for a play as Jake had done with Mom. I had my ear pierced, Jake's taste be damned. I bought her gifts—red earrings, a red bikini, red cowboy boots. In February she and I scrambled for beads at Mardi Gras parades and danced at Jake's Krewe of Rex Ball; in March we celebrated St. Patrick's Day at O'Flaherty's Irish Channel in the Quarter. Though I saw little of Evan, my roommate, I knew he disapproved. Alison would be home soon for spring holidays, and Charlie and I were more or less living together. For the first time, I had no desire to go out with other girls.

It was incandescent with Charlie, and the next stage was marriage. One rainy Sunday when she and I spent the afternoon in bed, she told me she loved me and asked if I loved her. Yes, I said. I also loved Alison, whose inconvenient existence I'd never mentioned to Charlie. I'd taken the path of least resistance, a familiar route.

At spring break, Alison came home and Charlie went to Baton Rouge, both of them expecting to see me all day every day. Charlie was thrilled that I'd be meeting her parents, and Alison confessed that, for her, dating others hadn't worked out.

Every day I commuted the eighty miles from woman to woman, my excuses becoming more and more inventive as my stamina diminished. I felt like air traffic control, guiding my sagging Cessna in for landing after landing. And it worked, almost to the end of the holidays, when a Cajun barbecue that Charlie's parents were holding in my honor coincided with the night of Alison's goodbye party, a must-attend function that I'd been certain wasn't until the next night.

I knew Charlie had a flair for the dramatic, but, overlooking her journalism minor, I hadn't considered her investigative skills. I got to witness both when she crashed the party at Alison's parents' house, bludgeoned me with a full Champagne bottle, and told Alison her colorful but fairly accurate reconstruction of my double life. I drove that night to Baton Rouge and told Charlie I wanted only her—I'd made the decision—but her burning love had chilled to the opposite emotion. My feelings did not change as fast or as radically, and one indelible drunken night I literally cried on Evan's shoulder over her. Alison I eventually won back (after all, we were supposed to be dating others), but my future with Charlie no longer existed except in my cabinet of might-have-beens.

Alison zapped the TV to black. I'd learned nothing new about Richard Flowers' death, except that Charlie Dumaine considered it more suspicious than the infamous, underpaid New Orleans police. She was no fool, though I had enough sense not to say as much to Alison.

Only the day before, New Orleans had been tied with Washington, D.C., for homicide capital of America; by all rights,

Flowers should've put us in the lead. As a port city, a drug entry point, and a destination for millions of tourists and thousands of prostitutes, New Orleans had a tolerant, wide-open attitude that either lured killers to it or lured its citizens to kill, I didn't know which. We offered the Mafia, Mardi Gras, Bourbon Street, a free-wheeling history of corruption, legal gambling, illegal gambling, the intimate juxtaposition of mansions with shotgun hovels, gangs, a disproportionate percentage of alcoholics and users, a robust porn industry, and weather hot enough to drive you mad. We even had food good enough to kill for.

"Do you know what I crave?" Alison asked.

It was Tuesday. "Shrimp remoulade."

"Am I too predictable?"

"I crave predictability," I answered, and it was mostly true.

As we waited in line outside Galatoire's, inevitable unless you camped out at their doorstep, Alison commented on my silence, and then, once we'd been served, on my lack of appetite.

"You love their trout meuniere," she urged, as if trying to reason with my stomach. Since she abhorred change or any deviation from the norm, I was a worthy lifetime project.

"Ate a big lunch," I claimed, nonetheless taking a large bite of the buttery fish to deflect suspicion.

In fact, I'd eaten no lunch. Nor, after the firm meeting, had I done any work. In my office with the door closed, I'd played and replayed mental snapshots of Laura at the meeting. At first I thought I was trying to gain insight. Then I realized I couldn't stop myself. Random jagged images jolted through me—her silk skirt over thighs toned enough to feel the hard along with the soft, her creamy blouse unbuttoned one button beyond Ginger's. Her lips full and lightly glossed, pinning you even before the eyes. The skin so rich and smooth you could live without other sustenance. Situations where surprise overrode improbability: against the wall, maybe in the supply closet, my hand gliding up her suede-smooth thigh and hooking her panties—the briefest, the softest—and bringing them down. Or riding in her car, my fingers manipulating her to pull to the side of the road where I would unbutton the final clasps of that same blouse while traffic whistled by.

The Galatoire's waiter filled our wine glasses.

Me appearing in Laura's shower, or she in mine, with no explanation, the sudden vision of all of her filling my throat with desire so thick I couldn't have spoken.

No, I hadn't counted on being attracted to Laura, not to this extent. But a simple physical attraction wouldn't harm what Alison and I had. I would damn well stick to that. I forced myself to raise the image of my father kissing her, and rage replaced lust.

"What ever are you thinking about, Kyle?" Alison asked, a perturbed look on her face, as if I might be coming down with something. She was determined that we were both going to live to be 100, together.

"Work," I said, and she nodded. Work meant Jake, and that explained anything.

After I dropped Alison off—I'd finished my meal, and hers, to allay her concerns—I considered stopping by the F & M. But this night I didn't want anything the F & M offered, and I headed home to the French Quarter, where I insisted on living despite Jake's railings about degeneracy and high rent.

My upstairs apartment on Saint Peter Street had a balcony, a private courtyard, and a miniscule, rickety, locked garage—originally a stable from the 1700's—that cost as much per square foot as my living space. On nights when I got home after midnight and drove past unlit black holes of doorways, I could feel my support of historical preservation begin to crumble.

I'd never seen a neighbor and, if need arose, they'd likely be more a source of danger than help. When I heaved open my two green stable doors so I could park, my gun was in my hand. If murder trumped everything in New Orleans, I planned to play the card.

Once I secured the garage, I opened the two substantial locks on the tall wooden gate that blocked an outsider's view of the wisteria-vined courtyard garden, then climbed ten winding wrought-iron steps to open the deadbolt to my apartment. Inside, my hand went first to turn on the life-support—known in other parts of the country as air conditioning—then to the overhead light switch, then to the alarm system. Such was the norm in the tropical murder capital of the United States.

Were they together now, this instant? I called home, hoping for the first time in memory that Jake would pick up.

"Yes?" That was the way my mother always answered the phone, as if the world were no larger than the immediate neighborhood.

"Just called to check in. Big doings at your end?"

"Very tiny doings. Infinitesimal." Her voice sounded fairly clear, a sign that Jake might be there to take the sharp edge off the night. But if he were, would she have said "infinitesimal"?

"Where's Tiger, asleep?"

"At the office." Concern crept into her voice; I never called for or asked about Jake. "Is something the matter?"

I cursed my stupidity at upsetting her. "Nothing's wrong," I said lightly. "Just a question about work."

"That's where you'll find him."

"You doing okay? Need anything from the store? I can drop it by."

"I'm stocked for the winter, honey." I could hear the slur purring its way into her voice. The edge of the evening was softening. "Like the honey bear and the honey bee." The conversation was heading into Wonderland now. There Jake would find her, struggling against sleep so she could see him at whatever hour he returned.

"I'll see you tomorrow, okay?"

"Bye, bye," she said absently.

I speed dialed the office, Jake's direct line. By the second ring I knew he wasn't there; Jake always picked up immediately, with a gruff "Cameron." Long after the fifth ring I still clung to the hope that he might answer.

Why not drive to Prytania Street, see for myself? And there sat Jake's conspicuous black Jag, across from Laura's house and a few doors down. Did he really think he was invisible, or even discreet? I blared my horn, or wanted to.

I drove home blindly. Alarm off, air conditioning on, I turned to the TV, anesthesia. Charlie Dumaine was droning on about some world crisis.

What were they doing now? Were they talking, comfortably, intimately? Or could they not wait, against the wall or on the floor, still half-clothed?

A close-up of Charlie filled the screen like a haunting. I heard her say an all-too-familiar name and zapped up the volume.

"April Cahill was moved from county jail today to Angola Penitentiary," Charlie announced.

My stomach whirled, bourbon and bile mixing unpleasantly. Onscreen, April, hands cuffed behind her, wore a demure pastel dress as she was escorted from a caged police car to a prisoner transport van.

"Though Miss Cahill testified she had been beaten severely and repeatedly by her boyfriend, she was found guilty of attempted manslaughter and sentenced to five years in prison. Her attorney, Kyle Cameron, who twice failed his bar exam before being hired by his father, did not return repeated phone calls."

In contrast to the noteworthy criminals New Orleans could boast, April Cahill had not rated a single line in the *Times-Picayune*. Yet, because I'd been her lawyer, she was getting exposure on the top-ranked news station in the city—and not for the first time.

Six years had passed since Charlie Dumaine had learned there was an Alison, but her revenge, apparently, had no statute of limitations. An unflattering shot of me, staring into the sun, mouth open, looking demented, stayed on the screen for two good seconds longer than necessary. I killed it with the remote.

At midnight my father's car was still at Laura's, also at 1:30.

At 2:30 it was finally at home.

I poured a bourbon, straight, electing to knock myself out the natural manly way instead of following my mother's chemical path to sleep. It would take more than one, I gauged.

I stripped down to my briefs and went onto my unlit balcony, sipping my bourbon, as I stood watching the addicts, thieves, and murderers stroll below.

Who was the first lawyer to arrive at Cameron & Munger the next day? Kyle Cameron was, preceding name partners Munger and even Cameron. Why? Kyle was beginning a new life of legal responsibility, one stellar enough to impress Laura Niles. He was hard at work straightening his files so that his office would be presentable. And he was busy re-arranging his furniture so that his view of the parking lot and all entrances thereto would be unimpeded.

By the time Jake drove up at 8:00 a.m., his usual time, I was seated behind my newly situated desk. Looking down at him, I could tell he was puzzled to find the Alfa there so early. He put his hand on the motor to see if it was still warm; it was not. He came directly to see me, Gumbo padding behind.

"What's wrong?" he wanted to know.

"Nothing."

"Why are you here so early?"

"I wanted to ask you something."

He nodded, certain I was in some kind of scrape, if not financial, then legal or domestic. Alison—or some other girl or girls—was pregnant perhaps, or there were bookies on my tail, or my real bar exam scores had just surfaced after two years in the wrong file. His frown indicated he was awaiting the damage report.

"I could stand to be a little busier. Maybe you could assign me a couple of more cases on my own or let me assist somebody."

A long pause ensued, as Jake's neurological wiring struggled to decode information so contradictory to its last twenty-seven years of programming. Is my good-for-nothing son really asking for more work? Could I have misunderstood him? Is he trying to torment me? For several seconds his face contorted and froze, as if his brain were undergoing a tiny ischemic stroke.

Once he'd finally processed what I'd told him, he was so hopeful and excited that I actually felt ashamed for the countless disappointments I'd provided him, or at least I did until I heard his response: "I always knew you'd surprise me one day."

"In other words, 'Your no-count son might at long last turn into a self-sufficient adult.'"

"That's not what I meant to imply."

"It's just what you meant."

He shook his head. We were back on familiar territory. "I don't know why I even try with you, Kyle. You have a world of potential but you squander it all. I've got a law firm to run. Maybe you can scare up some work to keep you busy till I find the right case."

Later, as Laura passed my office, I hurried into the hall to catch her.

"Thought you voted right. About remaining exclusive."

"Jake's the only reason I joined this firm," she answered unpromisingly.

I cast about for something to say. "Great color," I ventured, indicating her burnt-orange suit. "How'd you find shoes to match?" The line sounded juvenile, though it never had with other women.

She looked at me coolly, without affect. "Actually I found the shoes first."

"So I'm asking the wrong question."

"No, you're asking the wrong person." And she disappeared into her office, closing the door in my face and leaving me alone to consider potential subsequent witty rejoinders.

After that, I began to observe Laura more closely. Legally, the exact term for the kind of observation I was doing was "stalking." And legally speaking, it was illegal.

For the next week, I checked her office mail and, a few times, slipped by her home mailbox, finding nothing revelatory. I tried but wasn't able to break her answerphone code. Twice— Tuesday and Thursday— she left for lunch three minutes before Jake, enough time for him to watch her walk to her Saab, inform his secretary he was leaving, and hurry down to his Jag to follow her home.

On Jake's three regular evenings at the gym, I k surveillance on Laura's house from my Alfa parked two dooı down. One evening she went to the neighborhood grocery, once she went to the Prytania movie theater alone, and on Friday she went inside Jake's gym, then exited and drove home. Jake cut his workout by thirty minutes and followed her home. I'd never seen him abandon a workout, not even the time he sprained his ankle. In fact, on school nights when I'd left my homework half-finished, he would tell me that anyone who quit a small task before reaching his goal would quit an important one too. Apparently his goals had changed.

Saturday morning she left her house at 9:00, bought fresh flowers at the French Market, then browsed in the antique stores on Magazine Street. Good taste, like Jake's. I never saw her with a friend. Sunday she went to breakfast at the Camellia Grill in Uptown, drawing men's stares, as she did all week, everywhere.

That night came a change. I saw a lighted candle in her bedroom window and thought at first it was a signal for Jake. But it was merely her light source of choice. Behind sheer curtains, framed by the smooth slender trunks of her crepe myrtle trees, she slipped out of her bra and pulled on a top, her silhouette graceful and unbearably erotic. She blew out the candle and walked outside, wearing something brief and black. As she climbed into her Saab, I saw a flash of thigh.

Waiting until she turned the corner, I started the Alfa and pursued, surprised, once I'd made the turn, to find her already out of sight. I sped to Saint Charles, took a chance on a right turn, and caught up with her five blocks down.

Fast, reckless, tearing through the dark streets like she was bulletproof, she took us east onto the Mississippi River Bridge. Far below us, the water churned past the last part of the delta on to the sea. Behind us, millions of lights from downtown lit the sky. Across the river, darkness. Through that darkness, my eyes stayed locked on Laura's taillights. She sped through the ugly, charmless parts of town that New Orleans didn't like to claim, then onto a narrow road that snaked alongside the river. Finally I heard music, and the thick vegetation gave way to an oyster-shell parking lot filled with cars from every level of society. Jake's Jag wasn't there.

Beyond the parked cars stood a crumbling Creole mansion, its faded peach stucco devoured by ivy. Surrounding the house were giant oaks in the process of dying a slow, gorgeous death from Spanish moss.

Only then, at 10 p.m., did I remember to call Alison.

"Where in the world are you, Kyle?"

"The old man's got me working late." It was a half-truth anyway, my new standard.

"That's a first," she said dubiously.

"And last, I hope."

Normally we saw each other every night. But this week I was breaking more dates than I was keeping. Even when we were together, my focus was elsewhere, and it had not gone unnoted.

"I love you," she said as I started to hang up. It sounded more like a warning than an endearment.

"I love you too." And I did, in my way, for whatever that was worth.

I watched Laura as she walked inside, her purse swinging freely, her bare legs truly exquisite. No, this would not be a night for Jake.

The old house had a heavy wooden door, on which was fixed a small, rococo sign: "Demimonde." Inside was a very hip, very decadent crowd, on the edge even for New Orleans. I saw one extraordinary creature whose entire left side—hair, makeup, long red nails, jewelry, breast, purse, and short skirt—was female, and whose entire right side—trousers, beard, hairy muscled arms—was male. Definitely not a lawyer hangout.

Unlike at the F & M Patio Bar, where I was accustomed to being sought out because I stood out, at the Demimonde I was too understated even to be seen. My gold loop earring, which I usually considered daring, seemed the mark of a naive pretender. With just one step across a portal, I'd become not only alien but also invisible and undesirable.

And alone. Laura, my one link to a familiar world, had vanished. I threaded my way through the crush to the bar and sat at the far end, trying not to look normal. I was beginning to sweat through my shirt. The air conditioning system at the Demimonde consisted of open doors and windows and a high ceiling; nothing other than overhead fans had been added in the last 150 years.

Several seats down was a girl in her early twenties, probably once pretty, now wasted from drugs or booze, and a little grimy, with matted hair and raccoon-circled eyes. She craved a drink, couldn't come up with five dollars and was arguing with the bartender, to no effect, except to annoy a model-thin girl sitting nearby.

"You know me, Perry," she demanded, loud, coarse. "Just cash the goddam check."

Perry pointed to a bounced check pinned on the wall. "Once a fool, twice an asshole," he answered.

"You always say that, asshole," she snapped, then, trying another tactic, gave him a smile. Bored, Perry looked away.

The dirty girl turned to the model, who was leaning as far away as possible, so as not to pick up lice or herpes or a rank scent, all of which the girl probably carried.

"Buy me a drink?" she keened. Model-skinny slid off her barstool and disappeared into the crowd.

I would be next and I'd already decided to buy her a whole bottle just to go away. But she spotted someone familiar and click-clacked off on teetering heels to intercept her. Stunned, I realized that the woman moving toward her through the crowd was Laura, my prey. I watched from the shadows as they gave each other a loveless hug.

"You're late," accused the dirty girl.

"You're early."

"My time's valuable. Just like yours."

"Then let's not waste any more of it. Don't ever call me at work again, understand?"

They moved to a table out of my earshot. After they exchanged what looked like several unkind remarks, Laura took a plump envelope from her purse and slipped it across the table. The dirty girl looked inside and smiled, then walked away into the swarm. Was Laura paying to keep her affair with Jake secret?

She rose and headed into the sea of plumes and flesh.

"Laura," I called, attempting casualness. "Laura!" I yelled, as she was about to vanish. She turned, hesitating, as if trying to place me.

"You're a long, long way from home," she said, finally approaching. "I wouldn't have thought this was your kind of place."

I smiled my pirate's smile. I could shine all night if she kept tossing me lines like that.

"What would my kind of place look like?" I asked.

"Lots of suits, beefy guys, helpless girls, endless conversations about football and pussy. Pool table."

She'd nailed me but I didn't care. I realized this was the first time I'd ever looked directly into her eyes; they were steady, penetrating, utterly confident. When she smiled, my eyes were drawn to her lips.

"That shows you don't know me," I told her.

"Don't I? Let's see," Laura said, smoothly sliding onto a barstool. I tried not to look at her thighs.

"Drink, Kyle?" That should've been my line.

"Whatever you're having," I said. And that should've been hers.

"Absinthe." She raised two fingers to Perry. My smile faded as he poured from an evil-looking, smoky bottle.

"Wormwood rots your brain."

"Just a little." She sipped her drink. "You don't obey all the rules, do you, Kyle?"

She looked at my untouched glass. I hesitated, then downed it. "Rough." An understatement.

"Only the first time," she said.

"You never even speak at work. I figured you had a boyfriend." I immediately regretted the remark.

"You mean 'lover'?"

She was no longer feeding me easy lines. "Yeah. Lover."

Another absinthe glass materialized by me. Laura smiled and held up her glass. "To lovers."

We clinked, then downed them. The only evidence of its effect on her was a slight flush. But whether it was the absinthe, the heat or Laura, I felt like I'd been drugged.

"He doesn't care that you're here all alone?" I asked. She pretended to be puzzled, forcing me to clarify.

"Your lover doesn't care?"

"I like coming here alone. It leaves room for surprises. You like surprises, don't you, Kyle?"

"No. I like to be in control."

"No, you don't."She smiled, languid. "Dance?"

I nodded. Things were moving much faster, and much differently, from what I'd planned. She led the way outside to an intimate patio, a dance floor of sorts. The beat was insistent, hypnotic, like drums at a voodoo ceremony, and we were good together, the chemistry immediate. Next to us, two scantily dressed dancers stroked each other. Laura saw me watching them and let me move in closer. The few lanterns hanging from tree branches just accentuated the darkness. With the heat, the lush encroaching vegetation and the cries of insects, it could've been a million years ago, before man and woman began to creep upon the earth. Her blouse began to outline her breasts, and she danced closer, never touching me. She could see the way I was watching her.

I wiped sweat from my brow. "New Orleans in summer. If you ever need proof there's a hell."

"You can't fight it," she said. "You have to let it swallow you up."

The music segued to a slow dance, "New Orleans Lady." Her breasts and nipples were fully outlined now. "All the way from Bourbon Street to Esplanade," the song went, "they sashay by, they sashay by." The music flowed over us like syrup, and we melted together.

As the song ended and the other couples slipped away, she took my hand and led me through thick undergrowth from the patio into the darkness. I watched her move in the moonlight, smooth, sure and lithe. I'd never been more excited.

She took me down a rotting pier and into a vine-covered gazebo. It was dark, the smell rich with decayed leaves and probing newborn vegetation. My breath caught as I imagined once again how silky her thigh would feel if my fingers brushed inside it. I placed my hands on her waist and gently pulled her to me. Heat radiated from her body. She looked at me, knowing I'd kiss her.

I did and felt her lips curl into a smile. Moving her face away, just an inch from mine, she asked, almost in a whisper, "Why are you stalking me, Kyle?"

"I'm not," I stammered, jolted by being caught, by her body next to mine.

She shook her head, not impatient, just light-years ahead of me. Had she told Jake? Would she, now that I'd kissed her?

I tried my pirate's smile. "Because I want you." With her that close, it was hard to keep my concentration. And yes, God, I did want her.

"I'm going in now," she said, turning away. In a moment she'd be gone, my mother would be lost, and so would I.

"I know about you and my father," I blurted out, anything to keep her there.

She stopped, the most gratification she'd granted me that evening.

"And you want me to quit."

I tried to see her face. Was she angry or, worse, amused?

"Yes."

"Are you going to steal me away?" There was no anger in that ironic voice. I hadn't cut that deep.

"I can't go to your boss," I parried, trying to match her tone. "I'd prefer not to kill you. So, yes, that's my plan."

Laura appraised me, seeming to consider it. "Why should I let you?"

"Because I'm better than the old man. Younger, stronger. Better in bed."

Then she did laugh. She watched me absorb it, then turned away and walked through the woods toward the Demimonde. Lit only by the inconstant moon, she shimmered in and out of vision. Even after she disappeared, I still saw her.

I found myself on Prytania Street wondering if the old man would be getting out for a late date. After two hours, Laura still wasn't home. Was she drinking her absinthe alone? Not damn likely.

Finally I drove to my apartment, loaded with enough sexual energy to pole-vault myself, without apparatus, onto my upstairs balcony. I'd be spending a long night up there, sweating off the evening.

The next morning, despite a ferocious hangover, I arrived at work at my new early hour to find Jake waiting in my office. My heart literally stopped before slamming its next beat into my chest wall so hard I got dizzy. She had told him. His next words confirmed it.

"Just spoke to Laura," he said.

"I can explain." I felt physically sick, like I might throw up my breakfast along with my confession.

"Explain what?"

Because he had no idea I'd been with her.

"Laura said it's fine with her for you to take the Wittenhurst case," he continued.

"That's a big case," I said, stalling. Had she changed her mind about seeing me? Or just decided to toy with me a little more? Worse, maybe Jake had talked her out of the case, telling her how pathetic I was.

"Big as they come," he replied.

"So why do I get it?" It made me more than a little nervous imagining myself as the lead lawyer. Beneath the nervousness was a little burr of guilt.

"I think you're ready to handle a big one. You've been getting in early, working late, ..."

I'd simply been keeping Laura's hours.

"...you've asked for more responsibility,..."

The better to impress her.

"...and the Wittenhurst case is right up your alley."

"Date rape, you mean?"

"That wasn't what I meant."

"Then what did you mean?"

"I meant he attends Tulane, is a member of your old fraternity, probably goes to all your old hangouts. You're of the same generation and can speak his and his friends' language, which is the argument I'm going to make to his father when I tell him you're the lead."

"Who's second chair?"

"I am."

"Oh, no. I'm not going down that rabbit hole."

"Meaning?"

"Meaning I'd rather be second chair. Less frustrating. Let's face it, you're planning to be lead lawyer in everything but name."

"Absolutely not. It's your case. I'm just there to give advice when asked."

"What if I don't want any?"

That took him aback. He began imagining the mess I could make if I became too headstrong to accept his help.

"I hope we can work together on it but, if you insist, I'll stay out of it. I do think you'll need help from someone here," he couldn't help but add. Could Kyle be so obstinate and vindictive that he'd lose the case just to pay me back? He had to be wondering because, frankly, the idea was already crossing my mind.

"I should warn you about the prosecutor. Ray Sessums." I'd heard of him. Criminals called him Dr. Death Row.

"What about him?"

"He applied for a job here. The only firm he wanted. Had a great record. We considered him but finally turned him down. He was more than disappointed. I'd say he has it in for us."

"Why'd you turn him down?"

"You were due to take the only slot."

"Might have it in for me, you mean?"

"You and me both." He paused. "He and Munger got along."

So Munger had pressed to hire Sessums. My father had held the line for me. Even though I was the lead partner's son, I'd barely slipped in. It was a sobering realization. If the small, exclusive firm of Cameron & Munger hadn't taken me in, I'd be toiling in a nest of clientless attorneys, sharing garage-sale furniture with other prime examples of why there are too many lawyers. Jake had not only expended God knew how much political capital to get me in the firm, he was now giving me a case he had to know was out of my league.

"Well, thanks." I wasn't sure what I was thanking him for, my job or the case. I was equally undeserving of both.

"Good luck, Podner," Jake said, standing. He shook my hand. "I'll tell Tommy to send the file up to you."

"What does he think about my working his case?" Fraternity big brother was a southern kinship that on occasion went deeper than blood.

Jake smiled. "Thought I'd wait to inform Tommy when it was a fait accompli. If you feel the floor trembling in a minute, it's not an earthquake."

"More like spontaneous combustion." I returned his smile, one of the few times since I'd embarked on my law career. And I considered how ironic it was that Laura had brought us closer, if only for a moment.

• • •

Then, through my window, I saw her arrive, wearing one of her signature Laura dresses, devastating. Ten minutes later, after Munger's secretary had dropped off the Wittenhurst file, I fought down any residual guilt I felt over Jake's generosity and dialed his mistress' number. Because what had happened the night before made me even more determined to have Laura Niles.

"It's me."

"Jake."

"The other me."

"Oh."

"Appreciate the Wittenhurst case."

"Always glad to be a benefactor."

"Always glad to be a beneficiary."

"That makes for a nice symbiotic relationship."

"In that spirit I'd like to get your ideas on the case."

"Have you read the file yet?"

"In the process of." I opened the file folder for the first time.

"My ideas on the case are as follows: read the file, do the interviews, study the law, and ask your daddy for help. Speaking of whom...." I could almost hear the smile in her voice. In the background I heard Jake's voice as he entered her office. The line went dead.

Dammit! I opened the Wittenhurst file and began to read. Munger's secretary had ordered all the news stories on the case from our clipping service. Munger had postponed any interviews with the accused but did note that Roger repeatedly insisted, "I didn't rape her. She wanted it."

The later news articles were much less tentative in reporting the rape charge than the first had been, once Roger's accuser was found to have connections to an advertiser as munificent as the Wittenhurst restaurant empire. I hurriedly ingested the most recent story.

> Tulane student Roger Wittenhurst, 20, youngest son of restaurateur Joshua Wittenhurst, remains free on bail after being charged with the rape of his date, also a Tulane student.
>
> The alleged incident occurred after a fraternity rush party July 1 at Nottoway Plantation on the River Road outside New Orleans.
>
> The alleged victim, whose name is being withheld, is the 18-year-old daughter of a local hotelier. Police said she accused Wittenhurst of raping her in the backseat of his Rolls Royce as two of his fraternity brothers, Allen Sheffield, 21,and Conrad Couvecor, 22, drove them back to her Garden District home.
>
> Joshua Wittenhurst is the owner of some of New Orleans'finest restaurants, including Delta, Chez Faye, Jolie's, and Lagniappe.

The article included a Tulane yearbook photo of Roger, finely dressed and coifed. In his eyes I recognized only too well the expression of a kid with a safety net.

"The only problem with safety nets, Roger," I thought to myself, "is that it gets terrifying to work without one."

When I called Roger to set up an appointment, Mr. Wittenhurst insisted on accompanying him. I refused. If Jake and Joshua attended, they would do the strategizing, leaving Roger and me silently staring at each other, neutered by the dominant males.

Roger agreed to see me at 3:00 the next day, and I called Alison at work.

"Can't make it tonight, A. I'm really sorry."

"Again? You sure?" She sounded disappointed.

"Jake's given me a case, and I'm meeting the client tomorrow," I explained, a less than full vessel of confidence. "You know those dreams when you look down and you're naked?"

"I guess."

"Well, I'm awake."

"You'll do great," she exhorted me, with no basis in fact or limit in faith. "You're a natural."

I had several law professors and one father who would disagree.

"What kind of case?" she asked, hopeful for me.

"Rape. It's the Wittenhurst case." The smile I felt spreading across my face was almost embarrassing.

"Oh, Kyle! Congratulations! I told you Jake would come around."

"I'll call if I finish before 10:00 and stop by," I told her, this time hoping I'd make it. Maybe she could give me one of her pep talks about how smart I was and how much potential I had.

As I hung up, I heard Jake's footsteps pass my door. Laura would be free. In keeping with my strategy, I dialed her number.

"I heard a rumor your birthday's coming up in a few days," I said with an attempt at breeziness.

"Did you now?" Was there a trace of coyness in her voice? I heard Jake stalk by again, heading in the direction of her office. Did he not have any work to do?

"How about Emeril's for dinner to celebrate?"

"I have plans." No coyness, not even irony, just the same answer most men hear all their lives.

"Cancel them."

"Actually I should have just said, 'No, I wouldn't like to go.'"

Once again I heard Jake's voice in her office. Once again she hung up. I told myself it didn't matter, that I'd planted the seed, but my rage at Jake, in the past always mixed with other feelings, was absolute.

In my desk drawer were several strings of Mardi Gras beads, cheap glass that could withstand thirty-foot tosses from floats. Flooded with adrenaline and sudden fury, I flung a garish blue necklace as hard as I could and shattered the glass framing my law diploma. A thousand tiny plunks ricocheted as the beads came loose from the string, bouncing and rattling along the glossy hardwood floor. Above me in Jake's office, Gumbo, the consummate watchdog, sensed danger to his absent master and began to bark.

"This is something you'd better look at," Myrt said, sticking her head in my office. She held an official-looking letter with the words, "Louisiana" and "Attorney" in the return address.

I'd automatically given it to her unopened, thinking it must be either a bill for yearly dues (paid for, as were all things, by Cameron & Munger), or an accounting of my usually deficient Continuing Legal Education hours. It was only summer, and I had until the end of the year to locate a seminar that, though it might have no bearing on my practice, didn't take attendance. (The year before, I'd gotten into an anesthetizing two-day course in admiralty law where I met a lovely, ambitious, but ultimately distractable new associate from one of the two-hundred-person megafirms).

Studying the envelope more closely, I saw the forbidding words "Disciplinary Board." The letter inside read "Notice of Complaint." I groaned, more annoyed than worried. Complaints against criminal lawyers for incompetence were legion. Even

Jake and Munger received them. Although the chance of any action being taken was slight, convicts knew that a victory before the Disciplinary Board increased their chances of attracting the appeals court's attention.

The complaint contained citations to disciplinary rules, which I skipped, and a statement of the charge, which I didn't. "Violation of fiduciary duties to client because of sexual conflict of interest and violation of the rules of professional conduct in failing to disclose offer of a plea bargain."

This was a complaint about my ethics, not my mere incompetence. I skipped to the name of the complainant: "April Cahill."

"Dammit," I muttered. "April Cahill." Now I was a good bit more worried than annoyed.

"I never liked that girl." Myrt, ever loyal, was still standing at the door.

April, my first client to go to trial, and my only one to go to jail, had shot her boyfriend, Hank Chesny, and just barely failed to kill him. He'd beaten her numerous times, she insisted in our interview, and, on the night she shot him, "tossed me around the room like I was some ten-pound sack of dogfood." They'd argued after she'd danced with two other men, "good-looking guys, lots better-looking than Hank."

Couldn't I tell immediately she was trouble? Oh, I could tell, all right. I could tell before she even spoke. Tight jeans, white teeth, small waist. A fitness instructor, formerly an exotic dancer, with slim, graceful hands. We both knew she was trouble and that I soon would be in it. Frankly, I found that knowledge more attractive than not.

"April," I cautioned her, "there's a slight problem. You have no evidence whatsoever that he ever beat you. No one heard it, no one saw bruises, you never reported it to the police or to your doctor. You never even mentioned it to a friend. Why is that?"

"I was too embarrassed." April Cahill had never known the feeling, that much I knew.

"Some people need shooting" was her later explanation. Not an encouraging remark. In fact, downright alarming, because our physical relationship had passed a watershed mark the night before when she'd surprised me at my apartment. A vengeful woman and a hothead, she was a defendant who definitely needed to be kept off the stand.

And far away from a jury. The bad facts continued to accumulate, including two witnesses at the dance hall who'd heard April threaten to "gut-shoot" Hank if he didn't "cut her some slack." April's doctor, whom she'd belatedly remembered she'd gone to see about her beating, disappeared after I discovered his license had been revoked.

I explored a plea bargain with the assistant D.A., who, I'd heard, was trying to clear his caseload. One the day before trial, he finally offered aggravated assault and one year.

"I'm not giving up a year of my prime" was her response. Unfortunately, I had no witnesses that I'd communicated the D.A.'s offer except her tomcat at the end of the bed.

When the verdict came in, no one was surprised but April.

I had thirty days to provide a written report responding to April's allegations. The Board would then determine whether or not to proceed with an investigation. That gave me two months before the charges could become public.

I was in the familiar position of asking Jake, former president of the State Bar, for help. Whatever the outcome of the proceedings, my fear of the Disciplinary Board was far less than my fear of his reaction. I could predict, almost word for word, what Mom and he would say. She would know I'd done nothing wrong, and he would reach exactly the opposite determination, each of their conclusions based on no evidence whatsoever.

"These are serious offenses, Son," he began. I already knew it from the look in his eyes, worried rather than angry, which surprised me almost as much as it scared me.

"It could mean disbarment."

I felt a little bolt of fear whip into my throat, where it met the blood rushing from my head. I sat down.

"I told her about the plea, I swear." It sounded false but wasn't. "I begged her to take it. I knew I'd fuck up the trial." I was reduced to pleading my own incompetence to persuade my father.

I could see his legal-machine mind weighing the facts, the logical inferences from my past as a notorious pussyhound competing with the equally compelling evidence of my usual ineptitude. Hung jury. He stared at me, his hard stare that made you forget there was a human being in there.

"You told her." Testing around the edges of my story, seeing if it would give. I'd seen him do it to clients, not to mention me, all my life.

"You didn't fuck her."

I shook my head. "No. Hell no." The lie came out easily, so easily it surprised me. Though I'd never been a poster boy for probity, I'd never before flat-out lied to my father about something significant. As I weathered another few seconds of his stare, I remembered why. But I had another consideration, one that in my new priorities outweighed even Jake's fury, even, God help me, my career.

The allegations in the Complaint cast me in about a desirable a light as a case of genital warts. I met my father's stare, and, after a long moment, he nodded, satisfied.

"Can we keep this between us, Dad? At least until it has to come out." Jake's rule was always to inform the firm of anything that might concern them. So, it surprised me when, after a hesitation, he nodded yes.

He laid his hand on my shoulder, and I felt, despite everything, reassured. As he walked out, I started to call out for him to wait but I let the moment pass. I felt more than a tug of guilt at my plan. If I could've retracted the dinner invitation to Laura, I would've. But I couldn't, so it was an easy penance. As to my plan, there was my mother, so there was no going back on that either.

I spent the rest of the day preparing for my meeting with Roger Wittenhurst. At 9:00 p.m., nowhere near finished, I called Alison. She said she missed me. I told her I missed her, and I did. My intention remained to go back to her after my mission with Laura was complete. Ignoring the lesson of my earlier disaster with Charlie Dumaine, I still believed that Alison would never have to know.

When I left the office at 1:00 a.m., I couldn't stop myself from driving down Prytania Street in order to pass within fifty feet of the sleeping Laura Niles. Her birthday was in three days. Adhering to my strategy, I would make no further attempts to contact her.

Out of insecurity I'd overprepared for Roger, then found myself annoyed when, a half hour late, he hadn't yet arrived or bothered to call. After twenty more minutes, when he entered my office without knocking, wearing sweaty jogging clothes, I was infuriated. I debated whether or not to mention his lateness and thereby spoil our rapport. "My time is valuable" was what I wanted to say, a pure Jake-ism and probably a Joshua-ism as well.

Roger's mouth, which in the news photo had appeared cruel, now looked merely arrogant. "I'm the heir," he said, bored, sitting across the desk from me, not bothering to shake hands.

"No shit," I said. Roger looked a bit surprised. He tossed his head to get the hair out of his eyes, a characteristic gesture, I soon realized. He had the finest hair I'd ever seen on an adult—he would begin balding within a few years, and, barring a medical miracle, be down to a blond hat-brim fringe before he turned thirty. Thank God I'd inherited Jake's hair, I thought, relieved at any dissimilarity I could find between Roger and myself.

My initial intent—to be friendly to elicit his trust—changed when I saw that he was unredeemable, at least for the time I'd know him, and wouldn't be redeemable until he'd undergone protracted suffering. In the meantime, to command Roger's cooperation, I'd have to dominate him.

How in hell did I hope to manage that? If dominating a spoiled kid were easy, Jake would've handled me years back. I took my cue from the few times he'd come close. Firm and cool. Unconcerned with whether I cooperated or not. Willing to watch me fail. Tough love, as the self-help books called it. With Roger Wittenhurst, it would have to be tough love minus the love.

"Roger," I informed him, "you are in a world of shit that for once your father can't rescue you from. Juries are not made up of wealthy people, they won't take to you, and in New Orleans they are so fed up with crime they'd love sending you to prison. If you want my help, you'll arrive when I say, leave when I say, do as I say, and exhibit normal social proprieties such as shaking hands and asking permission to sit. Otherwise you can fuck off."

"May I please sit?" he asked sarcastically, not the least cowed.

"Get out of my office. And fuck off. And be sure to quote me to your father." Roger just shook his head and gave me a smile that said I'd soon be tangling with his old man. Then he strolled out.

Good Lord, had I lost my mind? Jake was wealthy, but Joshua Wittenhurst could crush him. I gave Joshua twelve hours maximum to corral Jake and Munger and insist I be removed. Munger would support Joshua and make another bid to hire Ray Sessums. Jake would have no defense for me.

From my window, I watched Roger shuffle slackly to his vintage Rolls, tossing on a pair of sunglasses. Then the horny little bastard took them off, to stare at Laura, who was emerging, like Botticelli's Venus, from her Saab.

After less than five minutes with the file, I'd lost the firm's wealthiest client and Laura's override with it. When I called Alison and told her what I'd said to Roger, even she was worried. I dropped by Evan's that night for a second opinion.

"Joshua Wittenhurst fired his executive chef for not calling him 'mister'," Evan said, the light from his computer monitor turning his face an unencouraging blue.

"So?"

"The executive chef was his brother."

My future unfolded in my mind, quick as a switchblade. In twenty-four hours, I'd be unemployed, calling suddenly busy family friends to ask for a job, any kind of job. I had no qualifications for anything, had never needed any. I couldn't even ask Evan for a referral as a waiter since he worked for Joshua. Incidentally I would be disbarred. I spent the rest of the night awake, rehearsing for a meeting with Jake and Joshua Wittenhurst as dual adversaries.

The next day, when the phone rang at 8:00 a.m., I'd already been at work for over two hours. "Mr. Cameron," a voice said, "I'd like to apologize for my behavior and request that you handle my case."

Was it Evan, playing a practical joke?

"Who's calling?" I asked.

"Roger Wittenhurst. Would you handle my case? Uh, please."

It was Roger. Thank God. I forced myself to hold off answering him, as if I had to consider my response.

"I'm open to discussing the possibility with you. No promises though. Be here in one hour."

"Thank you, sir."

"Myrt," I called out as soon as I hung up. "A little help?"

When she stuck her head in, I was on my hands and knees, tearing through files on the floor. "Have you seen the questions I drew up for my interview with Roger Wittenhurst?"

"Have you looked in your briefcase?"

"No, but they're not in there."

She opened my briefcase and produced the list, without comment or wasted motion. I grabbed it as if it were a roadmap to salvation. I had one hour to wipe out all doubt, all fear, all human feeling. People like Roger, once they'd been broken, had to be ridden relentlessly, or they'd fight to regain their head. I had to keep handling him the way Jake should've handled me.

Roger arrived in forty-five minutes dressed in a thousand-dollar suit—I should know—and after letting him wait thirty more, I allowed Myrt to escort him in. After he shook hands with me, I gestured for him to sit down. He jerked his head to the left, just enough to toss the shock of fine blonde hair out of his eyes, the first of many times that day.

"If I decide to represent you, I don't need or want to know if you're guilty. But I do need to know all the details of your relationship with Mamie Lawrence and all the details of what happened on the night she says you raped her. Who, what, when, where, how. Every single thing."

"It was our third date."

"When were the first and second ones?"

"A couple of weeks before.

"Was there any physical contact on those dates?"

"I patted her on the butt once. No big deal."

"Her response?"

"Vague. Anyway I pick Mamie up at 6:30. It's a Saturday and she's alone, parents in New York, and she invites me in for a drink. I have a bourbon straight, beer chaser, she has wine, no big deal."

"Any physical contact then?"

"Not unless she touched my hand when she handed my drink over. Anyway, then I stop by Conrad's house and pick him and Allen up and we drive to Nottoway. Mamie and I are in the front seat. Not touching and not drinking," he added, already anticipating the drift of my questioning.

"We get to Nottoway around eight o'clock, and there's maybe seventy-five brothers and a hundred rushees, most with dates, so about three hundred people. Some are outside on the grounds where we have kegs set up, some are in the ballroom we rented for the night. Mamie likes to dance, the band's good and it's hot as hell outside, so we spend our time inside."

"Open bar inside?" I figured nothing much had changed since I'd been in the frat.

Roger nodded. "But I don't get too drunk because I know I've got to drive home. Three or four more bourbons is all, and we're dancing for three hours straight and working it off. Mamie, on the other hand, gets wasted, you know that point of no return?" I knew. "Well, she's beyond that by 11:00 and I'm hoping I've packed an old beach towel or something because the ride home's not going to be pretty. You know...." He mimicked a barf.

"Can anyone testify that you weren't drunk?"

"Conrad, Allen, probably ten more."

"But you didn't drive home."

"No, because I've got to nurse Mamie so she doesn't puke on my original leather seats."

"Who drove back, Allen or Conrad?"

"Conrad. Allen was too drunk."

"Then I don't think he can testify you weren't. Did you and Mamie have sex?"

"Yeah, but she's of age, I'm of age, no big deal."

"She consented?"

"She damn sure didn't protest."

"Was she conscious?"

"Semi."

"Give me more detail."

"She was sitting up, she was talking, she said the band was good, she was glad her parents weren't home, I was nice. She kissed me back, took off her shoes, then she put her head in my lap and said she was going to take a nap."

"What happened to the nap?"

"I unzipped my pants and she started giving me a blow job. Not the best I'd ever had, I might add. Pretty toothy."

"She started it?"

"Most definitely. Practically swallowed it."

I gave him my best version of Jake's hard look. Roger didn't look away. "I unzipped; she licked. Swear to God."

"Did you use any force or hold her head down?"

"Not really, just enough to direct her." Not what I would call a promising answer. "Then we had sex."

"You had sex after the blow job?" I worked at not feeling competitive.

"Yeah," he said, his face reflecting his remembered perturbation. "She quit halfway through, so I got on top of her and pulled up her dress and we fucked."

"Did she protest at any time?"

"No. At least not until we dropped her off and she sobered up and started worrying what Allen and Conrad might say about her. Her parents are big Catholics."

"Did she explicitly say that?"

"No."

"Was she able to talk? Did she have a chance to protest?"

"We were kissing the whole time."

"Did she try to move away from you?"

"She squirmed but I just assumed she was humping. Not the best I'd ever had of that either."

"Were you rough in any way? Did you exert any force?"

"No. Just normal sex."

"Did you ever ask her if she'd like to have sex?"

"No! Ask any girl and she'll say no, even if she's dying for it. Anybody knows that."

So we did. I got names and phone numbers of witnesses from Roger, then dismissed him. He was unsure about the propriety of a closing handshake but decided he'd better extend the hand. I nodded in approval, then after he'd gone, made a note to set up appointments with Conrad Couvecor and Allen Sheffield.

About some things Roger seemed to be telling the truth. He could've easily claimed that he'd asked Mamie and she had said fine, but he didn't. He also admitted that he'd been the one to unzip his pants; he could've laid that on Mamie too. Conceivably, he was being truthful when he said Mamie was the toothy instigator. True, I'd learned in law school that defendants were often crafty enough to trick their lawyers, but I didn't know if Roger had the brains or the guile.

If he was telling the truth, I could be certain that Mamie Lawrence wouldn't. The verdict would come down to which of the two the jury would like more. Though I hadn't yet met her, I was leaning toward Mamie.

An hour later Myrt informed me that Jake wanted me to hold lunch open for him.

"Did he sound angry?" I asked her.

"No worse than usual."

At noon Jake drove us to Antoine's in the Quarter. We walked past the line of hungry tourists at the front door, to be escorted in through the side entrance for regulars by his assigned waiter, Gaston.

"Our soft-shell crab has been excellent, Mr. Cameron," Gaston said as he seated us at Jake's table. "Perhaps you can bring Mrs. Cameron in while it's still in season."

"Good idea," Jake said. "I believe we'll have some wine today. A bit of a celebration." Gaston vanished on soft feet.

"Congratulations, son," he said after Gaston had returned with Jake's regular wine and padded away. "Joshua Wittenhurst thinks you can do no wrong."

I smiled when I saw his smile.

"That's great." For once, I didn't want to be sarcastic or take a swipe at him.

"He wants to come in and meet you tomorrow. He says you've got Roger eating out of your hand."

Jake was so proud of me right that instant. And I was too.

That evening at Alison's, when I told her about lunch, I had to restrain myself from grinning.

"You see? You see?" she exclaimed, as if all had been forgiven and forgotten over the noontime Oysters Rockefeller.

We settled in like an old married couple. She thawed some of her gumbo—the best, Eunice's recipe—and we watched a tape of *Casablanca* while sailing through a bottle and a half of Chardonnay.

By force of will I was able, almost completely, to avoid thinking about Laura. But her presence hung about the edges of the room. I focused on Alison's blue eyes. I kissed her, at first lightly, for I knew she liked to go very slowly. Then with a rush of feeling, I kissed her more probingly. I felt her hand under the cover lightly touch me.

"Rising young lawyer," she said and smiled. We made love to the accompaniment of *Casablanca*, and when I happened to catch a line of Bogart's dialogue about lost, doomed love, I looked down at Alison's sweet face and knew I was lucky to have her.

"Let this moment last forever," she said, almost like a prayer, and at that moment I would've granted her wish. Whether it was from years together or the mesh of our personalities, there was no one I could talk to like Alison, no one outside of blood who knew me better or had forgiven as much.

Afterwards, we talked—about her parents, my mother, Roger—with Alison steering the subject away from Jake every time I brought him up, like an expert navigator avoiding a submerged rock. Then she said something that surprised me. "You know, Kyle, if you ever wanted to leave the firm, you could."

I'd honestly never considered it, mainly because I knew I'd have to face a question I'd avoided. But now with Alison I voiced it.

"'Who would want you?'" she repeated incredulously. "Anybody who has the least bit of perception can see you were born to this." She waved away my protests before I even had a chance to voice them. "Don't even bring up the bar exam. Einstein flunked math. Van Gogh couldn't sell a painting."

"Kyle Cameron flunked math too," I joked.

She propped herself up on one elbow, not to be diverted. "Or you could go out on your own."

The prospect was equally appealing and terrifying.

"I'd work in the office if you needed me," she added.

I'd never encountered anything like her loyalty. With the firm, I had security—and an income that would allow me to retire at fifty, if not earlier. Alison, despite her native optimism, was not a Pollyanna. She knew the survival rate of one-man firms. Yet, because she thought it might make me happy, she was willing to risk her future, even give up the job she loved.

"Or stay there, if you want. Just do what's best for you."

"I do have a dream."

"What?"

"You'll think it's stupid."

"Tell me."

"Med school."

For a moment she almost believed it. Then she laughed, half-exasperated. "You flunked math, remember?"

I kissed her then, and we made love a second time, needing no accompaniment from Casablanca or anything else.

Later, while Alison showered, I paged through one of her musty museum magazines.

"What are you doing?" Alison smiled from the bathroom door. She had on a fuzzy robe and bunny-rabbit slippers.

"Nothing," I said .

She padded into the room and saw Charlie Dumaine on the TV. I'd turned it on to see if she had anything about Roger. She did. Her videocam had caught footage of my client as he scuttled out of Cameron & Munger just that morning.

"'Nothing' is right," Alison said and disappeared into the bedroom without a goodnight kiss.

My dream was New Orleans, loosest city in the loosest state, where Daddy took us once on our best and longest-ever time together, nearly a month at the Royal Orleans, so sweet a time I even hugged Sissy. But at age seventeen the closest I could get was Baton Rouge, an hour north. Earl drove me to the bus station.

"You're now a freshman at LSU," he said. I planned to finish early (ambitious considering I hadn't gone to school since the eighth grade). Then I would go straight through their law school. Justice was blind, I damn sure knew that, but she carried a sword to protect herself since nobody else would.

Earl presented me with a high school diploma and a Social Security card. They looked perfect and I'd expected no less.

"Laura Niles," I said, trying it out.

The bus was loading, and Earl kissed me goodbye for a long time. When I got out of the car, I told him.

"When I disappear, it's from you too.

"You sure that's what you want, Babe?" he asked, and for once I was on top. He'd done a lot for me. He'd also done a lot to me.

"That's what I want."

Unexpectedly, I missed Sissy and Mama for awhile, then recalled what Mama used to say: "You even miss a headache when it's gone."

My roommate my first semester at LSU was a rich girl. We never became friends, but I didn't need her for a friend. Pretty soon people couldn't tell us apart on the phone. I saw how to book a flight, call a taxi, make a reservation, and leave a tip. I saw that some people spend $300 for one pair of sandals. What surprised me most was that parents took care of their children instead of the other way around.

My second year at LSU Law, I interviewed for a job in New Orleans. The founding partner was supposed to be the best in the state. He also happened to be as handsome and as intense about the eyes as Daddy'd been.

One day at Audubon Park, while I cried over this lawyer, a taller, even more handsome man in jogging clothes approached me. He was breathtaking—dangerous-looking and innocent at the same time.

The man looked to be about my age. Too young. When I motioned him away, I saw disappointment in his eyes. He wanted me.

I watched him jog away, graceful and strong. And then I left, still crying over his father, before Kyle could loop back around and ruin my life.

Two days before Laura's birthday, I drove downtown during lunch to the Saenger Theatre, where the recently discovered Tennessee Williams play was showing. When my mother had been in college at Sophie Newcomb with Jake next door at Tulane Law School, she played Amanda in *The Glass Menagerie* and Blanche in *Streetcar*. After Jake saw her in a performance, he was so taken that he called, arranged to meet her and, to my knowledge, never had another date with anyone else—until Laura.

I selected two tickets for the next night, conflicting with Laura's birthday, then dropped them off for my mother. Tennessee Williams was one of the few diversions that could still bring life to her eyes.

"But tomorrow's your daddy's regular poker game," she told me, almost in tears. "He'd never cancel. He hates to miss."

"Tell him it was the only night they had tickets available. He'll understand."

She considered it a moment, then smiled brightly. "I know, I'll call Buddy Longineaux and tell him Jake can't come. And then tomorrow night I'll surprise your daddy with the tickets when he gets home. By then it'll be too late for him to un-cancel. How does that sound?"

"Sounds like a plan to me," I said. Buddy Longineaux, a steely realtor, would have the presence of mind to cover for Jake.

That afternoon I found Laura in the coffee room and, all business, persuaded her to give me five minutes to discuss my interview with Roger. She could be magnanimous about giving up Roger's case because Jake had offered her a murder case that had just come in—a pretty battered wife, just twenty-five, who'd blown her husband's head off with his illegal sawed-off shotgun—an April Cahill case with better facts, client and lawyer.

During the short time she'd had Roger's file, she'd looked into Conrad Couvecor and Allen Sheffield's backgrounds and found that Conrad's family could barely afford to keep him at Tulane.

"Conrad would be very susceptible to Joshua Wittenhurst's financial persuasion," she told me.

"I thought the Couvecors were big in the Yacht Club."

"Until they sold their boats."

"They had a killer sailboat. Vanguard Laser." I could be an assiduous researcher when motivated. "By the way, you like sailing?"

"Depends."

"On what?"

"The weather, the boat, the company."

"Steady breeze, Laser, me."

"Two out of three."

"If you change your mind, I'm in the book."

"Right after Jake?" She watched me coolly.

For an instant I felt the stirring of an active dislike for her, a harbinger of the cold hatred I would come to feel. And that was when I would want her all the more.

I called Alison to go out that night, knowing that the next evening would be Laura's if she so deigned.

"Oh, Kyle, I'm uncrating Faulkner. Don't you remember? I told you." I didn't and she had, in detail, about some upcoming exhibit on Faulkner and New Orleans.

"What about tomorrow night?" she suggested. "There's a new movie at the Prytania." New Orleans, despite its size, had only one art movie theatre; my swampy city was given to less cerebral appetites.

"Tomorrow's bad. Work." The lies were becoming automatic. "How about if I come late tonight and stay over?"

"Kyle, I'm so tired. You don't know how hard I've been working on this exhibit, not to mention trying to persuade these mule-headed administrators to pursue the German Expressionists. I'm so sleep-deprived I'd just fall in the bed and never know you were there. Listen, they're calling me. I'll talk to you tomorrow, okay?"

"Okay," I muttered sullenly.

No woman, other than my mother when she'd accepted the tickets to the play, had given me an affirmative answer in quite some time, and the failure ratio was beginning to jar my self-assurance, ever so slightly.

"Wait," Alison said as I was about to get off. "What about lunch tomorrow?"

"What about Faulkner and the mule-headed Expressionists?" Though I'd relegated Alison to low-priority, I was finding I didn't much care for the status myself.

"Bring a good appetite and none of that bad mood," she instructed me and hung up.

Impulsively, I called Mom. I wanted to find out if she'd sprung the tickets yet, but she didn't mention it and I didn't want to agitate her by asking. At this point everything was set in motion, leaving me free to consider fully the consequences. Even best case, there would be casualties. If all the rats scurried back into their box, I would almost be glad.

In the meantime I put my affairs in order. First thing the next morning I asked Ginger to represent me in the disbarment proceeding. She was an effective lawyer, not averse to fighting dirty, with a lot of presence in the courtroom or any room she was in. Really, there wasn't much choice in my selection. Laura of course was out of the question. Turnage would enjoy it too much, and I'd never be sure he wouldn't try to sabotage the case to make up for all those nights he sat home alone with his dick in his hand. Jake, well, there were a million reasons and besides he hadn't offered. As for Munger, I was, frankly, terrified of him.

"Did you have sex with her?" Ginger asked, taking notes, after she'd reluctantly agreed to keep the matter in confidence.

"No," I said firmly, "never."

Her fingers formed the shape of a six-gun, which she pointed at my crotch. "Keep it zipped, buster," she ordered with a hard stare that contained not one atom of indulgent humor. "I'm not fucking around. Any new legal infraction and your next career will be pizza delivery."

The next morning Joshua Wittenhurst arrived, Roger in tow, and forty-five minutes late. Why was I surprised? I had Myrt tell him I'd had an emergency come up and would be through shortly. Then I made him wait. There was no joy in my retribution; it had to be done or Joshua would seize control. Myrt came in twice to report that Joshua said he couldn't wait any longer—he even had her cowed—but I shook my head no and kept my eyes on the clock.

At 10:46, the phone rang, startling me. It was Munger. "I understand you have a client waiting," he said, his speakerphone rendering his voice even colder and more inhuman.

"I'm finishing something up. Something urgent."

There was a brief pause. I knew what Munger was thinking: "What could you possibly have that's urgent?" But I resisted the urge to amplify, and the even stronger urge to capitulate.

"I suggest you put it aside," Munger ordered. "Now."

"Thanks for your help," I said, a non sequitur I knew would infuriate him, and hung up.

I forced myself to remain seated, watching the second hand's unhurried journey around the clock. By the time twelve more minutes had passed, I was sliding in little pools of nervous sweat.

"A pleasure to meet you, Joshua," I said, when I finally allowed Myrt to escort him and Roger in at 11:05. "This is my assistant, Mrs. Gravier."

Myrt looked at me oddly; she'd never heard me use her last name, much less refer to her as my assistant, but I had to keep Joshua from steamrolling her too.

"What do you think of my son's chances?" he asked. No time for pleasantries. He didn't look at Roger.

"It's too early to say. I need to conduct interviews with Conrad and—"

"He'll give you what you need."

"I'm sure he will."

"If he doesn't, let me know."

"I'll be able to tell you more after I've talked to all the witnesses. Not before."

"How long will that take?"

"I expect to complete the major ones within a week. That should give us some idea how to proceed."

He still hadn't looked at Roger, a measure of how much his youngest son apparently disgusted him. I tried to recall if Jake had ever withheld eye contact from me, finding me too loathsome to look at. It seemed possible. Maybe the night of my sixteenth birthday, which I'd spent in the drunk tank? The times I failed the bar exam?

"Money can be extremely useful," Joshua informed me. "If you think of a way—any way—that I can use mine to increase our chances of winning, let me know." He was telegraphing his willingness to bribe anyone—witness, cop, jury, judge.

"I want to get the best jury consultant in the country." Laura's advice. "That could cost $50,000."

He nodded his permission. "My oldest sons, Eric and Peter, are established at CeCe's and Delta." His two newest restaurants. "They're doing well, and I don't want publicity from this one's jail term hurting their chances. Bad enough he's putting them through this trial at all. Which for their sake I want expedited."

At least I didn't have brothers to compete with. I glanced at the still unnamed Roger. Gone was the old arrogance. In the presence of his father, he nibbled on the inside of his mouth and stared vacantly at a woodpecker drilling an oak outside my window. I felt oddly protective of him, annoying twerp and possible rapist that he was. As Joshua Wittenhurst declaimed about his family tree and the size of his stock and real estate portfolios and the wondrousness of his two older sons, I determined that I'd do my utmost, the distraction of Laura Niles notwithstanding, to unearth evidence of Roger's innocence and to convey that to his jury. It would be exhilarating to deny his father one more thing to bully him with. I didn't ask myself why I always chose competitors—first Jake, now Joshua—who were larger than life.

By the time Joshua finally decamped, I was running late for my lunch with Alison. The museum was in City Park, almost to the Lake, and I'd have to navigate every back route I knew to escape the traffic. As I grabbed my coat—a lawyer would wear his coat in hell—I saw something out the window that was strange even by my standards: Jake was walking with Laura to his car, making no attempt at concealment. As they got in the Jag, I saw Turnage shamble up behind them and shoehorn himself into the back seat.

Curiously, my first reaction was to Turnage, not Laura. Antoine's aside, Jake virtually never took me, his own son, out to lunch. No matter that the few times he did, the hour was spent sparring over cooling red beans and rice. So paralyzed was I by sibling rivalry—with, God help me, Turnage—that Jake was backing out before I realized Turnage was there not as a surrogate son but as a beard for Laura's birthday lunch.

They were headed toward the Quarter, and I followed from three cars behind, although City Park and Alison were in the opposite direction. I was officially late by the time the Jag eased up Dauphine Street and stopped at Bayona, the best Mediterranean in the city. The restaurant, a cottage surrounded by banana trees, would be a romantic spot, even with Turnage sprouting in the third chair like a toadstool.

Only someone born in New Orleans could've made it back to Mid-City in under fifteen minutes. I saw Alison waiting in front of the Museum, a classical Greek design set off by tropical flora that gave the building a seemly decadence. Her white linen looked wilted, and her eyes were cool under her blue sun hat. She got in without a word, holding our picnic lunch from the museum cafe. She looked, I noted, particularly pretty today.

"Traffic?" I tried, and when it didn't work, inserted one finger into her blouse and started tickling her stomach.

"Not funny. Stop it."

"Stop what? This? Or that?" I knew since childhood the location of her every nerve.

"Stop, Kyle, I'm going to spill our lunch." She was now laughing. Any more and I'd be into diminishing returns. I lifted her hat and kissed the sweat off her brow, then her eyes.

"Not here," she admonished before I kissed her lips. "That won't always work, you know," she added when I finally moved my face an inch away.

"Did this time."

"Only because I'm too hungry to fight."

"How does Mediterranean sound?"

"What about this?" She lifted the paper sack. The plan had been a picnic under the nearby Dueling Oaks.

"Too hot. Let's go to Bayona." She had a weakness for their mushrooms in Madeira cream.

"Mmmm," she said, putting our picnic in the back. "What about all the people starving on the gambling boats in Biloxi?"

"I'll drive it over after lunch."

Twelve minutes, three run red lights, and one argument about my driving later, we pulled to a stop on Dauphine. I tossed the key to the valet and opened Alison's door.

"We're running late," I urged. Desire expands, they say, in inverse ratio to availability. Alone, I was one of numberless predators tracking Laura. Accompanied—especially by someone as pretty as Alison—I was subject to reappraisal. Or so I hoped.

"You're the one who was late." Her voice had a little edge. "Remember?"

I took her hand and more or less dragged her out of the car.

"Stop it, Kyle."

"Sorry," I muttered, pulling her toward the restaurant.

"You keep a girl jumping."

More than one, I hoped. Inside, I could barely see the dining room through the crowd.

"Kyle, do you have reservations?" Alison asked, suddenly concerned. A waiter veered nearby with a tray of heartbreakingly aromatic offerings.

"We'll get in," I assured her and jostled my way to the front.

There they were, in a secluded corner table, with a view of the courtyard. Turnage was performing oral sex on a grilled quail, oblivious to Jake and Laura, who, I could tell by arm position, were holding hands under the heavily linened table.

Fortunately, Suzette was the hostess today, and fortunately we'd parted well. If Monique had been on, things might've been more problematical though not impossible.

I caught Suzette's eyes, gave her an I'm-at-your-mercy look and held up two fingers. She gestured to the waiting crowd—an unforgiving and vicious-looking pack of upmarket tourists and Garden District doyennes—with an I-wish-I-could look on her face. Remembering Suzette's apartment full of rescued dogs, cats and even a chicken, I gave her a look of true devastation.

A minute later Alison and I were seated at a tiny table that a busboy had somehow squeezed in. We had an unimpeded view of the courtyard and, more importantly, Laura. Jake nodded curtly; my presence was an inconvenient and no doubt inhibiting reminder of his other life.

Alison studied the menu. I tried to read mine but couldn't, not with Alison beside me and Laura just five—no, six—tables away. With the slightest turn of my head, I could see both the women in my life, my brain registering comparisons even as I tried not to. The categories of light and dark, good and evil, would've been too obvious to mention if they hadn't been so apt. Alison's skin, untouched by sun, was smooth and cool as alabaster. Laura's glowed with a natural year-round tan, striking with her light eyes. Alison's hair, like my mother's, was ash blonde, as fine and delicate as antique silk. Laura's was thicker, never quite controlled, a rare auburn shot through with red and brown and honey blond. Alison was slender, trim, with quite lovely legs, though she dressed conservatively for the museum and rarely showed them. Laura had, simply, the body of the concubines pictured in those sacred Hindu love tracts. Alison was for lifetime—meaning future—and Laura was now.

Laura had caught me staring, or maybe I'd caught her. I looked away to Alison, she to Jake.

"Decided?" I asked. The waitress was approaching.

"Mushrooms in Madeira. But I'm in an agony between the quail and the rabbit." Rabbit in Armagnac with green peppercorn sauce. Despite her delicacy, she was quite the carnivore, whereas I, since the night at Commander's, had less and less appetite for meat or, really, any food.

"I'd go with the rabbit," I said after an unintended glance across the room at Turnage and his bestialized quail.

"But the quail comes with a risotto cake," she argued.

"Then get it," I said, a little curtly. Knowing Laura was watching—or not watching—was making me jumpy.

Alison gave me a sharp look. "Just the rabbit, then." I ordered a relatively spartan crab salad.

I forced myself to focus on Alison. This was, after all, her time, and besides, the whole point of this exercise was to appear unavailable.

"What's your big project for tonight?" she asked, taking a healthy bite of rabbit. I'd abandoned the salad for the Sauvignon Blanc, a little sweet, Alison's choice.

My mind suddenly evacuated itself of thought. My project was ten feet away holding hands with my father. Frantically I leafed through my mental folder of cases, a brief excursion.

"Wittenhurst." It was either that or Munger's doorman's son's DUI.

"Wish I could be with you," she said and took my hand.

"Can't be helped," I replied, unable to stop myself from wondering if Laura was watching and whether hand-holding would make me appear a little too unavailable. I didn't want to appear unfaithful to the woman I had yet to be unfaithful with.

• • •

"Sweet bird of youth," Turnage proclaimed, suddenly materializing by our table, referring either to our young love or his lunch. Turnage, of course, knew about some of my lapses, most recently with the Tulane grad student from the F & M. Confidentiality was an understood corollary of male solidarity. I hoped it was understood.

"Jeb," I said, with attempted cordiality, "you know Alison."

"Jeb Turnage," he informed Alison and offered his hand. They'd met at least a dozen times but Turnage suspected women immediately forgot him. "I work with Kyle."

"I know you, Jeb," Alison responded, graciously not shrinking from Turnage's sticky clasp.

Jake hugged Alison.

"Didn't know you were coming here," he said to me, unable to completely hide his discomfort. "Tough reservation to get." Laura, studying one of the old photographs of Italian gardens on the walls, obviously wasn't going to greet us.

"Didn't have a reservation," I said, knowing it would infuriate him. "Came on a whim."

Jake's mouth tightened, my reward. "Say hello to your parents," he told Alison and walked away. Laura fell in with them, the old photograph having yielded all its pleasures.

"What a sweet surprise this was," Alison said, taking my hand again. "I'll be having sex dreams about this rabbit." She looked at me. "And you."

"Me too." I absently brought her hand to my lips as I watched Jake converse with the maître d', slip him a bill, no doubt large.

"Where are you, Kyle?" Alison withdrew her hand, leaving mine lying in the middle of the table like a prosthesis.

"What do you mean?"

"I mean I would've had more company in my office with Matilda." Matilda was her notoriously silent parrot.

I took her hand again, determined to make up the previous hour with a concentrate of attention.

"How were the mushrooms?" Through the window I could see Laura slip into Jake's Jag.

"I didn't order the mushrooms."

"I meant the rabbit."

By the time coffee had come and gone, Alison was as silent as her parrot, dispirited and perplexed by the joyless meal. I was feeling even less self-estimation than usual. In fact, I was considering telling Alison I would come over tonight after all, right up until the moment I asked for the check.

"Your father took care of it," our pretty waitress informed me, seeing me doubtless as quite the pampered pup. As Jake had noted at Commander's Palace, it was all coming from him anyway.

That evening in my apartment, I ordered a pizza and waited, not patiently. Curtain was at eight, so my mother would've sprung the tickets on my father no later than 6:00, giving him time to shower, change and eat.

He would also have to find a private moment to call Laura and break their date for her birthday. She would know by 7:15. She would be hugely disappointed and angry, because no matter how faithful my father had been about keeping their dates and seeing her often, this would certainly not have been the only occasion he'd stood her up. On her twenty-eighth birthday, would Laura then call me, out of vengeance, boredom, frustration or loneliness? I didn't care what the reason was, just so she called.

When the pizza delivery guy rang the bell, I carried the phone down with me, afraid of missing her call, then sat on the balcony eating one slice after the other, trying to stare the phone into ringing. By 8:00 when it finally rang, I was a desperate man with an expression on my face that would've rivaled Turnage's. Feeling my judgment becoming more impaired with each moment, I was glad that in my Alfa trunk, already packed and chilled in an ice chest, was a bottle of Cakebread Chardonnay.

"Hi there," the voice on the phone said. "It's me."

It was Alison.

"I thought I told you I couldn't make it tonight," I told her.

"You did. I just called to say hello."

"Hello." I couldn't stop myself from sounding abrupt.

"God, you're a grump tonight. What's wrong with you?"

"Nothing's wrong. Just Jake, exhaustion, stress, work, the usual." I tried to even out my voice, slow it down instead of hastening her off the phone. "How was your afternoon?"

"Good. I think I've gotten the German Expressionist exhibit lined up for next spring, and my boss said—"

Just then I got another call, a beep on call waiting.

"Alison, could you hold a minute?"

"Sure thing."

I frantically beeped her off. "Hello."

"I'll take you up on that sail after all."

"When?"

"Now."

"Great. I'll be there in 30 minutes."

She hung up, and I beeped Alison back on. She was in a talking mood, full of intricacies about her coup in snagging the Germans. She needed to debrief and wind down; I needed to catapult out of my apartment and over to Prytania, and if I didn't get off the phone in the next ten seconds, I truly might explode.

"Listen, can I call you back on my way to the office?" I interrupted her in mid-sentence telling a story about her boss's amazement after earlier being certain that New Orleans couldn't attract a significant show.

"Okay." She was puzzled, a little hurt. I grabbed my keys and was in the Alfa in under a minute, then called her back and mollified her a bit by making plans to see her the next night at my parents' weekly dinner. I knew already that if Laura made herself available, I would cancel. Alison was essential to me, but you don't miss air until you're drowning.

I was so damn nervous when I picked Laura up that I remember almost nothing of the ride to the lake. White shorts, bright orange top, matching polish on her toes, black bra strap showing on her shoulder, hot July night, quiet ride. I remember thinking hard but finding very little to say, even though she seemed less edgy than she had at the Demimonde.

Out on the lake the moon was full, the wind high. I was proficient at sailing Jake's pretty little boat. Even he'd conceded I was a good athlete, despite my bewildering indifference to team sports.

Laura seemed more innocent, less sure of herself. Several times I caught her watching me, then looking away. I poured us glasses of the Cakebread. The play would be letting out for intermission around now, and Jake, I knew, would be frantically calling Laura, getting her voicemail. A part of me felt triumphant; another part, I couldn't deny, felt inexplicably sad for him, going through the hell that I'd devised.

"How is it?" I asked her.

"The wine or the company?"

"Either. Both."

"Very, very nice." She leaned back away from me and stretched out her legs, pearl white in the moonlight, touching mine for the briefest moment. Nothing in my previous experience with women had prepared me for the jolt of desire that rocked me.

"But I told you this was going nowhere," she said.

"Then why'd you call me?"

She didn't explain, or maybe she did. "I love to sail. My daddy used to take me. He'd just whip us across the water." Her face became suddenly melancholy and even more beautiful.

"You're good," she noted as I tacked, and I felt as thrilled as a sixth grader. "Did Jake teach you?"

A quick, bitter laugh escaped me. "You could say that." Jake had pounded the rudiments of sailing into me on the Mississippi Gulf Coast when I was a teen. I'd loved the sport but lost interest after the Father-Son Memorial Day Race, which we narrowly lost due to an error on my part and for which Jake dressed me down in front of the judges and most of Biloxi.

"Jake prefers endeavors with opponents," I said. "Someone to trample."

"That's what makes him a great lawyer."

I tacked away from shore. "Tell me about your father," I said, diverting her. "The excellent sailor."

"Daddy was a professional gambler and a professional shit. Also the handsomest man I ever saw."

"Where is he now?"

"He died when I was fourteen."

"I'm sorry," I said. "Do you still miss him?"

"Only every day."

"What happened?"

"Shot," she said, and something in her voice told me not to press for details.

"What about the rest of your family?" I ventured.

"Gone."

"Are you from New Orleans?" I was determined to find out one damn thing about her.

"Lafayette." She smiled. "We can't all grow up in the Garden of Eden District."

"Are you quoting my father now?"

"Why don't you two like each other? Because you're so much alike?"

So Jake didn't even like me. My own father. "Did he actually say he didn't like me?" I couldn't stop myself from asking.

"I just mean the way you stay angry at each other. What's the story?"

"I can only speak for myself.

"Fine."

"The old man came up hard, and as much as he hated that life, he thought it had made him tough. So he wanted to toughen me up the way he'd been toughened. The only thing was, he made too much money for us to live in a three-room shotgun duplex in the Irish Channel—"

"Not Nola's style."

"Not his."

"I stand corrected."

"But he gives me everything he ever wanted when he was a kid—electric trains, camp, go-cart, trampoline, tennis lessons, clothes, cars, cash, you name it—and then he stays furious at me when for some reason I don't turn out in his goddam mirror image." I couldn't believe I was spending my precious time with Laura on the subject of Jake. But that was what she wanted to hear, and what I wanted to say.

I looked at her. "Why are you asking me this?" Do you care? I wanted to ask. About me?

"I just wondered. I only hear one side."

"Which is...?"

"You're brilliant but you don't apply yourself. You were a talented athlete but let it go to waste. You chose Nola over him. You're impulsive. You can be ruthless."

"Go for the throat." I managed a smile.

"He meant ruthless out of court."

I could hardly deny it. Not while I sat with his mistress on his sailboat.

She poured herself another glass of wine, exposing the smoothest, whitest part of her inner thigh. I'd never seen anything so soft, so perfect. I wanted to kiss her there. "So, Kyle, are you ruthless?"

Her hazel eyes, in the glancing moonlight, seemed warm yet unreadable. I was learning that not everyone's eyes are a window to their soul.

"I don't feel ruthless," I answered, truthfully.

"What do you feel?"

"Reckless," I challenged and held her gaze.

She looked away. "It's time for me to go home now."

I checked my watch. The play was letting out. Jake would be calling.

"Sure," I said. "But before, what say we take the sail down and dive in." I was already moving for the boom.

"I think not."

"Just a dip." I slapped at a mosquito. Now that I'd taken down the sail, they'd be all over us.

"I don't have anything to swim in."

"Yes you do." I smiled wickedly and stripped off my shirt and shorts. I stood on the boat for a moment in bikini briefs, hoping she liked the view, then dove into the black night water.

"God, this is great," I said truthfully as the coolish water lapped against me. "No mosquitoes."

"Have a great swim." She slapped at a mosquito, for once outmaneuvered and plainly not accustomed to the sensation.

I stroked a few yards from the boat, then turned back. "Nothing like a midnight swim."

"It's nowhere near midnight."

I did a somersault in the water. When I looked at her again, she was standing.

"Turn around."

I obeyed, aroused beyond all memory as I heard clothes being removed, then a splash as she dove in, surfacing near the boat. Her hair and skin glistened in the moonlight.

"Stay away from me, Kyle," she warned.

"I wouldn't dream of getting near you. In fact, you stay away from me. Get away." I splashed water in her direction. She laughed.

Didn't I know that only distance and detachment would allow me a chance with her? Didn't I have Turnage for an example of what desperation did to women? I dove and surfaced at the other end of the boat.

"I'm calling the skinny dip police on you," I said.

She laughed again, then swam toward me, seeming to trust me. She stopped several feet away, suddenly hesitant. We were treading water, looking at each other.

"You're different every time I see you, Laura."

"Am I? And you don't like surprises." "I like some."

"Who were you with today at Bayona?"

"Her name's Alison."

"I didn't mean her name. Is she your girlfriend?"

I hesitated, searching for the exact balance of desirability. "We've gone out for a long time, yes."

"Is it serious?"

"It could be." I paused again. "It depends."

"On what?"

"Me."

It seemed to be the right answer. There were no more questions.

I moved a few feet closer and waited. She didn't protest. I moved closer, then waited, the way I would've with a spooked horse. Closer. She backed off, just a foot, touching the boat

"This is crazy, Kyle." I thought I heard a catch in her throat, almost a sob.

"I know it. It's crazy as hell."

I waited till there was no resistance left in her eyes, then stripped off my briefs and languorously breast stroked the last yards. I slipped underwater, reaching for her waist, pulling down her bikini pants, putting my head between her beautiful thighs. As I licked her, I felt her shudder and then relax. When I came up to the surface, her eyes were still closed.

Feeling exultant, proud, possessive, I moved behind her and gently pulled her to me, with my body cupped around hers. I kissed the back of her neck, then touched her and she moved against it.

I very slowly made love to her, feeling as if I'd connected with what had always been lost, every cell straining to please her. Did I? I was crazy with wanting to ask but knew how it would sound, and there was already so much else I needed, like a promise to go out with me again. I was aware now—had been since the Demimonde—that I could never have enough of her. I had joined the ranks of the eternally hungry, the desperate, the powerless.

On the sail back, she was thoughtful, quiet. "When can I see you again?" I asked as we docked.

"Never. Tonight's all."

"After what just happened?"

"Because of what just happened." Her voice was less firm, and I saw something like panic in her eyes, not unlike that day I'd seen her crying in Audubon Park.

Nobody in New Orleans would've ever heard of Daddy, or really anybody outside the scrub pine woods a little to the north and east of Pensacola. But back around the Florida-Alabama line of the Redneck Riviera, he was who you looked for if you wanted to win or lose a lot of money.

Daddy liked high-risk (look at us as a prime example) and his luck was ours. Dependent on how they were falling, we might have a month-long run of eating Beanie-Weenies and sweating under the July sheets to keep off the screaming mosquitoes. Or we might get a spell at the Sandestin Hilton, with ironed linens and air conditioning so cold we had to use two blankets.

The last time we went, the very last, Daddy rolled up in a brand-new, paid-for, long-bed Silverado truck, strode to the door in his black alligator cowboy boots, and yelled, like on TV, "Honey, I'm home. What say I take all my girls to the beach?"

He stood in the front door, just about filling it up. "Where's my favorite daughter?"

"In here?" I hoped he meant me.

Daddy was a big man but graceful with longish dark hair and a lightning smile, like one of those TV riverboat gamblers, or maybe a pirate, or Rhett Butler except better looking (no big ears).

"How much did you win?"

"Just fair, Honeybabe."

"How fair?" I was the only one he'd tell.

"Forty and change," and I knew we'd have at least a week with him.

"Everybody ready?" he yelled out in his big voice, as if he'd given us more than ten seconds' warning that we were headed for Destin.

"I am." I dragged out my suitcase, kept packed for the day Daddy would decide it was time for a fresh start and take just me. The birthday before, he promised that the next year I'd be old enough, fourteen, for him to escort just me to the restaurant on the top floor. We would sit at a candlelit table, he swore, with a pink linen cloth, looking out at the whitest of sand while we ate filet mignon and butter pecan ice cream.

"Can we take Joker?" I asked. "I can hide him in a tote bag. Joker was the terrier I'd found the summer before, half-starved on the road in front of the trailer. He was scared of Mama and Sissy cause they could get frantic real fast.

Daddy smiled his answer and one second later I was dishing up dogfood.

Mama appeared from behind Daddy and put her hands over his eyes. "Guess who?" she said in her soft sweet little voice that always got her everything she wanted. In the short space since he'd been home, she'd lit out of bed and shucked off that duster she wore day and night and into some kind of slinky thing she was way too old for.

"Lady luck." Daddy wrapped her in his arms, and I quit watching.

Mama, they say, had been a real good-looking woman before she had me. Of course, I came along when she was sixteen, so Mama's years of beauty were pretty scant. She and I, we quit getting along right after I started developing and men started noticing.

"I can't find my purse," Sissy screamed. "I can't go if I can't find my purse." That was just the kind of thing that could delay Mama for an extra hour on top of all her natural distractions and you never knew when Daddy might just throw up his hands and walk out. Her and Mama was two of a helpless kind.

"Here it is," I said, dragging that ratty piece of shit out from under a pile of Mama's dirty clothes.

Our room at the Sandestin was the best ever, high up and facing straight out into the Gulf. Mama and Daddy had the big bedroom, Sissy and Joker and I shared the small one. The sun was close to setting when we got there, but Daddy rented their Sunfish and took just me out sailing, Mama being too scarey of the water and Sissy being left on the pier since the sailboat held only two.

"Take you next," Daddy yelled back, and Sissy lit up with a smile, though I knew, and maybe Daddy too, that the sun'd be down when we got back and there wouldn't be any next. When we got in just past dark, she was still standing on the pier.

Next day on the beach, Daddy wasn't looking for a game, at least not hard, but it found him, a loud, big-bellied Alabama fan who'd just checked in. "This'n's a flounder waiting for the gig," Daddy whispered, something he didn't tell the others. He started off after Big Belly. In the white terrycloth robe from the hotel men's shop, Daddy looked like some kind of desert sheik. Big Belly looked more like a camel.

"You're not gonna forget about my birthday tonight?" I yelled, fast, cause he walked fast.

"Bet your life on it, Honeybabe," he hollered back and we both believed it, I think.

At 7:30, only thirty minutes late, Daddy showed up at the room for my birthday dinner, except he was just in his bathing suit.

"Pack up quick," he said and we did, even Mama. We were on the road inside of twenty minutes, just ahead of Big Belly coming to collect the IOUs Daddy's left. Somewhere around Valparaiso, Daddy pulled over to a McDonald's and produced from his right sock a crisp hundred-dollar bill. He sat Mama and Sissy at one concrete picnic table and me and him at the other and we ate long past it tasted good.

"Filet Mig-Donald's," he said and toasted me with his large Coke. I was still wearing my gold sundress and matching sandals.

Back at the trailer, Daddy unloaded us and said he had to get going right then. I had no way to know when he might come back. Sometimes we wouldn't see him for a month. I thought fast and stepped on a nail sticking through the trailer steps. He felt bad for me, but after he washed off all the blood and wrapped my foot, he went on just the same.

Our weekly family dinners—back in those days when we still had them—were always difficult. The only thing that varied was whether Jake and I would start arguing during the shrimp remoulade appetizer course, the redfish entree or the profiterole dessert. Mom valiantly pretended nothing had happened, as did Alison, who always came. My guess was that my mother had wanted a daughter, after me, or maybe even instead of, but after an ectopic pregnancy, the doctors pronounced further pregnancies dangerous. So Alison was like my sister as well as my as-yet unannounced fiancée.

She'd been saving up her anger over my inattentiveness, and when I walked next door to get her, she discharged it. I was behaving, she said, like someone who regretted having gotten engaged. Not only had I been late to lunch, curt at Bayona, and short on the phone, I'd also failed to call her back last night at 11:00, approximately the time I was lost between Laura's legs in Lake Ponchartrain.

If I had changed my mind about getting married, she told me, she'd better be the first to know and not the last. Her blue eyes were hard, not the way I liked them. After Charlie Dumaine, a minor betrayal compared to this, she had not spoken to me for a month, not gone out with me for three months, not slept with me for a full six.

As I absorbed Alison's firestorm of accurate accusations, I wavered, an increasingly familiar motion. I could lose her, I realized. In Alison's sobering presence, I could see that my chances of winning Laura were slight; in fact, my whole scheme—even with its original, marginally noble goal of saving my mother—seemed implausible, my motivation mixed at best. Should I forgo Laura, let my mother fend for herself? Could I? I could avoid her at work. I could turn her away, even if she showed up at my doorstep wearing her white shorts. I'd wean myself, a little at a time if necessary, from fantasizing about her. I could do that, I thought, even as I felt my throat thicken with the memory of my body cupped around Laura's just the night before.

But was my plan to steal Laura really that implausible, even if that morning Laura had hung up when I called. Examining the evidence rationally, everything was working. I was ahead of schedule, in fact. As long as I could keep my head and priorities clear, I could pull it off.

"Are you listening to me, Kyle?"

"I have no consideration, I act like a different person, my mind's a million miles away," I repeated verbatim, and she continued, now dipping into the past for corollaries to my recent behavior.

Then Alison said something that penetrated. "You know, Kyle, there's a point people reach when something changes for them." She was looking at me very seriously. "They don't feel the same any more and they never do again."

"That's pretty dramatic," I said, trying to lighten the mood, but her expression didn't change. What the hell would I do without Alison? Imagining it, I felt like all the air had been sucked out of me. "I don't want that to happen."

"I don't either." She kissed me, a sweet innocent kiss.

At dinner I strained to play a part in the conversation and meet her eyes. Jake I could hardly face at all. Guilt? I didn't think so—he was married, dammit, and he knew what his affair would do to my mother.

What else did he know? The old man was such a good lawyer I was afraid he'd see last night on the lake reflected from my brain onto my eyes.

"Have you taken the sailboat out lately?" he asked as he finished his gumbo; he powered through food like everything in life, voraciously.

I looked up, making my eyes as blank as possible. "Couldn't sleep. Is it a problem?"

My mother and Alison tensed, and Alison was about to jump in with some diverting comment, but Jake unexpectedly smiled.

"Glad to see it getting some use. How's it handling?"

"Smooth." Careful, I had to be careful.

"Not hungry, Baby Doll?" Jake looked at my mother with concern. She seemed to subsist on air and coffee and, of course, Xanax and Prozac and Bombay gin.

Mom took a dutiful quarter spoonful of gumbo. "It's very good." As if Jake and not Eunice had cooked it.

"You need protein, Nola." Jake actually looked almost worried.

"I have everything I need," my mother said with a small smile, and what she meant was she had her faithful loved ones gathered around. Except I—and of course my father—knew how false her assumption was.

"And I hope it stays that way." I hadn't intended to speak so harshly. Jake looked up, unsure what I meant.

"Jake, I heard Kyle's doing great on the Wittenhurst case," Alison interposed.

"So far." He dipped his French bread in the rich courtbullion gravy, bad manners anywhere but New Orleans, where you'd be a damn fool not to get every drop. Jake, the man of appetites.

"Joshua mentioned a girl who's got dirt on the complainant," he continued. "What about it?"

"Roger just gave me her name this afternoon."

"Well, go dig up the dirt. Talk to the girl."

"I'll call her tomorrow."

"It's so unpleasant, isn't it?" Mom almost never commented on his dinner-table legal harangues.

"Sorry, Baby Doll. I can't help the way of the world."

"It's not your fault. It's just the whole dirty business."

I didn't know which Mom was talking about, law or sex, and though I agreed with her on one and probably both counts, it was my turn to redirect the conversation. Except I couldn't think of anything except sex and law. Jake, oblivious, just kept ramming through.

"Call her tonight, not tomorrow," he ordered.

"Okay, okay."

"What's the witness' name?" Alison asked.

"I'm not supposed to say."

"I forgot. Sorry.

"It's Jenna Farber," Mom said. Apparently Jake had told her. "Alison won't say anything," she assured Jake and me.

"I know that."

"I heard something about the Farbers," Alison said. She hesitated. "You can't say anything either."

"I promise."

"I heard Mr. Farber's about to go bankrupt." It was the kind of thing she would've heard from her father, a heart specialist, whose patient questionnaire elicited answers to inquiries such as, "Is anything specific causing stress in your life?" Yet another witness susceptible to Joshua's philanthropy.

I walked Alison home, the twenty yards to her parents' house next door. She took my arm, leaned her head against my shoulder. It felt so peaceful in the summer night, along the familiar little footpath that the two of us had worn in the thick St. Augustine grass, with the crickets chirping like they'd never stopped doing since I was eight years old and first moved to that perfect little spot. An ancient, gnarled wisteria vine arched over our path, and a light breeze carried the perfume of my mother's antique roses. Everything I needed should be right there.

Jenna Farber, worldly, brisk and assured at nineteen, faced me across my desk the next morning at 9:00.

"It was a revenge fuck, pardon the expression," she said, a mid-Atlantic accent still lingering from boarding school. Laura's Saab hadn't yet appeared in the lot; my new furniture arrangement allowed me to check frequently.

Jenna was an almost pretty girl but only because she worked at it unflaggingly. Beauty spas thrived because of Jenna. She wore an expensive suit and was perfectly made up, her dark hair tormented out of its natural curliness. This girl would not flourish without her daddy's money, and she looked smart enough to realize it. She had a few more years before she'd either have to do a strenuous daily workout or subsist on celery and cigarettes.

The Farbers lived in one of the monstrous new mansions on Lake Ponchartrain that squatted like stucco toads over the entire lot. A perfectly respectable cottage, a real house, had been razed for it. All that was left for yard was a three-foot fringe of new turf, like a green merkin. Laura and I'd sailed past the Farber home just three nights before. Could Jenna have been at her upstairs mirror, toiling over her curls, as our white canvas caught the wind?

"Why was Mamie after revenge?"

"She was pissed that her old boyfriend Britt had screwed DeeDee Major that night."

"How do you know?"

"She told me."

"So you two are friends."

"Not really."

"Then why'd she tell you?"

"You'd have to ask her." Though she was our witness, she was getting a little hostile.

"What's your guess?"

"She wanted it to get back to Britt. His father's in the restaurant business. But he just owns one restaurant. Roger's daddy owns ten."

"Did you tell Britt?"

"No."

"Why not?"

"I didn't want to hurt his feelings." Those who believed that could line up and fly.

"Did she tell anyone else?"

"Not that I know of."

"Why is Mamie now claiming rape if she planned it all and divulged her plans to a witness?"

"Catholic guilt, maybe. And the fact she got back with Britt and wants to come off innocent. She has a rich daddy who takes care of everything and she probably figured I wouldn't testify." Jenna smiled. "But she was wrong."

"Why'd you wait so long to come forward with your story, Jenna?"

For the first time her delivery faltered. "I didn't want to make Mamie look bad. I don't really like Roger all that well. You know, he's kind of a nerd, don't you think?" She tried her smile on me, and went from almost to pretty.

"That's one you can be sure the D.A. will ask you on the stand," I told her. "So you'd better come up with a little smoother way to say what you just told me."

Was any of Jenna's story true? It seemed doubtful that Mamie had confided in her. More likely, the miracle of Joshua's money was transubstantiating all my witnesses' stories.

After Jenna left, I finally saw a flash of copper-gold speed into the parking lot. Laura cut her wheel but not until she'd crossed the line two feet into Munger's empty space. Then Venus emerged from her shell. I watched her walk in, imagined her walking up the stairs, and dialed the second she stepped into her office.

"I saw you drive up," I said, then cursed myself for saying something so stupid. Nothing but silence at the other end, so I rushed to fill it. "Got a lot of work today?"

"If you don't, maybe your father can find some for you." She hung up. Damn her!

At ten I dialed her extension but managed to stop myself before the last digit. At 11:12 I hung up before she answered when it struck me that my father might be in there. Right after lunch I called again. It rang and rang until her secretary picked up.

Without realizing how I got there, I found myself knocking on her locked door until Munger stuck his head out of his office. "She's obviously not in there, Kyle."

"Yes, she is, you praying mantis fuck," I wanted to yell. It struck me that she really might never see me again, that nothing I could do would persuade her.

Late that afternoon, when I knew Jake was locked in a meeting, I let my fingers press the now familiar three digits, like a junkie tapping for a vein.

"Yes?" Odd, that she answered the phone the same way as my mother. In Mom it was an endearing quirk; in Laura it wasn't.

"I need to talk to you."

"I told you."

"That this wasn't going anywhere? Let me tell you, we're making great strides in that direction."

A small laugh. And she hadn't hung up.

"At this rate," I continued, "we'll be nowhere soon."

"But it's where we are, Kyle."

"What about the other night?"

"That?"

"Yes, that," I said unable to keep the anger out of my voice. "Don't pretend you don't remember. I was inside you. You came. More than once."

She took a long breath. "It was a mistake. Don't call me again. Ever."

I sat with the phone frozen at my ear for several seconds. Only Myrt's beeping in reminded me to hang up. I'd managed in the space of a few moments to be pitiful, petulant and incomprehensible.

The phone immediately rang. One ring, in-house. My heart pulsed once in hope. In the instant it took me to answer, I checked off Jake (with Munger) and Ginger (in trial), leaving Laura.

"Hello," I said. It was actually more of a yelp.

"You jerking off in there, Cameron?" Turnage.

"Trying to get some work done."

"Work's done. Time for a beer. Or ten."

I hesitated. I'd considered calling Laura once more, prevented only by the suicidal stupidity of such a move. But even that wasn't going to stop me much longer.

"Caught me in a weak moment," I said.

"How could I miss?"

It was, thus far, the hottest day of the year and, at the F & M, the women wore their shortest dresses. Turnage, on beer number three, was recounting his latest debacle.

"I prime her with a two-hour feed at the Grill Room," he said. The Grill Room in the Windsor Court Hotel was the most formal restaurant in the city, and I'd specifically counseled him not to take his date there. The girl, Turnage had told me, was a free-spirited yoga teacher, which he'd imagined would translate into promiscuity. The yogini would likely be a vegetarian, unstirred by the steaming gobbets of blood-rare wild game.

"I got a room beforehand, king bed." He paused to observe a girl whose perfect breasts were battling gravity for possession of her topless tank top. "I figured we could just migrate upstairs," he continued. "Convenient, except she wanted to go dancing."

I didn't need to hear any more. Turnage on the dance floor was like an untrained bear on ice skates. He wildly windmilled his arms as he hopped, first on one foot, then the other. Usually he cleared the dance floor before the song was over.

"She told me she was going to the ladies' room," he said ruefully. He'd heard that one before.

"Tough," I said. Normally I felt either pity at his misfortune or incredulity at his ineptitude. Now I felt a new emotion, one I didn't welcome: empathy. In the space of forty-eight hours I was right down there with him, no Olympian advice to dispense. I looked at my watch. Too late to call Laura at the office, and she'd changed her home phone number.

A girl in a clingy silk dress, a model maybe, wove her way through the crowd. I automatically plotted her course; she would pass right by us.

Turnage stared at her. "Plenty of beaverfish in the sea tonight," he observed, looking over at me hopefully. I knew Turnage's main reason for drinking with me was his belief that my success might somehow include him. The fact that it had never happened only increased his certainty.

I casually glanced up at her, out of habit more than anything else. She looked European, maybe French, with retro glasses that gave her a sexy bookish look. I raised my smile. Her gaze seamlessly slid away.

"Not biting tonight, I guess," Turnage said, disappointed, finishing beer number five. I watched the girl stop to talk with some cocky bastard with his shirt open to his navel. She'd smelled it coming off me, the desperation.

My pleas and offers to Laura grew not only desperate but absurd, including absinthe (procured with difficulty) and, God help me, homemade (by me) pralines. One day at the new cappuccino machine (La Marzocco, commercial model, five figures) I hoisted my pirate's smile, much diminished, more like a tugboat pilot's, and, remembering her interests, asked her to go horseback riding. She walked away with her half-filled cup, leaving the rest to froth down the drain like Onan's seed

As Laura's rebuffs became stronger and stronger, I allowed Roger's case to swallow me. I was firing off briefs and motions, setting up witness interviews, trying to cull usable half-truths from outright lies. For maybe the first time, I felt like a lawyer.

As Laura had predicted, Conrad Couvecor seemed eager to please Joshua. His story of the evening echoed Roger's except he portrayed Mamie as the sexual aggressor. Allen Sheffield, more financially sound and less inspired to be mendacious, was better acquainted with his own dry heaves than with a possible date rape occurring two feet behind him.

Roger had taken to calling me every day, sometimes several times a day, for updates and reassurance. He'd been more or less neutered by his father and was weak through and through, with lots of money and an inverse amount of character. Even so, though he was only seven years younger, I had the curious sensation of feeling paternal.

He showed up at the office one afternoon around six, feeling particularly low after his father had disinvited him to a family gathering at his oldest brother's restaurant "because of bad publicity." I'd intended to drop by the gym, but Roger asked me to have a beer with him at Cooley's. He seemed so forlorn that I scratched the workout, though I'd been looking forward to a long, purgative sit in the steam where I might forget Laura, my father and everything else.

As we walked out of the firm, I saw Munger occupied with several Trust Life officers, sleekly well-fed to a man, as if their diet consisted of nothing but premiums and unpaid benefits. They were gathered in a porcine cluster, with Turnage in their midst, managing without difficulty a laugh at some joke about women, Jews, blacks or all three. Richard Flowers' death had been ruled a suicide, and the Trust Life case would soon come to trial. So New Orleans had lost a notch in the ongoing competition for murder capital.

I hurried past but not quickly enough.

"Kyle," Munger called, detaching himself from the group and gesturing with one long finger for me to come over. I had the errant thought that he would've made a fearsome proctologist.

"You haven't kept me apprised of Roger's case."

"I didn't know I was supposed to."

"Joshua was my fraternity big brother," he said, as if that were a response.

I synopsized the events, forcing myself to maintain eye contact.

"I assume Jake is supervising you," Munger said dubiously when I finished.

"We're working together." An unsatisfactory answer.

"I'd like a daily report."

"Fine." I walked away before he could say anything else.

"Sorry," I told Roger. "He's above me on the letterhead, and shit rolls downhill."

"I know the drill."

Roger brightened a bit when we stepped into Cooley's, a Tulane hangout, with several pool tables and reputedly the widest selection of beers and ales in New Orleans. He ordered a Bud Lite. I convinced him to try a Pilsner Urquel, a potent Czech brew. He grimaced but took another swallow.

"Puts hair on your chest," I said, trying to evoke some kind of heartiness from him.

"I had three but one fell out," he said, and it was a moment before I realized he'd made a joke, his first. Did he have so few friends that he was reduced to drinking with his lawyer?

Roger was characteristically inept at pool. I dragged out the game so he got some play before I slammed the 8-ball in the corner. Roger winced. Unbidden came the memory of Jake beating me at darts (age ten), at golf (fourteen), and of course boxing.

"Close one," I encouraged.

"I'll get you next time," he said with fragile bravado. We fought for the tab and I let him win. As we waited for the harried bartender to find change for Roger's hundred-dollar bill, the smallest he had, I glanced over at a nearby table where three wan-looking freshmen were watching internet porn on a laptop: a man and woman, grimacing with mock pleasure, athletically switched positions like acrobats linked by a baton. My life's pursuit, reduced in pixels to its indecorous, elemental expression.

"Ever watch it?" Roger asked.

"Not really."

"Joshua does," he volunteered, now calling his father by his given name. Roger was silent on the way back, leaving me to turn over in my mind the significance of his cryptic revelation.

I called Laura once again, perhaps twice—idiocy abhors a vacuum—in case I'd somehow misinterpreted her signals or she'd changed her mind. I hadn't and she hadn't.

After that, I quit calling altogether, not through strength of will—I had none— but from the realization that with each call I was diminishing my already minimal chances. As much as possible, I avoided the vicinity of her office. I rearranged my office with my back to the parking lot so I wouldn't have to see her heart-stopping entrances. Every time I heard her car door slam in the firm parking lot and swiveled in my chair to watch her leave, then saw, precisely three minutes later, Jake stroll to his Jag without the slightest concern for the needs of his clients and speed after her, I told myself that at a certain point the raw nerve has to become dead. If I could cut it, just one quick slice, I would. As to my mother, and separating Laura and Jake, I realized even then there might be another way.

I was seeing Alison again every night. Mondays at her house, Tuesdays at Galatoire's. Wednesday meant Cajun shrimp mache choux at the Palace Cafe on Canal. As we made our way though the corn and cream sauce, I asked her if she knew any of Mamie's sorority sisters.

"Why?"

"Witnesses."

"They're very young," she said, as in "too young for you." The waitress, who looked as wholesome as I imagined a sorority sister might look, had stayed overlong explaining specials and kidding around.

"And I'm very old," I assured her. Though for Laura, apparently, not old enough.

"You still seem so distracted," Alison said.

"Antihistamines."

She spent the night, but we'd eaten so much white chocolate bread pudding that sex was out of the question.

Alison needn't have worried about Mamie's sorority sisters, whom I questioned the next morning. I'd been rendered monogamous, just not to her.

What emerged, from the girls I found most credible (or the most accomplished little liars) was that Mamie had stayed sober until she learned about her old boyfriend's infidelity, and that it wasn't until the next morning, after they'd reconciled, that she reported Roger's alleged rape. So Jenna Farber's story held, if not her motive for telling it. By this time I'd started believing Roger's story, at least the part that went to whether the sex was consensual. Proving it was another matter.

When I returned from the Garden District, my phone was ringing. I almost hoped it wasn't Laura.

It wasn't. I heard the imperious voice of Joshua Wittenhurst. "I want you to explore a plea bargain."

I'd recently told Roger that he might have to testify. He was my most credible witness; that was the sorry state of our case. Apparently, Joshua had recalculated the algebra of public embarrassment.

"You're not the client." I was finding I could barely be civil around him.

"Here's the client," Joshua said, and a moment later I heard Roger, sounding more diminished than usual.

"Just explore it, Kyle, okay?"

"Is this your idea?"

"My father says sometimes you have to cut your losses."

"Your damn father is not the one on trial."

Silence at the other end. I could imagine Roger, nodding, trying to think of something to placate me without offending his father. Between his newly acquired habit of nodding and his old hair flicking, he looked like a candidate for Tourette's syndrome. Not desirable in a witness.

"We can win this thing, Roger."

He laughed sharply, or what sounded like a laugh.

"You know, you don't have to take this crap from him," I exploded. I barely had a degree in law, much less psychology, but somebody needed to tell him.

"Yes he does. And so do you." It was Joshua, who had commandeered the receiver.

I kept my voice as even as I could. "I believe he's innocent."

"That and $300 will buy dinner for two. You haven't seen my son in action."

"He has a right to testify."

"Not if he doesn't choose to exercise it. You have an obligation to explore a plea. Do it."

I hung up. The loss Joshua wanted to cut was his son.

In contrast to my high-ceilinged, Persian-carpeted, antique-furnished office, Assistant D.A. Ray Sessums' was a windowless cell. On his metal desk was a photo of a prematurely gray, heavy-boned woman, the painter, I guessed, of the awful still-lifes of grapes and daisies that constituted the decor. The woman wore a large cross on a chain around her neck. Sessums wasn't getting a lot of sex, or, if he was, he wasn't enjoying it much.

"The junior Cameron," Sessums greeted me with a firm handshake. He looked down at me—he was four inches taller—with an almost affectless face and deceptively placid eyes. I saw him take in my thousand-dollar suit, my hell-with-it floral tie, my

Italian calfskin loafers. I was the sole reason he was here making maybe $35,000 a year instead of in my office making ten times that.

I could see why Cameron & Munger had wanted him. According to my research—actually all I'd had to do was look in the firm's files—he had a 170 I.Q. Top of his night law class at Loyola. Highest bar scores in Louisiana since they started keeping records.

"Please, move those files, make yourself comfortable," Sessums said graciously. "Water? Sorry, it'll have to be tap."

"Tap is fine." Anyone who drank New Orleans water was courting cancer, but I'd be damned if he'd make me out to be as effete as he thought I was. To prove my point, I took a sip. It tasted like my childhood chemistry set.

"Nice haircut," he commented as he settled behind his desk.

"Thanks." At $100 excluding tip it should be. Sessums' own hair looked like a home-job.

"You defense guys, ...we could learn a few things about style. That suit...." He shook his head in apparently sincere admiration. "Very cosmopolitan."

"Nice watercolors." I wasn't about to be outdone in the insincere compliment department.

He smiled deprecatingly. "She's just a dabbler, as she'd be the first to tell you. Now, the Wittenhurst case." He picked up a file from one of around twenty tall stacks on the floor. Each stack represented a case. Twenty cases to my maybe four.

Sessums opened the folder but didn't look at it. I remembered he had a photographic memory.

"Roger Wittenhurst. What was it F. Scott Fitzgerald said, 'the rich are different from you and me'? Not from you, of course."

"Actually, he said the 'very rich.'" I'd gotten it from a crossword puzzle in the *Times-Picayune*.

He just smiled and again shook his head as if in admiration. "Night school. Leaves gaps. Thanks."

Sessums with his little verbal daggers was as toxic as the water in my glass. I took another drink, to show my immune system hadn't been incapacitated by growing up rich.

"I feel your case is weak," I began. Damn, that sounded bad. Sessums nodded encouragingly.

"And we're not considering a plea." I wasn't, and if I could convince Roger, neither was he. I stammered on. "But my duty to my client, all that, would you consider sexual battery?"

Sessums' face didn't harden like Jake's did when he got down to business. Sessums just became more reasonable, infinitely reasonable, as if the only end we could come to was my just flat out agreeing with everything he said.

"You've reviewed our evidence," he asked. Then with apparent concern, "You did receive it?"

I nodded curtly.

"Well, based on that evidence, Kyle, this office couldn't consider a plea. Of any nature. I could be wrong, of course. Your take on the case could be dead on." He smiled, as if this were a joke we could both appreciate.

He stood, offered his hand. "That tie. I'd get thrown out on my ear for wearing something like that here." He shook his head. "Could never carry it off anyway."

I found myself in the hall, still holding the damn glass of water. I didn't need Jake to tell me it hadn't gone well.

When I got back to the office, I called Roger, who seemed both relieved and terrified about the denial of a plea. Then I checked in with Alison. Our date that night was still perfect, she said, and could we please go to Pascal's Manale for raw oysters and barbecued shrimp? Ginger had given me a research project, so with enough time left in the afternoon to get a start on it, feeling virtuous, I went to make an espresso.

Laura was there, her cappuccino almost made. I had a moment when I could've turned back before she saw me and, remembering my date with Alison, I tried. I was starting to sleep again, Alison was happy. But thinking of my mother and of course myself, I failed, the path of least resistance again being the shortest distance between two points.

I hoped she'd ignore me. Maybe she would leave. Or Jake would come by. Even Munger I would've welcomed. Instead she looked over and caught me in the high beams of her hazel eyes. The same helpless hunger, undiminished, filled me.

"Nice shirt," she said. "How'd you ever find a tie to match?"

"Little tag on the back that says 'wear with blue, brown, gray or green.'"

"You stopped calling."

"You noticed."

"What happened to your grand strategy?"

"Awaiting a thaw in the Russian winter."

She smiled and it wasn't wintry. "Where do you live, Kyle?"

"The Quarter. Saint Peter Street, a few blocks down from Pat O'Brien's." I could still pretend it wasn't going to happen. Though I mentally kicked myself for mentioning Pat O'Brien's, a sing-along tourist bar she'd find hopelessly straight.

"Nice location," she said, sipping her cappuccino. To Munger, who walked by, we looked, I hoped, like nothing more than two diligent attorneys with nothing more than money on our minds.

• • •

"I like it." Nice neutral reply. I was going to walk away now, say I remembered something, a hearing, a deposition, an oral argument before the United States Supreme Court.

"I thought I'd come see you tonight."

In my office, I desperately tried to catch Alison before she left the Museum. It was after 5:00, too late. I dialed her cell, which wasn't on, then left a message: "Alison, something urgent at work has come up, and I'll be tied up tonight after 7:30. I'm heading over now, should be there by 6:00."

I waited in her front porch swing until 7:00, when she finally pulled up after stopping off to visit my mother. By that time my shirt was spotted with tiny blood streaks from swatting the clouds of mosquitoes.

I stood. "I'm here. Didn't want to startle you."

"Has daylight savings time suddenly changed in the middle of the summer? You're not due for another hour," she said, coming to sit down by me in the swing. She had on a cerulean blue dress, her best color.

"I left a message. I had something urgent come up at work and I have to go back to the office, so I wanted to see you before."

"How about if I go with you and bring the book I'm reading?"

"I wish but this'll take all my concentration."

"What came up that's so urgent?"

"Mr. Wittenhurst wants to come in with Roger and go over my strategy. I don't think I can quite pass Joshua's muster, not without some major preparation."

"That's odd," she said quizzically.

"What?" I didn't like the tone in her voice.

"I just left Nola. She said Mr. and Mrs. Wittenhurst left for Europe today." She paused, waiting. All I had to do was say I must be confused, and I could keep her. But if I did, I'd have to stay, and I wouldn't be home when Laura came over. I remained silent.

She looked at me, absorbing it.

"Why are you lying to me?"

I tried to come up with some magic words to save myself but the trap I'd devised was perfectly engineered.

"I...," I began. Nothing else came. I could see that change in her eyes she'd told me about. She shook her head, as if the last decade had been a hallucination from which she'd finally awakened.

She stood, leaving me rocking back and forth in the swing.

"I'll miss those poison pen news reports. You might tell her red is a little tiresome, not to mention trashy. One viewer's comments."

Charlie Dumaine. If God had a sense of humor, I wasn't laughing.

"I'd give you back your ring," she said, with what was almost a smile, "if I had one." Then she walked inside, and only as she shut the door, when she thought I couldn't see her, did she start to cry.

I walked to my car, numb, feeling like half my body had been severed but the nerves hadn't yet transmitted the extent of the damage. I arrived home twenty minutes before Laura was due. I heaved open the stable doors, not bothering to get out my gun—if someone had jumped me, I had enough adrenaline in my body to toss him over the river levee. Thirty seconds later as I showered, the alarm, which I'd forgotten to disarm, screamed like a police siren. Startled, I banged my forehead into the showerhead. I felt something warm drip down into my eyebrow. I raced out naked and wet to the alarm controls, slipped on my wood floor, landing on my hipbone, and careened into the sofa.

The alarm was still blaring but the phone rang, and I reached for it instead, slowly rising from my fall like an arthritic.

"Hi. It's me." Laura said. "Great view."

"What do you mean?"

"You should pull those curtains or else charge for the show."

She was outside. I could see her lights. I'd have asked her to drive around for a minute, but I feared she'd arbitrarily decide not to come back.

"I'll be right out." I switched off my alarm, grabbed a white bath towel and my key, and catapulted down the stairs to open the courtyard gate.

I peered out. Unfortunately, there were no parking places, and my garage was at full capacity with only one car, just as years before it had housed only one horse.

"Get in," she called, and I limped out barefoot, nursing my bruised hip, and climbed into her car. Two taxis were behind her by then, blaring nonstop, but she was laughing too hard to drive.

"White's your color."

"Just drive," I said.

She turned the corner. "I'm sorry I laughed. You do look pretty grand naked." I forgave her everything.

"Nice outfit," I told her as I looked at her. Cream-colored skimpy sandals with a short slipover silk dress. "How'd you ever find a dress to match those shoes?" That tired line again, but my brain, as always when I was with Laura, had migrated south.

"Actually I bought the dress first."

"You're saying I can't win."

"Depends on what your goal is."

She tugged at a corner of my towel until it came unfastened, and I let her open it and glide her hand up my thigh. How many times driving in traffic had I slipped my hand in a girl's panties? I killed the disconcerting thought that she was, again, assuming my role, then leaned back and closed my eyes.

The glare of flashing neon brought me back. We were stopped in traffic and two jaywalking college girls were approaching the car. Startled, I reached for my towel.

"No. Leave it off," she told me. I obeyed her, powerless not to as she moved her hand faster. Outside, the girls' eyes widened as it began to register what we were doing, and they froze for a moment in the street. The car in front of us moved on, and another taxi behind us began an insistent honk as Laura bent her head over my lap and began to lightly lick me, then took me inside her lovely mouth. That was all I needed to have the most powerful, shuddering orgasm of my life, and I threw my head back, not caring if the police were called or Nightwitness News, so truly unable to form a thought at that instant that I couldn't have told anyone my name.

She drove back toward my apartment. "Those girls thought you looked pretty grand naked too."

"I'm happy they're so easily entertained."

"Not at all. A show like that on Bourbon Street would cost $500."

"I've never seen anything like that on Bourbon Street."

"You don't know where to look."

"I know right where to look on Saint Peter if you'd just find a damn parking place."

The closest spot was a block away and I limped back home with her, towel corners reattached, drawing a few stares from tourists, none from the locals.

Back home, my security service patrolman was searching my apartment, and I left Laura waiting in the courtyard, while I finally convinced him that I was who I was. I phoned in the code and he left.

"No wonder he didn't believe me," I told Laura when I'd seen my face in the foyer mirror. My forehead was bleeding and needed a stitch, maybe two. She handed me a lipsticked kleenex to dab off the blood, and rather than throw it away, I went into the bathroom and hid it in a drawer, ashamed to let her see I was saving something intimate of hers.

"You should go to a Doc-in-a-Box to sew up that cut."

"I'll live." At the moment of orgasm outside O'Flaherty's, I'd permanently lost any remaining capacity to leave her presence of my own volition. Forever after that night of my exhibitionistic ride through the Quarter, I would wear a tiny scar.

"Mind if I look around?"

"What if I did?"

"But you don't." She was right. I went to get us some wine so I wouldn't seem like an anxious realtor.

From the kitchen I watched her move through the living room, running her fingers lightly along the chest-high dark wood wainscoting that encircled the apartment. She studied a photo of my mother, exquisite at age twenty-three, holding the infant me as she beamed up at the taker of the picture, who, undoubtedly, was Jake.

"I see why he married her."

"Why is that?" I asked, handing her a wineglass.

"She was beautiful."

"She still is." I like to remember the way her face tightened ever so slightly.

"Are you trying to hurt me, Kyle?"

"Isn't it obvious?"

"Why would you want to do that?"

"You enjoy seeing me twist in the wind. Why should I be any different?"

"It would please me if you were."

I was infuriated at being so in her thrall.

"Then quit seeing my father. Don't break my mother's heart."

She just smiled, not even deigning to address my demand. "You favor mahogany too," she observed.

"Yes." I didn't know if she was referring to her or Jake or to them both.

"I like all your paintings," she noted. I had a modern nude above the mantel. "And your hardwood floors."

She lightly, almost caressingly, trailed her sandal along the wood. "I have heart of pine too."

"No, you have heart of stone."

She seemed to enjoy my unaccustomed attacks, as if I were an amusing, fangless pet.

"Would you like to fuck me again, Kyle?" In her lovely mouth, the coarse Anglo-Saxon word was resonant with exquisite possibilities. She looked at me ironically, as if simultaneously parodying and being the femme fatale. I could only nod, my dick having paralyzed my vocal cords.

She sat down on my sofa and slipped off her sandals. "Turn off the lights."

I obeyed, then lit a candle I'd recently bought for that moment. The flame brought out strands of gold mixed in with her dark auburn hair.

I undid her dress and my lips followed her panties down. When we fucked—that is the word for it, there being no element of love and little of humanity in it, just the deepest million-year-old hardwired craving—she came several times before I let myself go, then thirty minutes later I fucked her again.

"I bet the old man can't do that for you," I heard myself say afterward.

She looked at me, surprised I'd stepped over the line that any damn fool would've known was there. She wordlessly walked into the bathroom. For the second time in a day, to the second woman, I'd said exactly the wrong thing. I heard the water run. When she came back out, she reached for her dress and let me watch her slip it on. She picked up her keys.

"It's dangerous out there," I warned. "Wait, and I'll walk you out."

As I grabbed my pants from the bedroom, I heard the front door close. I ran to the balcony and saw a drunk approach her threateningly. She said something that made him step back and reel off balance, then she walked on without a glance back.

When I went into the bathroom, her lipsticked kleenex with my blood on it floated in the toilet.

The next night and the next she was with Jake. I parked a block away and waited, drinking out of my debonair flask, staring at her darkened house. I didn't see her at work, even in the halls. Finally, at the end of the week, I spotted her at the cappuccino machine.

I watched her for a moment, just admiring her cool efficiency, her utter focus, as she expertly piloted the baffling settings. She wasn't thinking about me or for that matter Jake.

"Sorry about what I said the other night," I said.

She looked puzzled. Had she forgotten my stupid remark about besting Jake? Was it that unimportant to her?

“It doesn’t matter,” she said, and smiled, a smile so warm and innocent she looked young enough to believe in anything, even love.

I lost myself in that smile, but then her cappuccino was made and she was leaving, and I remembered that food was one of her interests. I knew, as did Laura and everyone else this side of the Mississippi, that Mosca’s would in soon close for the entire month of August.

“Do you like Oysters Mosca?” Dying men had been known to rise when a platter of the pungent dish arrived before the priest. As to other appetites, the long hour’s drive across the river made the Creole roadhouse safe for an illicit evening.

“Is that a rhetorical question?”

“Hell, no. Eight o’clock.”

“Nine,” she corrected, and walked away.

Turnage appeared at my side, his eyes following Laura down the hall. How long had he been there?

“Just like her not to clean up after herself. Too good for it."

How much had that dolt heard?

“It's one thing if a girl says no, it's another if they laugh. Never had one outright laugh before."

He studied the Marzocco, then poured himself a cup from the adjacent Mr. Coffee.

"I saw her smile at you just now."

As long as I didn't actually look at him, there was the possibility he might leave.

"Anything I should know about? Or shouldn't know about?" I could feel his calculating little eyes on me, but I assiduously set about making my espresso, hoping I wouldn’t have to resort to the instruction manual as often happened.

"No on both counts."

• • •

"You know, I always liked Jake." Something about the way he said it made me look up.

"Regular guy," he continued with his usual affable smile. "Munger didn't want me in, but Jake held out. Appreciated that. Still and all, he's giving her cases that by all rights are mine. Been trying to figure why."

"She's a good lawyer. He gave you Myron Jones, remember?" Once again, I found myself unwillingly defending Jake.

"No, Munger did. Jake took it away, remember?"

He walked away. For the first time in my life, I found myself caring about what he thought and worrying about what he might do.

Laura was funny that night at Mosca's, a side I'd seldom seen, doing a remarkably fluent imitation of Munger and his precise rasp. "Kyle, I don't believe I've given you permission to use my first name. That is granted only to partners and rapists." We laughed together like fools over a second bottle of Merlot (no white wine could stand up to Mosca's artillery of garlic).

And she was, uncharacteristically, helpful with Roger's case, telling me the names of some of Mamie's Boston prep school friends who might know something. After I'd paid with cash, Mosca's strict policy, we walked out to my car, passing a new black Mercedes Kompressor like the one Munger had incongruously bought, supplanting his hearse-like Lincoln. Never would I have placed Munger in a convertible. I hadn't yet fallen through the rotten planks of my most basic assumptions.

"Oh, God," Laura said with sudden panic. "Munger's here."

"It might not be his car."

"It's his, I have a feeling." She was totally undone. "Go back in. See where he's sitting, see if he could've seen us together. Hurry. And see who he's with," she pleaded.

Inside, partially blocked by a booth, a man who resembled Munger was devouring an entree of Chicken Grandee with potatoes and artichokes. Munger would not be eating that heartily. But he was. Across the table, starting in on the Spaghetti Bordelaise, was Trust Life CEO, Randall Chaney.

It was unlikely Munger had seen us, unless he'd looked up at the exact moment we exited. More important, I didn't want Laura to have a reason not to see me again. So I decided to simplify my report and tell her he couldn't possibly have spotted us.

"It was him, wasn't it?" she asked.

"How did you know?"

"I'd know him if he were cremated," she said with more loathing in her voice than the colorless Munger usually elicited.

She was still unnerved, I was satisfied to see. Out of character for her. I didn't puzzle over it though, just, as always, took my pleasure where I could find it.

More liaisons have been contemplated, if not consummated, in New Orleans' eateries than its hotels. Even so, only someone with the profound arrogance of Joshua Wittenhurst would open a restaurant named "Jezebel" while his son was charged with rape.

Every lawyer in the firm was invited to the opening night party—Joshua's way of reasserting dominance. No one but Turnage wanted to go.

"Free Wittenhurst food?" Turnage exclaimed at the firm meeting. "That's like legal ethics. You know, no such thing."

"I'd rather eat my brassiere," Ginger responded.

"Woo, that'd be a full meal!"

Munger ended the merriment. "Attendance is mandatory."

"Last I heard, my free time was free," Laura said, her eyes hard as two minted pennies.

"Now you hear different," Munger replied.

"Jake?" Ginger turned to my father as if to the good parent.

Jake reluctantly nodded in assent. "Make an appearance. Eat. Smile. Leave early if you want." He'd pushed Munger too far with Joshua to object now. Otherwise, he'd never expose Laura or himself to one of Joshua's notoriously bibulous spectacles, especially with my mother on his arm.

Except he arrived alone, as did I.

"Where's Mom?" I asked as we walked up to the columned antebellum mansion just off St. Charles. I'd wanted Laura to see them together, a pair.

"Too much of a scene for her."

And it was, with sleek evening-gowned second wives and their pork-fed self-pleased husbands, all talking about food and travel and deals in the secret language of money. We stepped inside, father and son, looking for the same person, who had not yet arrived. Together we observed the overblown opulence of the décor from the days of eating cake while guillotines were sharpened. The walls assaulted with outsized oil murals of Cleopatra, Salome, Delilah and other temptresses of history, accented with Arabian harems, French court concubines and Kublai Khan's thousand wives. Buttocks and bosoms strained at cruelly restraining garments.

Though it looked like a top-scale "gentleman's club," the imprimatur of the Wittenhurst name would draw both genders. In the men's restroom, I later found, was a rendition of "The Rape of the Sabine Women" over the self-flushing black onyx urinal. Roger was not the sexual offender in this family.

"Nothing exceeds like excess," Jake said with no small contempt. Joshua would've been pleased that Jake's taste—and mine—were violated.

"Bought out Royal Street," I commented, referring to the center of the antique trade in New Orleans.

"And Bourbon," Jake replied, referring to Royal's seedy neighbor.

A sylph-like Asian hostess (according to Roger, Joshua hired only "USDA prime pussy" and exercised his prerogative over the more vulnerable) greeted us, took our invitations and handed us menus with the prices crossed out but still readable.

"Your place cards are on the table," she said. "Mr. Wittenhurst instructs that substitutions may be made on the menu but not on the seating arrangements."

"I'll sit where I damn well please," Jake growled, to me, being far too well mannered to harass Joshua's helpless minion.

"This is Joshua's piss rock."

"Don't drink too much," he said as if I were fourteen instead of nearly twice that, and set out to reconnoiter the tables, specifically his and Laura's placement. He wouldn't be happy at what he found.

Not offering an explanation, and Roger requiring none, I'd asked him if he could manage some discreet rearrangement. He didn't dare to shuffle Laura, seated directly next to Joshua at the main table, but he was able to exile Jake to the second dining room and to place me, alone among the firm's lawyers, at the main table directly across from Laura.

Munger I consigned to the upstairs Siberia between a notoriously garrulous society reporter and a deaf legislator. I felt like God. I installed Turnage at an all-female table of hostesses where he would eat too much and humiliate himself. Ginger I deposited next to Jake so she'd have someone to talk to.

Laura arrived more than fashionably late and seemed uneasy to be seated next to Joshua.

"Laura, queen of the Nile," Joshua greeted her, making a show of pushing her chair in. With the slightest movement of his right hand he signaled a waiter to bring her the two courses she'd missed. Since Joshua employed the firm, he apparently thought it appropriate to bed its most desirable employee.

"I'm not really hungry," she said, as a large—larger than the rest of us had received—marinated crab salad was placed in front of her, with at least a pound of claw crabmeat. Next to it steamed a formidable bowl of Andouille sausage gumbo.

"I'm really not," she said more sharply.

"Appetites can be created," Joshua pronounced, his voice hardening. Laura took a bite of crab.

The rest of the table was filled with the burgeoning torsos of young Wittenhursts, the faultless older brothers, and their cowed wives. Roger had been relegated to a single table near the kitchen door and didn't dare, despite my urging, switch. As for me, Joshua reached with apoplectic consternation across the table to check my place card and consulted with his maitre'd, who shrugged in mystification as to why Munger's chair of honor was thus beturded.

Laura seemed equally displeased I was there and resisted my efforts to talk shop, instead listening to Mrs. Wittenhurst, who had the shape and high color of a stuffed shrimp, maunder on about Art.

Soon after the redfish—grilled and topped with oysters and crawfish—was served, Laura became utterly silent. I watched her lean over and whisper something harsh in Joshua's ear, saw him lean back and utter something that must have been persuasive, because she sat there rigidly, ignoring even the Lady Wittenhurst.

Slow student that I was, it took me several minutes to realize that Joshua had eased his pink, manicured hand onto Laura's perfect knee. Except by this time, judging from the increasing tautness in Laura's face, that hand had not been stationary.

Reaching in my pocket, I dialed myself on my cell phone.

"Hello," I said loudly, drawing irritated stares from all around. Cell phones were a faux pas in any restaurant, especially Joshua's, where they were confiscated.

"Cameron, don't you have any goddam manners?" Joshua bellowed, gesturing with his non-groping hand to a waiter to advance on me.

"Yes, she's right here," I said, concern in my voice. "We're on our way."

I looked at Laura. "It's your father. An accident in the breeding stables."

She stood, Joshua's hand dropping off like an old scab. "It's been lovely," she told him and hurried away with me right behind her. She was laughing as soon as we were out of Joshua's line of vision, and so was I, like two kids who'd tricked the ogre.

We wove our way through the tables and found ourselves in the foyer, alone.

"My hero," she said, kissing me lightly on the cheek, the gesture meaning more to me than anything we'd done.

"Laura?" It was Jake, looking more stunned than I'd ever seen him.

"Your son saved me." She tousled my hair like I was a younger brother, age ten.

"Joshua's hand was trespassing," I elaborated, happy to shift the focus off Laura and me. It was, I realized, the first time that the three of us had been alone.

"That bloated son of a bitch," Jake rumbled and I knew, from my own feelings, that there was nothing he would rather do than wade back through the tuxedos to drown Josh in one of the large silver bowls of steaming rice pudding now being served.

Laura put her hand on his arm, as if all of New Orleans weren't in the next room and nobody but us chickens in this one. "It's all right, Jake." And damned if she didn't kiss him on the cheek, while Nola's son watched. Then, with a smile for both of us, she stepped outside. Jake and I could see her hair, rendered almost chocolate by the moonlight, all the way to the street.

"What the hell's going on?" Jake asked, bringing us both back to an unpleasant place.

"I told you—Joshua Wittenhurst had his hammy hand—"

"What's it to you?"

"She's in the firm," as if Cameron & Munger were family instead of a fractious bunch of backbiting wolverines. "Anyway, you always brought me up to be chivalrous."

"First time I've ever seen you do anything I taught you."

"I'm growing up," I said and started out the door. Laura would likely be going straight home. If I could catch her before she went in, I had a fair chance of persuading her to go for a drive to the lake, maybe even a sail.

"Where in hell do you think you're going?" Jake barked.

I automatically stopped, not feeling one bit grown up. "Home. You said we could go early."

"Not those who got themselves seated at the head table," he said, appraising me. "For whatever reasons."

"Trying to get back in good with Joshua," I offered.

"Then do it," he said, not taking his eyes off me. I turned back to the dining room, but not before watching Jake step outside, in the direction of Laura. When I got back to my chair, I found it taken by Munger, so I spent the rest of the night shouting at the deaf legislator and, after an hour of the gossip columnist, wishing I too were deaf.

Given my history, the least Jake could suspect was that I was pursuing Laura. The most would be that she'd caught me.

My birthday night I lay in my sandy, sticky bed next to Sissy and listened to her whine about her sunburn and not going sailing. Mama had taken to the bed. My foot ached from the nail, throbbing with every heartbeat.

I knew everything'd be up to me, just like everything always was. Like Daddy always said, even if your cards are bad, you can still win. It was near light when I realized what I had to do.

I took off for Daddy's house, a good hour away even at a dead run. His wife opened the door. Except she wasn't ugly like he'd said. Not much taller than me, wearing spike heels around the house. And she was carrying a baby in her arms, in a pink blanket.

I froze to the ground, too scared to say a word, much less my speech, so I just shoved the pictures in her face—Mama and Sissy and me with Daddy, going deep-sea fishing in Biloxi, eating crawfish in New Orleans, playing chase at the trailer with Mama waving from the shade. Now she wouldn't want him any more, and he could move in with us like he always talked about.

I heard Daddy call out, "Who is it, LuAnne?"

"Nobody," his wife called back. But she was shaking all over, about to drop the baby.

She handed the baby to me and she walked to the closet tap-tap like a hammer on those heart of pine floors and took out something dark and long. She left the room, me following her with my new little sister. She stopped when she saw Daddy. Everything was clear and bright, like there was two suns. It must've had a hair trigger cause she barely moved her finger and it shot once into Daddy's chest. Like an echo my new sister started crying.

"Honeybabe?" Daddy asked with wonderment looking up at me from the floor, where the blood foamed into his mouth and onto his lips.

"Come home, Daddy." I tried to pick him up but his blood was seeping out onto the floor and all around my shoe.

When his wife moved again, I saw she had the shotgun pointed my way. I stood up real slow, still holding that baby, and pushed the barrel up to point at the ceiling. She stepped back and caught her high heel on the throw rug and fell, and the shotgun hit the floor not even bouncing before it fired and peeled off the right side of her head. I put the baby, squalling to beat all, in her crib, and found some ante-up money, $2200, hidden in Daddy's billfold. It would be all we had. I took his favorite dice and shuffling deck too, cause that would be all of him I had or ever would.

Too crazy to cry, I ran home through the scrub grass, chased by a hellfire sun. Out past the trailer mailbox was my Joker, waiting under the short pine where I'd left him with a bowl of fresh water.

August brought a cannonade of hundred-degree days to New Orleans. At ten at night, it was still in the nineties. Drivers fought in the street like gladiators over perceived slights, the weak and the elderly silently died in closed rooms, and husbands and wives knifed each other over ancient indiscretions. For the first time it occurred to me that I might be happier if Laura were dead.

Where once I'd been ecstatic over any fraction of Laura's attention, now sharing her had become intolerable. So that she'd be home in case Jake came by early, she never spent the night with me, always disappearing sometime around four, like some kind of sex vampire, and appearing the next morning at work as fresh and, if I chanced to see her, as cool as designer water. Intermittent reinforcement may be the most effective treatment for dogs. It will make a human crazy.

One night, as I was debating between bed and bourbon, I heard a short beep from a car in the street, like the peremptory bell calling a servant. I was both aroused and furious. She was dropping by (I knew from her calendar) after an assignation with Jake.

"Did I get you out of bed?" she asked.

"I might ask you that."

"It would be a mistake." She looked at me levelly with those hazel eyes, a color I'd once thought of as warm. The old Kyle Cameron with his trademark never-fail smile would've had a snappy comeback. But he was no more. She walked to the back, and I followed.

By my massive four-poster bed I kissed her and she coiled one leg around mine the way she had with Jake. When I lifted her sweater over her head, she held her arms up high, the way a child does. The familiar drowning feeling washed over me.

"It's worth it," she said softly, as if to her own, and my, unasked question, and it was.

We had sex three times that night but I never experienced a moment of satisfaction; instead, I stayed on-guard, off-balance, afraid of losing her at any moment. It made me enraged and frantic all at once.

The next morning, when I left for an appointment to meet Mom's psychiatrist, I almost felt in need of one myself.

For the last year, every Wednesday at 3:00 it had been my responsibility to drive my mother to see Dr. Hart. Otherwise she wouldn't go. She despised the sessions, pronounced them useless except as a source of drugs, and hated talking about her personal life. One time, as I drove her home, I gingerly asked her how it went.

"Fine," she answered with a bit of triumph in her voice. "He kept waiting for me to say something, and I waited for him to ask a question. So there we sat for an hour." She smiled.

"Is that how it usually goes?" I asked.

"Oh, sometimes we talk about travel, and sometimes about movies. Chit-chat and this and that."

"Don't you ever talk about—" I hesitated. Mom refused to acknowledge the existence of any troubles in her life, despite her suicide attempts and cabinet full of pills. She only agreed to go to the psychiatrist because I'd pleaded and Jake had insisted. "Don't you ever talk about how you feel?"

"Lord, no, I wouldn't bore the man with my problems."

"He's paid to listen, Mom. That's what you're supposed to talk about."

She looked over at me and I knew I'd gone too far. "It's my life, Kyle."

I didn't ask her again. Instead, I made my own appointment with Dr. Hart. I didn't tell Jake and I didn't tell Mom. It was her life, but she was taking more and more pills as Jake, enfolded with Laura, was home less and less.

The guy, Dr. Hart, didn't look too impressive considering my mother's life was in his hands. He was a scholarly-looking man about forty, with a neatly trimmed beard, wire-rim glasses and tweedy-looking suit, though it was summer. Seeing him study me as we shook hands, I wondered how silent my mother had really been.

"You recognize, of course, that I am extremely constrained in what I can discuss with you." He spoke deliberately, as if much depended on his choice of words.

"I understand. But I'm worried about her."

"Of course you are. You saved her life. In many cultures that binds you to her forever. Not our culture, of course."

"So she has talked about me."

"Yes." It felt strange to hear it. But what if he'd said, 'No, she's never mentioned you'?

"And my father?"

"Oh, yes."

"Their marriage?"

He hesitated, sensing this might be classified material, then deciding in my favor.

"Quite a lot."

"It's a major issue."

"A major issue."

"For how long?"

He shook his head. I took another angle.

"Is she suicidal now?"

"My opinion is no."

"As I recall, that was your opinion before she tried last time."

"Psychiatry isn't a science. It isn't even an art."

"Eight years and a hundred thousand dollars later and you're telling me she might as well have been going to a podiatrist?" He watched as my face flushed with impatience and anger, the old standby Cameron emotions. "What's the point in her even coming?"

"Damage control," he responded after a moment, as he observed my fists unclench. "Your mother has been—continues to be—injured."

"By Jake."

"That's as far as I'll go. Farther than I intended."

"What about all the pills?"

"She needs them. If the situation changes, she won't."

"Has Jake ever bothered to come up here and talk to you?"

He looked at me for a long moment, weighing it, then said, "No."

I stood. "Thanks for your time."

He remained seated. "You paid for it." He looked at his watch. "You have forty more minutes. We could talk about you, if you like."

I felt a quick jab of terror—that would not be overstating it—and wondered, irrationally, if the door were locked. Because I had the strongest sensation of wanting to run.

"I'm doing fine, Doc, no snakes in my head." No, nary a one. "Healthy all-American boy. Eagle Scout." Expelled, actually, girl in my tent, same old same old.

He just sat there, with a pleasant smile on his face. A nice guy actually. And for one second I was tempted to sit back down and let it pour out. Except that I didn't know if I'd ever be able to stop.

When Laura, at the very last minute, cancelled a midnight date I'd lived for all week, I sought out Evan, with vague plans for an all-night binge. I hadn't specifically told him about Laura and me, but I suspected he knew.

We started out at the F & M. Evan was quiet, just putting away beers and fighting me for the tab with an odd insistence. After awhile, the crush of bodies made the heat unendurable, so we left and drove, top down, with the wind feeling like it had come off the Sahara—the prehistoric Sahara, back when it was still a sinkhole sea. We headed toward The Columns, a decadently overdecorated mansion-cum-bar on Saint Charles.

Evan was usually a benevolent drunk, reminiscing about old times together that I'd forgotten, but that night his mood was turning fouler the longer I kept talking my way around the subject of Laura.

"I guess you know," I finally said.

"I guess I do."

"How?"

"I know you." I couldn't see his face in the shadows but guessed it wasn't wearing a friendly smile.

"You won't say anything?" I asked.

"I never have."

"Thanks. I can think of a few hundred women who'd enjoy seeing me now." I took a solid drink of bourbon. It joined its cousins in my stomach, all steeping in a stew of self-pity.

"And a few men," I heard him say from his rattan high-backed fan chair. He leaned forward. His eyes were angry, and he looked like Zeus, or more appropriately, Jehovah, on his throne.

"Prince Cameron in extremis. For the first time he drinks the piss of life."

There was no humor in his voice, but I chose to pretend otherwise.

"Hey, don't forget the thrice-taken bar exam, Jacobs."

"You never gave a damn about her, did you, Trojan?" It was my high school nickname, which he knew I hated.

Alison, of course, was who he was talking about, Alison, for whom he'd always been there with a comforting shoulder—and what else?--whenever I wasn't. This was way beyond masquerading as humor and in fact I could feel a gorge of anger rising.

"I guess that doesn't much matter now, does it?"

"Matters to me."

"Stay out of it. That's a friendly suggestion."

"Don't see any friends in the vicinity."

If I hadn't known Evan so well, I'd have thought he was going to come right out of that fan chair and take a swing at me. And frankly I didn't know if I could take him. He'd put on some heft since high school and had studied an obscure branch of martial arts, though he told me it was for the philosophy and that Jews didn't fight.

But one afternoon on Saint Charles when I was giving him a ride to work, I had rear-ended a Cajun's brand new truck. While I was pulling out my license, the crawfish-sucker poleaxed me. Evan stepped up—this was college and the guy had five years and thirty pounds on him—and did something with his hands. The next thing I saw, the guy was on the ground crying. The good old days.

"Call her," I challenged, keeping an eye on his fists. The idea of them together turned the bourbon foul in my mouth.

He didn't respond, just looked anywhere but at me.

"Go ahead," I pressed, perversely, wanting my world pushed into utter ruin. Like most of the guilty, I craved justice. "Call her," I repeated, finishing my drink in a show of callous nonchalance. Sometimes I got a little tired of Evan's being right all the time.

"Leave it alone," he commanded.

"Because you wouldn't do that, right? As opposed to me?" Me, who'd snake anybody's girl, including my father's. That's what he thought, and obviously who could argue? Jake had told Laura I was ruthless, hadn't he?

The waitress glided by, slender, dark, coolish, a Laura type though merely pretty instead of fatally lovely. It was a mark of my addiction that I wasn't even tempted by the counterfeit. With my credit card, I signaled her that I'd pay both tabs.

Evan grabbed my wrist. "I've got this one."

"Twenty-two dollars," the waitress said.

He opened his wallet. Took out three tens and handed them to her. "Keep it," he said.

"Thanks," she uttered, with all of Laura's indifference.

An eight-dollar tip, his wallet now empty.

I knew not to interfere. The summer after high school, we'd gone to Europe, the trip paid for, lavishly and in full, by Jake, who at my urging had secretly siphoned cash to Evan's father, a gentle guy with a failing optometry shop. I let it slip one night in Spain, and Evan flew back the next day, leaving me to wonder which was worse, foolish pride or none at all. He'd paid Jake back, with interest, and I vowed never to offer him unsolicited aid.

Evan looked at me, really for the first time all evening. “There’s nothing underneath, is there, Kyle?”

“Just more Kyle.”

“That’s what I mean.”

Nothing I hadn’t said to myself. But the corroboration from such a well-informed source made all the heat go out of the night, and the sweat that trickled between my shoulder blades felt like a tiny icicle.

I sped down Saint Charles—Evan had just loped off into the darkness, preferring a five-mile jog in the New Orleans steam bath night to my company. I slowed automatically to make the turnoff for Prytania.

Jake’s car wasn’t at her house. He was at home where he belonged.

He would be asleep. Mom wouldn’t. When I was a child, I’d awaken at 3:00, 4:00, to find her downstairs, reading, watching television, knitting. I wouldn’t go back to bed, and she’d let me nap on the sofa, near her, vigilant. I suddenly wanted to see her.

The lights in the living room were on. I let myself in with my key, then called out so I wouldn’t frighten her.

“Mom. It’s me.”

“I was just thinking about you,” she called out. The same soft voice from my earliest memory, when my parents were infallible and together.

The TV was on, the sound almost inaudible—no doubt so as not to disturb Jake, though his sleep was as deep and untroubled as mine wasn’t. Several opened books lay about her on the sofa and floor like sampled chocolates. She was knitting, and on the coffee table was not coffee but a 3 a.m. martini.

I joined her with a pre-dawn bourbon.

“Long night?” I asked.

"Not so bad. Yours was, though."

I nodded, wishing I could explain, somehow be absolved.

"You feeling okay?" I asked.

"Happy as a cheerleader." She tried to pull off a smile but it got lost on the way to her eyes. She was thinner, and for the first time she seemed to have lost the young, even childlike, quality that she'd retained through all her troubles. I didn't think she knew of, or even suspected, Jake's infidelity. Her devotion was the kind that didn't question. But all those hours alone, when Jake was supposedly at work, were cumulatively crushing her.

"I saw Alison today." Her eyes were sad, not reproachful.

"She probably didn't ask about me, did she?"

"She wasn't here long."

I'd told Mom I was too unsettled and that Alison deserved better, two true if incomplete assessments. What Alison had told my mother, I couldn't guess.

"I guess the old man's up there snoring away like a big old bear."

"He's exhausted. He went to the gym, ate next to nothing and went right to bed. Then the phone rings and he dashes out, another legal crisis. I wish he'd get some clients who had their emergencies during normal business hours."

"What time'd he go?" I asked, trying to keep my voice casual.

"Just before midnight. Back after 2:00 and fell right asleep."

That was my midnight date, I wanted to yell. I wanted to drag him out of the bed and throw him down the stairs.

"He's getting a little old for these escapades," I said.

"That's what I told him when he came home."

"Jealous mistress, the law."

"I just wanted him to hold my hand a little while." She never spoke about her feelings, but the last martini, and the dark room, must've loosened her brittle barrier for just a moment. Even so, I had to strain to hear her soft confession. "He said he was too sleepy."

When I heard that, I took the stairs two at a time.

"Kyle, stop, what are you doing?" I could hear Mom call after me, but it seemed from a long way away. I didn't knock, just surged into the bedroom. Jake was sleeping the heavy sleep of a sated carnivore.

"Wake up," I demanded, and when he didn't I grabbed his shoulder, hard, and shook him.

"What the hell?" Jake was immediately alert, sitting upright, on the attack. "What are you doing here?"

"Your wife is downstairs. Crying. In case you haven't noticed, she needs you."

"I believe that's my business."

"Then tend to it."

The wild thought came to me that he was off balance, and that I could pummel him down, right there in the bed. Scared of what I'd do, I forced my fists to open.

Jake looked at me for a long moment. He was the least bit uncertain of his position, the first time I'd seen that. He put on his robe and walked out without another look at me.

I stood at the top of the stairs, saw him sit by Mom on the sofa and put his arm around her. She relaxed her head so gratefully onto his shoulder that it almost made me cry. She was happy now, if only for these few minutes.

Roger's trial date was set for mid-October, less than two months off, and Jake and I met almost daily. Sometimes for whole afternoons, as we planned our strategy, it felt like we were partners instead of mortal adversaries. Working with him closely for the first time, I saw what a brilliant lawyer he was. He moved the facts of the case around like knights on a three-dimensional chessboard.

Our theory of the case was "the revenge fuck," as Jenna Farber put it, but gone awry.

Mamie had anesthetized herself for the procedure with Roger, then, the next morning, as her relationship with Britt began to resuscitate, had retroactively retracted her consent. This we would support with phone records, which showed one phone call from Britt to Mamie at 7:13 Sunday morning and subsequent calls from Mamie to Britt, culminating in a twenty-nine minute conversation that ended at 11:03. At 11:04 Mamie called the police.

I'd be cross-examining Mamie's friend Ashley, who was set to testify that Mamie had been too drunk to give consent, and I'd also be setting Mamie up for Jake, the bad cop, who would brutalize her in a soft-spoken manner ("Do you get drunk often, Miss Lawrence?" and "If you were that drunk, Miss Lawrence, then how can you be certain you were not the initiator?")

He had me write out my opening and closing arguments, which he then critiqued. He then had me deliver them to an empty jury box while he videotaped them. He showed me a tape of him delivering the same arguments, had me practice again, and taped me again. I was shockingly improved. Despite my best efforts, he was turning me into a lawyer.

I met with Roger to review his testimony, though he still balked at taking the stand, having no more confidence in his credibility than in any other matter. Since I'd last seen him, he'd taken incompletes in all his courses and checked out for his family's villa in St. Thomas. When he came to my office, he was darkly tanned—an unhelpful reminder to the jury about the difference of the very rich—but otherwise the trip didn't appear to have been restful. He'd dropped perhaps twenty pounds. Whereas before he'd been carrying a little beefiness from the Wittenhurst menus, he now appeared unhealthily gaunt, his custom suit coat gathering about him like a caftan. His eyes, once casually arrogant, wore a constant shadow of fear. One month in the tropics contemplating ten years at Angola Prison Farm had broken him.

"What's the most they could give me?" he asked for the second time in our meeting, hoping I'd give him a better answer. It was 10:00 a.m. and he'd been drinking. I didn't blame him.

"You're not going to lose." Whether Roger was guilty or not, he sure as hell looked it.

"Rape's one of those things they don't like in prisons, isn't it?"

"You're not going to prison, Roger. I want you to stop thinking you are, do you hear me?"

"Yes, sir," he answered, and he wasn't being sarcastic.

"Now listen to me," I ordered. "First, sit up straight, dammit." He complied as best he could, considering his lifelong slouch. "I want you to put on some weight. That means eating. Meat, vegetables, fat, the seven basic food groups. And exercising. You know how to exercise?"

"Dad has a gym in the house. Nobody ever uses it."

"You are. Now stay out of trouble," I said sternly. I didn't want him going back home to nurse on the bourbon bottle. "And stay out of the sun."

Roger shakily made his way out, so bedeviled he didn't even notice Laura as she passed. As the sunlight flamed her hair, she looked so lovely as to be of another, higher species. According to the pencil jotting on her calendar—which had been there this morning but not yesterday-- she and my father were going to rendezvous at 3:00 p.m. And there was nothing I could do to stop it.

Myrt said something but, watching Laura, I didn't hear her.

"Anybody seen Kyle Cameron?" Myrt asked me.

"What?"

"This is what," she said, holding a single envelope in her hand. My eyes asked, From them? And she nodded.

The paper cut I received ripping open the envelope was a preview of its contents. The Bar was filing formal charges based on April's complaint. My case was the one in a thousand deemed to have merit. No more confidentiality. April Cahill would now be public record.

I found Jake in his office and immediately told him. I'd expected to see anger, even disgust in his dark blue eyes—the same as mine—but what I saw there was something akin to sympathy.

"That's a tough break," he said, I knew he was already calculating how to combat it. "I'm calling Joshua to meet, preferably immediately, before this gets out to the media."

I nodded. Curiously, the biggest disappointment I felt was that I'd let Jake down once again.

"Dad," I began. He stopped; I almost always called him Jake, had for years. I don't know why I called him "Dad."

"I'm sorry." I was, and not only about April. He nodded.

"It's not over yet, Son."

Joshua commandeered the head of the table, his accustomed spot in life, while Roger sat in my corner chair, looking like nothing so much as the dunce.

"What the hell is he doing here?" Joshua challenged as I entered the conference room. I hesitated but Jake waved me on it.

"I believe you're making a mistake, Joshua." Few called him by his first name, compared to the hundreds who called him "sir," and—behind his back—"Sir Prick."

"The fact that both Kyle and Roger are unjustly accused could work to your son's advantage. It will put the multiplicity of these claims before the jury's eyes every day of the trial." I marveled at Jake's attempt to transmute a serious liability. But Joshua wasn't moved.

"What it'll put before the jury is two pretty boys who can't keep their slippery dicks in their pants. Dammit, Cameron, I agreed to let your boy take this case on your specific recommendation.

"Kyle has told me the charges are a fabrication. I believe him."

The lie I'd told Jake about the sex caught in my gut like a fishhook. My father was behind me, for once in my life, and he was dead wrong.

"I believe him," Jake repeated, pulling the hook back through. "The majority of these formal filings are dismissed."

Ninety-nine out of a hundred, Ginger had calculated, not quite the one-in-a-thousand edge she'd given me at the outset.

"If you wish to change representation," Jake continued, and I watched him chill down the temperature of his stare, "that is your privilege. However, it won't be with our firm."

What was Jake doing?

"You're saying you won't represent my boy?" Joshua said slowly, then raised the bet. "After all the years Tommy and I've been friends?"

"It's a package deal, Joshua." I never believed he'd go that far for me.

Jake fixed him with his Medusa stare. Joshua stared back, one of the few people I'd seen survive it.

"Then to hell with all the Camerons," he cursed us and stood to leave, gesturing with a curt hand movement for Roger to follow.

Roger had a look in his eyes I'd seen in dogs hit by cars. But he didn't move.

"I have something to say. About this case. Which is my case and my life. And that is that Kyle is my lawyer. And therefore he's not fired."

Roger's words seemed to have sucked every other sound out of the room. In the vacuum he sat tensed, as if awaiting a cudgel. It wasn't long in coming.

"Since when do you decide anything?" Joshua asked, both angry and a little amused, as if a Chihuahua had tried to nip him. "Since when, boy?"

Roger was silent, having expended all his courage.

"Since never, that's when," Joshua railed. "And that's never going to change."

He turned to us. "Damn boy soiled his pants until he was six. Had to hold him out of school a year so he wouldn't make a fool of me." He turned to look at Roger, something he seldom did.

"Tell me this, boy? Just who do you expect would pay your legal bill? Who? Answer me, boy."

"I'll do it pro bono," I heard myself saying.

Joshua rotated his gaze over to me, like a tank gun moving its sights. But there was no comeback.

"What do you say to that, Jake?"

I couldn't read Jake's expression. "Our lawyers are encouraged to take on pro bono cases. Usually the clients are indigent. But I leave the decision to the individual attorney." Jake was giving away $100,000, something he'd have to explain to Tommy Munger.

Joshua turned his gaze back to me. "You two deserve each other," he pronounced in exquisite disgust and walked out.

Jake gave me the most minimal of nods, his "good boy" nod, so subtle nobody but blood kin could read it. As he left the room to let Roger and me confer, he lightly clapped me on the shoulder, something he almost never did. Once again I was surprised at the feelings he evoked from me, just as once again I knew how little I deserved his confidence.

It was then I noticed the clock. I didn't believe it but my watch confirmed the time: 4:12, over an hour past Jake's scheduled date with Laura. He'd forgone her.

I almost admired Charlie Dumaine's efficiency as she broadcast her discovery that same night. Behind her was an artist's rendition of a man and woman copulating on a skewed scale of justice.

"In an ironic but logical twist in the Wittenhurst rape case, Kyle Cameron, attorney for the alleged rapist, has some serious sexual problems of his own. Ethical charges were filed today by the Louisiana Bar that Cameron had sexual relations with a client."

I felt an awful inertia, as if I were strapped into my chair, Charlie's words coursing through me like the lethal injection she'd no doubt be delighted to administer. "Then when she rebuffed him, he took his revenge by failing to disclose the offer of a plea bargain. We go to Angola Prison."

April Cahill's image filled the screen. Charlie had moved fast and with the right connections to get this interview. Of course, she was well motivated. The phone rang, my private number that only a few people had.

"Kyle, what are we going to do with you?" my mother chided, as if I'd been caught in a picayune roguish scrape. I knew Jake had prepared her and that she'd retreated behind an extra chemical cocktail. In that stratosphere, everything always worked out fairy-tale perfect. On the screen, April was still talking. She started to cry but bravely continued, makeup perfect, courtesy NightWitness News.

I assured my mother that, indeed, she needn't worry about her mischievous only child. Immediately, the phone rang again. I quickly calculated who had the number. Alison? Not likely, especially after this. I picked up the receiver, heard a guffaw. Turnage.

"I'd call that snappin'-turtle pussy. You're a poster boy for abstinence."

"That's your specialty," I said. I hung up and turned up the volume.

"It just about amounts to rape," April explained, following Charlie's line of questioning or maybe she didn't need any prompting. If one day I wound up dead absent a dick, they'd have to search a lot of houses to find the trophy.

The phone rang again.

"You definitely leave an impression on women, don't you, Kyle?"

It was Laura.

"She's lying. I begged her to take that plea." I didn't mention the sex, and she was too good a lawyer not to notice.

"I'm free," she announced, radically changing the subject. Either she didn't believe the charges or simply didn't care. On her moral radar, they might not even register. As Charlie continued, interviewing an expert on legal ethics, I noticed I had an erection just talking to Laura. I clicked the TV off; they could be broadcasting the immediate solution to all of mankind's problems for all I cared.

"Come over," I suggested.

"I have trial tomorrow. You come here."

She'd never invited me over before. I'd always figured her house was reserved for my father. Maybe I was making some kind of progress. Maybe my sexual notoriety was an enticement. All that really mattered, though, was that I was going to see her. I followed my dick out the door.

I parked down Prytania Street, as directed, then hurried along the old cracked sidewalk toward her cottage. After a summer's full bloom, her crepe myrtle blossoms were still glorious.

She'd given me instructions on finding her key, under a clay pot holding a giant mother-in-law's tongue. I didn't question why she couldn't simply answer the door; it would be too ordinary. I took advantage of the opportunity—I'd long ago planned this—and pressed the key into a small rectangle of wax I'd warmed with my car cigarette lighter. I blew on the wax to cool it, then slipped the impression into my pocket and let myself in.

I was afraid I might be disappointed if her home were less than flawless, but the house, like Laura, presented a perfect surface. An antique cut-glass bowl held a single headily fragrant magnolia blossom. The heart-of-pine floors had a reddish tinge that evoked her auburn hair. The living room was, by intent, sparsely furnished and, like her office, without clutter, dominated by a mirrored mahogany armoire reflecting a rich green sofa. Knowing how she would look in that mirror, she would've lain on that sofa with my father.

The shower was running. I let myself into her bedroom and knocked on the bathroom door.

"Hey, I'm here."

"Just put my key on the dresser. I'll be out in few minutes."

I watched the door like a hungry dog. "I could join you in there."

"I'll be out in a few minutes."

I stepped over to her dresser and lightly ran my fingers over the items on top. Her perfume was a French brand I'd never heard of. I drew its paralyzing scent deep into my lungs, poured some on my handkerchief so I could sleep with it. Opening her jewelry box, I saw a pendant inscribed, "I love you, Jake." What the hell else had he given her? I opened a drawer and found his framed photo, tactfully slipped out of sight.

The shower stopped but I didn't notice. In another drawer were a pair of ivory dice in a green suede pouch and a well-worn pack of black playing cards. I fondled the dice, then rolled them for an omen. Snake eyes. Definitely not an omen. I picked up the pack of cards and started to cut them for a more accurate reading.

"What in the hell are you doing?" Laura's sharp voice demanded.

She stood in the bathroom doorway wrapped in a towel.

"I was looking for a pen."

"Those are private things. Personal things. Very private and very personal. Got it?"

She slammed the drawer.

"I just want to know more about you. I don't know anything." I was only too aware of how craven I sounded.

She threw open the towel. My eyes filled with more than desire, something akin to worship.

"This is all there is, Kyle. There is nothing else."

"No. I want all of you."

"This is all you get."

And for that moment it was enough.

She lit a candle as I stripped off my clothes, then she lay down in her canopied bed and stretched out naked in my arms. I ran my fingers feather-lightly over her. Aroused, she glided her hand down my chest and stomach. As she held me, I would've come in her hand if I hadn't kept uppermost in my mind the knowledge that bed was the one arena where I might best Jake.

The phone rang. She released me and reached for the phone. I grabbed her hand but she pulled away.

"Yes?" She smiled. Jake. "A little busy," she replied to what was obviously an invitation. "Sanders trial tomorrow."

She spoke softly but I could make out what she said. "Tomorrow night's fine. I love you too." She hung up.

"I can't stand this," I told her. "I can't take any more."

"Then leave."

"I can't."

She moved over me. "Then enjoy it."

I buried my face in her breasts. She moved on me, bringing me close to orgasm, then stopped, smiling at her power. I grabbed her waist, forcing her up and down until we both cried out.

Within minutes I was ready again, my body rallying from sheer fear that she'd turn me out otherwise.

She let me penetrate her again, but after a few strokes she softly asked me to stop. "Please, Kyle."

Unthinkable.

"Kyle, I asked you to stop."

"Why?" I kept moving, finding her refusal a powerful aphrodisiac.

"I'm just not in the mood any more."

I rolled away and stared up blindly. She'd weighed me against my father, and I'd been found wanting. Erased were the final vestiges of twelve years of easy confidence. I was drawing my payback for Alison and all the others. I'd never be so cavalier with another woman, wouldn't have the heart, or anything else, for it. Laura was the high point, or low point. After her would be, in every sense of the word, anticlimax.

As I wordlessly dressed, Laura unpacked her briefcase, her mind already on trial or Jake. She escorted me out. For a moment we stood framed in the lit doorway as I tried to salvage a kiss and got only her cheek.

Reluctantly, I walked down the street to my car. A skateboarder approached and I hid in the shadows. As I drove away, headlights turned on behind me.

Dousing myself in whiskey was my first idea, but I didn't want to be with anybody and I didn't want to be alone. Instead, I drove to the gym. Jake the beneficent had gotten the firm a membership and a large communal locker for the men. I dressed out, appearing to anyone who cared to look to be a fit, if haggard, young man instead of someone who'd just been expertly denutted. Upstairs, I began fiercely skipping rope in front of a mirror.

Then suddenly I saw Jake in the mirror right beside me. He had a jump rope, holding it by both handles in one hand, like it was a whip. It wasn't one of his gym nights.

"Working out mighty late," he said. His face was tight and for a second I had the wild image of him strangling me with the rope.

"Got to stay in shape," I said, watching him.

"I'll bet you do." His voice had dropped very low, and I was scared.

"What do you mean by that?"

"You know exactly what I mean, you little bastard," his voice so low it was a growl more than human speech.

Those headlights had been his. I felt like I had those ten thousand times he'd caught me and punished me. I fought down my fear and forced myself to look at him in the mirror. His eyes were hard but I could see pain there too. Had he suspected before? From the night at Jezebel? Or had he trusted Laura, trusted me? Was his realization as staggering as mine had been? Then I thought of him calling Laura, and Laura saying she loved him.

I did a fancy maneuver, crossing my wrists in front, and Jake matched me. I skipped faster and Jake kept up, in great shape for his age. I skipped on one foot, and he followed, pushing his heart rate into red-line, but after twenty seconds, he tripped on the rope and fell. He got up like the floor was a hot skillet, but Ben, the earnest fitness counselor, stopped him.

"You okay, Mr. Cameron?" Ben held a blood pressure device. In the gym Jake was known as a likeable guy who could be an asshole in court, and the gym was paranoid about lawsuits. Jake threw him off. His eyes were frightening.

"Take his," Jake said, indicating me. Ben looked over sharply at me. He had an innocent, trusting demeanor that told me he'd grown up in a normal family—surely some must exist somewhere—and he didn't know what to think of, much less do with, a father and son who were apparently pushing each other to the brink of death.

"That's okay, Ben, we can rest," I told him and stopped, but Jake wouldn't quit jumping until I'd thrown down my rope.

"How about we go a few rounds on the punching bag?" I challenged, once Ben was out of earshot. Jake didn't even answer, just turned his back and walked toward the heavy bag hanging in the corner.

"So now you're a fighter," Jake derided as he held the big bag. I slammed it with punches. He braced, surprised at the strength of my blows.

"A lover and a fighter," I corrected, keeping my breath even, so he wouldn't guess how exhausted I was.

We took turns holding the bag while the other slammed blows as hard and loud and intimidating as we could. Jake was getting wobbly.

"Getting tired?" I said between blows. "Maybe you ought to compete with someone your own age."

"Save your breath."

"Remember when you taught me to box?" I'd been twelve, facing him in a makeshift ring in the basement. There was the raw smell of the dirt floor and the feeling we were in a cave a long way from help. I asked him to stop, but he told me life didn't work like that.

I pounded the bag again and again until he was breathless, barely holding on. Then I kicked it, making him stumble back.

"How about some racquetball?" I proposed, breathing deeply from my diaphragm, as he'd taught me to do.

"Just going to suggest it."

I had the speed and stamina, Jake the technique, so for quite awhile he was able to stay even. After one tough volley, he slammed a corner kill shot.

"19 all," he announced and served a long low shot to the left corner, my backhand. Unexpectedly I slammed it back.

"How's Mom?" I asked as he ran up for it. He missed.

"Still 19 all," I said, stepping into the service area.

"Nola's fine. How's Alison?"

I served, hard. Jake roused himself for a hard return.

"I don't think Mom's fine." My return smashed, satisfyingly, into his back.

"Ow! Damn, boy, watch it."

For my next serve I slammed a low one that sent him running. "I don't think she's one bit fine."

He got to it somehow, a testament to his amazing competitive drive, and smashed it back, almost hitting me. I whizzed one by his head. It was a shooting gallery.

"20-19 mine," I said.

I served, this time keeping the volley going just to tire the old man. Finally he could hardly move, standing flat-footed in the center spot like a winded old bear. I slammed one down the line, and he took a futile swat at it. "Game," I gasped. "Another?"

He shook his head, too tired to speak. As he limped off toward the shower, I stared after him.

"We'll do it again," I promised.

"Any time."

As he showered, I opened the Cameron law firm locker and got out my things, leaving his clothes, wedding ring and—what else?--his damn briefcase.

Even in extremis, knowing the limits of our control, neither of us had directly mentioned Laura, a pattern we would maintain. Of course, in the end, which was not far away, none of that would matter. Except of course it wasn't the end, not near, for Jake and me. But for Laura, soon.

I ran home, limping from the nail, and told Mama and Sissy we had to cut our hair, leave town, go North. I gave Mama a thousand and I hid the rest for when Mama ran out. They were screaming and crying and falling down, so I had to pull some clothes and food together and shove them in the car.

Mama left Joker at some vet while I was asleep, and we were already in Houston when I woke up. She said she forgot where, some town that started with a T or D, and the more I begged her, the less sure she was, it could've been a C, and I never wanted or got another dog.

I was only fourteen but looked older and got a job at a Popeye's Fried Chicken. Sissy got one at a sno-cone place. Between us, we kept food in the trailer. Mama took to going to revivals and tithing my paycheck and praying for money.

At a prayer meeting, or bar, she met Earl Hutchison. He wasn't the looker Daddy was, but he had something Daddy didn't, which was a going business. All of a sudden we got regular meals to fatten us up (Sissy had gotten scary skinny on those sno-cones), we got a makeover at some spa. Though he was never nothing but nice, I had the idea he could turn real easy. Sissy was scared of him and I was too, a little.

Mama started working on Sissy, and she didn't have much trouble, them being two of a helpless kind and Mama having trained her good from day one. Sissy quit her job. That left me feeding three people on $3.75 an hour.

Earl took us out to the Sizzler one night. None of his movies were ever shown in theaters, he said. He did quality stuff for a select audience, so hardly anybody would ever know. I asked him how that squared with him also saying we'd be famous, so he substituted rich and took me off to the side. He said he'd pay me double what he told Mama, and I could put my part in the bank. I told him no, even after he promised me a tutor, Mama having never gotten us registered in school.

That very week, a cop started coming by Popeye's every night for a bucket of thighs. I quit wearing makeup and hid my hair in a bandana, but one night he tailed me from work and pulled me over. He was pale, clammy-looking, like he'd been brought out of the oven too soon. He always had little sweat drops above his lip.

"License, missy," and when I told him I'd lost it, he outright laughed. I could barely see over the wheel even with a pillow stuck under me. Driving age was eighteen, but Mama couldn't or wouldn't drive in the city.

"Little lady, you're in a pile of trouble." It was so hot my uniform was sticking to me. He looked at me the way the men at the mall did. If he ran my name, he'd find more than no license.

He smelled like old sweat and fried chicken, and his hands felt like hard-scraped leather. "Girl looks like you, it's just a matter of sooner or later," he said after.

Earl took me to his doctor friend, when I figured I was pregnant, and he took care of things.

Popeye's let me go and with nobody working, no food in the house, and too many years before I could go out on my own, I finally gave up and gave in to Earl. To Mama, really. Sissy loved the attention, and the free drugs got her through. I did what Daddy always said, keep your eye on the game, and my game was never anything but getting out.

The day Daddy died was when I learned the true power of hard. The reason more people don't know it is you can't be hard unless you can take losing everything. Cause, eventually, sometime or other, you will, you'll lose it all and then some.

TWO

THE POLICE NEVER FOUND MY footprints in Laura's crepe myrtle blossoms, nor my fingerprints nor any evidence I'd ever been there. On the morning after her murder, everyone at Laura's--Balthazar, Sessums, the surviving members of the firm—seemed to be moving through shimmering waves. I tried to reconstruct my interrogation by Balthazar, but my thoughts were like alphabet blocks scattered by a deranged baby.

I found myself back in the van with the rest of the firm, just as we'd been before we'd arrived at Laura's. Only now Ginger ate no pastries, Munger unfolded no spreadsheets, even Turnage, after one gauche comment about going on to the resort since we'd paid for it, retreated into unaccustomed silence. I didn't look at Jake and he didn't look at me. Of the ride, I recall nothing else except the sharp rush of pain as I cracked a tooth from clenching my jaw.

Though my apartment was out of the way, Jake dropped me off first, either out of protectiveness or simple repugnance. No one said goodbye.

I didn't go up to my empty apartment. I never wanted to go to the office again or see anyone there.

I drove to Evan's. We hadn't spoken since our night on the town but technically we were still friends.

"Evan," I yelled, too far gone for knocking. Looking through the window, I could see him making love to the computer screen.

"What are you doing here?" His voice was hard, but he got up to let me in.

"She's dead. Murdered."

"Who?" he quickly asked, his face tightening. He was thinking that I meant Alison.

"Laura."

"Sit down," he commanded, and I did. My eyes were closing. I fought it, but the weight of the last eighteen hours was heavy as a corpse.

"Do they know who did it?" He looked at me strangely.

"You mean me, don't you?" I leaned my head onto the arm of the sofa. My only semi-conscious awareness was of Evan putting my feet up on the sofa and then talking in the next room, saying he'd be late. When I woke up, after four hours' sleep, I found a cover on top of me and a note: "I had to go. I'll call tomorrow. You're the lawyer, but I do know this—don't tell anybody, including me, anything."

I waited there until after dark, then drove to the firm and parked a block away on Carondolet. No cars were in the lot, so I let myself in the back as I'd done two months before when I searched Laura's personnel file. This time the stakes were significantly higher. If Munger happened to come to work, or

Ginger, or even Turnage, I was in no frame of mind to explain what I was doing.

Upstairs, I put on gloves, unlocked Laura's office, and stepped inside. A car light from the street flashed through her window, briefly exploding the shadows and framing my face before I dropped down out of view.

What if the police were waiting outside? Paranoia shot through me—or was it paranoia? They could be marching up the thick-carpeted steps at that instant. They could be taking photographs of my parked Jeep. I jumped as Laura's phone rang, froze until they hung up.

Quickly I forced open her locked desk, scarring the beautiful wood. I ransacked the drawers, finding a snapshot of Jake but nothing else of interest. I took it and her desk calendar, with its little jottings, then turned on her computer. There was only one note, a humiliating entreaty from me. I erased it and then, to lessen the chances that her e-mail would be reconstituted, I removed the private e-mail program from her computer altogether. It was getting easier to think like a criminal. I relocked her door and ran downstairs, slowing to a walk when I left as I'd done the night before at her house. No one was waiting at my Jeep on Carondolet. No one followed me.

Back on Saint Charles, I sped, changing lanes, inviting an accident. Stoplights turned yellow, then red, and I gunned my new Jeep through again and again. Cars swerved and I passed by untouched, charmed or the opposite.

At home I sprawled shirtless on my balcony chair, falling deeper and deeper into a bottle of bourbon. My eyes felt dead, beyond tears. I poured a drink and looked at the bottle: a ways to go to hit bottom.

I called Alison again. It rang and rang. Finally, a sleepy voice answered. It sounded like Evan, but it couldn't be because he knew I hadn't meant it when I said to call her.

"Hello? Who is this?" he asked.

I hung up and sat down with my bottle like a very old drunk. Around the dead black star of Laura at the center of my universe now rotated two lifeless planets that had once been Alison and Evan.

At work the next morning, the firm felt like a funeral home, somber, hushed, bearing the death smell of chrysanthemums. Jake, tight-mouthed, approached Wendy. "Firm meeting in five minutes. Tell everybody."

"Yes, sir."

She handed me a message slip, "Call Evan," which I crumpled and threw away. As Jake strode toward the conference room, Ginger, dressed in a black silk knit that showed off still-great calves, came out of the copy room and swung into place beside him.

"Thought you might take the day off." They didn't hear me behind them on the soundless plush carpet.

No answer from Jake.

If you need to talk, you know where I live." Her eyes held an invitation as she turned into her office, but Jake walked on.

"Ginger," I thought to myself, shaking my head. Ginger was a damn good-looking woman—like a big sister, the kind who figures in porn fantasies about incest. No wonder she and Laura had hated each other. Was I slow or just blind? Nor, likely, was Ginger the first, if the block resembled the chip.

As soon as the lawyers had gathered in the conference room, Jake moved as always to the head of the table. Even standing in back, as far from him as I could get, I could see he wasn't wearing his wedding ring. He never went without it, except when he was working out at the gym. Had he removed it out of some kind of symbolic deference to Laura? Nothing else made sense. Mom would notice. As soon as the meeting was over, I'd demand that he put it on.

"Laura's funeral is Saturday at ten-thirty at Saint Alphonsus cemetery," he said. "We've all suffered a shock. Anyone who needs some time off, just let me know. The police will probably be back. Cooperate with them. Any questions?"

"Who's gonna get all her cases?" Turnage asked immediately.

"I'll take the Duval rape case," Ginger offered.

"It might be the decent thing to wait till after her funeral," I couldn't stop myself from saying, "if we can control ourselves."

"Excuse me for living," Ginger said. "No pun intended."

"It's not like she didn't snake all the good cases before we had a chance at them," Turnage said.

"Maybe she was just better than you, Turnage," I said.

"May be." He looked over at me. "But at least I'm pulling my weight. Unlike some." That silenced me.

"Do they have any suspects, Jake?" Munger asked.

"They think it's one of us."

I looked up sharply.

"Why?" Munger demanded.

"Someone broke into her desk last night. Her calendar's been removed." Jake deliberately looked away from me, but I could see he was furious at my stupidity.

I determined that it wouldn't be the best time to ask why he wasn't wearing his wedding ring.

That Saturday, Cameron & Munger gathered at the old Saint Alphonsus graveyard in the Irish Channel district. Inside the church, the famous stained glass Black Madonna gloomed down her ambiguous blessing. I walked unsteadily [illegible] toward Laura's open coffin. Because Laura had [illegible] law firm arranged for her funeral. Ordinarily, J[illegible] assigned all the decisions to Ginger, but he handle[illegible] himself, selecting Laura's cemetery, coffin, burial outfit, and tomb. He'd opted not to have a church service, intending, I assumed, to spare himself some of the strain, since my mother would be on his arm, but he instructed that the coffin be open. He couldn't deny himself his last look ever upon Laura's face.

In somber suits, the bickering lawyers stood together, roasting in the September heat under the funeral tent. Ginger nodded when I arrived, not yet hating me. Turnage stared intently away from me, as did Jake; Munger, as was customary, looked at no one. In their own group, the firm secretaries clustered together, required by Jake to attend. Laura had no friends among them. Jealousy of her beauty, and awe, and distaste for her coldness, were what they'd felt, and, now, relief at not having to compare themselves to her any longer. Along with a few of Laura's curious neighbors and several of her criminal clients, we comprised a disparate crowd. Though Jake stood away from me, with Mom in between us, I was able to observe his left hand, still ringless.

He'd arrayed Laura in her cream-colored slipover silk dress; he'd searched for her favorite, gold and green like her eyes, even breaking our now accustomed silence to inquire about it, but I told him it was no doubt smothered in plastic at some dry cleaners, never to be claimed.

At the sight of Laura, my hand went to the scar on my forehead, just beginning to fade, a diligent reminder in case I forgot her for one blessed moment.

A very wayward Catholic, Jake had had some difficulty finding a priest to perform Laura's service, and the eulogy was delivered by a macabre priest-for-hire who'd never known her.

"We come to say our farewells to Laura Katherine Niles, a hauntingly beautiful woman," he began. I was unable to look away from her. With the scrape on her cheek masked by the mortician's art, she remained flawless.

A tear came to Jake's eye and he didn't dare move to wipe it. I hardened my face.

"She was so pretty," my mother whispered to me, "and so smart." Too pretty, too smart.

"Do not grieve her for her rare beauty," the priest chastened, "for in this world it is an affliction on both bearer and beholder. In the lines of the poet:

Beauty is that Medusa's head,
Which men go armed to seek and sever.
It is most deadly when most dead,
And dead will stare and sting forever."

He delivered the last line almost like a curse, then crossed himself. I repeated it to myself. As usual, poetry trumped prayer.

"May God have mercy on her soul," he petitioned with little hope. "And may God have mercy on all our black hearts."

Jake signaled the paid pallbearers to close the coffin, and the mourners began to make their first tentative steps toward their cars. As the lid was lowered, he and I stood side by side at her coffin, fixed on her lovely face until the final tap of wood on wood.

"And dead will stare and sting forever," I thought I heard him whisper.

As we lawyers slowly dispersed, sweating in our sun-absorbing blacks and grays, my mother spoke. "I ordered that coffin spray of yellow roses for the firm. She was from Texas, wasn't she?"

"Louisiana. Lafayette," I corrected her.

"I'm the one from Texas," Ginger put in.

As we neared the street, we saw Balthazar and Rimers, leaning against their car.

"Here come the buzzards to pick the bones," said Ginger.

Jake, our leader, stepped out. "We'll all make ourselves available back at the firm for questioning."

"We're here to make an arrest," Rimers announced.

Jake and I looked at each other: which of us would it be? Turnage's hand flew to his stomach. Ginger emitted a little "Oh." Munger remained expressionless. Balthazar and Rimers headed toward me—I tensed—then on past.

"Sorry, Jake," Balthazar said as they cuffed him.

"What?" Mom's knees buckled, and I grabbed her arm. "You're making a mistake, Bal," Jake told him.

They led him to the police car. "Tommy, get down to the station," Jake ordered.

"Dad, I'm coming, too."

"No you're not."

"What's going on, Kyle?" Mom demanded.

"I'll tell you as soon as I know."

I turned to Jake. "I'm coming," I told him. "You need all the help you can get." He shook his head. Rimers pushed him into the car.

"I'm your son, dammit!"

In cuffs, helpless, Jake looked at me for a moment and finally nodded.

From the police station I called to assure my mother that he'd be home later that night; I thought it unlikely that she'd try to commit suicide without knowing the details of her husband's arrest, so for once I gave myself permission not to worry about her.

As I waited with Jake in a locked holding room, I again noticed his ring finger. It looked naked without the band familiar since childhood, heavy gold with a Greek key design.

"Why haven't you been wearing your wedding ring?" The answer to that question suddenly seemed crucial.

"Can't find it."

"The gym's the only place you ever take it off."

"I know that, Kyle," he said with elaborate patience. "Did it not occur to you to think I checked there?"

I started to retort, then didn't. He needed an ally; he would have more than enough inquisitors.

"Just asking."

He looked up, perhaps surprised at the unprecedented conciliation in my voice.

"The only other time I remember taking it off was when I washed the car." It was his pass at conciliation.

Together, we guessed at what the police had. Jake's fingerprints throughout her house (I didn't mention I'd wiped the doorknobs clean). A neighbor identifying the Jag as a frequent visitor to Prytania Street. Cell phone records could be a problem.

"What about that last little piece of jewelry you gave her?"

"I'll discuss it with Tommy," he snapped, closing the subject and reminding me of my status.

We sat in hostile silence, both of us no doubt again realizing the wisdom of never discussing Laura. Finally, chafing, he sent me out of the holding cell to get briefed.

In his genteel yet persistent way, Munger had wrung out some information from Balthazar. "They have your father's wedding ring," he announced.

"What for? How'd they get it?"

Munger didn't like conversations to be hurried along. He operated at his own decorous speed, and attempts to skip ahead only resulted in greater delay.

"They have it as evidence. That's all he would reveal."

"As evidence of what, that he's married?"

"That was all he would reveal."

"Would he reveal how they got it?" I asked, assuming his cadence.

"Yesterday your mother's maid invited them in to wait while Jake was washing his car. He had left the ring in his study, and they seized it as evidence."

"Can they do that without a warrant?"

He looked at me. "Didn't you take Constitutional Law, Kyle?"

I remembered something about items in plain view. That was the totality of my Sixth Amendment knowledge.

"Was it in plain view?" I asked to demonstrate I had a functioning brain.

"We have a basis to argue the point. The judge will decide in a pre-trial hearing."

"Why do they want it?"

He looked down at me with minor annoyance. "We don't know yet, Kyle. Perhaps you'd like to speculate?"

"Somebody saw it when they were together. They want to place Jake somewhere with Laura."

"Perhaps."

"Any sign of forced entry?"

He shook his head.

"Somebody she knew, then," I observed. Anybody with a law degree or a TV set would know that. "What about the murder weapon?" I asked.

"An antique sterling silver candlestick. Three blows to the head."

She'd fought to live.

"They assume the candlestick belonged to Laura," he continued. "It was found in her bed under the covers with her blood and her and Jake's fingerprints all over it. She was killed on the floor—"

"How do they know that?"

"Blood-spatter pattern. Also, the angle of the blows. The first blow came when she was standing, the other two after she had dropped. The murderer then took the time to drag her to the bed, rip off her gown, and pose her arms above her head."

I made my voice casual. "Any theories as to why she was killed?"

"What are your theories, Kyle?"

"Jealousy. Sexual obsession. Vengeance."

Munger nodded, as if in approval of my answer or the act itself. "Balthazar argued against arresting your father, because an experienced criminal lawyer would've disposed of the murder weapon or at least wiped his prints off."

So he would.

"Sessums believes that, in his haste and possibly remorse, Jake misplaced the candlestick, panicked and ran. That, subconsciously, he wanted to be caught. A less obvious and more elegant theory," he added gratuitously, reminding me yet again of his championing of Sessums for my slot. "Finally," he continued after he was sure I'd comprehended the insult, "they have witnesses that Jake was having an affair with Laura."

"They worked together," I argued. "If all Sessums has is Jake at Laura's house every day..." I said, then stopped. How could I have known that?

Munger smiled faintly, either at my imprudence or my fervor. "A few months ago, two teenage boys constructed a treehouse, which happened to give them a vantage point from which to view your father and Laura copulating."

I felt a surge of fear. "Eyewitness testimony."

"Worse. Photographic."

"Of who? Just him and her?" I asked, too quickly.

"Who else?"

"The real killer."

He looked down at me, with that odd praying mantis cock of the head, as if x-raying my brain for later dissection. For someone whose law partner had been accused of murder, he seemed remarkably calm. But that was his way. "To my knowledge, the photographs with your father are all they have." And with the slightest gesture of his patrician head, he dismissed me.

Back in the locked holding room, I hunkered with Jake on metal chairs at a metal table and started down my notes. Ever the defense lawyer, he began to argue his case, point by point, before I could even finish.

"Ring's inadmissible, warrantless search. Fingerprints on the candlestick are easily explained. We were working on the Petty case at her house—verify it with our computer billings—and the electricity—"

"Two kids saw you in bed with her from their treehouse. They have photos." I took no pleasure in the stunned look in Jake's eyes.

After a long moment of silence, he sat back. "Well, that changes things."

"You'll have to tell Mom."

He hit the table with his fist. "Dammit, I've been trying murder cases for twenty-five years. If I'd killed her, wouldn't I have had the sense to wipe the murder weapon clean?"

"Sessums thinks you subconsciously wanted to be caught."

Agitated, he looked toward the door. "Where the hell is Tommy? How long does it take to post a no-hold bail?"

An hour later, after I'd been caged with Tiger for twelve hours, Munger finally maneuvered the papers through, and a cop in the station lockbox area began checking out Jake's possessions to him.

"Where're my keys?" Jake demanded. Munger hushed him. Outside the station, he told us they were evidence.

"Of what?" Jake challenged.

"Did you have a key to her house?" Munger asked. Jake's expression said it all.

"Jake," he admonished.

How was it that the idiot son had been quick enough to steal, erase or wipe clean anything incriminating, yet the practiced criminal attorney had already been caught twice?

"Why didn't you have the sense to throw that key away?" I was suddenly furious at him.

"What do they want with your ring?" Munger asked him.

"How the hell do I know?"

I drove Jake home from the police station—he wanted to drive, though it was my car—while Munger followed in his funeral-director black Lincoln, to which he'd returned after his fling with the Kompressor.

"Tommy's not to know anything about you," Jake ordered, breaking a long silence during which, I knew, he'd already been constructing his defense. "Is that clear?"

I nodded.

As we passed Prytania Street, our heads turned almost in unison to look down Laura's block. Longing, remorse, fury--I'd lived with him long enough to know we were feeling the same things.

After a long silence, I asked, "Why were you washing your car the day after she was killed?"

"It was dirty."

"From what? Fingerprints?"

He stared back at me, his eyes hard. "Get this straight. My life is on the line. I will not discuss my guilt or innocence. With anyone. And if you're smart, you won't discuss yours either."

We drove on, silent again. As I turned in his driveway, I looked over at the desolation in his eyes.

"Dad?"

"What?"

"I never thought it would turn out this way. I wish I could make it right."

"You can't. She's gone."

It was dark, and I was glad. Seeing each other's tears was more than our deteriorated relationship could withstand. As we parked in front of the house, Munger waited, leaning against his Lincoln, a grim dutiful look on his face, as if he'd rather be home nurturing one of his migraines.

"Tommy, why don't you wait in the kitchen while I tell Nola," Jake suggested.

"Fine," he said, an understatement.

"I'm coming in," I insisted. "Moral support."

"For whom?"

"For whoever needs it."

I followed him into the den. He joined my mother on the sofa, but at the other end. I sat across from them like a chaperone. My mother was waiting, waiting, but Jake just stared at the floor.

Finally, she said, "If someone doesn't say something, I'm going to scream. Why on earth do they think you killed her?"

He looked up but didn't speak. Mom looked more and more frantic. "Tell me!"

I began, "Because—"

Jake broke in. "I'll do this. Because I was having an affair with her."

At that, my china-doll mother sank into the sofa. "I see," was all she said, so softly I didn't know if Jake heard it.

"I'm sorry. I never wanted to hurt you, Nola."

She shakily walked to her purse and got out her tranquilizers. She tapped out two, then two more and swallowed them without water. She reached for another bottle.

I grabbed her hand. "Don't. It'll get better. This is the worst."

She collapsed into a chair, her face ten years older, and tried to make sense of her new world. "She was just a girl. She was Kyle's age, wasn't she, Kyle?"

"Yes, ma'am."

"Did you, Jake... kill her?"

"No."

When she got up her courage for the toughest question, there was still the tiniest quiver of hope in her voice.

"Did you love her?"

I prayed he would lie.

"Yes."

I winced as she squeezed back tears. "All those nights. What a fool I've been." Her voice was dead. I hated hearing her sound like that again.

"You need to know something else," Jake continued, "because it could come out. She wasn't the first."

My mother stared at nothing.

"Will she be the last?" I demanded.

After the briefest delay, Jake answered, "Yes. The last. Nola, whatever happens, I never stopped loving you."

Did you ever start, I wanted to say, but she looked at him, believing even this, even now.

"What time did it happen?" she asked.

"Somewhere between ten and two a.m.," I told her, quoting the police report.

"Between ten and two we were together," she said to Jake, her voice very determined and with an unaccustomed focus in her eyes. "You were asleep. I was reading. *Gourmet* magazine."

I stared at her. My mother could be remarkably efficient when the occasion demanded—her parents' opposition to her marriage, my expulsion from the fraternity, a city order to cut down her favorite live oak.

"Nola, I won't let you perjure yourself for me. Not after–"

"I'm still your wife. Give me that." Her eyes were fierce, maybe a little crazy, and Jake finally acquiesced with a nod. "You'd best have Tommy come in," she said and he went to get him.

Munger, a familiar figure in the house since my childhood, sat down in his usual ladder-backed chair. "As you well know, Jake, the jury will be trying you for adultery too—"

He didn't get another word out before Jake stood, unable to tolerate the inferior position one second more. "Here's what I've decided. I want Kyle sitting second chair with you."

Munger studied me thoughtfully. "That's an interesting idea."

"Whoa," I said, and my hands went up like I'd been offered rat poison. "I'm the last person you want for any number of reasons. I could be disbarred by then."

I could see Munger's lips tighten at tawdriness upon tawdriness; if he had his way I'd not only be disbarred but unborn.

"It won't happen," Jake said.

"But they'll know I was accused. I'm tainted," I argued, desperation creeping into my voice.

"Juries have short memories."

"They don't have lobotomies." I'd seen Jake before when his instinct guided him against all prevailing reason. Usually he was proven right. But not always.

"I need my family," he pressed. "Behind me and by my side. As for the bar situation, you're innocent and Ginger doesn't lose that kind."

"But you always say I don't know my ass from my elbow," I said, once again pleading my own incompetence.

"I believe you know enough to sit in a chair and act like a devoted son. And that is what I need most in this case. A devoted, forgiving family."

"Then that's what he'll have," Mom stated, with her new firm voice. Crisis strength. When I next visited Dr. Hart, he predicted it would last as long as Jake was in trouble. She could rise to the occasion when others were in need—but not herself.

Under his breath Jake said, "You owe me, Son."

My mother looked at me.

Finally I nodded. "God help us all."

Later—much later—after Munger left and Mom wandered upstairs, it was just Jake and me. He allowed himself a drink, and after a moment's hesitation offered me one.

"Ground rules," he decreed. "We never talk about Laura, except as the victim of a murder. I don't want to hear about you and her."

I nodded. Fine with me.

"Except for tonight. I want details. Now."

"That's private," I protested.

"I'm your father," he suddenly roared. "And your lawyer and your client. And I'm scrambling for a trial strategy. They may not have motive, and they won't unless they find out about you. Does anybody know?"

"Evan."

"He won't come forward," Jake said in one of his snap character judgments. If Evan would steal my girlfriend, how far could you trust him? "What about your neighbors?" he probed.

I shook my head. It had always been dark and no neighbor shared my entryway. Most of the Quarter had sexual habits more outré than mine. Laura and I had taken chances—repetition legitimizes anything—but the city itself, in all its seaminess, had provided us protective coloration.

"What about fingerprints?" he asked. "In her house? Her car? Your car?"

"I don't think so." I'd done an extremely thorough cleanup job, excepting of course the murder weapon. And I'd returned after Alison slammed her door on me and made a good, if rushed, pass through Laura's car.

"Where else did you go with her?"

I told him about my bath-toweled ride through the Quarter and Mosca's and seeing Munger there. He closed his eyes for a moment at that.

"You damn fool." Likely not trusting himself to speak further, he gestured for me to continue.

"Her nightclub. Her house that once. Sailing."

"My sailboat, I presume."

I nodded, feeling nothing like the contender I'd considered myself that night on the lake.

"You little bastard," he said in a low voice. Laura was not a good topic for us.

My defense, that I'd seduced Laura to protect Mom, now sounded implausible, even to me. Better to leave it unsaid. Let him think me wholly ungrateful and selfish rather than a fool.

"Jesus. What a gamble." With that, he brought his fist down onto the table, as if he would've liked to be cracking open my skull. In the interest of self-preservation I omitted one other tryst.

He finished his drink and looked at me for a long moment. "Then that's it," he said by way of goodnight and started up the stairs.

As much as it confirmed his opinion of me, as much as I feared his rage, I couldn't let him head into trial not knowing.

"April Cahill."

He stopped.

"I had sex with her."

"What about the plea bargain?"

"I told her. In bed, in fact."

He looked at me for what seemed like a full minute. "I see."

"What happens now?"

"You fight it."

"I mean with your case. My representing you."

"It's a risk. You're just second chair. I'll take the risk."

"What about the Disciplinary Board? You're obligated to report me."

"If every attorney who screwed a client were disbarred, they could hold the bar convention in the restroom of the Royal Orleans."

He headed upstairs, playing it as if it were a trifle. But as past president of the Bar, he knew it wasn't, just as he knew his failure to report my violation was a serious ethical offense. They'd recently disbarred a husband for failing to report his alcoholic wife's theft of a client's funds. Jake was regarded in the legal community, and outside it, as that rare animal, a lawyer with integrity. I was a little awed that, facing murder charges, he'd bend his rule for me.

He stopped at the landing. "I'm glad you told me."

As he climbed the rest of the stairs, I just stared at his back, as confounded by his reaction as I was by virtually everything he did.

It was an hour before dawn when I drove home. For almost a day and a night, consumed by Jake's arrest, I'd managed to keep Laura away, but she found me now. The longing was so strong I had to fight to breathe. Was this worse than having her alive? I'd thought it wouldn't be.

I climbed my stairs. Half my courtyard garden was already dead from heat and neglect. Only the hardiest plants would survive my dereliction through the coming winter, one when it would turn suddenly cold and the leaves die and fall in one day.

As soon as I bolted the door, I yanked a suitcase out of the closet, opened it and removed a used Mexicana Airlines ticket. I ripped off a Mexicana luggage tag.

Out on my balcony, with the erratic shuffle of drunken footsteps below me, I struck a match and touched the flame to a corner of the ticket, then to the luggage tag. Flames crept up the paper, devouring, but for my scar, the last tangible thing I had of Laura Niles. There was no place for sentimental attachments that also happened to be evidence.

As I watched the ashes writhe in their last glowing twist, someone knocked. I stared at the door, not breathing. Who could be out there? And how the hell did they get in the outer gate at—I checked my watch--5:00 in the morning? I tapped the ashes flat with my fingers, but they still looked suspicious. Another knock, and I felt compelled to answer it.

Through the peephole I saw the last person—the very last—I wanted to see, Charlie Dumaine.

"Go away, Charlie, I'm asleep," I said through the door, slurring my words.

"I saw you come in not ten minutes ago. Why are you lying to me? Force of habit?"

I opened the door, knowing if I didn't she'd concoct a story about my refusing comment. She walked in, noting the open door from the balcony. She took in my artwork, my antiques.

"Exactly as I imagined it," she announced. "Exotic"— she touched a full-hipped Cycladic goddess—"to enchant your lovely victims." She continued around the room, indicting me with my decor. "Eclectic to confuse them." She peered into my high-ceilinged bedroom. "And a deliberate touch of decadence to let them know that the path to hell will be sweet." With that she sat on my bed, striking a mock-overcome pose.

"It's late, Charlie. It's been a long day."

"And not over yet. You keep a reporter hopping."

"Maybe your journalism would improve if you found another subject." Though it was near dawn, I found myself pouring myself a drink.

"On the contrary," she said, joining me at the bar and helping herself to a tequila, "you are the grindstone upon which I whet my talents."

"You mean fangs."

"Same thing. So, am I to assume the arrest of your father was a miscarriage of justice, soon to be rectified?"

"Go home, Charlie."

"So soon? I haven't even taken my clothes off, much less had the obligatory Olympic gold medal fuck."

Charlie had, I suddenly realized, been drinking. Her current tequila had several predecessors in her—I couldn't deny it—lovely flat stomach.

"When's this going to end? When you cover my funeral?"

"That would be a sweet story. 'Kyle Cameron and his dick died today. His dick will be deeply mourned. The New Orleans police force had to work double shifts, ladies and gentlemen, just to hold back the crowds of stampeding women who'd lost their virginity—'"

"I apologized for that. I'm going to call a taxi for you. You've had too much to drink."

Unfazed, she continued. "But today's viewers want to know about Jake and the notably desirable Laura Niles. This news is definitely sordid, fully satisfying the Cameron standard, not to mention the journalistic one. You'll have the national media in for this one, Kyle."

She was right. Another thing among many that I hadn't yet thought about.

"But I'll have the inside scoop, won't I?"

"Not from me."

"'Noted attorney kills beautiful woman. Attorney's son, a longtime Satyriasis sufferer, says he never visited the forbidden garden. Or does the apple not fall far from the tree?"

For literally the ten thousandth time I wished I'd never touched Charlie Dumaine.

"What were you burning on your balcony while I was watching from the street? Pieces of paper, right? Medium stock because it burned nice and slow. Mind if I inspect the ashtray for telltale Dick Tracy clues?"

"There's nothing out there."

She grabbed my hand. My fingertips were smudged black with ashes.

"Of course not. Not any more."

I felt a surge of panic in my chest. What if a tiny shred of paper had been left unburned? It could be traced by a dogged enough reporter. She might not know anything but she could find out everything. I opened the front door.

"Goodnight."

"Use 'em, abuse 'em, but you can't lose 'em."

She finished her tequila in one long swallow, then circled her arms around me and pulled me to her. After the first sensation, of shock, came the warmth and softness of her body, fully pressed against mine, melting into me.

"It doesn't work with anybody else," she said. Her voice was choked with a pain that was familiar to me, pain from wanting someone you could never hope to have.

For a moment—it couldn't have been longer—I returned the kiss of my enemy. Then somehow I wrenched myself away, surprising myself even more than her.

"Damn you," she said.

She walked out. The fires of her vengeance, as if they needed it, were fully restoked.

The defense blearily reconvened three hours later to question Eunice, my parents' maid, about the day the police seized the ring. Excepting my mother, Eunice had been the most constant figure in my childhood. Now she was past sixty, and what she called her sweet-diabetes allowed her to work only part of the week, supplemented by a brisk cleaning service with the personal touch of Roto-Rooter.

"How's my baby?" she asked, hugging me.

"Without a paddle."

"I believe it's me up that creek today."

"You didn't do anything wrong," I told her. "The police did, not you."

"Hemp. 'Spect it was Goldilocks let the po-lice in the house."

"You were supposed to."

"That's why I got three lawyers at the house this morning. Only other time I seen three lawyers roosting in one spot was after the Chantilly bus hit me."

The other two, Jake and Munger, were waiting in the dining room. "Your father ain't never been nothin' but nice to me," she said as we walked down the familiar hallway that now seemed like the last mile. "But I seen him light into you," she added darkly, and I realized that, like me, she had a healthy fear of Jake. I'd never seen her frightened before; when I was nine, wielding a flyswatter, she'd saved me from a mauling German Shepherd, yelling, "Scoot! Scoot!"

Munger, like a machine, showed no fatigue and had taken the time to select a natty handkerchief for his suit pocket. The Camerons revealed more human frailty. I had no handkerchief, or tie for that matter, and I could feel Munger staring at my unbuttoned collar button. Jake, unshaven, looked the worst of us. It was a shock to see the stubble, and even moreso to see that it was gray.

Eunice sat down, unaccustomedly and uncomfortably, at the head of the dining room table. With Jake and Munger at the other end, the room seemed transformed into an inquisitorial chamber.

"Can't we do this a little less formally?" I asked. "This is quite informal," Munger said, opening his crocodile-bound brief-pad and clicking on his microcassette recorder. He attempted a smile, which undid Eunice further.

"Not necessary," said Jake, clicking off the recorder, and for once I was grateful for his commandeering ways. "What we need to know, Eunice, is exactly what you said to the police when you answered the door."

She looked at me. I nodded.

"I told em, 'Y'all come on in and make yourselves at home.' I know that for sure cause that's what I say to all the visitors. Even those ain't got no business here." She gave Munger a look.

"Which room did you show them into?" Munger asked, with no attempt at a smile.

Eunice looked at me. "It's okay, tell him," I said. Munger's brow tightened with irritation.

"Living room," she said to me. "And then I went straight and got Mr. Jake from out back."

"How long were they were alone?" Munger asked.

"Lord, I don't know. I stopped to stir the peas. Had to salt em and—"

"We don't care about the peas," Munger interrupted. "Approximately how long?"

"She's trying to help," I told him.

Munger raised his eyebrows, waiting for Jake to chastise or, preferably, eject me, but he did neither.

"Just try to remember, Eunice," Jake said, as gently as I'd ever heard him. "How long from when they walked in, to salting the peas, to getting me?"

"Three, four minutes. That's all."

"Were the two policemen in the living room when you came back inside the house?" Jake asked, trying to keep the urgency out of his voice. I had to admire his control.

"One of em was. And one of em wasn't."

"Where was the other one?" asked Munger, hoisting that smile again.

"The tall one"—Rimers—"he was near to the study door."

"How close?" Munger pressed.

"Any closer he'd a been in there."

"Did you tell them they could go into the study?"

"I said, make yourselves at home, like I say to everybody. If I'd a known—"

"Did you tell them they could go into the study?" Munger pressed.

"I ain't crazy. That's Mr. Jake's study," she said incredulously, as if Munger lacked all good sense. But I could see Munger preparing to ask her yet again.

"Just tell him 'yes' or 'no' and he'll be happy," I interposed.

"No," she said to me firmly. "I never told them that. I wouldn't never tell nobody that."

After Eunice left, Munger looked at Jake, his head slightly cocked in his version of Jake's stone-stare. "Once again, Jake, is there anything I need to know about the ring?"

"You know as much about that damn ring as I do." And Jake gave him his stare, the original article.

In the kitchen, I sat Eunice down and got her a glass of orange juice—her blood sugar was plummeting.

"Like I said, baby, your daddy ain't never been nothin' but nice to me," she said, then added, "That other'n is a different kettle of worms."

My oldest memory of Munger was the precise slap to my face that he delivered when I was nine and, rampaging around the firm like it was a playground, broke a piece of his Chinese porcelain. I never told Jake, knowing I wouldn't be believed, just tried to avoid my father's partner, a pattern that continued into my adulthood.

We were both crime scene witnesses, so we had to secure permission from Sessums to represent Jake. As we drove to Sessums' office downtown, Munger was mute, and ours was not the comfortable silence of friends. His opposition to my joining the firm had probably forced Jake to outright overrule him. Sad to say, my performance to date had proven Munger, not Jake, right.

Halfway there, as we made the turn onto Lee Circle, where the fifty-foot statue of Robert E. Lee had once stared down from antiquity, Munger started talking. "It's fine to share what you're thinking, Kyle. When Turnage and Ginger were associates, they always did. I wonder why you never have."

"Jake's my father, you know," I said, inanely. "So I just talk to him." Which he knew was a lie.

"That's natural, I suppose," he said, making it sound perverse, "though Jake sometimes has a habit of putting his big boot into things. As you must know better than I."

I felt as if a tentacle were sliding across my back and around my shoulder.

"If you have ideas on the conduct of his trial, let me know." He looked at me full on. "I'm not closed to another perspective."

"Ask Sessums what he's doing with Jake's ring."

"I believe we can wait until the witness list arrives."

"Why wait?"

"Because it indicates fear. Every question you ask gives something of yourself away." With that we relapsed into a clammy silence for the rest of the journey.

Sessums went through the pleasantries, the offer of tap water, the clearing of seats for Munger and me. I noticed a new watercolor by his wife, of a cow or possibly a sheep, disproportionately large, between two miniscule haystacks. On the floor of his office, neatly arranged like live mines, were thick files, competent files, many labeled "Wittenhurst." Spread across his desk was "Cameron." If Sessums granted his permission, I'd be facing him in both trials, a statistical improbability, given New Orleans' sixty prosecutors. It had to have cost him more than a few political nickels for the chance to go after Jake.

Sessums nodded respectfully while Munger argued there'd be no need for us to testify, since Ginger and Turnage had witnessed exactly what we'd seen. At the end there was the slightest consternation on Sessums' face.

"I do understand your point. Well argued, by the way, Mr. Munger. I'm just a bit concerned about losing the opportunity to question Kyle. I have some interest in his view of the crime scene, though I'm sure it would exactly parallel what the others saw. For instance, his perception of the demeanor of the defendant."

He favored me, not with Jake's turn-to-stone gaze, but with a steady stare, just a reasonable guy making a reasonable request that I tell him right there that Jake had behaved like nothing so much as a guilty man. I looked back at him, taking a sip of reclaimed New Orleans sewage water.

Munger started to speak, but Sessums held up his hand as if overcome by sudden largesse. "Of course, as you noted, the other witnesses could testify to that as well."

Sessums looked over at me with his same steady look, only now with a smile.

"Kyle," he said, "the last thing, the very last thing I want to do is impede you from working on your dad's case, no matter what your function." He was thrilled, in other words, to have me fucking things up in even a minor capacity.

"You're very gracious," Munger said in his tight, formal way.

Sessums nodded his head to me in mock bow. "Noblesse oblige. Oh, wait. I'm wearing the wrong hat for that, Kyle, am I not?"

"Night school," I said, looking at him. "Leaves gaps."

I saw the slightest tightening of Sessums' mouth, major emoting for him, so I seized the moment, Munger be damned.

"Care to share your plans for my father's ring?" I had to know. Because the trail of blame for Jake's arrest led to me like slime to a snail.

There was an edge in Sessums' voice, so he probably said more than he normally would've. "If I were a praying man—which I am—I'd regard that ring as a gift from heaven."

Munger waited until we were entombed in the Lincoln before saying, "Never contravene me again," and such was the frost in his voice that he didn't need to elaborate. After that, the ride back was wordless, I turning over and over Sessums' last remark, Munger for all I knew deciding between a shrimp or oyster po'boy for lunch.

Oyster, as it turned out. He ate it fastidiously with a knife and fork, folded the wrap into a neat quadrant and creased the bag shut, all the while studying my father.

"We will be the subject of unrelenting scrutiny," Munger said finally. "Two cable tabloids are doing features next week."

No surprise. Already, media or tourists (there was no distinguishing them) slowed like drive-by shooters to photograph the firm. The case had enough hooks to draw in every demographic over twelve: prominent older man seducing beautiful young mistress, Irish Channel husband betraying Garden District wife, top criminal attorney fighting own murder charge, and wastrel son defending adulterous father. In the short week since the arrest the *Times-Picayune* had run the Garden District wife angle on the front page , the *National Enquirer* exhibited a skin-shot taken by the teenage perverts, while *The New York Times* bloviated about decadence in the South.

"If there are any undisclosed elements to this case, this is the moment to inform me." Munger's gray eyes, bisected by his half glasses, focused on Jake as through a microscope, and it was Jake who looked away.

Munger's head pivoted back to me, his eyebrows raised questioningly. I shook my head, holding his stare as long as I could.

"As hoped," he concluded, exiting.

I looked at Jake. "Should he know?"

"About what?"

"Me."

"I know. That's enough," he said, leaving no question as to who sat first chair in State v. Cameron.

Over the years, a recurrent theme in Jake's dinner table rants was clients who lied to their lawyers. Perhaps he now appreciated the value of selective mendacity. I did.

My disclosure to Ginger about April Cahill had been somewhat incomplete. Initially, I couldn't tell her about the sex because I didn't want Laura to know. Later, I assumed Jake had told her about it. Then, when Ginger didn't say anything, I didn't either. Lying in my sworn answer to the complaint constituted one of those "new legal infractions" Ginger had warned me against. Actually, I was following her advice by not telling her about the sex. In any case, I'd been avoiding her.

One morning she was waiting for me in my office.

"I thought you'd cleaned up this dunghole," she greeted me.

I had, for Laura. No more Laura. "Office is the mirror of the soul," I tossed off.

"Call a priest," she snapped. "Why haven't you returned my calls?"

She motioned me to the overstuffed sofa, standard firm office decor to unsettle clients. I sank into its depths and found myself looking up at her defensively.

"I've been working on your little bar problem," she said. "And your lawyer has one basic question. Do you know what that is?"

"Why do bad things happen to good people?"

"Why the hell is April Cahill claiming you had sex with her if you didn't?" Her eyes had that cynical, knowing look that can only be observed on the faces of certain women, those who are almost—almost—old and smart enough never to be fooled by another man.

I made a quick calculation about the costs and benefits of the truth. The ratio remained as before. "You'd have to ask her."

"I asked Jake. He said ask you." So he'd honored my confidence.

"If I told you I had and you didn't report me, you could lose your license," I temporized.

"You will lose yours, you little snatch hog," she exploded. "Before or during Jake's trial. How's that going to look to his jury?"

I twisted on the sofa to try to get a higher perch, failed, sank back again.

"We had sex," I mumbled.

She stared at me. If she quit the case, the fool would have to represent himself.

"Why the hell didn't you tell me?"

"It looked bad," I said. That really had been one of the reasons.

She laughed at that. "How many times?"

"Twice." Somehow she'd proven an exception to my one-time rule, which had been my pass at fidelity to Alison. Maybe I hadn't been engaged. In any case, an exception.

"I figured once. Gave you credit for better taste than you deserve."

"You knew?"

"I knew you." Just as Evan had once said. She got up and started out.

"Are you still my lawyer?"

"Contingent."

"On what?"

"On how I feel any given day."

She didn't bother to close the door as she clacked out on her bright red heels with toes pointy enough to pierce soft tissue. Anyone looking in would've seen me gracelessly struggle up from the sofa, a thousand times a liar, one more time caught and counting.

Jake often said that the ability to compartmentalize is essential for a lawyer. I also read that adulterous lovers and killers, the ones who do it in cold blood, share this ability. As jury selection began in Roger's trial, I was able to place my case, as well as Jake's, in tightly secured, individual boxes at the back of my brain. Laura was a more difficult capture.

It was mid-October, and Roger's tan had faded enough that it wasn't a flagrant announcement of his privilege. His father was absent from the courtroom, though again paying the bills after the *Times-Picayune* discovered I was representing a billionaire's son pro bono. Their relationship had deteriorated to the point that Roger had been banished to the guesthouse, a move he embraced.

By contrast, I'd found myself missing Jake's company. We'd worked surprisingly well together, or so I liked to think, until his arrest forced him to step down . Whatever our disagreements, I knew I could trust him. Whereas with Turnage, who became second chair, I never knew. I glanced over at him, fleshily flanking me at the defense table; he seemed as pink, robust and carefree as a farm-fed shoat. He was experimenting with a new cologne or colognes.

We had spent the day before with our jury consultant—as promised, the most expensive in the country—financed out of Joshua's pocket change. Barbara Kaplan was a tightly focused, sleekly tailored New Yorker with degrees in law, psychology, and statistics and a fierce energy that made me feel in perpetual southern slow motion. She'd known who we'd need on the jury long before the moment we picked her up at the airport.

"Black women," she prescribed as she stepped briskly down the concourse, refusing my offer to carry her bag and Turnage's proffer of a praline. "They won't like Roger but they'll despise Mamie. Little white girl had her fun and wants someone else to pay the bill."

"What about black men?"

She shook her head. "Inner city, maybe. Middle class, absolutely not. Law and order, straight down the line."

We walked outside. October, and it felt like August. Turnage's past-the-season seersucker hung on him like a limp tarpaulin. Nobody out and about except the desperate and their soothsayers.

"Look for attractive, educated white women who would've had some loose behavior in college," Barbara mandated. "They'll project their own self-blame onto Mamie. Jesus, how do you live in this heat?"

"You can't fight it. You just have to go with it," I advised, quoting Laura, my muse.

Barbara stepped into the street and stared down a shuttle driver who honked at her. "No—repeat, no—rednecks of either sex. The men will have fantasies about Mamie, and the women will think they know men for what they are: shitheels." She gave Turnage and me an encompassing look.

In the firm conference room, we listened as Kaplan analyzed the jury questionnaires with machine-like precision. At $30,000 a day she was an expensive machine.

"Dreck," she said in conclusion, almost accusatory, as if I'd had something to do with the panel's makeup. I drove her back to the airport, a long silent ride. As she got out, I hoped for an encouraging word, but all she could manage was, "I'm sorry."

In the courtroom I studied Mamie, seated across with her parents. She looked a good bit healthier than Roger, than me, for that matter. I didn't know whose family had more money, Roger's or Mamie's, but Mamie acted wealthier: supercilious, highly-strung and melodramatic. In favorable contrast was

Roger's new, humbled demeanor, accentuated by the firm's gray polyester tie.

He'd need more than humility to save him from five years' minimum, if he even stayed alive that long. Roger was simple, shallow, with a simple, shallow story about drunken, joyless copulation. Mamie had maybe thirty I.Q. points on him, her mind and motives infinitely more complex.

At the prosecutor's table, Sessums sat alone, disdaining assistance, radiating competence. Earlier, as we'd entered the courtroom, he'd commented on my "splendid" custom-made shoes, disparaging his own thick-soled wingtips as "farmer shoes."

"All rise," the bailiff commanded, and Judge Harmon Lyles entered.

"Fucked," noted Turnage, not for the first time. And we were. Judge Lyles, a squat, crablike man with suspicious eyes, was a barely functioning alcoholic who'd stayed on the bench through family connections and mulish tenacity. If his grasp of the facts of a case were tenuous, or if he were going through a wet spell, he compensated by siding unfailingly with the prosecution, blindly banking on the mathematical probability that most defendants were guilty.

I watched the fifty members of the jury panel file in, an anonymous mass I knew only from reading the runes of their questionnaires and Barbara Kaplan's determination that they were, for Roger, "as bad as they come."

And the first twelve were among the worst. I had six peremptories that allowed me to exclude any potential juror—and I might end up using most of them on this batch, leaving me vulnerable to more fatal prospects later.

One challenge went to an ex-cop, who was replaced in the jury box by a young hotel manicurist, certain to know privileged men at their worst. A young black man I'd hoped would be from the underclass was instead the son of a Tulane physics professor.

I had to settle for an angry-looking mechanic and a tired-looking but still pretty cocktail waitress. By the time they came along in the jury draw, I'd used up most of my peremptories on even more problematical candidates, such as a highly empathic poetess/activist.

"What do you think?" Roger asked, as if my opinion would've altered in the five minutes since he last asked.

"Only way out is through." It was what I'd heard Jake tell the hopeless ones.

"Get on with it, Cameron," Judge Lyles barked as I pondered a middle-aged woman who, though her niece had been raped, insisted she could be impartial.

"I'll excuse Mrs. Jeffries," and I was down to one challenge, and then, as Mrs. Jeffries was replaced by a newly divorced young tattoo artist, zero. I watched Sessums cherry-pick the rest of the jury while I watched, impotent.

Outside, after we adjourned, I tried to offer some encouragement to Roger that even he, ravenous for hope, didn't believe.

I watched his slight figure enter his father's limousine. Then unexpectedly he turned back to me. "How's your father's case going?"

I was surprised to see him evince or at least feign interest in someone else's troubles, particularly given the magnitude of his own.

I shook my head. I didn't have it in me to lie about the prospects of another doomed case.

"I know he didn't do it," he said with what seemed like certainty. I looked at him sharply but saw nothing accusatory, just an awkward attempt to show solidarity.

"So do I," I replied without expression and watched his limousine drive away.

Turnage and I spent the rest of the day and night cramped together in the small attic study, pre-empted from the main conference room by Jake and Munger.

"What do you think?" I asked Turnage, who was cleaning his fingernails with a secreted lunchtime toothpick.

"About what?" he asked, his shrewd little eyes on me.

"The jury." I hated to be asking Turnage's opinion but he had forty trials to my five. I still hoped my estimation of Roger's chances was too low.

He looked at me and farted to express his opinion. He could do it at will. "I think this firm's on a losing streak," he added.

Shortly after 1:00 a.m., Turnage stood. "I'm ready," he pronounced himself.

"I'm not," I said, though I was ready for his absence. We'd been together in ninety square feet for ten hours.

"Happy dreams," I said, but he just stood there.

"So you're sure Jake didn't do it." It was one of those questions that isn't supposed to be asked, but something in his tone made me look up.

"You think he did?"

"I think that stuff was too fine to waste." There was an odd note in his voice, and it was good for both of us that he did leave then.

I moved down to my own office. Time oozed past 2:00 and 3:00. In Joshua Wittenhurst's guesthouse in Audubon Park, Roger was, I knew, no less sleepless than I. His life, like the others I'd failed, was in my hands.

I looked through the wilderness of papers and notes on my desk, trying to find Turnage's revision of my opening argument. I had no idea how to excavate it from the cyber-cavern of Myrt's word-processing program.

Using the passkey—I'd long since made my own—I opened Turnage's door and was hit with the rank odor of fast food and dirty laundry. On his desk, balanced atop a heap of documents, rested a grease-stained paper plate holding a mound of sucked-clean chicken bones. I placed the plate on top of the overflowing trash basket and rummaged through his papers. Using the key he'd left in the lock, I opened his drawer. There was his printout of my argument, crumpled but clean, edited in his uneven, blocky scrawl.

Beneath my argument was a packet of pornography, the kind vendors dangle for tourists in the Quarter. A quick look verified its cheapness. Typical Turnage, earning $250,000 a year and unable to procure decent porn.

As I was closing the drawer, I saw another, larger envelope, this one white and unsmudged and therefore suspicious. Intrigued despite myself, I undid the clasp. Inside were photographs of Laura, naked.

Had she been fucking him too? Gap-toothed, moon-faced, hee-hawing Turnage?

Then I realized they were copies of the crime scene photos, but with every mark of death expertly, painstakingly, and expensively digitized away. I'd underestimated Turnage. More than underestimated him. Like me, perhaps even more than me, he knew how conjoined hatred and desire could be. Quickly, before I could change my mind, I shredded the pictures, allowing myself one last look at each.

I stayed at Laura's grave until dawn, not the first time I'd spent an entire night lying above her on her tomb. Stretched out below me in her cream-colored silk and matching shoes, she was, for once, unable to waken before daylight and slip away.

The next day Judge Lyles was forty minutes late and looked as if a raging hangover had gripped his head in its teeth and tossed him against the wall. Roger looked even paler than the day before, and he seemed to have shrunk a suit size. The ranks of reporters had multiplied, like flies on a dying carcass. Whether it was my mood or my reality, the jury in its now-official position seemed even more hostile.

In his opening argument Sessums met each juror's eye, seemingly at random but—I knew from voir dire—at the point that each juror would find most telling. "He went after her when she couldn't defend herself." Sessums's gaze swept the hotel manicurist, accosted daily by her wriggly-fingered clientele; then the housewife with three daughters in their teens; and on to the cocktail waitress, whose fanny was patted nightly like a pet dog. "Equal application of the law" went to the black professor's son, whose car was regularly pulled over for drug searches. The angry mechanic got "back-seat of a college boy's Rolls-Royce."

I was caught between wanting to object and applaud. The pauses, the pacing, and most of all the never failing reasonableness that made you think he was playing fair—it was a masterful performance, one that supported the maxim that juries make up their minds in opening argument.

Compared with Sessums, I was merely adequate, though the sessions practicing with Jake had at least raised me to that level. I walked up and down the length of the jury box, feeling naked without my notes but determined to maintain eye contact as I laid out our case.

"I am sure that Mamie Lawrence did not set out to bring us where we are today," I said, looking at the mechanic. No welcome lamps burning there. Suddenly the words flew out of my head like bats at sunset, and for an eternal five seconds I fought down panic until my mind caught the beginning of the next sentence.

"I am sure if she could rewind the events of that evening and the consequences of her accusation, rewind them into nonexistence, she would. But no one can." I went on, carefully setting out our case, knowing the risk of further alienating a jury already predisposed against us. No matter how I put it, it came down to blaming the victim. By the time I concluded, the manicurist had quit listening and, as for the rest, I might've been better off if they had too.

"Bad?" I scribbled on the notepad to Turnage. He turned the paper upside down and changed the question mark to a noose.

After each prosecution witness, Turnage drew another little noose. As for Mamie, she was magnificent. Watching her, seeing her eyes change at the moment her story veered from Roger's, I was again struck by the certainty that she was lying. But not the jury. By the time Sessums had finished with Mamie's account of the evening, I could see tears in most of the jurors' eyes, including the men's. What had begun, before voir dire, as a 55-45 shot was now looking 99-1.

Judge Lyle ordered a ten-minute break for Mamie to compose herself and for him to absorb a couple of Delta Airline gin miniatures. When we reconvened, I would cross-examine Mamie.

"With this jury," Turnage observed helpfully, "Sessums could whip it out and piss on them, and they'd think it was Mountain Dew." Roger heard it but didn't even bother to seek reassurance from me. Too far gone.

"Shut up, Turnage." I couldn't stand seeing Roger's defeated shoulders; the jury was seeing them too.

I watched Mamie resume the stand. Turnage was right. It really didn't matter what I did with Mamie on cross, or how Roger performed on the stand if we put him on. The case had been decided, not in opening arguments, but way before, when Sessums drew his dream jury.

The only way to save Roger was to get rid of the jury. There was only one way to do that. I would be violating the Bar's ethical code and I knew the violation was serious and would exacerbate my existing difficulties. The only person I knew who'd been disbarred was Franklin Temerry, a bloated old drunk who still wore a coat and tie, though it was the same one every day, and hung out around the courthouse like a ghost trying to get back home.

I found myself studying Mamie, wondering how she hoped the trial would go. Guilty, and her reputation would be intact but she'd know she had destroyed a life. Innocent, and she'd look a fool or worse. I felt a sudden jolt of sympathy for her; she was riding the train she'd engineered and now couldn't stop, life having no emergency brake.

I looked at Roger, his hands folded, head bent as if for the axe. A fuckup, born and raised. Still, I felt somehow protective of him, maybe the way Jake had once felt about me. Every time I saw Roger, I wanted to shake him into shape. The closest I could describe my feelings for him was somewhere between an unwanted little brother and an unadoptable foundling cat. He wasn't the brother I would've picked, but he'd picked me.

"Mr. Cameron," Judge Lyle rumbled. "Do you wish to cross examine or not?"

Mamie watched me approach. It seemed strange that anyone could be afraid of me when I thought of myself as harmless. Of course, others too had made that assumption.

"I don't have many questions," I began, and I didn't. "The week before the party, what was the status of your relationship with Britt Cowley?"

"There was no status."

"You had broken up?"

"Yes."

"Otherwise you wouldn't have accepted Roger's invitation."

"Obviously."

"Yet you and Britt continued talking to each other on the phone."

"As friends."

"Had you reconciled?"

"No, we had not."

"Had you almost reconciled?" Too many people knew the truth for her to lie.

"'Almost' doesn't count."

"May I take that as a 'yes'?"

"If you like."

None of which made a bit of difference to me. I was simply building the gallows. Now the only mercy I could show was to do it quick.

"You'd dated Britt since you started college?"

"Off and on."

"Not in boarding school?"

She looked the slightest bit uneasy.

"No."

"Correct. Because in boarding school you had an affair–"

"Objection!" Sessums shouted.

"Sustained!" Judge Lyles roared back. Mamie's train had left the station and we were all hurtling a hundred miles an hour off the cliff. I plunged on without pause.

"—with your biology teacher who was married—"

"Objection!" Sessums came thundering toward me. Judge Lyles was gaveling hard, and I had to raise my voice to get it in so the jury could hear.

"—and you subsequently had an abortion." It was done. I knew, as did every lawyer, that prior sexual history was absolutely inadmissible in a rape trial. I also knew that seven of the jurors were devout Catholics.

"No!" Mamie exclaimed, not a denial but a cry.

The courtroom had erupted in outrage. I could see Turnage looking at me, his mouth literally gaping open. Judge Lyles stood up, leaned furiously down at me. If he could've reached me with the gavel, he'd have bashed out my brains.

"Did you not hear me gavel you down, you little bastard?" He didn't bother keeping the jury from hearing. It was beyond that now.

Sessums stared at me, fury seeping out from underneath all that bland civility. He knew what he had to do. "Your honor," he said, his voice at the back of his throat," I am forced to move for a mistrial. The jury has been irrevocably tainted."

No jury instruction from the bench could eradicate the damage. "State's motion for mistrial granted," Judge Lyles spat out, looking down at me, his eyes red with gin and rage. "I'm reporting you to the Bar," he vowed.

Such gratitude was in Roger's eyes that I had to look away. He knew I'd gone over the edge, buying him a reprieve at the probable expense of my legal career.

"Thank you," he stammered, all he could manage before sitting and crying in relief. This once, at least, my plan had worked as intended.

We hacked our way through the thick tangle of reporters at the courtroom door. Charlie Dumaine, the most persistent, thrust her microphone in my face. "Exactly how low will you go?"

I let my silence be my answer.

Turnage looked at me warily, like he would at a harmless puppy who'd suddenly ripped his master's throat out. The ride back to the firm was eerily quiet.

When we walked in, everyone fell silent like I'd ridden in on Death's horse. My popularity rating, never high, was now subterranean. Turnage separated himself from me. All the secretaries became very busy.

"Shithead," Ginger said concisely as I passed her in the hall. Munger stared directly at me, assessing; usually when I looked at him, his eyes slid away like egg yolks.

I saw Jake pause at the other end of the hall. He looked at me, then nodded his head. For what I'd done there could be no congratulations, just the acknowledgment that when the necessary had to be done, I could damn sure do it.

That wasn't quite the way Charlie Dumaine phrased it that night on the 10:00 news, no doubt taped for every member of the Bar Disciplinary Board. I didn't need to ask Ginger, who in any case now wasn't speaking to me, whether this qualified as a new legal infraction. I forced Mamie out of my mind, cramming her away in a locked compartment along with all the rest I'd done. It was getting pretty full back there.

I'd long since given up trying to call Alison. All I got was voice-mail at work or answerphone at home, and I didn't want to receive another pained message from my mother relaying Mrs. Ford's request that I stop calling. I gathered that Alison was daily bolstering my mother. I'd forfeited her bolstering.

Self-pity is not an attractive feature, but I found myself slipping into those soft waters. With Roger's trial euthanized and no date set for its resurrection, I had no piles of documents on the floor signifying work. As for Jake's case, my only document was Munger's lunch order for the next day. I could now see that the reason people worked constantly was not for money but for the narcotic of distraction.

The firm was deserted. Jake was having Munger over for dinner and a strategy session. I wasn't invited. Ginger had bustled off to the gym, and Turnage, if he could be believed, had a date. Laura was dead.

The fact that I didn't deserve Alison—never had— didn't diminish how much I needed her now. The fact that Evan, who was more or less living at Alison's, did deserve her was of even less comfort.

I forced myself to get up from my desk, pulling away from the inertia that could've left me paralyzed there all night. I formed a plan. I wouldn't call Alison. I'd go see her. She'd just now be getting in from work, and Evan would just be starting. I only wanted to talk.

In my car, energized with sudden purpose, I evaded the Saint Charles traffic and arrived at her house in less than fifteen minutes. I caught a glimpse of myself in the rear mirror and saw there, for the first time since Laura's death, life in my eyes.

I bounded up the steps, knocked my familiar knock, waited. I could hear movement inside. It was then that I saw Evan's bicycle on the porch—he had a damn car but insisted on biking everywhere to absorb local color and be bohemian—and Alison opened the door.

"Bad time," I said through the unopened screen door.

"Any time's a bad time," Alison replied. She was wearing an old terrycloth robe, Evan's. I prolonged the conversation, despite Evan's lean, arty presence somewhere in the house.

"I thought you'd be just coming home from work," I said idiotically.

"I took the day off. So did Evan."

Evan appeared behind her, his hands resting comfortably on her terry clothed shoulders. He'd thrown on jeans and nothing else.

"Gang's all here." That was all he said.

"Could I come in for a second?" That was what I really wanted, just to be with friends. Former friends would do.

"That's not a good idea," Alison said, her icecap eyes not changing expression.

"I just want to talk. Okay?"

I watched her look up at Evan for his opinion. His eyebrows gave a little shrug. Alison unhooked the screen door and warily, as you would a half-wild dog, let me in.

Damn, he had moved in. Alison, supposedly so independent, had allowed him to hang his—I'm speaking objectively here—crappy abstract paintings over the mantle, supplanting the 1924 Expressionistic poster she supposedly had loved so much. The Grim Reaper, my portrait, was also absent, perhaps being used by Evan for canvas.

Evan padded in his bare feet to the sofa, stretched his long legs out familiarly on it. I saw he'd moved over his antique bookcase of leather-bound first editions; he might disdain money but not what it could buy.

"Would you like something to drink?" Alison offered, unable to be uncourteous though she'd very easily managed moments before to be hard as blue steel.

"A bourbon would be nice, thanks." I kept a bottle of Makers Mark in her kitchen cabinet.

"I threw it out. There's some wine Evan brought home." She smiled at Evan. "It's great. Latour '70, almost a half bottle."

"Latour '70 is fine."

Alison hesitated, debating the wisdom of leaving us alone, then disappeared into the kitchen. I took a seat in my old easy chair. My territory. I looked across the room at Evan, who stared back with the expression he always wore, the one that said, Aren't we, every last one of us, ridiculous?

"You seem to have moved in," I noted.

"You moved out."

"You know why."

"Don't I though."

"I told you that in confidence."

"Where it remains." He placed his finger to his lips in mock conspiracy.

"You didn't tell Alison?"

"Unlike you, I actively try to avoid hurting her."

I could feel the same helpless rage that had inhabited me so many times with Laura. Incongruously, I also wanted to cry. "Things are screwed up, aren't they?"

"Who screwed them up?"

Alison should've returned by now with the wine but, perfect girlfriend that she was—to Evan—she was allowing us time to resolve our manly differences.

"This was intended to be a friendly visit."

"No, it wasn't. Guess what, Kyle? You don't get the girl this time."

"All the women in New Orleans, you had to go after mine?"

His transcendent cynicism dropped for a moment. "That was the one I wanted. The only one." Back up went the mask. "Isn't that your approach, Trojan? Dickfirst into the breach?"

I wasn't getting angrier as I might've expected, just more and more tired, like I'd never be anything but tired again. Practicing for being dead. I didn't have any position, any argument.

"I guess I would've appreciated it if you'd said something."

"Like you did me?"

"What do you mean?"

"I was with Alison first, if memory serves."

"You'd just had a few dates."

Evan just shook his head. "What's the secret, Kyle?" he asked. I recalled having this conversation a lifetime ago with Turnage.

"Not caring," I said automatically. It was a knack I'd lost the first night with Laura and would never regain.

I got up. "You two finish the Latour. Half bottle's not enough for three."

As I walked out, I glanced into the kitchen. Alison was looking at me but she turned away.

I stopped off at the neighborhood all-night grocery, where I used to go at 2:00 or 3:00 in the morning for a pint of Ben & Jerry's to cap a night of excess. It was only 8:00 but I was ready for bed. After Laura died, I didn't sleep at all. Lately, I'd been pushing fourteen hours a night. I selected a bar of soap—I'd been showering with shaving cream for two days, not having had the energy to shop. As I was debating the wisdom of a Slim Jim Salami Stick for supper, I heard a voice behind me, soft and female.

"Hey, Mr. Cameron."

Turning, I saw a striking girl, trim, tan, her hair a blonde flag down her bare back.

"Remember me?"

I tried to match the face with a memory but my card file was too full. God knew who she was or what we'd done.

"Commander's Palace?" she reminded me.

The hostess. So many other events had filled the night of my mother's birthday that I'd forgotten. I remembered her leading us up the stairs and saying her name loud enough for me to hear.

"Holly Lefoldt," I said.

"I'm impressed."

I found myself outside with her. The streets looked empty but the alleys and shadows never were.

"Which way you going?" she asked, her voice softly southern. I gestured toward my apartment.

"I'm this way," she said, pointing the opposite direction. She hesitated for a moment, then with a little wave started down the dark street. I noticed, almost dispassionately, that I was attracted to her. The first woman since Laura.

"I'll walk you there," I offered. She smiled and took my arm, an old-fashioned but surprisingly intimate gesture. We walked the short block, talking about nothing. I hadn't touched a woman in almost two months, hadn't wanted to. I could smell Holly's perfume, something light, sandalwood. Her hand resting lightly on my arm felt like I remembered a woman's hand feeling.

"This is it," she said as we stopped at a heavy colonial gate outfitted with a fearsome lock. She put her key in and looked at me, raising her eyebrows in a delicate question. I didn't owe any fidelity to Alison, that was for sure.

Inside the gate, I pressed her against the wall and we hungrily kissed, my hands exploring her taut body as we moved down the walkway. By the time we were inside her apartment, her dress was half off. She moved her hand up my thigh but I gently diverted her. I kissed her more fiercely, cupped her lovely ass with my hands and pressed her against me, trying to goad my instincts to life. Because I was dead down there, with all the feeling of a stick of wood but none of its consistency. Her hand, insistent, moved slowly back up my leg, and in a moment she would know.

I'd never felt the need or inclination to resort to fantasy. The woman I was with was always an overpowering experience--as heroin warms his veins, does the junkie pretend it's Demerol? But now I desperately conjured Laura, Laura's smiling lips, Laura's bare skin, Laura's expert hand. Holly, now inhabited by a dead woman, instantly came alive for me.

"Nice," she murmured as she slipped her hand inside my pants.

Throughout, every time I released the image of Laura, I felt myself go dead and had to resummon her. As I came, it was that first time, in the lake, with the waters immersing us in unholy baptism. Afterwards, as Holly and I lay in silence, I knew that for the rest of my life, whenever I was with a woman, I would be Laura's marionette.

When I got home, it was only 9:30. The homeless guy who lived on my block shuffled past as I closed my garage door. Since the morning I'd given him the contents of my wallet, he always looked at me with whatever hope he was still able to spark. But tonight I could swear what I saw in his eyes was sympathy or, even worse, pity.

Since I was asleep by 10:00, I didn't hear Charlie Dumaine break the news that Sessums was seeking the death penalty for my father.

When I joined Jake and Munger in the conference room, Jake looked at me in a way I'd never seen, as if he needed something. I didn't know what to give him, so I laid my hand on his shoulder, something I don't think I'd ever done. In Louisiana, capital punishment wasn't an abstraction— we ranked tenth in the nation in executions.

My father looked over at Munger, his long-time partner, and Munger looked back for a long moment. I saw sympathy in his eyes, something I'd thought him incapable of.

The morning turned into afternoon without more than a few words exchanged. Ginger and Turnage came in to offer encouraging words that sounded like condolences. I remembered the time Jake talked to my law school class about lethal injection. You look like you're very peaceful, but your organs are on fire.

"It'll never happen," I said vehemently. "It'll never come to that." Jake just nodded. Munger gestured for me to follow him into the hall.

"Maybe Sessums miscalculated," I said in wild hope. It had happened before in Jake's cases, a juror who wouldn't send a man to his death.

He shook his head. "I believe it's part of his strategy."

Ginger walked by, curious to overhear, and Munger simply quit speaking. When her footsteps had descended the stairway, he continued. "Sessums beyond question has turned up what our investigator has."

He'd found out about me and Laura. "Which is?"

"Our investigator tracked Laura from LSU to high school in Lafayette. He found no record she attended. Her Social

Security number was acquired with a counterfeit notary public seal and a forged birth certificate. Both exquisitely rendered."

An accomplishment for a seventeen-year-old. Laura Niles was born of herself. I'd never even known her name.

"If she got by the state bar and the U.S. government, there's no culpability on the firm's part for not uncovering her," he added. His desire to escape blame was legendary.

"What does this have to do with Sessums' strategy?"

He looked at me as he always did, like I was an idiot. "Because she has no history, Kyle, there are no other suspects." Our investigator hadn't found, or maybe even looked for, a link between Laura and me. He had assayed every degree of moral decline, but ours was apparently beyond his compass.

Munger lowered his voice, as if we were conspirators. "I believe it's Sessums' strategy to encourage us to seek a plea. And, under the circumstances, I believe we shouldn't dismiss the idea out of hand. It's possible he would consider manslaughter and fifteen years. Jake could be out in ten, in time to enjoy his retirement."

"Did Sessums make that offer? Did you tell Jake?"

"Not specifically, and Jake wouldn't discuss it. Perhaps he would with you, or more particularly, your mother."

"Hell, no," I argued. "We've got a shot. A good damn shot."

He looked at me, twenty-five years of experience to my not-yet three. "Consider that you might be deluding yourself."

I'd never known Munger to be wrong.

That night I set out to find Laura a history. I laser-copied her photo from her personnel file and drove across the river to the Demimonde. I pushed my way through the crowded bar, showing her picture to the night crawlers: a body-pierced model in see-through black, a socialite in lingerie, a coked-out jazzman, an aging gay billionaire. The only way to save my father was to find another suspect, preferably someone other than me. I didn't want to contemplate what I'd do if I no longer had the luxury of that preference.

"Ever seen this woman?" I questioned, receiving the same negative from them all, or at least those whose minds weren't yet dimmed by their drug du jour.

A lovely woman in a slit-skirt offered me her hand. "You're beautiful. Dance?"

Neutered by duty, and by Laura, I shook my head and moved on. Perry, the bartender, didn't recall the beautiful lady who loved absinthe. I ordered one in her memory.

"You like surprises, don't you, Kyle?" she'd said.

"No. I like to be in control."

"No you don't."

I downed my absinthe, this time enjoying the flush racing through me. As I stood to go, I saw a check pinned on the wall.

The dirty girl's. The one who knew Laura.

Sarah Loretta Lugar lived on the border of the French Quarter, Rampart Street, in a squat shabby shotgun house just five blocks and one world away from my apartment. I waited until full mid-day brightness for my visit; tourists who wandered into this area often lost their wallets or more.

She answered, dirtier than before in a robe with the underarm ripped out, and escorted me through the kitchen and bathroom to the bedroom suite, outfitted with two stained mattresses on the floor. The wan autumn sun tried to fight its way through cardboard-covered windows. Around us lay a six-months' accumulation of damp oily dirt and empty TV dinners, and the stench made me gag. An anorexic cat, all eyes, walked the windowsill, meowing hungrily. I predicted it wouldn't eat that day.

Sarah Loretta sat down on a sagging lawn chair, already occupied by her equally filthy boyfriend, whose name, I learned, was Wayne. As she took a joint from him, I sat on the edge of the stained sofa.

"I understand you knew Laura Niles," I began.

"We were like that," she said, holding two fingers far apart. She took a long drag. "Hit?"

"No, thanks."

"Scared you'll catch something nasty?"

Not scared. Certain.

"How did you know her?"

"From way back." The cat gave a plaintive violin-like wail. "Shut up, you fuckin' cat," she shrieked.

"Way back where? School?"

"Yeah. Same sorority."

Wayne, whose drugged eyes remained half-rolled back into his head, emitted a shadow of a laugh. Sarah Loretta rearranged herself on the chair, and her housecoat hiked midway up her thigh. She gave me a half-sardonic, half-appraising look, which I ignored as I explained the case to her.

She listened with mock-raptness. "I've got it all in my archives." She gestured to a mound of newspapers in the corner, a yellow-stained hostel for rats. Wayne pinched her leg and they both shrieked with laughter.

"Do you have any idea who might've done it?" I pressed.

"Sure. I got ideas."

"Would you care to share them?"

"Happy to." She leaned forward. "CIA."

"FBI," Wayne offered.

"UFO," she countered.

"PTA." She and Wayne again dissolved in laughter.

"Just think, please." But every question I asked—from Laura's first job to her real name—elicited similar gibberish. I restrained my strong desire to snatch her up by her white trash neck and shake till I heard a loud snap.

"Who were her other friends?" I persisted. I fervently hoped she'd never heard of me. I also suicidally wished Laura had cared enough to tell her.

"Women like Laura don't have friends." She looked at me. "Not women friends anyway."

My eyes jumped to hers. Did she know? She coolly stared back. Suddenly she didn't seem stoned at all.

Our investigator got even less from Sarah Loretta than I had. Despite Munger's counsel that we needed time to find another suspect, Jake was insisting on a speedy trial—within sixty days. Munger was constitutionally unable to do anything speedily, one of the increasing number of disagreements they had on strategy. Each argument ended the same way, with Jake casting the final, incontestable vote.

I agreed with Munger, for once, and, on the day of Jake's arraignment early in November, I tried again to convince Jake of the insanity of rushing the trial.

"I know we've gone over this before," I began cautiously. Though a fragile cease-fire held in our relationship, for unknown reasons he'd refused to speak to me all morning. "They've got more manpower, more resources. We'll never—"

"We?" he thundered, and I could see he was enraged. "Tommy's my lawyer, Kyle." He looked at me for the first time since I'd walked in. "You're here for show. Period. You won't be making a peep the whole goddam trial."

At the arraignment, I slumped in my chair, peepless. It was the first time I'd seen Sessums since Roger's mistrial. As he and I passed within inches of each other at the courtroom door, for once he didn't comment on my attire. Our relationship had altered. If before he'd felt contempt, now there was loathing.

Judge Evelyn Barber took her seat at the bench. In her late thirties, petite, good-looking enough to know men at their worst, she had a reputation for an unpredictable temper and rulings to match.

Jake stood and pled not guilty to first-degree murder. Munger stood. "Your honor, my client demands his right to a speedy trial."

"Are you certain?" Judge Barber looked irritated, a characteristic emotion, as I was to learn.

"I have warned him of the risks involved," Munger replied sourly, obviously displeased. Munger had been known to drag out a murder trial for two years, winning through attrition, whereas this was typical Jake—try them fast, try them hard, listen to no one's opinion, move on.

"Sixty days it is," she announced and, making allowance for the Christmas holidays, set a date for the middle of January.

Jake conferred with Munger, no doubt giving him his marching orders for the day. Still stung over Jake's sharp words that morning, I childishly stalked out unnoticed.

Except I wasn't unnoticed.

"Not so fast, boy," Jake barked. "I'll ride back with you."

Jake as passenger was not a role that suited him. "Damn, this Jeep rides rough," he complained.

We darted into the midday traffic. An oppressive, overcast day and not just the weather.

"Construction up ahead," he pointed out.

"I see it."

Suddenly he grabbed the wheel and jerked the car left.

"What the hell are you doing?" I demanded. When he'd taught me to drive, it was with his foot on my foot.

"Why aren't your eyes on the road?" he growled.

"They are on the road."

"What happened to that turn signal?"

"I did signal."

"What happened to my Krewe of Rex photo?" he asked. Perfect rhythm, 1-2-3. Not a question I wanted to hear, though it provided the unwelcome answer as to why he'd been treating with barely suppressed fury all morning. It wasn't going to be suppressed much longer.

"The one on your wall?" It was all I could do to keep the car on the road.

"Only one I know about."

"Did you ask Mom?"

"Your mother hasn't changed the decor in five years, as you well know."

"Why do I feel like I'm being cross-examined?"

"Because you are." From his faithful briefcase he brought forth a large official-looking envelope.

"The District Attorney's office returned this to Tommy early today. The police found it in Laura's closet. Sessums won't be needing it, since he has far more direct evidence."

He withdrew a framed photograph, one familiar to me since childhood.

"How did my Krewe of Rex photo get from my wall to Laura's closet?"

My merino wool suit suddenly felt like raw horsehair. "How?" I temporized.

"That is the mystery, Son."

It had been in late August, the bludgeoning dog days of summer. She'd been in trial all week, winning of course. Too busy for me, though not for Jake. Friday I waited in my office in case she called. Every five minutes I promised myself I'd leave in five minutes. Finally at 7:20, I did, not to preserve the remnants of my dignity but because I thought the odds might've shifted to her calling my house.

The firm was dark. Though I knew she—and everyone else—was gone, I couldn't stop myself from going by her office. When I turned the corner, a pool of light blazed through her door, which I'd never before seen open. My first thought was that it was a sadistic hoax; after never returning my calls, she'd left her lights on to raise my hopes until I looked inside and saw her empty chair.

Except she was sitting in it.

"You know what I'd love? A stiff drink and all the trimmings." she said with a smile that seemed utterly guileless. I stood in her doorway, pinned like a butterfly by the mere sight of her. I half-expected that I'd blink and she'd be gone.

"I'm your man," I managed to say.

"Are you?" she asked, suddenly serious, as if my feelings and not hers were in doubt. I felt the power shift for a moment, and everything I knew screamed to keep her wondering.

"Yes," I said, because if I didn't she might not want the trimmings any more or even the drink.

She came around from behind her desk and kissed me, molding herself against me.

"Let's go," she said, her face very close.

"My place," I said, our usual.

She shook her head. "Something different."

I suddenly knew where she wanted to go, just as surely as I wanted to take her there. If character were fate, as Evan said, I was going down fast.

How many times had I driven up that driveway? Or been driven by my mother when I was a child, past the banana trees, between the ancient azaleas, up to the columned porch. It had been risky in high school sneaking girls in while my parents slept down the hall. I'd been punished swiftly and fiercely the one time I'd misjudged Jake's arrival hour. This, of course, was on an entirely different plane.

Laura pulled up behind me. To anyone who saw our cars, bumper to bumper right out front, they looked like they were mating. But if Laura was willing to risk it, so was I. Jake and Mom had gone to the Prytania to see an art film that would transport my mother and stupefy my father. Depending on the length of the film, we had until at least 9:00.

Inside, she looked around, hungrily studying the mundane objects of my parents' life. She seemed to forget me as she prowled from room to room. I followed, a mere docent. Gumbo ran in and buried his nose in Laura's crotch, no doubt sensing his master's recent presence there. I grabbed his collar and hauled him to the back yard. He growled at me, the usurper.

"Drink?" I asked Laura when I returned, to remind her of my existence, but she didn't bother to answer as she studied my mother's cache of pills, one of many, in the kitchen.

"I'll damn sure have one," I announced, keeping up my end of the conversation, and reached for Jake's twenty-five-year-old Laphroaig scotch. It tasted like wet ashes but Jake treasured it. I mixed in plenty of water, ruining it according to Jake.

Laura opened the freezer and removed my mother's bottle of vodka. "May I?"

"No."

"How inhospitable."

Staring at me, she opened the bottle and took a leisurely drink, marking it with her lipstick.

"Damn you," I said, wresting the bottle from her. It was nearly full. One blow would be all it would take, at most two.

I wiped the lip and put the bottle away.

Laura was studying my mother's to-do list from two months earlier, still posted, still unaccomplished. "Ambitious."

"Let's go," I said, surprised at my backbone.

"So early?"

"This was a mistake."

"No, it wasn't. You know it wasn't." She smiled then, as if we shared something no one else could. "Don't I get to see the young prince's chamber?"

I escorted her upstairs. Laura's tour had taken longer than expected, and we now had only forty-five minutes left.

Laura dallied over the family photographs lining the upstairs hallway.

"I see where the looks came from," she said of the photo of Jake's father, dressed in a tie for my parents' wedding, probably the only time he'd ever worn one.

"And here's the family culture," she determined, studying my mother at her debut with her parents. I looked at the picture, trying to see it as Laura might, but all I could see was that my mother's eyes held a shadow of sadness even then. Standing behind her, I kissed Laura's neck to forestall another slur against my mother. We now had thirty-five minutes. Damn, did she want to get caught?

I turned the light on in my room. My Tulane pennant looked juvenile, I saw. On one high shelf, wearing two decades' dust, was a damned model airplane.

"Untouched since excavation," I joked. There was my adolescent single bed, site of ten thousand solitary ejaculations and some not.

I stepped inside but she didn't, just looked at me. A dare. I took her by the shoulders and pushed her against the hallway wall, kissing her deeply.

She responded immediately, her tongue alive in my mouth. Slowly I maneuvered her down the hall, Laura writhing against me, as we undressed each other. We were both naked by the time we crossed into Jake's bedroom.

In my entire life I'd been in that room perhaps twenty times, and almost all were by express invitation. Now it felt like I was invading an ancient pharaoh's tomb, incurring his curse. And it would easily be worth it.

We both stood naked in front of a gilt dressing mirror, watching our hands move over each other's bodies as if reading some frantic braille message.

"You like this," Laura whispered.

I didn't know how long we had left, and at that moment I didn't care. My thumbs lightly circled her nipples, then pinched them until she gasped.

"Don't you?" she insisted, running her fingers thrillingly down my stomach.

"Damn right I do." In one movement I ripped the covers back, pushed her to the cool pressed sheets and entered her. She thrashed wildly beneath me, wilder than I'd ever seen her. We twisted and rolled and violated every inch of that king-sized bed, finishing together with a cry with her perfect ass right on Jake's pillow.

I don't know how long we lay there. Finally my breath slowed and I opened my eyes. Jake's old-fashioned clock read 9:15 but I didn't move. I felt fear, yes—I still had some semblance of a normal organism's survival instinct—but the presence of Laura in that room on that bed was like a honeyed drug.

Still inside her, I felt myself growing hard again. 9:20. My brain noted the time, made the calculation that, unless the movie were one of those endless, incomprehensible Japanese epics, Jake and my mother were surely enroute home. My body, utterly in command, began moving slowly in and out of her.

"We have to go," Laura suddenly announced.

"We have time."

"Now," she said vehemently and with surprising strength twisted out from beneath me. All business now, efficient as a hotel maid, she moved about the bed, straightening the wrinkled sheets, turning over the wet-stained pillow. I watched, my dick still snapping its unanswered salute.

I dressed slowly, as if I'd forgotten how. By the time I came downstairs, she was pouring my untouched shot of Laphroiag into the sink and putting the glass exactly where it had come from.

"Let the dog in," she commanded, and I restored Gumbo, glaring at me with disapproval, to the house.

When I got out front, she was gone. That's when I noticed she'd stolen the photo--Jake when he was king of the Rex parade, standing on a float, looking like some barbaric warrior-lord with his finery—and replaced it with a similar-sized photo from my mother's closet. I heard Jake's Jag pulling into the driveway and was sitting at the breakfast room table, drinking a glass of milk and eating a piece of Eunice's incomparable chocolate cake, when they came in.

"Kyle," my mother said with surprise and delight, hugging me and, I hoped, not smelling Laura. "Just like when you were little."

"I couldn't resist," I said. "How was the movie?"

"Wonderful. It was a revival of *Ran. King Lear* in kimonos, sort of."

She laughed and I did too. I looked up at Jake. He hadn't said anything, just stood there studying me, knowing something was amiss but unable to puzzle it out.

"What time did you fall asleep?" I asked him.

He laughed suddenly, and I was reminded, once again, of why so many people liked, loved, him. "Twenty minutes in."

Mom shook her head, and we were all laughing together, as if the last two hours and the last twenty-seven years had never happened.

Now, chauffeuring Jake back from his arraignment, I didn't know whether to slow the car to avoid an accident or speed up to encourage one.

"Going there was her idea. She wanted to."

"And you couldn't tell her 'no'?"

"I could never tell her no."

He blew out a long breath. Careful to signal, I turned into the firm parking lot.

"Why didn't you tell me?"

"I was scared."

"What else haven't you told me?"

"Nothing. I've told you everything. I swear." For some reason I sounded like a criminal.

"They all say that," Jake said and walked alone into the firm. I remembered what Alison had said, about how you go too far and feelings change, and they never change back.

If before that November day I had little to do on his case, afterward I had nothing. I picked up Munger's laundry, knocked on doors for research projects, took my mother for her psychiatrist appointments.

Her depression seemed to have deepened beyond the reach of Prozac, and I had taken to stopping by every day. Usually she was alone—Jake was her life and she had few friends—but one day I saw Alison's Honda out front and felt an unaccountable joy. The second I walked in, she stood and placed her still-full coffee cup on the table. "Nola, I'll stop by some other time when you aren't busy,"

"That's okay," I said to her. "I'm not staying long. You don't have to go."

"I'd rather." She walked out, closing the door with finality.

"Far be it from me to tell you what to do," my mother said, "but love is rare, and you have to fight for it."

"She's gone. I pushed her too far."

"Yes, you did. You're very like your father." It was the first time I'd ever heard a word of criticism from her about Jake, or for that matter about me. She went back to her stitching.

"I know you always wanted us to be together," I said, wanting somehow to make it right, one of my many fatal flaws.

"What I want doesn't matter, Kyle. It just seemed so perfect. Too perfect to be true in this sad world."

"But what if I don't have an explanation for what I did?"

She looked up from her lacework. "You're a lawyer, aren't you?"

Without another word I tore after Alison as she strode across our front lawn to her parents' home next door. "Alison, wait!" She kept going. "Just listen to me. I know I hurt you. Will you just listen?" I grabbed her arm and she furiously wrenched it away from me. Her mother, next door gardening, stood up, concerned.

"You must think I'm the biggest fool in the world," Alison exploded.

"I know I just vanished from your life. I know I lied. But I have an explanation if you'll just hear me out."

"I've heard them. First it was work, then more work, then more lies." She shook her head quickly, as if those lies were persistent little insects. "I'm with Evan now. He makes me happy. He never lies."

"I know." And I knew too that happy wasn't enough for Alison. I felt a sudden pang for Evan, who would never have her, even if they lived together for fifty years.

"Just listen and I'll go. I found out about my father and Laura Niles. I hated him. Mom was slipping back down to hell. I didn't want to be close to anyone." It rolled out smooth, without hesitation.

She looked searchingly at me. "Why didn't you tell me? You always told me everything."

"I don't know," I said, a troubled look on my face. "I just couldn't talk about it. I was wrong. I have a talent for that."

She was guarded, as I worked my way through the five stages of making up—the same as for dying and everything else in life: anger, bargaining, denial, etc.—until I finally reached the pivotal lie I'd told her about having to meet with Joshua Wittenhurst.

"Then where were you, Kyle? With your woman in red?" Charlie Dumaine again, 720 degrees wrong.

We were back at anger, and I knew I didn't have time for any more buildup.

"I'm seeing a psychiatrist. That night was my first appointment." It had just come to me as we stood there.

"You would've told me that, Kyle."

"There's nothing wrong with me," I declared, a deliberate non sequitur. "I'm not crazy."

"You don't have to be crazy to see a psychiatrist, you know that."

"This is what I didn't want to tell you."

"Then don't," she said, and I probably didn't have to but I wanted to.

"I want to die." The part about the psychiatrist was fabrication. But the other wasn't. First, it was a fantasy of escape. But lately I'd been taking the gun out. To the temple or in the mouth? I'd researched it. Wouldn't want to botch it, a final fuckup. Inexplicably, I found myself crying, as if I really did need to see a shrink.

Mrs. Ford walked up, wary and protective, offering me her unsmiling profile. "Honey, you ready to go shopping?" She moved between us.

"I'm ready." Alison, my sole link to sanity, walked after her into their home without a glance back.

As the last daylight of the weekend became shadow, I carried a single red rose to Laura's tomb at Saint Alphonsus, replacing the wilted one I'd left the day before. Laura's tomb came chin-high on me, just as she had done. I traced the carved letters of "Laura Katherine Niles" with my fingers, as if inside her still.

In simpler times I'd been accustomed to stopping by Felix's Oyster Bar nearly every day. Not that I believed the myth about the connection between raw oysters and sexual prowess, but during my run with Laura I consumed sometimes three dozen a day. Since her death I'd lost my taste for them.

I pushed my way through the other carnivores to the steel-topped bar. Behind the counter, several shuckers, dressed in uniforms that had once been white, expertly split open oysters, their blades faultlessly finding the weak spot in the shell. All morning I'd been trying to divine why Ginger wanted to meet away from the firm.

"Saved you a spot," she called out, and I squeezed in beside her and automatically ordered a dozen.

She watched me shake a liberal dose of Tabasco directly onto my oysters. "You and your father," she commented.

"Puts hair on your chest," I said, offering her the bottle.

"That's his line," she said, but smiled. She seemed to have forgiven me for Mamie, and, after a beer and a dozen raw, we settled back into our old relationship. She chatted away about what an asshole Munger was and speculated on why it had taken his wife so many years to leave him. She offered her opinion, not complimentary, on Roger Wittenhurst and gave me a few ideas on strategy for Roger II. "Forget that New York advice and pack that jury with men, no matter what flavor. Esprit de testicle."

We were both halfway through our second dozen oysters and I still knew no more than when I'd walked in. I speared another oyster. As always, I'd stirred so much horseradish into my red sauce that each in-breath felt as if flames were being drawn into my sinuses. I doused the fire with Dixie draft, locally made and possibly the worst beer in the United States.

The Disciplinary Board, Ginger told me, was aware of my cross-examination of Mamie, and, in spite of Jake's confident predictions, she was concerned about my chances. The head judge was Leland Upshaw, a patriarch with a distinguished mane of gray hair and a penchant for young girls at his firm. "That," Ginger said, "will cut against you."

Worse, one of the other judges was Carrie Louise Howorth, the tireless, sugar-voiced sponsor of the Young Christian Lawyers' League. My hearing was set for the Monday after Thanksgiving, three weeks away. But it wasn't my case Ginger had come to talk about.

"Word's around that the Jake Man is uncomfortably short on witnesses. And that the D.A. isn't."

"And?" I drained my Dixie, just one step above Sessums' tap water.

"I know where you can get another witness. Somebody who'd be happy to make Laura look bad and Jake look good. Who heard him talk all the time about how much he loved Nola."

She looked me in the eye, and we both knew she was offering to perjure herself—quite a risk for a lawyer, who if caught could be disbarred—to save my father. Still, it didn't give us much, which is what I told her.

"It's better than nothing. Which is what you've got now." Ginger was plain-spoken, a refreshing but not always reassuring approach.

"Thanks, Ginger. We'll see how it goes."

"Keep me posted, okay?"

"As much as I can." I felt my cell phone vibrate on my belt. "Munger wants me."

She grimaced. "Better you than me."

As I jostled my way out, I heard an almost familiar voice softly call my name when I passed one of the booths. I looked down. It was the Tulane grad student from the F & M a million years ago, eating with a friend.

"Hey," I said, trying to put enough warmth into the greeting to make up for not remembering her name.

"You never called," she said.

"I never said I would." That was a rule, one of the few I respected. It was the only reason my approval rating among former lovers stayed somewhere above 50%.

"A girl can hope." Her friend watched our interchange with interest.

"Nice tan," I observed, to divert. She was the color of warm cocoa.

"I got an au pair gig in Barbados. Tan all over." She smiled with a beguiling mixture of lasciviousness and mischief. "Want to see?"

The strangest thing was, I didn't. Women now seemed behind glass, as if in a museum. When Laura had been alive, I'd wanted no one but her. Now I wanted no one.

"I wish I could," I said. Munger beeped me again, the first and only time I was glad to hear from him.

"Gotta go. Good to see you, Danielle," I said, remembering thank God her name.

As I walked away, I heard her friend say, "Bastard," and Danielle's response, "For sure. But what a fuck."

I found them in the conference room, Jake staring out the window, Munger sitting with his long legs crossed like two well-tailored matchsticks. It felt as if nothing had been said since I'd been summoned.

"Your father had told me there would be no more surprises," Munger announced. "However, I just received the prosecution's evidence."

He handed me a document. I frantically skimmed it, looking for my name, but saw instead, circled in red, "Memphis Hastings, neighbor of decedent, will testify she saw defendant's Jaguar at Laura Niles' home at 10 p.m. the night of the murder."

"That's an extremely bad fact, Jake," Munger said, "which you neglected to tell me."

"I'll tell you what you need to know," Jake replied.

"You were there?" I asked him.

"Ah, so you didn't know either," Munger noted. "He's lied to both of his attorneys. Consistency is always comforting."

"She was alive when I left."

"What's the next surprise, a semen match?" I asked, feeling jealousy burn through me strong as ever.

Jake gave me a direct look. "Not if she brushed her teeth."

"That's hardly the worst of it," Munger said, and I looked again at the evidence list.

"You hit her with your fist?" I yelled at Jake.

"Hell fuck fire no."

"After she was dead. Jesus."

"Wait. It grows far more interesting." Munger read from the list: "Tissue scrapings found under raised ridge of defendant's ring match DNA of victim." He looked at Jake. "Ring pattern matches facial abrasion. Now your attorneys know why the police seized your ring."

"It's impossible," Jake argued. "I never hit her. Dammit, this is insane."

"It's all over, Jake," Munger said. "We've got to try to plea bargain this down."

"I'm not going to jail. I'm innocent."

"As you know, Jake, they all say that."

"Am I the only person around here who thinks I can win this?"

Munger and I were silent.

"I see," Jake said finally.

"I'm calling Sessums," Munger said. "For your own good."

As he reached for the phone, Jake clamped his hand over Munger's. "You're fired."

"Have it your way, Jake," Munger responded, calm. "But then, when don't you?"

As Munger started out, Jake put his hand on his shoulder in what looked to be a sincere gesture of friendship. "Tommy, wait. Let's talk."

Munger shook off Jake's hand. "I told you, no lies. You lied. There's nothing to discuss." With that, Munger walked out.

"Fine," Jake said to no one in particular. "I don't want a lawyer who's not on my side." He sat down slowly. I'd never before seen him wounded, except by me.

"I'll request a continuance for you," I said, "until you can get new counsel."

"No," he said after a moment.

"You don't even think I can file—"

"I have counsel."

It took a moment to sink in. "Oh no. No way. You need somebody experienced. Somebody good."

"I've got a good lawyer. The best there is."

"Me?"

Jake gave me an odd look. "No. Me."

He was unaware of how hopeful and complimented I'd been, if only for one moment. I felt very foolish.

"I won't do it."

"We've got over two months. Enough time to rehearse everything. I'll write out all the questions—"

"I said no. Hire somebody else."

"Son, I want this trial behind me. I can't wait for a new lawyer to get up to steam. You know the facts. I need you on this case."

"Bullshit. Any decent lawyer could get up to steam on this case. I know why you want me to do it. Because any other lawyer would want to do it his way, and for you there's only one way--Jake's way. Any other lawyer would last about as long as Munger did. I'm the only one you think you can bulldoze. Well, I've done it Jake's way for twenty-seven years and I resign."

Jake smiled in spite of himself. "I guess you didn't just fall off the turnip truck."

"I guess I didn't."

"Glad to see that."

"Answer's still no."

"Your mother needs for this trial to be over soon. You can make that happen if you agree to represent me," he urged, proving no tactic was too low for a criminal lawyer.

I shook my head no.

After a hesitation, during which he visualized all the ways I could screw up his trial and jeopardize his life, he relented. "Okay, then. We'll be a team."

"You don't even know the meaning of the word."

"I mean it. We work together. Partners. A team. Like on Wittenhurst."

"There's the issue of who killed her."

"I don't see that as an issue," he said.

He didn't? There'd be times later, sitting next to each other in court, when we'd look at each other and think of what we'd lost, and we'd both have to look away.

Jake offered his hand. After a long hesitation, I warily took it. He smiled his wide warm smile, the one that had made me worship him as a child.

That night at home I watched myself on the evening news, a nervous amateur attempting a publicity interview. "Every piece of evidence they have is circumstantial," I told the reporters, "and it points to one conclusion. Somebody's trying to frame Jake Cameron."

"Is this the first time a son has ever defended his father for murder?" one reporter asked, shoving the microphone under my face.

"There was an instance in England in the 19th century." I'd researched the point minutes before, knowing it would be asked. I didn't mention the outcome, conviction and hanging. "To my knowledge this is the first time in this country in a capital trial."

"You have only two months to prepare. You think you'll be ready?"

"I know the facts. I know the defendant. And I know he's innocent." I nodded confidently to the camera."

"Why did your father ask you to defend him when he could afford the best lawyer in the country? And when he knew you'd been charged with a serious ethics violation?" That was from Charlie Dumaine, recognizable from the back in her red beret. Facing yet another woman who knew me too well, I felt my vocabulary vanish.

Jake stepped in, polished, charismatic. "To answer your second question, Charlie, he's innocent. As to your first, I did get the best." And, for the cameras and for the second time that day and since Laura, we shook hands.

Munger moved out of the conference room and I moved in, with as little ceremony as succeeding residents in a hot-sheet motel. I seldom saw him in the hall and, when I did, his eyes fixed on some distant point until we'd passed. As it turned out, we wouldn't speak again, except once, until I faced him at trial.

Over the next several days, as Jake and I eased into working together again, I considered the strange circumstances that had thrust me into first-chair position on the most notorious homicide case in the country. Was it simply coincidence that I—the alley cat of faithless lawyers--had become my own father's defense attorney? I'd never even sat second-chair on a murder case.

It made no sense that Munger had quit so abruptly. Yes, my father was infuriating but so were most criminal clients. And yes, he'd lied about the ring, or so Munger thought, but most criminal clients lied to their attorneys. Even more inexplicable was Munger's attempt to push Jake into a plea bargain. After working with Jake for twenty years, Munger would know only too well the answer to the question my mother had asked me, "Have you ever tried to make Jake Cameron do anything?"

What kind of reptilian motive might Munger have for walking out on Jake? Could he have guessed I'd be the new first chair? Had he quit so I—inexperienced, inept, reckless—might render Jake's problematical case unwinnable? Munger wanted to expand and had enlisted Turnage as a foot soldier in his campaign—that I knew. He chafed at the way Jake ran the firm and made every strategic decision—that much also seemed clear.

What more effective way to take control of Cameron & Munger than to send Jake off to Death Row at Angola Penitentiary? Could Munger be that calculating, that cold-blooded? Would Jake even consider the possibility? For someone whose profession demanded that he judge human character daily and daily find it wanting, Jake was given to baseless trust of those closest to him. Munger was one of two examples who sprang readily to mind. No, I doubted if Jake would believe it of his long-time partner, not when I was having trouble believing it myself.

Even so, one day after lunch, when satiety made him relatively quiescent, I broached my theory to him.

"Wouldn't it be much cleaner, Kyle," Jake said finally, with what looked like patience but wasn't, "for Munger to simply leave and take his clients with him? Doesn't that produce the same bottom line as eliminating me?"

"No, because he'd be starting over," I argued. "What about this building, the furniture, Ginger, Turnage?"

"What about the pens in the supply closet, Son? The case of grapefruit juice in the safe?"

"What about the firm's reputation? He wouldn't have that."

"Reputation?" He almost snarled the word. I hadn't expected this reaction at all. "Wouldn't it be more logical to walk away from this?" His hand, sweeping in disgust, seemed to take in his hopeless case and all of Cameron & Munger. I had never seen cynicism in him, never wanted to again.

"Forget I said anything."

"As for Turnage," Jake added, walking out, "he'd go with Munger."

As for Turnage, whenever I saw him, he would try to wheedle some explanation about my apparent rise in fortune, but I gave him the party line: I had been second chair and was the obvious choice.

"Obvious my blue rectum," he retorted one day when he had waylaid me at the copy machine. "Obvious is me. Nepotism is you." I looked up, surprised at the vehemence from my erstwhile pool buddy and trial partner.

"You've been hanging around Munger too much."

"Why did you think Jake didn't want any more associates? Because he knew you couldn't have kept up with them."

"Bullshit, Turnage."

"Too bad Laura's dead. She could've told you."

"Jake didn't want to dilute the vote."

"Jake didn't want his son to wash out when the going got tough. Who else would hire you? That's why he made it so goddam easy for you."

As I tried to digest it, he kept stuffing more down. "The Wittenhurst case? You? Make me laugh. And how about Nadine Chisholm? That cute little black girl? Jake gave you her pro bono just so you'd have a case to call your own."

"He tell you that?"

"He didn't have to."

I was quiet, trying to calculate it but Turnage kept on. "Ask Munger. Hell, ask Ginger. We all knew it. You didn't?"

My father had been protecting me.

"Jake doesn't make many bad decisions. But when he does, it makes up for all the rest." Turnage walked away.

That day's quiver of poison arrows was far from exhausted. Not an hour later, Ginger knocked on the conference room door.

"Don't kill the messenger," she said and handed Jake a document.

Jake skimmed it. "They've subpoenaed Munger. He's testifying against me."

"But he can't. Attorney-client privilege."

"Doesn't apply to the time before he was my lawyer," he said and I watched him as he surveyed the changed battlefield. Jake had a fortress mentality. Those inside were to be protected and trusted; those outside, battled and destroyed. There weren't many of us left on the inside for Jake, and it hurt to watch that number diminish by one. There would never be another thought of Munger except as enemy. I didn't ever want to be on the outside of that gate.

"What if Munger killed Laura?" I asked, as long as Jake might now be in the market.

"Motive?" was his two-syllable dismissal.

All I had to support my improbable hypothesis was a question Munger never should've asked. He'd stopped by my office the day before, something he'd never done

"Have you chanced upon any suspects?" Munger had asked me, leaning in like a long plank, his feet never crossing the threshold. His face was impassive, all but his eyes. Munger, who had told me never to ask a question because it showed fear.

"Why do you want to know?"

"Concern for Jake."

"Ask him."

You give something of yourself away, he'd told me. Jake dismissed it with a flick of his hand. But I remembered Laura's loathing for Munger the night at Mosca's. I couldn't tell if it was instinct, vengeance, or my need for a scapegoat, but I sensed a linkage between Munger and Laura. And I was ever on the lookout for a suspect whose last name wasn't Cameron.

As to my own case, Ginger was growing increasingly pessimistic. My amatory reputation, she had heard, was known to the New Orleans Bar and would create an unspoken presumption against me. A few days before the hearing, she came into my office and shut the door.

"I want some details," she said. Precisely what Jake had demanded about Laura. Was this what my hell would be, interrogated for all eternity—it would take that long—about every girl I'd ever been with?

"I told you. We had sex. Twice," I added as if that were a detail

"Specifics," she demanded. Why did I again feel like a criminal? "Graphic."

"I used protection, if that's what you mean."

"That's not what I mean." She took out her notebook. "Did you have oral sex?"

I shook my head.

She looked at me skeptically. "Let me rephrase so there's no confusion about terminology. Did she suck your dick?"

I thought back to be sure. "No."

Her skepticism deepened. "This is critical. I want the truth."

"I told you no. She's a very basic girl."

"She's going to testify that you made her perform oral sex."

"It never happened."

She sat for several moments, probably determining why she should believe me.

"Did she ever hold your dick in her hand?"

"No."

Ginger snorted in disbelief. "What did she use, barbeque tongs?"

"She's a bronco-buster."

"Meaning?"

"No foreplay."

"None?" I'd succeeded in the impossible—shocking Ginger.

"None. She just hops on and rides."

"You like that?" she asked wonderingly.

"Sometimes, I guess." I didn't see why my tastes were relevant, not to mention any of her business.

"Did she get a good look at it?"

"My dick?"

"I believe that's the dick under discussion."

Again I thought back. At my apartment it had been quick and dirty, with most of our clothes on. The night in her apartment April had consumed Southern Comfort before, during and after.

I shook my head no.

"How can you be so sure?"

"It was either wham-bam or dead drunk."

"Then we may—may—have a chance," she said, smiling oh so briefly. "Now drop your pants."

"Damn, Ginger. What the hell--?"

"You heard me. Drop your pants. As your attorney, I need to see it. Believe me, my interest is purely professional."

That's why it was so intimidating. "No way."

"It won't be to Jake's advantage if his lawyer is disbarred."

I locked the door. Then I just stood there, sweat drenching my lower parts.

"This isn't the Kyle Cameron of legend," she noted.

I dropped my trousers, then my underwear. If Ginger was impressed by what she saw, she did a good job of hiding it.

"Up sesame," she commanded.

"God, Ginger." I was now as pink as Turnage and every bit as sweaty.

"Do you want to keep your license?"

"Not that bad."

"Let me rephrase. Do you want to defend your father?" She reached in her purse. "Now, you do it"—she pulled out a pair of rubber gloves—"or I'll do it."

"I'll do it."

Finally, finally, I was ready. All those times I'd been naked and erect, with all those women, and I'd never once felt modest or ashamed. Providing pleasure to women was my gift, my single talent.

"Any identifying marks, moles or scars?" she asked, relentless.

"I don't think so."

"Don't think so?" Out came the rubber gloves again, only this time they made contact.

"Damn, Ginger." She was none too gentle.

"No identifying marks," she concluded. Then, pulling an old Godchaux's tape measure from her pocket, she handed it to me.

"No, dammit!" My voice cracked. I'd never even done this to myself. Well, once.

"You've gone this far, Kyle."

"No! Jake won't okay this strategy of your, whatever the hell it is."

"He already has."

The only dry part of my body was inside my mouth.

"Turn around first," I begged. I could feel the blood rising in my face. I was blushing like a virgin.

"I'll watch. I want it accurate."

Stripped, underwear exposed, sexual organs scrutinized, prodded, measured, and discussed in clinical language. This, perhaps, was how rape victims felt on the examining table. Mamie Lawrence had undergone this humiliation to accuse Roger.

I gave Ginger what she wanted. She wrote down the dimensions and handed me a business card. "Be there at 9:00 a.m. tomorrow."

I read the card. "No. I refuse."

"Look, kid. Your three judges have got five teenaged daughters between them. That means every Saturday night, somebody like you comes calling with a smile and a hard-on." Mine, impervious to nuances, still stood at 11:00 high.

"Get dressed and put that thing out of its misery," she directed. On her way out, she flung the rubber gloves into my recycling bin.

Thanksgiving passed uncelebrated by unspoken agreement of all three Camerons.

The following Monday, Ginger and I met before the hearing at 8:00 in the Cameron & Munger parking lot. I was not erect.

"Okay, kid, one more time," Ginger directed.

"I never touched Miss Cahill." As with Roger's case, my hearing would be a test of credibility, mine versus April Cahill's. Since we'd both be lying, it was a question of who lied better and less.

"Too pious," she said. She was risking prison by encouraging—suborning—my perjury. Nor was I comfortable about committing it. That much of Jake's code had stuck. Never mind that I'd lied so fluently with women; that fell under the "love and war" exception. Never mind that I'd already lied in my answer to the complaint; lies on paper were standard in my profession and most even had a name: legal briefs. Perjury, under oath, would be a deliberate step over the line into felony.

I'd envisioned the hearing room as a windowless Bastille cell or Inquisition star chamber staffed by hooded guards with truncheons, but it was just a small courtroom, like I'd seen in moot court at Tulane. My judges—the flowing-haired lecher, the religious fanatic, and someone else with some unknown but no doubt valid reason to despise me—filed into the room without glancing at me but with a familiar, unsettling nod to the prosecutrix, Teresa Levault.

Like all prosecutors, she assumed I wouldn't be there unless I'd done something. Of course, she was right. She led the state in disbarments.

"Did the defendant forced you to perform oral sex?" she asked her witness.

"He did," April enunciated.

"What else?"

"Anything he wanted. He said, quote, 'If I'm not happy, you won't be when your case comes to trial.'" The only person she was quoting was herself, but it sounded more plausible—though no more true—than my "I never touched Miss Cahill." Charlie Dumaine had remarkably improved her delivery.

"You testified you performed oral sex?" Ginger asked April on cross-examination.

"Anything he wanted. He said, quote, 'If I'm not happy--"

You remember his exact words?"

"I remember everything."

"Specific details."

"Very clearly."

"You saw his penis?"

"I have eyes."

"And felt it?"

"How could I not?"

"And you still remember it." Ginger seemed dubious.

April grimaced. "As long as I live."

Ginger then introduced defendant's exhibit 1. Levault objected, and I watched them argue it before the judges. Though everything depended on our exhibit being admitted, I prayed—I'd taken to prayer—it wouldn't be, that if I went down at least it would be with my boots, and everything else, on.

The sugar-voiced judge made several fervent points. Flowing Mane seemed ambivalent, but it was the third judge, a man in a wheelchair, who carried the argument. Sugar-voice sat back, defeated but not forgetting.

"We reluctantly admit the exhibit," announced Judge Flowing Mane.

Ginger unfastened a folder and removed six 9-by-12 color photographs of erect male genitalia culled from medical books and pornographic magazines. Some were smaller than mine, some were larger, all just bodyless meat stretched out next to rulers. In the cropped photos, their condition appeared more like paralysis than arousal. I was #1, and I could see Charlie Dumaine, seated among the press, making an immediate eyewitness identification. I knew the display would, via Charlie and the *USA Today* stringer seated beside her, find its way to Jake's jury and beyond.

"What about it, April?" Ginger said matter-of-factly. "Name that tuna."

The reporters bent down as one to write. I prayed it would go away, knowing it wouldn't. Sure enough, Ginger's phrase boomeranged from the news directly into the national consciousness. Late-night shows, cartoons and comics, even a rap album hopped on it. One of the courtroom guards had slipped a cell phone past security and videoed the testimony and it went viral. Tabloids and namethattuna.com soon had the six of us displayed side-by-side, and my answerphone ran out of message space every day.

In court, the spectators, the reporters—even Charlie Dumaine—were already looking at me differently. It was an expression I would come to spot instantly. From that day on, whenever I met anyone, or even saw someone glance at me, I would—like the Rose Bowl football star who ran the ball the wrong way and scored for the opponent—wonder if they knew.

From April's hesitation over the photos, I could tell she didn't have an immediate recollection, that mine was just another tree in a dense forest. She was trying to make an educated guess, but that would be difficult. A vagina, Ginger told me, had far less tactile sensation than a hand or mouth, which April had never employed. April knew she didn't have long to think it over, especially given such disparate specimens. The possessor of penis number 6 would have trouble finding an orifice if he limited himself to the human species. Number 5 was not circumcised. Number 4 was bent at a forty-five-degree angle. Three matched its number in inches. Number 2 had a large mole at the tip. And Number 1, mine, was unremarkable except to me.

"Number 6," she said with a show of certainty, choosing the largest specimen. I felt no pride over leaving that impression. I had discarded pride in the recycling bin with Ginger's examining gloves.

With a little flourish, Ginger removed the cardboard hiding my name under Number 1, then introduced statistics contrasting April's pick (13.6 inches) and me (7.5). There was laughter. After calling the photographer—my 9 a.m. appointment on the business card—to authenticate the photo, Ginger sat down.

"What do you think?" I whispered.

"I think you've made legal history, kid," Ginger said drily. "Again."

My time on the stand wasn't noteworthy except for the number of times and ways Teresa Levault asked me if I had sex with April, as if she were trying to amass counts of perjury.

"Do you find Ms. Cahill attractive?"

"Not at the moment."

"What about at other moments?"

"She is a lovely lady. Also a client,"

"Yet you had sexual relations with her, didn't you?"

"No," and except for "I never touched Miss Cahill," that monosyllable constituted my response to the rest of Teresa Levault's hour-long cross examination of me, in which she claimed I'd dressed seductively, behaved promiscuously, and called April repeatedly after the act—the same line of inquiry used to discredit rape victims.

"Did the photos help us or hurt us?" I asked Ginger after the hearing as we walked outside.

"If we win, that'll be why." she answered, putting on her sunglasses in the midday brightness. It was one of those New Orleans winter days that are as hot as June.

"What about my testimony? How'd I do?" I was determined to squeeze some hope to hold onto.

Ginger looked at me flatly. "Kid, your credibility as a witness is even lower than your reputation as a lawyer. Does that answer your question?"

Silence greeted me at the firm, just as it had after my cross-examination of Mamie. Whereas then I had sensed fear behind the silence, now there was laughter. Someone—Turnage—had tacked a Chicken-of-the-Sea label to the door.

Even Jake, who unblinkingly kept the company of killers, couldn't quite meet my eyes when I reported on the hearing and seemed relieved when I concluded.

"What now?" I asked.

"Work," he said gruffly. It was his catchall solution, and the only one possible under the circumstances. If the panel recommended disbarment, the decision would automatically be reviewed by the Bar. The final decision would come, unannounced, in the form of a certified letter to me. Any guesses as to when that letter would arrive would merely drive me crazy.

Jake and I picked up the rhythm of trial partners. As the Christmas holidays neared, we were together virtually every waking hour, even moreso than on Roger's case. Jake never became a patient teacher, but I determined to be a quick study, and I was. For every hour I'd fucked off in Evidence, for every cold rainy Saturday I'd skipped the bar review, I was now putting in ten-fold time. As for trial practice, Jake drilled me as mercilessly as when he'd taught me to box.

"About time," he said after a heated run-through in which I apparently displayed the potential he'd always cursed me for not living up to. He began to listen to my ideas with something resembling respect, though not the level he accorded Turnage. As Jake had foreseen, it was to no one's advantage to discuss who did it, and the issue remained submerged.

At night we moved to his house, where my mother seemed to brighten at the sight of her son and husband working as a team. Once, as we argued some point of strategy at the dinner table, I saw her unconsciously take a few sips of gumbo and even a bite of bread.

Jake remained unconvinced about the wisdom of her testifying, but my mother wanted to help, and we needed an alibi witness to counter the neighbor's sighting of Jake's Jag. I believed Mom could be practiced into credibility for a one-time life-and-death performance. Hadn't she been an actress in college? Of course, then she was playing Tennessee Williams' heroines, which for her required little acting. And she'd been working from much better scripts.

"Now then, Mrs. Cameron, how many years have you and Mr. Cameron been married?" I asked. Behind me, Jake paced the room like a coach on the sidelines, dying to get into the game. He'd started out rehearsing Mom but got angry so quickly that he passed the job to me, to everyone's relief.

"Twenty-nine years. No, thirty. In May." Her face was so taut I was almost afraid the skin would suddenly crack and blood pour forth. Xanax would not work against this kind of anxiety; it would take heroin.

I glanced at my notes. "How would you describe the relationship—"

Jake was in my face. "No crutches," he demanded, snatching the notes out of my hand.

I flushed. "No crutches it is. Mrs. Cameron, isn't it a fact that your relationship—"

"Objection. Leading the witness."

"Maybe I'd do better if you'd let me do my job."

Jake forced himself to swallow his retort, as, unprompted, my mother plunged back into her obviously memorized and bizarrely inflected lines. "We have had our ups and downs—"

"Hold it, Nola. Wait until he asks it."

"He tried to ask it," she protested. "If you had let him."

"I'm doing this, Dad, remember?"

"Then do it right."

"Your way."

My mother shook a Xanax out of her bottle.

"Okay, okay," he conceded. "I'll back off. Go."

"Please describe your relationship—"

"Keep eye contact with the witness. And don't mumble."

"I'm the lawyer, remember?"

"I'm still your father."

"Not now. You're my client. That is our primary relationship. Understand?"

His jaw muscle flexed from clamping it tight. "Go."

My mother began yet again without cue, "I was reading *Gourmet* magazine, about a recipe for black bottom pie..." Her finger was tapping nervously, like Morse Code for S.O.S.

"That's a little later on, Mom. Remember to wait for the question. Here it comes, okay?"

She nodded wide-eyed, as if I'd asked if she were ready for me to signal the guillotine operator.

"Mrs. Cameron, do you think—"

"Objection, speculation. Jesus. Barely a month to go and you're not ready."

I gathered up my notes. "No, you're not ready. We'll pick it up tomorrow, Mom, just you and me." I kissed her goodnight and walked out, surprising myself as much as Jake.

Driving home on Saint Charles, I caught a glimpse of two people from my past and future entering the Columns Hotel bar for a drink. It was clearly a business meeting because they didn't go together at all. The man was tall and wore a shapeless brown suit and thick-soled wingtips and carried a battered lawyer's briefcase. Beside him, a nicely built, energetic brunette in an expensive black suit trimmed in brilliant red.

Christmas and New Year's passed without a nod as, through bolted breakfasts and lunches of untasted po'boys and past the last dregs of midnight coffee, my father and I worked to construct a strategy out of what Munger had called "the worst set of facts this side of Judas Iscariot." Our primary defense remained "no motive," and Jake decided not to testify because of the risk they'd find out about me. Our auxiliary theory, "framed," was equally weak without a "by whom" to add. Anyone with access to all the facts would have to conclude I was the principal candidate.

We had so many potentially fatal holes in our case and I worried over them so constantly that Jake forbade me to mention them. Ten days before trial, the parties convened in Judge Barber's chambers for her determination on perhaps the most fatal hole in our case.

"You each have ten minutes," she decreed at the outset of argument on Jake's ring, coated invisibly with Laura's DNA. I kept it under five, as instructed by Jake, spewing what Jake had siphoned into me. She then listened with increasing impatience as Sessums parsed the legal meaning of "make yourself at home."

"It's in your brief, is it not, Mr. Sessums?" Judge Barber interrupted.

"Yes, your honor, but certain points need emphasis."

"Underline them," she said and abruptly ordered us, along with Bal and Rimers, out to Jake's house to re-enact the scene.

There unfolded the dumb show. Jake placed his ring in the half-open top drawer of his desk and withdrew. Eunice opened the front door.

"New Orleans police," said Rimers. "We're here to see Mr. Cameron."

"Make yourselves at home," Eunice enunciated, pointing fiercely to the living room, then exited, leaving the detectives in the foyer. Bal shuffled offstage to the living room. Enter Rimers. He paused outside Jake's office, looked in, and crossed the legal threshold.

"Back up," ordered Judge Barber. She retraced Rimers' footsteps. "I can't see it."

"You're too short," Rimers said curtly, and I had the pleasure of watching a wince constrict the imperturbable prairie of Sessums's face. Judge Barber was perhaps 5 foot 2, and the height of her heels made it obvious to anyone who ever studied women that she would've preferred willowy to petite. Eunice brought out a metal footstep ladder which, with a murderous glance at Rimers, Judge Barber mounted to attain his height. She leaned farther and farther into the room.

"I don't see it, Detective."

"I could see it," Rimers retorted despite Sessums' attempt to stop him. "It was in the drawer."

"If you could see it," Judge Barber said, "you were in the study."

Sessums smoothly interceded. "Your honor, even assuming Detective Rimers stepped into the study, he was well within the scope of the consent granted."

"Eunice didn't have the authority to consent. Mr. Cameron doesn't even allow her in the room," I countered.

"Is that true?" Judge Barber asked, stepping down from the hated stepladder.

"Not even to vacuum," Eunice told her.

"Your honor," Sessums argued, "she said 'make yourself at home.' The study is part of the home."

"Do you expect me to credit that construction?"

"Frankly, I do, your honor."

"You're not from the South, are you, Mr. Sessums?"

"South Boston, your honor," Sessums responded with an attempt at a smile.

"The evidence is excluded."

I nodded gravely at justice being done, while the most profound relief I'd ever experienced swept through me, like air to bursting lungs. The exclusion of the ring took with it both Laura's DNA and the unpretty fact of the post-mortem blow to her cheek.

The second the others were out the door, my father grabbed my mother and me in a hug, and we danced merrily around the foyer like children in a three-legged race, while Eunice watched with amazement. I didn't remember his ever hugging me before.

So we danced and skidded and bumped toward the day of trial in mid-January. I never located another potential suspect. Nothing in Sessums' evidence indicated any proof of motive. Ginger repeated her offer to perjure herself. My mother made it through her testimony rehearsals, if not with smooth credibility, then at least in response to the questions; her nervousness, we hoped, would be attributed to fear instead of mendacity. I'd written my opening argument; Jake had added and subtracted, and finally, as God had once done, pronounced it good.

The night before trial, he and I walked out to our cars together at midnight. I didn't know which of us was worse off, him from exhaustion or me from routine terror.

"Remember," he said.

"The throat."

He held out his hand and I shook it.

I gave up trying to sleep at 5:00 a.m., an hour before the alarm was set to ring. My mother, doubtless, hadn't even gotten into bed, just watched the clock as its hands wound her tighter and tighter. Alone of us, perhaps Jake had slept, discipline overcoming reality.

Shaving, I held my notes in my left hand and rehearsed my opening argument in the mirror. "Jake Cameron loved Laura Niles. And Laura Niles loved him." The practiced words never lost their bite. I stared at my reflection. I had sliced my cheek but didn't notice until I tasted something metallic and then saw the stripe of brilliant red.

At court I led them up the steps, breaching a phalanx of hysterical, jabbering reporters by shoving hard with my shoulder and elbows, then tromping on any wires and equipment in our way. Jake pulled Nola through the hole I opened. Inside, we passed beyond the metal detector ordered by Judge Barber after

Jake had received several death threats by the lunatic feminist and Christian fringes, who for once had found common ground.

I heard a low buzz of anticipation among the spectators, the same noise that must've filled the Coliseum before net-and-trident went against the short sword. I saw reporters from all the networks (Charlie Dumaine had managed to seat herself among them), journalists from the big dailies, the T-shirted representatives from tabloids and blogs. The only reason Court TV wasn't featuring it gavel-to-gavel was the inconvenient Louisiana law barring courtroom cameras. As it was, they were broadcasting a simultaneous simulation from a rented courtroom with actors. This was the big time.

I wasn't ready, nowhere near, might never be. My chest felt like I was driving a car flat-out and topping a high hill without knowing what was on the down side. No matter how many gulps of water I drank, my mouth was so dry I didn't know if words would form.

"Remember, start off slow," Jake instructed as the jurors filed in. "Look at the jury."

"I got it, I got it," I said, adrenaline coursing. Jake believed in his gut, not consultants, and out of a bad pool we'd managed to cull a marginally better jury than Roger's. Still, most of them were staid, permed and polyestered, more women than men, not likely to appreciate a fatcat lawyer who fooled around.

Two women in particular worried me. One came from money, expressed an interest in "crime of all forms," and had been too eager to serve; the other was twice divorced and not yet thirty, leaving me to draw my own inferences. Then there was the gardener, who toiled in the Garden District and was "very happily married."

Sessums' opening argument was larded with references to the Ten Commandments, two in particular, and he wore his Sears suit like the mantle of Moses.

"The defendant's wife—his college sweetheart—sits behind him," Sessums went on, allowing just a teaspoon of righteousness to flavor his tone. "And his son represents him. But, make no mistake, the defendant is no family man. He had a young, beautiful mistress half his age and more money than any of us can imagine. Thousand-dollar suits, flashy vintage Jaguar, palatial home in the Garden District."

I stood. "Objection, your honor."

"The best country clubs, the best restaurants—"

He was riding over me, the same tactic I'd used with him and Mamie. "Private school, private lake stocked with bass, a pony for his son—"

"Objection!" I cried out.

"Approach the bench."

"Your honor," Sessums began, "I object to his breaking into my opening argument. Any seasoned lawyer knows—"

"I believe the objection was by Mr. Cameron."

"Your honor, being wealthy is not a crime and my client's not being tried for it."

"Sustained. Tone it down, Mr. Sessums."

It was but a tiny victory, made even less significant by the fact that Judge Barber, who lived in the Garden District, was my natural ally on this point. Yet when Jake gave me a little nod of approval, I felt as exultant as if I'd just won the Powerball.

In my opening argument, my delivery was as uneven as my feelings were mixed. Nor could I forget that my mother was ten feet away. "Laura Niles loved Jake Cameron," I told the jury and the world. "And Jake Cameron loved her. Their relationship, though no one denies it violated the rules of society, was more than a mere affair. He had no motive to murder her. More than anything, he wanted her to live, to be with him, always."

I forced myself to focus on the jury. "Would an expert criminal lawyer, one of the best in the state, with twenty-five years' experience, leave his prints on the murder weapon? Would he leave Laura Niles' door key on his key ring? Of course he wouldn't. Not-unless-he-was-innocent."

That night my father reviewed my performance.

"Emotional," he said.

"Is that bad?"

"Depends on the emotion."

"I guess that's unavoidable, given the circumstances."

"Avoid it. That's over. This isn't." It was the closest we'd come to discussing Laura since the night of his arrest.

My mother appeared in her nightgown, in a rare ebullient mood, buoyed by Prozac and an absolutely baseless belief that my father stood a good chance of winning his case.

"Anything I can do?" she asked.

"Thanks, Mom. We're just finishing up."

"What day do I testify?" She looked at Jake.

"Not for a few days, Baby Doll."

She nodded and walked back toward the bedroom. My father and I looked at each other, both of us silently reassessing whether she'd survive Sessums' cross-examination.

My alarm didn't ring the next morning at 5:00 because I pre-empted it by getting up at 4:00. As I shaved, I rehearsed in the mirror for Sessums' first witness, the teenaged voyeur who would authenticate his photographs of Laura and Jake in her bedroom.

"You fantasized about her, did you not?" I accused. "You were consumed by her."

I stared at my reflection, at the man who, on one hot August night, had also watched Jake with Laura in that bedroom.

I'd been granted a late date with her, confirmed that very afternoon, and I'd been hoarding the prospect, allowing myself to anticipate it a little at a time all through the evening, so that, when I pulled up at her house, I was as aroused as if she'd been in the car with me naked.

As I parked, though, I spotted Jake's Jag and the light on in the bedroom window. I hit my steering wheel so hard I gave myself a stone bruise.

"Damn you, old man. Damn you!" I silently climbed over the door of my convertible and crept up under Laura's crepe myrtles to her darkened bedroom window. What did he know, have, do that I didn't?

Inside, Jake held the heavy silver candlestick that she kept by her bed and lit a candle. He kissed Laura on the neck, and she languorously held her arms up for him to slip off her sleeveless sweater. Laura's hands twined above her head in the same vulnerable position as with me. Jake kissed her nipples. When she began to undress him, something she'd never done to me, I turned away. Jake, the ultimate competitor, would've forced himself to stay for the advantage it might've given him. Of course, there are other ways to gain advantage.

Steam had covered my bathroom mirror by the time I returned from the irretrievable past. I was now late to court, my only chance to retrieve at least the present. I was surprised to find, months and many cathartic events later, that I was still angry over the image of Laura undressing my father.

I finished shaving in the Jeep, old habits for once serving me, and by the time I arrived at Jake's for our drive of family solidarity to court, I looked as wholesome as I ever would.

• • •

Vic Ezell was a thin fourteen-year-old with very light blue eyes and matching spiked hair, whose body listed to the left like a sinking boat. His hand was barely off the Bible before Sessums introduced his first exhibits: three monumentally enlarged photos of Jake making love with Laura, their private parts censored.

"Vic, did you take these pictures?" Sessums began.

"Me and Mel Champ took 'em," he offered indolently.

Sessums handed copies of the photos to the jury. I looked back at my mother, enduring it, as the jury passed them along.

"Was this the only time you saw the defendant there?" he continued.

A snort of derision. "We watched all the time. Three, four times a week. He couldn't get enough." A smile traced itself across his lips, where a flesh-colored salve inexpertly masked an impressive herpes blister.

"The throat," Jake said to me when I stood for cross-examination.

"You never saw Jake Cameron harm Laura Niles, did you? Hit her, yell at her, raise his fist to her?"

"He had other things on his mind."

"Answer the question."

"I never saw him hurt her."

"Did you watch them every day Mr. Cameron was there?"

"Every time we saw that Jag drive up. Wouldn't you watch?"

I'd tried but couldn't. "I'll ask the questions, Vic. Did you masturbate after watching her?"

"Objection," Sessums cut in. "Irrelevant."

"Goes to the mindset of the witness."

"Where are you going, Mr. Cameron?" Judge Barber asked.

"I'll link it up," I promised.

"See that you do. Overruled."

"Did you, Vic? Masturbate?"

Vic was now leeward at close to a 45-degree angle. He knew a denial wouldn't be believed.

"Yeah, a little," he confessed, barely audible.

"And Mel masturbated too, didn't he?"

He hesitated. We were getting into territory even Vic recognized as unseemly. "I don't remember," he equivocated.

"Don't remember? He was right next to you in the treehouse, wasn't he? Very close?"

"Okay, he did," Vic admitted, anything to stop the train.

"With your clothes off?"

Sessums objected and Judge Barber overruled, perhaps herself curious where I was going.

"We didn't," he said in a low voice, bravado gone. He was now sufficiently broken.

"You saw her naked?"

"Yeah," he answered uncertainly.

"Her legs were spread."

"Uh huh."

"You saw her arms raised above her head."

"She did that sometimes."

"Sometimes? How many times did you see that?"

"Lots." His voice was becoming smaller and smaller.

"How many is 'lots'?"

"Twenty, thirty, I don't know."

"The way she was when she was dead."

Now that he'd glimpsed our destination, his voice suddenly rose in volume and pitch. "I never saw her dead."

"No? Did you find Miss Niles attractive?"

"She was all right."

"She was a good-looking woman, wasn't she?"

"She was okay."

"But she didn't give you the time of day. A fourteen-year-old kid with pimples."

"She liked me fine."

"You were obsessed with her. You daydreamed about her. You fantasized about her doing all that to you."

"No, man." He shifted in his chair, leaning even more to the left, eyes blinking like two headlights on hazard.

"No? Vic, you masturbated. You said you did. You saw her with her arms up. You said you did. And that was how you left her after you killed her."

"We just watched." It was a plea. His voice was tiny again, like a gerbil caged with a snake.

While Sessums tried without result to rehabilitate his compromised and now capsized witness, I busied myself with some notes, not wanting to look pettily triumphant. We now had one potential suspect to divert the jury. More would be needed.

Jake scribbled something on a pad and slid it over. "Good boy," it read. I'd heard him say it to Turnage after he got some worthless scum off against all expectations. It was my first.

The only thing Vic's testimony proved was the existence of the affair. Since he couldn't place Jake at Laura's at the time of the murder, the damage was controllable. Likewise with the other voyeur, Mel Champ, who was so scared I'd ask him about masturbation and murder that he was eager to confirm that Jake had been surpassingly gentle with Laura. I was unable to shake the certitude of Laura's neighbor, Sessums' final witness of the afternoon, about the presence of Jake's Jag the night of her murder. Even so, the day hadn't gone badly, and I said as much to Jake as we pulled into the firm.

"Tomorrow's the physical evidence," was all he said, and I offered no more blithe summations. We worked until after 2:00 a.m.

As we drove to trial the next morning, Jake was silent, as was I. My mother, however, percolating with caffeine, was unusually talkative. "That boy really might've done it. Watching every day. Perverted, isn't it, Kyle?"

"Yes, ma'am."

"Those awful pictures were nobody's business. Everyone has a right to some privacy." My father and I listened without comment to my mother's bizarre condonation. We both knew how tiny, and temporary, our victory had been. Now would come the fusillade Sessums would pound us with.

First was Balthazar, veteran of a thousand trials, his sleepy Cajun voice laying out the unshakable evidence: the crime scene photos, the ripped-off nightgown, the head injuries, the murder weapon under the covers. The one thing Balthazar didn't describe, and certainly the jury must've been curious about, was the wound on Laura's right cheek. Only because it had been excluded, along with the ring, were we still breathing.

I stood for cross. "Detective, have you been involved in cases tried by the defendant, Jake Cameron?"

"Many, many cases."

"Murder cases?"

"That's all I do."

"So Jake—" I slipped in the first name, likable old Jake—"is an extremely experienced criminal attorney?"

"He's the best I've seen."

He was giving me a gift; he and Jake went back a long way.

"The best," I repeated. "And in your years as a homicide detective, have you ever before seen a murder weapon hidden under the same sheets as the victim?"

"It was a first."

"In your experience, wouldn't a crime professional—the best criminal attorney you've ever seen—have the good sense to wipe his fingerprints off the murder weapon?"

It called for speculation, and I expected an objection, but Sessums let it pass.

"In my experience, a professional would've wiped them off." Another gift; we'd anticipated only getting the question in.

Now, for the ice cream on the cake, as Turnage was given to saying. "Detective, did you find Jake's fingerprints on the front doorknob?"

"No. It was wiped clean."

"Were there fingerprints on any of the doorknobs?"

"None. All of them had been wiped clean."

"In your experience, wouldn't that ordinarily suggest that the killer was trying to cover his tracks?"

"That is the pattern."

"And so, was there not an inconsistency in behavior—carefully wiping off doorknobs yet ineptly leaving the murder weapon in bed with the victim."

"Yes."

"Unless Jake Cameron were being framed."

"Objection. No evidence to that effect."

"I just supplied it."

"Overruled."

"There is an inconsistency," Bal confirmed.

I sat, pretty damn satisfied. Sessums rose for re-direct.

"Detective, you investigated the Melorette murder, didn't you?"

Something about the expression on Bal's face made me realize everything was about to turn to shit.

"I investigated that case, yes." Bal looked the way I'd seen him when Jake was about to skewer him.

"Could you summarize the facts of that case, Detective?"

"A detective—

"What kind of detective?"

"Homicide."

"Experienced?"

"Fifteen years."

"Sorry to interrupt you. Please proceed."

"A homicide detective strangled his girlfriend with his necktie."

"And where did you find the murder weapon?"

"He was wearing it when I arrested him."

"What about fingerprints at the murder scene?"

"Wiped clean."

Why hadn't I known about that damn case? And why hadn't Jake known? Now I remembered the case, remembered Jake's talking about Anthony Melorette. But when we planned my cross of Bal, leading up to the any-damn-fool-would've-wiped-his-fingerprints whammo conclusion, he hadn't mentioned it. I knew my father had many flaws, but in the courtroom I'd always considered him infallible. That moment was the first I realized otherwise.

I looked over at Sessums, younger than Jake, hungrier, angrier. He wouldn't have forgotten the Melorette case.

Lunch was dismal, gray sausage-and-preservative sandwiches from the vending machine; no one wanted to fight through the thicket of reporters. Mom was silent and distant as we sat in a witness room, Balthazar's testimony having neutralized her medications as if they were so many M&M's.

• • •

"My fault," Jake said finally. Quick to assign blame, he was equally ruthless with himself. "I remember that case. I missed the connection."

"I should've quit when he said you were the best defense attorney."

He waved it away. "Bal was giving. You took. That was my plan." Jake finished his sausage sandwich. "Our plan," he amended and reached for my discarded half sandwich. Anything to survive. No one commented on Mom's untouched—unopened—sandwich. She put it in her purse.

"For later," she said, later meaning the nearest trash basket.

I went to get us some cardboard coffee from the machine, and when I returned, my parents were holding hands. I stood outside the door and watched for a moment.

Dr. Lucius Quintus Catullus Lamar, the police pathologist, looked like someone who would flourish in a cold damp place: watery gray eyes, skin and hair almost colorless. As the namesake of a Supreme Court justice from Mississippi who served during Reconstruction, L.Q.C. apparently came from an old-line southern family. Maybe the bloodline had gotten so attenuated that all it could produce was a sort of human mold.

As Sessums established Dr. Lamar's credentials, my mind explored the contours of his upcoming testimony, seeking some way to weaken it, undermine it, and I suddenly saw how to do it. I probed my idea for weaknesses but found none. It would add weight to our theory that Jake had been framed, which needed all the heft I could give it.

"Do you recognize this candlestick, Dr. Lamar?" Sessums asked, predictable as a tire tread. His prize exhibit, complete with Jake's fingerprints, looked substantial, crafted in a time when bludgeons were the Saturday-night specials of the day.

In a low voice that seemed to issue from a deep hole, the pathologist informed the jury about Laura's blood and hair and skull fragments on the base of the stick, about her standing then not standing, about the long arc of the final blow.

I led off my cross-examination with standard obfuscation, trying to cast doubt on tangents of the pathologist's testimony, with little success. Science, after all, was science, but I was about to use it for my own purposes. To set up anew our he-was-framed theory, I elicited from Lamar the unremarkable admission that if someone wearing gloves had killed Laura, he would've left no prints on the candlestick and Jake's could've remained intact. "Now, Dr. Lamar, you have stated that the blows to the head were delivered while Ms. Niles was alive?

I could feel Jake looking at me, almost hear his thought, "What the fuck is he doing?" I was about to show him.

"I have stated this several times."

"What you haven't stated—" I glanced over at Sessums to see how he was going to take my little twist of the evidentiary knife--"is whether the blow to the cheek occurred while she was alive."

This after-death blow was the strongest evidence I could think of that Jake had been framed. If Jake had killed her, whether in heat of passion or in cold blood, he would've struck the final blow with the heavy candlestick. Only someone who wanted Laura's DNA to be found on Jake's ring would have delivered a far lesser blow to an already dead victim. This was a key undermining of Sessums' case.

I heard an audible intake of breath from my father, and Judge Barber was staring at me strangely, when suddenly my father hissed to me, "Withdraw the question."

"What?"

"We withdraw the question," my father interposed, standing.

Sessums, alert as a rattlesnake, turned toward the court reporter. "Ask that the question be repeated."

"It was withdrawn," Jake argued.

"Sit down, Mr. Cameron," Judge Barber ordered Jake.

"It was withdrawn," my father all but roared.

"The defendant is not the attorney here," Sessums replied calmly. "Repeat my request to have the prior question read."

"Object," my father desperately ordered me.

"I object," though I had no idea at what.

"Overruled," said Judge Barber. "You gentlemen better get your lawyering straight."

While the court reporter repeated my brilliant query about the blow to the cheek, my father said to me, "Didn't you take evidence, you damn fool? You opened the door to the ring."

I felt my head get light and I quickly sat down. Behind me, Mom gripped the bench, hard, unsure what had happened.

"You fuckup," Jake said. "Now it all comes in."

And on Sessums' redirect, it did.

"Was there any injury to the victim's face?" he asked Dr. Lamar.

"Yes. There was an abrasion on her right cheek."

"Could you ascertain which hand the assailant used?

"His left hand."

"His wedding ring hand?"

"Yes."

"How can you tell?"

"The left hand is the natural hand to use to strike a blow on the right side of the face," he answered, pointing to his right cheek. "Also, the damage was discernible under magnification, revealing movement of the blow from left to right."

Sessums had Dr. Lamar demonstrate.

"Did you find anything unusual about the abrasion on the victim's left cheek?" Sessums went on.

"The abrasion did not bleed."

"What is the significance of the abrasion not bleeding?"

"That indicates that when the victim was hit, the blood had already pooled in her heart." Dr. Lamar's voice, with its muffled, hollow quality, carried the echo of the tomb, making him all the more effective a witness for Sessums.

"And what does that signify?"

"The killer hit her after she was dead." There was no overestimating the effect this literal overkill would have on the jury. Nothing, of course, compared to the DNA evidence, which I had also let in and which would, according to the soon-to-be-revised witness lineup, be offered first thing the next morning.

By the time I'd pushed through the reporters and gotten to the restricted underground parking, Jake and my mother had left me.

"How does it feel to kill your father?"

It was Charlie Dumaine. I punched the elevator button but the damn thing had already gone.

"How do you think it feels?" I said, still exerting a steady pressure on the "up" button.

"What I think has no bearing. You occupy a different moral sphere."

I took the stairs, two at a time, but not quickly enough to escape her last question.

"How much of your letting the ring in was accident, Kyle? Or do you even know?"

I worked late that night, preparing for the unexpected DNA witness. "Client ditches his own lawyer in parking lot" had led the evening news, as expected. Jake didn't come back to the office, and my mother, though she assured me she forgave me, wouldn't put him on the phone.

Wisely so, because Jake damn sure hadn't forgiven me. More than that, I knew he was weighing whether to fire me from the case. He'd done it four months before on Wittenhurst, at the end of the summer, a time when everything I'd begun neared its finale.

* * *

The August heat had become cumulative from week after week of blood-temperature days. Everyone came to work early, stayed late, and never ventured outside unless forced. Trapped together, breathing and rebreathing the same air-conditioned oxygen, our incestuous little firm felt even more inbred.

It was at this point (I could tell it from Jake as well as Laura) that natural selection chose youth. After our contest at the gym, he'd quit going and his stomach was starting to go soft. He'd show up at the firm mid-morning, seeming exhausted, as if he'd spent the night trying and failing to propitiate her. As we practiced in his office for Roger's trial, he took a savage pleasure in correcting my every mistake. When the phone rang, once for an in-house call, his face would brighten then fall. Because it was never Laura. On her calendar—the resemblance to a scorecard was inescapable--fewer and fewer pencil notations appeared for Jake, more for me.

Whatever guilt I felt, whatever pity I had for Jake, reduced now to the state of Turnage or, formerly, me, was swept away by what I'd have to call a continual state of ecstasy, like the crawfish's 24-hour-long orgasm.

Before, a week might gape between our visits. Now I saw Laura every night. As soon as the sun set, I'd speed to my apartment, and she'd follow. Sometimes I met her at the gate and I'd be inside her before we reached the top of the stairs. Wearing my robe, she made chilled gazpacho. In bed, I rolled the icy bottle of Chardonnay over her warm thighs where it left dewdrops of cool that I kissed away.

One night after lovemaking, as we lay facing each other, I brought up marriage. Before, I would never have been so foolhardy, knowing she'd exploit any weakness, mock any sentiment, but I sensed something had changed.

"I know it's crazy," I half-apologized.

"Crazier than this?" she asked, and I left it where it was.

To incite me, she wore briefer and briefer clothes to the office, short skirts of clingy material, bare-backed blouses with no bra. One gold outfit looked like a negligee. Her nipples, hard from the air conditioning, were impossible to ignore. It required no imagination to envision her naked.

One morning I saw Jake and Laura arguing near the espresso machine. Her outfit was particularly brief that day, and Turnage abandoned work as he tracked her through the halls.

"Go home and put on some damn clothes," Jake ordered.

"I don't believe you're my couturier," she answered breezily. Before, I'd been the target of her arch little arrows, and I almost felt sorry for my father.

"I do believe I'm your boss," Jake said, more loudly, trying to summon his Medusa-stare.

"Oh, is that what you are now?" she answered, unfazed, and walked away. I was at the far end of the hall. Turnage, who'd been gorging his optic nerve on Laura, wasn't so fortunate.

"What the fuck are you looking at?" my father thundered, and as Turnage debated whether to answer or run, my father grabbed Turnage's throat and slammed him back against the wall. He slid to the floor like a hawk of phlegm.

That day, as every day, I waited for her afternoon visit. She knocked, a mockery of propriety, and sat in my client chair. Then—the rite was as unvarying as a catechism— she started touching herself, strumming her already hard nipples, stroking her bare legs. I forced myself just to watch. She edged her hand higher and her dress—today the flesh-colored faux-negligee—gathered in silky folds. But that day I knew I wasn't going to wait for dark.

Quick as an animal, I moved to her, lifted her from the chair.

"We can't," she whispered. "Not here." But I knew Laura and she knew me. I quickly stripped off the dress, her hose, her panties. I wanted her completely naked, utterly compromised, as I would be.

"The door," she gasped as we slipped to the floor.

"Locked," I lied.

We were both so excited, and so scared, that it didn't take long. But just before we came, I saw the door open, not wide, but wide enough. And I'd been wrong; he didn't have the stomach to watch.

Later that day, as Jake and I silently worked in his office, I saw him get up and stare out the window. I heard him say something, very low.

"Are you talking to me?"

"You're off the case."

"Roger wants me on."

"Get out. Send Turnage up."

And so Turnage became second chair on Wittenhurst, and Jake assumed his usual position, on top, though of course as events transpired, he'd have very little time left to concern himself with other people's problems.

And now, on trial for his life, no time at all for a son who was a fool and a fuckup. Now that I'd let the ring into evidence, he had even more cause to fire me, not to say disown me. Laura was dead because of me. Jake would be too. I drove over through the still-muggy January rain, expecting it to be my last morning to pick up my client.

He was in the foyer waiting for my mother, who operated on SBT, southern belle time. I pretended to study the antique botanicals on the wall, while a few feet away he silently emanated rage. I prayed that for once she would not go through three wardrobe changes.

"Am I fired?" I finally made myself ask.

"Why shouldn't I?" he asked, his first words to me in fifteen hours. His voice was very soft, the way it got when the next level was a roar.

"Lots of reasons." I'd had enough sense, at least, to prepare an argument. "Number one, you'll look desperate."

"Better that than a fool."

"Number two," I argued, "what kind of man hires his own son? A loving father. What kind of man fires his own son? A ruthless, domineering tyrant. The kind of man who doesn't care who he hurts. The kind of man who could kill the woman he loves. You want to send that message to the jury?"

"I considered that," he allowed. His face was impassive but I knew the law machine was processing every nuance.

"Number three," I pressed, "you'll have to wait six months for another attorney." That would get him, I knew. "If—big if—you could find one you could work with."

"Why the hell didn't you consult me?" he snapped. I knew then he'd keep me on, that he felt he had no other choice.

"I wanted to surprise you."

"You succeeded. It goes without saying that what you did was quite possibly fatal."

I looked over at Jake, and was suddenly overwhelmed, by his utter familiarity. There was no separation between us. For some reason my eyes filled with tears and I quickly turned back to the wall, hoping he'd be disgusted, would say something to infuriate me, anything to stop what I was feeling. I could count on him for that, couldn't I?

But all he said was, "Your mother's on about dress number four," and he went to get her.

Martin Rosen, M.D., Ph.D, was a compact man with short-cropped gray hair and an air of barely suppressed impatience. Nothing was wasted about Rosen, his precise movements, his abrupt speech, his valuable ($5000 an hour) time. From reading his testimony in previous trials, I knew that his religion was science and his god infallible. He answered each of Sessums' questions with his head tilted back, eyes half-dimmed as if bored by the foregone conclusion of a guilty verdict. His findings were so certain that jury appeal was beneath him.

Though Sessums questioned Rosen for three hours on the elaborate procedures employed by Advanced Biotest and the reliability of DNA evidence in general, the greatest impact was made by Rosen's answers to the two simplest questions.

"Did you find tissue scrapings on the defendant's ring?"

"Yes. The tissue was identified, by DNA testing, as belonging to Laura Niles."

"What are the statistical odds it was her tissue?"

"The scientific certainty is 200 million to one."

After more questions about those numbers until they became as familiar to the jurors as their birthdays, and after my feeble cross-examination, Judge Barber recessed. The next day was the prosecution's final witness, Jake's former attorney, Tommy Munger. That night at the firm I typed my scrawled notes after a lengthy session in Jake's office. Jake hadn't brought up Rosen's testimony, or how it had come to be admitted. Another in the long catalogue of my father's admirable traits was his refusal to harbor a grudge. A quick flare of anger and he moved on. Unfortunately for all concerned, I'd inherited my mother's more convoluted makeup.

"Tomorrow's going to be your toughest," my father cautioned, appearing in my doorway. In court I'd seen Munger garrote hostile witnesses with nuance and contradiction and had no doubt he could do the same to a hostile attorney.

"Hard to believe you two used to be friends."

"Munger doesn't have friends."

I recalled similar words from Sarah Loretta about Laura.

"Better get some sleep," my father advised.

"Got miles to go."

He unexpectedly laid his hand on my shoulder, left it there a moment and walked out. I turned to look after him, then watched through the window to make sure he got safely into his car.

Three doors down, no light spilled out from Munger's office, and the darkness pulled me out of my chair. I moved softly along the carpeted hall, remembering the night of my mother's birthday when he'd surprised us both, stepping out of the elevator at 3 a.m.

I forced myself to go inside his shadowed office. It felt like the tidy lair of a snake. I sat down across the desk and stared at his empty chair, trying to overcome my nervousness—hell, my fear—over having to face him in court. Seconds later, mistaking the clang of the Saint Charles streetcar outside for the chime of the elevator, I jumped up and bolted back to my office. Three years old again, and the monster was in my closet.

The next morning Munger took the stand, wearing his favorite black suit. "Your honor," Sessums began, "given Mr. Munger's close relationship with the defendant, I ask that he be declared a hostile witness."

We had decided not to object. Although it might appear to the jury that Sessums was having to press Munger to testify, it wasn't worth raising suspicions about why Jake's law partner had quit being his attorney.

After establishing at length that Munger and Jake had been partners and friends for twenty years, Sessums set about his main business: establishing Jake's potential for murder. "Last March, Gary Longo, a CPA who visited the office, made advances toward the victim, correct?"

"Yes." Munger seemed pained to be testifying against Jake.

"You were in the firm conference room later when the defendant walked by with her."

"Yes."

"And you overheard the defendant threaten to kill her if she ever let another man touch her."

"I believe the threat was merely rhetorical."

"Did he grab her wrist?"

"Yes."

"Did she try to break loose?"

"Yes." Couldn't the jury see he was lying?

"Did the defendant threaten to kill her, Mr. Munger?"

A hesitation and, again, the feigned reluctance: "Yes."

They still didn't have motive. But they damn well had predilection.

My cross-examination of Munger, at first, went as planned. I'd practiced it enough, God knew, and all I had to put in the jury's mind was that Munger had a reason to lie.

"You would become senior partner of the firm if Mr. Cameron went to jail, wouldn't you?" I posed after my preliminary questions, during which Munger made every effort to be helpful, overanswering and, not coincidentally, breaking my rhythm.

"Yes, but it is a very small firm." He smiled, an uncharacteristically winning smile. "There aren't a lot of people to supervise. Only five of us now."

"But you would have no one to supervise you, correct?" I was asking, not telling, but I couldn't help it.

"As you know, Kyle, the firm doesn't work that way. Jake and I decide by consensus. I have my cases, Jake has his."

"You wanted to add more associates, didn't you, and Mr. Cameron didn't. There was no consensus there." I was supposed to build to this point, but suddenly all my questions seemed unpersuasive and I had skipped right to the end with nothing else to back me up. At that point Munger took control. I could feel it go.

"We frequently considered expanding the firm," he explained with sham thoughtfulness. "Every time we hired a new associate, it was accompanied by growing pains, as when I agreed, out of friendship, to let Jake take you on when no one else would because of your law school grades."

Sessums smiled then, I knew, without even having to look. The night before, with Charlie Dumaine's perfect timing, NightWitness News had broadcast the details of my wretched school record to the world, contradicting Jake's public front that he'd wanted me because I was the best lawyer he could find. And I was about to prove Munger right, being utterly incapable of deciding if his comment was objectionable, knowing only how objectionable it was to me.

"But you were angry nonetheless, weren't you?" I asked, plunging on.

"Jake and I've disagreed over numerous matters," Munger continued with utter composure. "All resolved amicably. Otherwise we couldn't have stayed partners for twenty years."

I had nowhere to go. "No? You argued over tactics for this case."

"I believe that's protected by the attorney-client privilege, Kyle." Munger smiled condescendingly.

I flushed. What he'd—what I'd—communicated, once again, to the jury was that whenever I had the floor, they were not in competent hands, that they shouldn't trust any direction I led them in. When I glanced their way, a few looked embarrassed for me, the rest hostile.

"No further questions," I mumbled, cutting our losses if any remained to be cut.

I sat, looking to Jake for a reaction. He gave none.

"Redirect, Mr. Sessums?"

"No need, your honor. The People rest." Sessums sat, well pleased.

"You were right. Munger's tough," I said to Jake, trying to forestall his fury and criticism. When he just nodded, his eyes tired, instead of berating me, that was the moment I knew my father had changed, and I hoped it wasn't forever, because even my fear of his highest pitch of rage and disgust with me was preferable to my fear of seeing him weak.

Judge Barber adjourned for the weekend. As we walked out, we passed Sessums, surrounded by reporters, prolonging his moment. "Fingerprints don't lie. Neither does DNA. With his partner's devastating testimony, this will be Jake Cameron's last trial."

I looked at his aging face. I couldn't deceive myself that his decline stemmed solely from Laura's murder and the trial. It had begun in August when he learned I was seeing her and it had slowly pulled him down. I alone had set it into motion, couldn't have helped it according to Evan's philosophy. But not mine, not while I had a breath left.

When the reporters spotted Jake and swarmed over onto us, I shielded him from the onslaught, more like a parent than a lawyer or a son. Charlie Dumaine, I noticed, was uncharacteristically hanging back, as if there were no more meat to be plucked from my bones.

We dropped my mother off, then rode in silence to the office. Monday we would put on our case, such as it was.

"What are you going to do after this is over?" I asked finally. I was simply, by force of will, going to assume it would be over and life would continue in some semblance of what it had been. I was going to do more than assume it; I was going to compel it to happen.

"I'll take that when it comes," Jake replied, ever pragmatic. He didn't, as would most, say that it was never going to be over; Jake didn't indulge in self-pity. When we parked behind the firm, he made no movement to get out of the car, and I saw this was a rare moment when we could talk, father to son or whatever the hell relationship we had.

"You've taught me a lot," I said. "I don't just mean law."

He looked over at me and, if I didn't imagine it, I saw a smile. "You can lead a horse to water."

"Make that mule." Now I had a smile, not a big one, but enough I think for him to see it.

"Mule it is. Give me an ornery mule any day."

Then his face settled back into its familiar grim lines as he readied himself to go inside. His law firm, once his undisputed kingdom, now was a second front, one that he was also losing.

"Mom's still for you. And me. For what that's worth."

He looked at me a long moment, then gave me his nod. I felt an unaccountable joy.

We went inside, and Jake headed straight for his aerie. We'd abandoned the conference room for reasons unexplained by Jake until he had the investigator sweep it for hidden recorders. Everyone at the firm seemed a potential traitor, even the poor, addled runner, who worshipped Jake. I saw Turnage step without knocking into Munger's office. Given Munger's Prussian insistence on decorum, this informality told me everything about their new relationship.

Jake and I worked together until midnight, when he said, to my surprise, "I'm going to leave it with you."

Around 2:30, after a twenty-hour day, I fumbled open my apartment door. Inside, I went through my routine, dead bolts, alarm, air conditioning, not bothering to turn on the lights. I shed my clothes in a heap, then froze—quit breathing—when I heard someone else breathing. It was happening—what every sane French Quarter resident expected and rehearsed for. I edged toward the drawer where I kept the gun. I would blast that fucker through the French doors. My hand was wrapping around its reassuring shape when the high beam from a car below lit the room.

Alison looked up at me from the bed, lying under the sheet. She didn't say anything, didn't need to.

I slipped under the covers, caressed her hair, as I knew she liked for me to do.

"I love you, Kyle. I never stopped."

I kissed her, softly at first. Then I stripped off her camisole and panties, rough, the way I would've liked to have done with Laura. Alison gasped, her eyes blurry with desire. She lay there, open and vulnerable.

"My pirate."

I moved over her, angry at her for being who she was, before I transformed her in my mind to who I needed her to be.

When I worked up the character to call Evan, remarkably he talked to me, though it was mostly in fractured aphorisms. Alison never mentioned what she'd told him, nor his reaction, though both were uncomfortably easy to imagine. Alison was a believer in meant-to-be, and nothing Evan did could roll back time to put him next door, climbing out the window for a precocious assignation, while adolescent Alison watched.

"He who lasts laughs last," Evan quipped, and I was surprised not to hear the familiar computer keys preserving the gem.

"I'm not laughing," I said, trying to evoke a human response, after which, maybe—I was a veritable Don Quixote after semblances—some vestige of friendship might be reestablished.

"Irresistible object met irresistible object."

"Are you writing?"

"Erased it."

"The novel?"

"All 345,112 words. All 27 drafts. All 149 returned manuscripts covered with coffee, blintz jism, and, if I'm not mistaken, actual sperm, though I'm not certain of its species of origin."

"You crazy bastard. That was a great novel. You always said John Kennedy Toole should've stuck it out." Evan regarded *A Confederacy of Dunces* as the top novel of the last century, though its author never enjoyed its success, having killed himself before it ever saw print.

"Toole's mistake was trying."

"You forget. I've got a copy."

For the first time the distance left his voice. "I didn't forget. I expect you to give it to me."

"Can't do that."

"If we were ever friends, you will."

I don't know whether it was the abjectness in his voice or the use of the past tense, but later I did as he asked, placing it on his doorstep like a baby left to die in a dumpster. As requested, I didn't knock. I listened through the door, hoping to hear typing, but all I heard was the moronic television, some mindless but commercially viable sitcom.

I put the copy I'd made of the novel in a locked drawer of my desk at home. I knew too well the irrevocability of desperate actions.

I worked straight through the weekend preparing to put on our case. Jake came up late Saturday afternoon for an hour but just sat in silence unless I asked a question.

Around 2:00 that night I finished typing my notes, then opened my drawer. In it was one of Turnage's photos, the only one I'd not been able to make myself destroy. She looked as if she were only sleeping. I picked it up and stared a long time.

As I drove home, I slowed when I reached the turnoff to Prytania. I looked down the street, as I did every night. This time I turned.

Standing on her front porch in the shadows, I unpeeled the no-cross police tape and unlocked her door with my key. In the yard, the crepe myrtle blossoms were long gone and the branches were bare of leaves.

I stood in the dark at the foot of her bed, remembering the one night we'd made love on it, and Jake's call and her telling Jake, as I lay beside her, that she loved him. I opened her dresser and touched her lingerie. I caressed her dice and cards, then took them. Mementoes, all I had of her, excepting my scar.

I breathed in her perfume deeply. "Damn you, Laura Niles," I said and slammed my fist into the wall.

I went home to my balcony to let the poison seep from my cells. As I drank my bourbon—the first since Jake hired me—I took Laura's cards from my pocket and held them. I turned over the top card. Ace of hearts. I made a noise resembling a laugh, then turned over another. In the center of the deck, a small block had been cut out of a third of the cards, about two inches long, an inch wide, less than a quarter inch deep.

What had she put there? A note? A photo? Not much room for money, not enough to make her desecrate her father's keepsake. It was the size of something very familiar to me. I could almost feel it with my tactile sensory memory as I held my fingers apart.

When I went in for another drink, I noticed my small tape recorder on the desk, identical to every lawyer's in the firm, and felt compelled to pick it up. Opening it, I saw why. The microcassette inside fit perfectly within the carved-out space in Laura's deck of cards.

I drove to the firm and played every cassette in Laura's office. On one tape still in her recorder, she'd dictated a motion for the Duval rape case, and I listened to every legal word, as intent on her unearthly voice as if she'd been begging me for sex or even love. Predictably, the tape contained nothing but arid law, but I pocketed it, another memento, and softly closed her door.

Sunday night I went to my parents' house, our last supper before we began our case. Eunice cooked my father's favorite, redfish courtbullion, and my father forced himself to eat, fuel for tomorrow. Mom ate nothing, and her thinness made me feel as if I were watching her die before my eyes. She rose, unsteadily, and I moved to help her up. She kissed me on the cheek. I saw no evidence of the crisis strength the psychiatrist said she'd have.

"Goodnight, you two," she said, the first words she'd spoken. As she walked past Jake, he held out his hand and she took it, squeezed it lightly and left.

"Going to do some work," my father muttered and went toward his study. His wine glass was untouched; Jake confronted his enemies, within himself and without, unaided. I finished my wine and had another; I wasn't strong enough to go it alone. I also needed it to prepare for what I had to do the next morning.

On the way out, I walked past Jake's office, expecting to see him absorbed in work. But he was asleep in his wing-backed chair, looking more grandfatherly than the Tiger I was accustomed to. As I studied his face, so vulnerable in repose, he awoke and looked over at me.

"How you holding up over there, Podner?" he asked.

"You haven't called me that in awhile, Dad." How often did I call him that?

"How do you think your mother's holding up?"

"I talked to Dr. Hart this morning. He says she may crash when it's over but not yet."

"I know you'll take care of her," he said. He looked worn to the marrow. "If it comes to that." If they convict me, imprison me, execute me.

I nodded, suddenly unable to speak, tears being the last thing either of us needed.

Then he asked, “You think we have any kind of shot?”

I looked over sharply. We’d reversed roles. “We’re going to win this thing, hear? All we need is reasonable doubt it wasn’t you, and we’ll get that tomorrow.”

I gave him a thumbs-up. But he just sat at the desk as if pole-axed, his eyes far away.

The next morning I watched the twelve skeptics on the jury file in. Fourteen-year-old Vic with his blue spiked hair and sideways list had provided them a momentary distraction from Jake, but he lacked the wile and wit to frame a doghouse much less a criminal attorney. Somehow I had to create reasonable doubt. Certainly none existed now. By the time Judge Barber asked if we were ready to put on our case, I’d managed to cram nonessentials, such as conscience, into my brain’s capacious back room. There wasn’t space left up front for anything but the means and the end.

Jake leaned over. “I wish there were another way.”

“There isn’t.” I stood.

“Defense calls Ginger Allred.” Two rows behind us sat Ginger’s parents, whom I liked. Her father, Jimmy, was a stevedore though he was in his 60’s, unloading huge crates of bananas as they came onto the wharves on overhead conveyer belts from South American freighters. He told me he’d gotten off work especially to see that smart daughter of his testify and that he’d told all his buddies. He laughed, saying he wore his funeral suit for the occasion. Ginger’s mother, Bev, the source of Ginger’s voluptuous looks, was a café waitress with a deep Texas twang, who'd fought aging hard but didn't have the money to keep her natural gifts in condition. Her hair was self-tinted a flame red, and she'd miscalculated in thinking her bright pink suit would set it off. Ginger would note it, might even inwardly cringe, but she wouldn't be ashamed. She was from a world where children loved their parents and never doubted that it was returned.

Jake looked away as Ginger, dressed in Armani for the photographers, walked past him and took her seat. I began slow and friendly, establishing that Ginger was a good lawyer who'd been with Jake for twelve years, since she'd passed the bar, that she'd worked her way through school, and that she loved criminal law.

"Was Laura Niles an asset to the firm?" I asked her. We were on familiar ground, having practiced all these questions and responses several times.

"Only with her legal skills. She was bad for morale. Whenever a good case came in, she rushed to Jake and he gave it to her."

"Did the rest of the firm know she and Jake were having an affair?"

"I don't know if the men did—it was clear to me, almost from the first."

"Did Jake give her a disproportionate number of good cases?"

"Yes."

"That must've been very frustrating for you."

Ginger looked at me, puzzled. We hadn't rehearsed this.

"Maybe a little." She did know, when taken off guard, to qualify her answer.

"The day after she was killed, did you ask to take over one of her cases?"

"I may have." Smart girl, to keep hedging.

"Did you request in the next firm meeting, the day after you discovered Laura dead, for Jake to assign you the Duval rape case?"

"Yes."

"After you found Laura's body, did you call her a total bitch?"

Ginger knew she was being ambushed then. Jimmy and Bev shifted uncomfortably in their seats; though they didn't know exactly what I was doing, they knew their daughter didn't like it.

"It was just an expression," she said. "You know that."

"Please answer the question. Yes or no."

"Yes."

"Were you in love with Jake Cameron?"

"He was a very good boss."

"Were you in love with Jake Cameron?"

"I cared about him."

"Did you have an affair with him?"

My mother, whom Jake had prepared for this, remained stalwart. Behind me, I was sure, Bev and Jimmy were frozen in pain for their daughter.

Ginger didn't want to answer. I pressed her. "You had an affair with him, didn't you?"

Sessums leaped up. "Objection. He's leading his own witness."

"Overruled," said Judge Barber. "I believe she's a hostile witness at this point."

Now that I was allowed to ask her leading questions, my job was to slam them into her, one after another, bruising her with my hard voice and arousing her anger. The jury needed to see her temper flare, enough combustion to kill Laura Niles.

Jake stared at his hands when I held up a packet of pink envelopes he'd given me. "I have your letters indicating you had an affair with Jake Cameron for five years."

Now that she was finally faced with the incontrovertible evidence, it was almost a relief to have somebody say it.

"Yes. We had an affair," she said, blinking back tears.

"Until Laura Niles seduced him over a year ago and filled your shoes, correct?"

"Yes."

"And she got all the good cases even though you had ten years' more experience."

"Yes." She was showing a little anger.

"And your office got moved down to first floor and hers upstairs so she could be closer to Jake." I knew all the sore spots to punch, all the indignities.

"Yes." Her cheeks were flushed, her jaws tight.

"Laura Niles was not friendly to you, was she. She was not a gracious winner." I was telling, not asking.

"Never."

"You hated her and loved him."

"I didn't hate her."

"No? She was eleven years younger, her looks hadn't started to fade, she got all the good cases and the man you loved. You certainly stood to benefit from her death. Didn't you?"

My eyes were hard. I didn't look away until Ginger said, almost snarling, "We all did."

My job was done. The judge recessed for the day. Jake, my mother and I escaped into an elevator as Ginger, eye makeup smeared, was swarmed by video cams. Jake watched, pained, as Jimmy and Bev stood protectively around her, helping her absorb the body blows of a national journalistic assault. They held their heads high, knowing that their friends and priest and Bev's customers and Ginger's business associates would all be watching. Jake's father had been a truck driver, a teamster and a family man like Jimmy, and Jake hadn't capitulated happily, not until I'd pressured him ruthlessly, convincing him that Ginger could never be indicted for Laura's murder because no evidence led to her. Nor, according to the investigator I'd hired, did any lead to Tommy Munger.

I forced myself to watch the locusts strip Ginger bare, just one of the afflictions that issued from my decision to take Laura Niles from my father. I could no more cure them than prevent what more would follow. All I could do was try to save my father.

Jake and I debriefed in the parking garage while my mother waited in the Jag.

"I was right, wasn't I? Admit it," I demanded. I was not going to let him weaken, not from discouragement or from guilt over sacrificing Ginger.

"You destroyed her. I'll give you that. Killer instinct."

"Just like you taught me.

"And then some."

"I'm on a roll. Mom's up tomorrow."

"No, she's not."

"What are you talking about?"

"We've got a shot now," he said. "Not much of one but a shot. I've changed my mind. We're not calling Nola."

"She wants to testify. She wants to help you."

"Frankly, I don't care what she wants. She's not on trial for her life. Sessums'll split her open like an oyster."

"But without Mom, you have no alibi. I was right about Ginger. I'm right about this too. I can do it. I've rehearsed her." Suddenly I found myself back in the inferior position, and I didn't care for it.

"She's the kind of witness who can sink your whole case. I've seen it happen too many times. End of discussion."

"You said I was running the show."

"I said we were partners. I'm senior partner. Tomorrow you fuck up their ring evidence. Is that understood?"

I stared in fury as he got into the driver's seat and took my mother home. Who did he think had given him his shot if not me?

That night, finding myself a bit less inclined to work for Jake's release, I took thirty minutes off and strolled down Bourbon Street, where I saw every type of faceless love: a veiny-legged prostitute disappearing into the shadows with her john, barkers in doors hooking tourists inside with glimpses of onstage flesh, a hardware conventioneer leering down the blouse of a drunken college girl. New Orleans being a big small town, I was surprised I didn't see someone from my lifetime there.

Then I did. Walking back up Royal, I passed a thin girl in a skimpy skirt, talking on her cell phone. It took me a moment to realize it was Sarah Loretta, shaky, coming down too fast.

She was making a pitch, possibly to a dealer or to a money source. I could tell because she was arguing with the same stance and gestures as the night she'd tried to finagle a drink out of the bartender at the Demimonde. When she hung up the phone, she smiled, satisfied, just as she'd smiled after Laura had handed her the envelope.

"Sarah Loretta," I called. When she turned and recognized me, the strangest look passed over her face.

"Are you following me?" she asked, her bluster gone.

"I live in the Quarter. Out for a walk."

She tried to calculate whether or not I could be telling the truth but she was too far gone.

"Did you get your money?" I asked. "From the person you called?"

"What do you know about it?" She was trembling, whether from fear or needing a fix I didn't know.

"I know you were blackmailing Laura Niles." It was a guess but, I thought, a reasonable one.

"How would you know that?"

"She told me."

That made her smile. "You don't know shit, pretty boy."

A taxi approached, and she raised her hand to hail it, ever the survivor. It swerved to the curb amidst a flurry of honks. Sarah Loretta stepped into the backseat, opening her legs in my direction to reveal she wore no panties, laughing when I looked.

In our cloistered little firm, it was, of course, inevitable that I'd run into Ginger. I avoided thinking about how unpleasant it was going to be, and would continue to be, just as I'd swept aside considerations of our friendship. My father had been my only concern.

Now, however, came the consequences, and sooner rather than later. I'd hoped she wouldn't be at the firm the next morning, would take some time off, like a decade, but that wouldn't be like Ginger. Confrontation was her style, with all the winds and thunder of a tropical storm. Sure enough, her dented Mercedes coupe, bright red with its license tag "LAWGIRL" was in its spot.

I took the back stairs to my office, trying to avoid her until time came to leave for trial. I phoned Myrt, asking her to bring me coffee. Ginger's office was near the espresso machine, and I would be easy prey there, like an antelope devoured at the water hole.

By 8:00 I felt safe enough to look out into the hall and duck into the restroom. Turnage was in there, trying to form a side part in his hair, same as every morning.

"Go for the throat and then some," he greeted me, grinning widely. "Man, I wouldn't be you for all the pussy in China."

"Have you talked to her?" I was reduced to gathering intelligence from Turnage.

"Hell no. Scared to, and I didn't even fuck over her. Who came up with that little razor up the ass, you or the Jake man?"

"Me." It was all mine and I wasn't going to pass it off to Jake.

"Whew," Turnage said with exaggerated awe. "And you two were supposed to be friends. Remind me never to piss you off."

"Don't piss me off."

At that moment, Ginger entered the restroom. Her emotions were always easy to read and today they were exclamation points. Turnage literally ran out. Under the bright fluorescent lights, everything seemed to freeze. Her hand flashed out. I knew she owned a gun—owned several.

Her fist connected neatly with my mouth, a very strong punch for a woman, and I staggered back against the sink, blood dripping from my split lip. I waited for the next punch, not raising my arms to defend myself, just holding a handkerchief to my lip.

"You're a cold-blooded little son of a bitch," she said.

I nodded.

"I used to think you were too nice to be a lawyer but let me tell you, sonny boy, you're prime material."

"I'm sorry. I know it doesn't mean much."

"You're damn right it doesn't mean much. You're a devious little bastard. Ruthless as hell."

She studied me carefully, some insight percolating underneath all that rage. "A devious little bastard," she repeated. "I've watched you fuck up a lot of things. You're a bright kid. Somebody with your brains couldn't fail the bar twice unless they were trying."

"I don't know what you're talking about." I'd forgotten how damn smart she was.

"What else are you trying to fuck up? Jake's trial?"

"No. Hell no."

"And why?" She looked at me. "Who killed Laura, Kyle?"

"I don't know."

"I don't think it was Jake."

"I don't either."

She looked at me for a long moment, nodding her head as the cylinders clicked into place. "Don't tank this trial. Or I'll shoot your balls off, one at a time."

I nodded. I knew Ginger was a very literal person and that she had not only the resolve to do it but the aim.

I watched her leave. She was crazy. Why would I fail the bar on purpose? What the hell else did Ginger know? Nothing. Anything she'd know would be supposition.

I looked at my lip; the bleeding had stopped. I washed the blood from my hands, and, unlike Lady Macbeth's, it came right off.

My first witness of the morning was Leo Altadonna, a manufacturing jeweler for thirty years. He had a warm, hearty personality that I hoped the jurors would associate with Jake.

"How is a ring copied, Mr. Altadonna?"

"All it requires is RTV rubber compound and one hour to make the mold."

"Only one hour?"

"No more."

"Would it require a trained jeweler to copy it?"

"Oh, no. It's a fairly simple process. You can buy the compound at any hobby shop. You mold it around the ring and let it harden. Slice the mold in two and you have two perfect halves of the ring. Any manufacturing jeweler can make the ring from the mold.

I held up Jake's wedding ring in its plastic evidence bag. "Could this ring be copied with RTV rubber compound in one hour?"

He inspected it. "Easily."

"So this ring—supposedly Mr. Cameron's wedding ring—could be a copy and no one would know?"

Sessums leapt up. "Objection. There's been no evidence whatsoever that the ring is not genuine."

"That's exactly what I'm establishing, Your Honor."

"Overruled. The witness may answer."

"No one but God would know if this ring were a copy or the original ring."

Jake nodded almost imperceptibly in satisfaction. "Good boy," he wrote on a pad, now that I was again firmly in yoke.

My next witness, dependable Ben, the fitness counselor from the gym, bounded to the stand. He, like Mr. Altadonna, should be an easy witness, but Ben was so cooperative that the jury might discount his testimony. To counteract this, I stayed at counsel table, creating an illusion of distance between us. A good idea, even if it was Jake's.

"Does Mr. Cameron wear his wedding ring when he works out?" I asked Ben, whom I'd instructed to wear his work outfit—a gold "Crescent City Fitness Center" T-shirt, black pants and tennis shoes. Not only did the uniform suit him and make him feel comfortable, but it also made him an authority figure in the eyes of the jury.

"Never. He leaves his ring in his locker, ever since last year."

"What happened last year?"

"The ring got caught in a weight machine and nearly took his finger off. We offered to pay his medical bills but he said it wasn't our fault." Nice touch. That rarest of all creatures, the gentleman lawyer.

"Does he ever work out for more than one hour at a time?"

"Monday, Wednesday and Friday. Two hours."

"Two hours. Leaving his ring in the locker."

"Yes," he said, nodding emphatically. Ben had told me when I joined the fitness center that I was lucky to have a father as nice as Jake. On the stand he was doing all he could for him. I frowned, to show he was getting too enthusiastic. He made himself quit nodding.

"How can you be sure he's there two hours?"

"Our computer registers the time a member checks in and leaves."

"In the last year, up until the day of the victim's death, how many times was Mr. Cameron at the gym for an hour and a half or more?"

"Ninety-three."

"Does anyone other than Mr. Cameron have a key to that locker?"

"The fitness center has two extras behind the desk, and the men in the law firm each have a key."

"And their names are...?"

"Jeb Turnage. Of course you. And Tommy Munger."

I paused, looking at the jury to indicate that Ben had just given them something pretty damn significant. I still felt there was a link between Munger and Laura. And Jake was willing to let me hang Munger if I could.

"During any of those ninety-three times when Mr. Cameron was at the fitness center an hour and a half or longer, was Jeb Turnage, Tommy Munger or I at the fitness center for over an hour?"

Though Munger despised the gym, he'd gone under duress because one of his clients felt safer talking in the steam room. To maintain his dignity, Munger had kept on his T-shirt and boxer shorts while his flabby, naked, drug-pushing client sweated and told him lies.

"Yes," Ben said. "Our computer shows all of you were there."

"Good boy," Jake whispered again as I sat down. I suddenly became too busy with my notes to look at him.

Sessums wasn't able to extract much from dependable Ben other than the fact that he couldn't personally be sure Mr. Cameron always left his ring in his locker because he wasn't always on duty. Sessums tried to get him to admit that the gym offered no areas where a member could stay hidden for an hour while he copied a ring, but Ben insisted that someone could stand in a toilet stall for an hour without drawing attention to himself.

When Ben was through, I stood. "The defense calls Nola Cameron."

Jake grabbed my arm. "No, dammit."

Behind us, my mother stood. She looked too delicate to withstand a cross exchange with a deliveryman, much less a battering from Sessums. Nonetheless, Jake, not Nola, was the parent in danger, and he needed an alibi. Jake had been adamant about keeping her off the stand. But I'd been right about Ginger, hadn't I? And Jake wrong about Melorette?

"Withdraw," Jake hissed. His hand closed tighter on my arm, like the talon of a hawk. My mother still stood, almost swaying with uncertainty.

"Withdraw the witness," he ordered.

I reluctantly obeyed.

"Break," Jake muttered intensely.

"Request a fifteen-minute break, Your Honor."

"I believe we could use more than a break," she said and recessed for the day.

Jake followed me into an anteroom, practically on my heels, and slammed the door. "I told you, goddammit, I told you, but you wouldn't listen. You deliberately disobeyed my order."

"We'd practiced it—"

"Sure you had, in your usual slipshod half-assed way. I never had any intention of calling Nola. That alibi was just for the press and to humor her." He stepped closer, into my space. "I told you she's the kind of witness who can sink a case." He looked at me steadily. "Or is that your intention?"

"What the hell does that mean?"

"It means you're either the stupidest fuck I've ever seen or smarter than I ever dreamed."

"Which would you prefer?" We were back to square one in our dealings. For a second I thought he was going to hit me. Instead, he said, "I thought you'd changed, but I was wrong. You don't have it in you."

I stared at the floor.

"It's too late in the trial to fire you," Jake continued, as hard as I'd ever seen him. "But from here on out I'm running this show. Jake's way. And you're just the puppet. I write the questions, you ask them. Your input is nil. Your only decision is what tie to wear in the morning, and that's subject to my approval. Understood?"

I didn't say anything. I'd forgotten what I'd always known, that you never grow up. The only change is your fuckups get bigger.

"Is that understood?" he roared, startling me. I'd also forgotten that I was afraid of him.

"Understood," I snapped, trying to summon manly anger as a camouflage.

I stormed out through the halls, as humiliated as the child he'd painted me to be. Taking a back route, I managed to avoid all reporters except the one who'd interviewed me at our first press conference.

"Does your father still feel confident he has the best attorney he could get?"

"Fuck off, asshole," I said, shoving him away. His station ran the shot, bleeping my comments, though any speaker of the English language could read my lips.

Back at the office, I stormed into the lobby. The paralegal and the secretary who'd been dissecting my trial skills scattered, leaving Wendy up front.

"Kyle? Are you all right?" Wendy asked, my tender young advocate whose heart I'd sworn never to toy with.

"You want to get a drink, Wendy?"

"I'll be off in twenty minutes. Is that okay?"

"No."

Wendy hesitated, then picked up the phone. "Lynn, can you cover the desk?"

Soon we were at the F & M Patio Bar, and I was drinking bourbon, not beer, and running the pool table while Wendy cheered me on. I was shooting hard and the balls cracked angrily before falling into the hole.

"You're great, Kyle," Wendy said when I dropped the last ball in. There was no artifice about her. She truly thought I was wonderful. A long night of adoration, if not worship, would be required to build me up after my father's demolition job.

"Nothing half-assed about that," I told my unhappy opponent, a Tulane kid who looked like he could use a free meal. "I won. Pay up, friend." He handed over a twenty, the last spot of green in his wallet. I was teaching him not to gamble with what he couldn't afford to lose.

In Wendy's bedroom, with its sad little first-apartment decorations, I went the rest of the way downhill. In my career with women, this one made me feel the worst. But that didn't stop me.

"God you're good, God you're good," she said, what I needed to hear, as I held her wrists above her head and expertly made her come. She wore one of those rings with tiny semiprecious stones that only very young girls wear.

When I got home at 4 a.m., my message light was blinking. Jake had called after seeing me on the evening news and left a message, his voice barely in check: "Do not talk to any media. You've given the impression that my lawyer is out of control and therefore by inference that I am."

He hadn't called again and I didn't call him back. There was one message from Alison, "Kyle? Where are you?"

The next morning, looking very rough, I dragged in a half hour late to trial. I took my seat at the counsel table and gulped a glass of water.

"Glad you could make it, Mr. Cameron," Judge Barber said. Any possible goodwill she'd had for me, as an outgunned novice or for whatever reason, had dissipated minute by minute waiting for me. "I want to see counsel in chambers."

Jake and I walked together, a display for the jury.

"Should've started without me," I mumbled. "I'd just screw it up anyway." I felt and sounded age fifteen.

"Grow up." He sniffed the air. "You reek of pussy."

"Eau de Cameron," I replied, and we carried our little war right into Judge Barber's chambers.

"You honor, we regret the short notice," Sessums said, with the bland sincerity of the blatant liar, "but this witness only turned up yesterday. She's vital to our case."

What witness? I started to respond but Jake cut me off. "Mr. Sessums is known for trial by ambush," he argued. "He's likely had this witness lined up for weeks. Give me the opportunity and I'll prove it, your Honor."

"I'll do this," I actually elbowed my way in front of Jake while Sessums watched, no doubt in delight. "We're not prepared, your honor. I don't even know who the witness is."

She glared at me. "You might if you'd gotten here on time. I'm allowing the witness. You have until tomorrow to get prepared."

Jake closed his eyes. "It's over."

That night, whenever I had a break, I tried calling Alison from the office, but she never answered. Finally, in desperation, I called her parents' home, getting her still-chilly mother, who talked with Alison every day. She said she had no idea how she could be reached. As for Jake, he said more to the pizza delivery boy than to me.

It was after midnight when I got home and checked my answerphone. “Kyle, it’s me. My boss sent me to Atlanta, just overnight. I love you.”

The night was the longest since Laura’s murder. I called Mrs. Ford again for the name of Alison’s hotel but she hung up. In the dark front room, sitting in a chair looking out at Saint Peter Street, I watched the moon die. I was too far gone to drink.

The next morning I stopped by for Jake and my mother, as planned, a feeble array of family solidarity. There was little talk and even less solidarity. Mom looked panicked, and Jake was closed inside himself. As for me and my hard-won new confidence, it had whirled down the drain after my mother’s aborted testimony, with Jake’s appraisal of my character as a chaser. I wondered if I now stood outside his gate. As the judge took the bench, I saw Alison slip into a seat in back. She smiled encouragingly.

Ana Lopez was a sturdy Mexican woman who’d never before in her fifty years gone more than a few miles from her native village. Sessums had been very thorough. After he’d found her, he arranged her appearance for the moment of maximum impact. Now all his meticulous preparations would be rewarded. All his indignations would be vindicated. And there wasn’t a damn thing I could do.

“What is your occupation?” he asked in English, and the interpreter translated.

“I am a housekeeper,” she answered, “at the Hotel Americana in Cozumel, the nicest hotel there.

“Have you seen this man before?” he asked pointing at Jake and stating his name for the record.

"He stayed at the hotel the American Labor Day weekend."

He handed a photo of Laura to Ana Lopez.

"Have you ever seen this woman?"

"She was there also," she said.

"And were they together?"

Here it came.

"No."

"No? Who was she with?"

"Him." She pointed at me, delivering unto Sessums a grand motive for Jake to kill Laura, one directly substantiating Munger's testimony about Jake's murderous jealousy.

Sessums allowed himself a smile. "Let the record show she has identified the defense attorney, Kyle Cameron."

All twelve jurors stared at me, trying to absorb this revelation.

"Now, Mrs. Lopez, tell us what happened."

She told it very succinctly and simply. She didn't know all the details but she knew enough.

From his palm-secluded patio outside his adjacent room, Jake had watched Laura and me in our room until Laura came out in a thong bikini and headed to the beach. Then he intercepted her and caught her arm.

"Why are you doing this? Are you trying to make me crazy?" I overheard him through our open window. He wasn't even trying to keep his voice down.

Laura pulled her arm out of his grip as I ran outside.

"Leave her alone," I ordered.

"Stay away, Son. She doesn't want you. Let's go, Laura. Get your clothes." I stepped between them. He may have had her first, but he damn sure couldn't have her now, not after she'd flown down with me, not after I'd proposed. Not after I was winning.

"Get out of my way, Kyle," he said softly.

Eyes wild, I hit him. He wiped his mouth, and his hand came away bloody.

"Don't do this." He still hadn't put up his hands.

"Go for the throat, old man. Like you taught me."

I hit him again, a quick left jab. His eyes hardened, carnivorous, and his fist flashed out, knocking me to one knee. I got right back up, and we went round and round, him stronger, heavier, but amazingly quick with his left, bruising my right cheek and upper body.

I kept to my strategy from the night I'd beaten him in racquetball, jabbing, feinting, wearing the old man down. His nose was bleeding, then his mouth. I'd opened a cut over one eye, and it was closing fast. We would later tersely agree that I would wreck the Alfa to explain our injuries. Finally, Jake couldn't get his arms up another time and I pummeled him to the ground, a very accomplished boxer. Laura watched, strangely calm.

"El Viejo salio ese dia. Solo," Mrs. Lopez concluded.

The interpreter translated: "The old man left that day. Alone."

The jury stared at me like I was something from under a rock. So did my mother. Alison left.

Jake looked down at his ringless hands. For the first time in his life, he'd given up.

I had no questions of Mrs. Lopez, nor would I have been able to formulate them if I had. There were no nuances to her plainspoken account, no crevices to wheedle my way into and confuse the jury. Jake, whose fingerprints were on the murder weapon, whose ring was covered with Laura's DNA, now had a motive and I, his son and attorney, was it.

The courthouse hallway was a jungle of reporters, cameras, microphones. This was better than they'd ever hoped, one of those stories that people would read and then wonder, as I once would've wondered, how such a person as I could exist. Jake walked ahead of me with Nola, leaning, it seemed, on her frail frame.

"Who had her first?" one screamed.

"Was it worth it, Kyle?" yelled another.

And, from a network reporter who'd managed to worm her way right into Jake's face with her microphone, "Will you ever forgive your son?"

Jake just tried to keep moving, as through a deepening snow bank. I roughly pushed aside several reporters, trying to get ahead of him and Mom to run interference.

"Please let us through," I called out uselessly, as bulb after bulb popped in Jake's face, each one like a tiny electrical jolt.

One moment he was standing, the next he was crumpling up, supported only by the crush of reporters, who stepped aside for the photographers to get their shot. As they did, he fell to the floor. My mother screamed, again and again. Photographers swarmed over Jake like maggots. I threw them aside—they seemed weightless—to kneel by him, and they all had their shots—sin, betrayal, murder, and retribution.

My religious upbringing had been negligible. Jake was utterly lapsed, and my mother was only nominally an Episcopalian, which I gathered was regarded as more genteel. Jake's mother, my grandmother, died when I was no more than seven or eight, but she did not care much for gentility, and when I was left with her for the day, she invariably took me to church. She didn't say much about heaven, or even hell, only purgatory, which in her view constituted all of life.

The Coronary Care Unit at Touro Infirmary vindicated her belief. The place looked like a vast indoor refugee camp. Relatives huddled under blankets, some approximating sleep as they molded their torsos to stiff-backed chairs, others just silently enduring. Some people had lived there for weeks, as close as they could get to their loved ones.

It was only my first night and I knew I'd be one of those who never left, who waited for the tiniest shards of news and the twice-daily visits which could be capriciously delayed or even cancelled because of mysteries as unknowable to us as God's expectations.

I sat slumped, my natty tie askew. Next to me, my mother sat upright, unblinking, wound tight enough to implode. There'd been no words between us. Finally, after many hours, she said, "You killed him."

It was a knife, and no one could plunge it deeper. Her voice was flat, more terrible than anger. "None of this would've happened if you hadn't pushed him into her arms." She wasn't looking at me, probably couldn't bear to. "He would've come back to me."

"I did it for you," I said.

Now she did look at me. "Do you actually believe that, Kyle?"

I didn't answer.

In one corner of CCU was a wide-screen television, the gift of someone who'd served his time here. Only a few people, mostly kids, were watching, but when the 11:00 news came on, a small crowd gathered. I knew what was drawing the crowd. I didn't intend to join it, but my mother said, "Go see what they're saying about your father."

Perhaps twenty people pressed near the screen, bathed in its lurid glow as they watched the soon-to-be-classic footage of Jake, Mom and me fighting our way through the hallway crush, of Jake crumbling, of me yelling for help.

I realized it was national, not local news, when the anchor said, "We go to Charlene Dumaine in New Orleans."

Charlie was doing a stand-up outside the hospital. If I wished, I could walk a few feet to the window and see her. A few people by the TV looked at me, and whispers sped through the group. I watched Charlie, her first national spot.

"Charlene," asked the national anchor, "how did you discover Ana Lopez?"

"It's Charlie," she said, correcting the anchor without hesitation, "Charlie Dumaine." She addressed the camera, smooth, professional. She'd be going bigger places than New Orleans after this.

"It was instinct, Ron," she began. "I just knew there was something rotten at the center of this case, given the parties involved. I put out feelers. One of them led to Ana." Ana, first-name basis.

"So you informed the D.A.?"

"This past Friday," she reported, and the lie was swallowed nationwide without a burp. More accurately, it had been a month ago this past Friday, the night I saw them walking together to the Columns Hotel Bar. She'd been wearing the same black suit trimmed in brilliant red.

I could imagine Charlie in her snug-fitting custom explorer outfit, tromping into Ana's dusty little village. And then I didn't have to imagine it, because Charlie had taped the whole epochal encounter—hacking through jungle, the surprised villagers, then a dramatic zoom to the door of Ana's hovel. Charlie in every shot, wearing a chic red safari hat to set off tailored khakis.

"You had a lot of dead ends before this payoff," the national anchor fed her. "What kept you on the story?"

Charlie looked at the camera.

"Justice," she replied, without hesitation.

"Stroke," the doctor had told us as we sat in the CCU waiting room chairs that by constant occupation would come to be regarded to be ours. Jake was slipping in and out of a coma. If he survived—the doctor wouldn't hazard an opinion--he would be disabled, to what extent he didn't know.

I hadn't seen my father in three days, nor had I left the waiting room except to appear briefly in court to secure a continuance. Judge Barber was formally polite, as was Sessums, both not quite looking at me, as if I'd departed the pale of humanity.

The hospital only allowed one visitor per patient, and there was no question who that visitor would be. Each time I saw Mom return through the glass doors, I sat up, hoping for the slightest shading of good news, but she always said, "No change." That was all she said to me.

The other groups in the waiting room maintained a grim camaraderie, sharing newspapers and boxes of candy, grieving when someone was summoned to the front by the doctor for final bad news, then disappearing to be replaced by a new family who would be quickly absorbed into the group and the changeless days and nights.

But no one spoke to me. After Charlie's expose, a shortened version of which was shown every night with a medical update on Jake, they felt there was something repellent about me and my vigil. On the fourth day, when the nurse came by to announce the morning visit, I didn't move, waiting for my mother to join the rush of rumpled husbands, wives, children who pressed toward the door. Without looking at me, she said, "He asked for you."

At that moment, if I'd been asked to wager that there was a God in the universe and that He was good, I'd have bet my life on it. I followed the other relatives into CCU, washed my hands as instructed, and found my way to the curtained section that constituted Jake's room. Once there, I hesitated; I didn't want to see Jake reduced, though once it had been all I'd wished. I parted the curtain and stepped inside.

I was sure I'd gone to the wrong room, the room of some frail white-faced old man who lay with his eyes closed, overpowered by all the machinery—the tubes, the oxygen, the catheter—that tied him to the bed like a spider's web. So changed was he that I had to verify his name on the doctor's chart.

I sat down by the bed and put my hand on his. Then I bent my head to my hand and silently cried.

He tried to speak. It was just a whisper. "Hi, Podner."

"You're going to make it, Champ," I said.

Jake gestured weakly at all the equipment. "Saving me for Sessums."

At the thought, the life seemed to drain from him and he closed his eyes. For the rest of my allotted time I sat watching his pulse, weak but steady, on the ECG.

A few days later he stabilized and they moved him to a regular room. Our spot was taken in the waiting area by a Vietnamese family, and Mom and I set up camp in his room. She spoke to me now, just essentials like, "Tell the nurse his drip is almost empty," but I was thankful for even that.

One night, late, I awoke from a shallow sleep to see Munger standing in the hallway, just looking in, a bloodless appraising look. Determining Jake's chances. Before I could stand, he was gone.

I finally went home, for a shower and change of clothes. The doctor had said, guardedly, that he would make it. He wouldn't say how much of him would be left.

A dog always returns to its vomit, and the reverse is also true. While Jake slowly recuperated, I received notice that State v. Wittenhurst had been reset for trial for late February. Even as I steadied Roger, I braced for State v. Cameron, set at Jake's insistence for just eight weeks after. My schedule, once so uncluttered I could've vanished for a full term of court and no one in the judicial system would've noticed, now rivaled that of the most ambitious super-associate at the downtown 300-man lawyer mills.

I visited the hospital in the mornings and spent most evenings there. Mom was speaking to me again, if somewhat formally, and as long as Jake was improving, I didn't have to maintain a suicide watch.

"Wittenhurst?" he asked regularly. I kept my case reports sparse, fearing he'd rise up and charge back to the office, trailing tubes.

"Coming up fast."

"Don't know if they'll let me out." At first I was afraid he was serious, that the stroke had affected his mind, but then I detected a sardonic half-smile.

"I'll break you out," I proposed.

"Don't let Turnage fuck it up," he instructed.

"I can manage that myself," I told him.

I didn't tell him about the firm. Ginger had her resume out. Wendy was gone, quitting without notice the same morning I apologized for taking her to bed. And Turnage was no longer making any show of being Jake's hire.

"Morning, fuckup," was how he now greeted me.

"Morning, dickhead," I returned.

"Gettin' any?" he asked. Turnage's eyes were red-rimmed and hostile, and I could smell last night's sour beer on him, all he had to show for another worthless evening at the F & M.

"Too busy," I said and tried to push by, but he stood in front of me like a lumpish schoolyard bully.

"I'll bet you are. You and your daddy ever do a threesome?" I paused, my muscles tensing, then edged on past; Turnage was again my second chair on Wittenhurst.

Munger had assumed control of the firm, though he abjured any overt sign of it, keeping his old spot at the side of the conference table. Jake's chair remained at the head, pushed tightly to the table.

"I've interviewed several candidates for the two associate positions," Munger began the 7 a.m. firm meeting, his second that week.

"As I recall, there were objections to expansion," I said.

"Those have been resolved."

With Laura dead and Ginger betrayed and Turnage co-opted, no one occupied Jake's camp except me, his former enemy. In small ways Munger encouraged me to leave the firm. Myrt was reassigned to Turnage. The cleaning crew was told to skip my office. Firm meetings were held without notice to me. All typical Munger—secretive, oblique, nonconfrontational.

Secretly, obliquely and nonconfrontationally, I began to rifle Munger's files and computer for evidence of a link with Laura.

One night late, I walked upstairs to Jake's office, as I often did. It was always restful there with the tall windows and the stars seeming to fill the room. In the winter silence I could almost think that none of it had happened, that Jake would step through the door, whole, and reclaim what Munger had taken.

This time I saw no stars. Tall shapes blocked every window. My hand shot out to turn on the light. Storage boxes from the firm's overcrowded dead files room were stacked halfway to the ceiling. Munger, who would never move directly into Jake's office, was simply replacing him with ancient history.

Every day at the hospital, I asked the nurse if he'd had any other visitors. The answer was always no. No lawyers from the firm, none of his former friends and colleagues. The only thing visited upon Jake was the sins of his son.

I'd thought Evan would've come. When his father died when we were in college, Jake had more or less adopted him, having him over for dinner constantly, going sailing (he was hopeless), once even taking him to the Sugar Bowl without me. Remembering those times, and knowing how much Jake would brighten to see Evan, I called him.

It had been an unspoken rule of our friendship that I never come to his restaurant, see him "in servitude," as he put it. But after three unreturned phone calls, I broke that rule, as I had all others, and reserved a table in his section at Jolie's, one of the smaller gems in Joshua's crown.

"I recommend the menhaden," Evan said when he finally came over. Menhaden was a tiny, greasy trash fish used in chicken feed.

"How about just a couple of minutes of talk?"

"I'm a waiter, not a whore. What'll you have?"

"Redfish Joshua." The highest priced item on the menu. I then ordered the most expensive wine on the list. Another waiter brought the wine, which went untasted, as did the redfish, which could've fed a family in China or wherever people led simpler lives of simpler miseries.

"Jake's been at Touro since December," I said to Evan the next time he passed. "I thought you might go by and see him. It would make him feel good."

"You mean make you feel good." Since we'd last talked, Evan's little aphorisms had soured into sermonettes.

"He always liked you."

"He's your father. Just because you never did him right, don't expect me to take up your slack." He started away, to tend to less demanding diners.

"Who anointed you saint?" My hand snaked out and grabbed his arm, pulling him toward my table. It was a testament to his balance or years as a waiter that the full tray he was carrying didn't topple to the floor.

"How about just desserts?" he said, and neatly tipped my plate of redfish into my lap. He did it so gracefully that no one noticed.

"I came here as a friend," I said, ignoring the sodden mess soaking through my pants.

"You won't leave that way."

"It's not my fault she didn't love you," I said, half-rising, the $50 redfish falling onto the $50,000 Persian rug, my hand still gripping his wrist.

"No, she doesn't love anyone now." And he did something with his hand, freeing it, then damn near breaking my wrist— all this while still balancing the tray in his other hand— then left me there, the center of my own circus.

When Charlie Dumaine caught me later that night at the hospital, I thought to ask her the question that had played off and on in my mind for eight years: how, on the night she broke up with me, had she found out about Alison and her college goodbye party?

"Your friend called me. I can't remember his name. The one who disapproved of me."

So Evan had betrayed me, couldn't have done otherwise according to his damn philosophy, which didn't even require him to feel bad about it that night I'd cried on his shoulder over Charlie Dumaine.

At my apartment that night I removed Evan's novel from its locked drawer and wrote a cover letter to Jake's publisher friend at one of the large trade houses in New York. Jake had gotten his son, down for Mardi Gras, out of a potentially nasty statutory rape situation with just a few phone calls. It never made the papers, the record was mysteriously cleared, and the father remained deeply grateful. I'd offered to ask Jake to intercede with the publisher to get Evan's novel to the top of the stack. But Evan the pure artist refused, determined for his masterpiece to make it on its merits or molder and be posthumously discovered by subsequent, more enlightened generations.

I was reasonably confident that Evan's book was publishable. I also knew he wouldn't be able to refuse an outright offer, even though he'd know with inescapable certainty how it came about. Wherever his career took him, it would always lead back to me. Evan the pure, the disapproving, the independent, would be compromised. At 11:59 p.m. I Fedexed his manuscript to the publisher.

I would not say I slept well, but I didn't sleep badly.

I managed to get to the office a little after nine, late enough to reinforce Sessums' notions of my laggard existence but in time to receive his second phone call of the day.

"Hope the Wittenhurst trial date isn't too inconvenient," he said in a tone of faux-concern. "You must have a rough schedule." It was our first communication since Jake's continuance, and it seemed a gratuitous one.

"Just serve the subpoenas," I told him.

"They've already gone out." I started to hang up but felt a hesitation at the other end, the screw he'd called to tighten. "Philosophically speaking, Kyle, and I'm out of my element here, you ever think about how things work out for the best?"

My taking his slot at Cameron & Munger apparently was still as sore as the day Jake had sent him the letter concluding, "We know you'll find an excellent position elsewhere." Sessums must've thought Jake was good as dead to bring it up.

"Philosophically, Ray, I think society needs its civil servants. Great benefits, I understand," and I hung up, because Roger was on the other line, having just received his subpoena. For months he'd awakened every morning, forgetting for a moment that it hadn't gone away. After that moment passed, he spent the rest of the day in the house with curtains closed.

"Hope your father's better," Roger muttered when he came into the office. In the weeks since I'd last seen him he looked to have foregone all nourishment, surviving on nothing but air and adrenaline. "What do we do now?"

"Get ready."

In the days remaining I met with him every day, and when I wasn't micromanaging Turnage to make sure this case was his priority, I was drilling Jenna and Conrad Couvecor until they were as dependable as little human tape recorders. I took Roger to the gym and dragged his sorry, skinny butt onto the racquetball court, where he stood like a scarecrow with a racket but at least worked up a sweat.

Three days before trial, I got a call from the court clerk's office. I heard the familiar voice of Amy Harris, deputy clerk, a willowy black woman not much older than I but possessing an unshakable calm and utter immunity to my pirate's smile. Once we'd established the parameters of our relationship (none), she'd treated me with the same good-natured competence that every other lawyer received, but, I was convinced, just a bit more warmth.

"Kyle, I don't know if this is good news but Mr. Deputy D.A. Sessums has gotten a continuance until Tuesday."

It wasn't good news. I was ready. I might never be this ready again.

"Based on?"

"'Conflict' is what it says on the order."

"What's the real reason?"

"This office can't say."

"What does this person say?"

"Shake you up, throw you off your stride. That'd be my guess. Unofficially."

I hung up. That sanctimonious bland-faced bastard, in bed with that vodka-pickled little crab of a judge. Another weekend to nurse Roger through. At this point our rehearsals were in danger of diminishing returns.

On Monday I got another call from Amy at the court. "Continued for two more days."

"More 'conflict'?"

"'Illness.'"

My calls to Sessums' office went unreturned. Roger was so terrified he was becoming almost incoherent in our rehearsals so we just sat in silence. By the end of the second day, I'd lost my focus and a good bit of my nerve and was beginning to hope for another continuance. We waited for a call from Amy. Then I heard the six chimes of the antique grandfather clock in the reception area. Usually its deep chords were a reassuring evidence of constancy in the world, but today they meant that the court clerk's office was now closed. Trial was set. I looked across at Roger. If my eyes mirrored his, Sessums had accomplished his goal.

The next morning I watched the dawn make its way up Saint Charles Avenue. In the previous forty-eight hours I'd slept perhaps four. By 7:00 I shook Roger awake from his fetal doze on my rug.

"It's time, Podner," I said.

The phone rang.

"Continuance!" Roger cried hopefully.

"Clerk's office isn't open yet," I told him and picked up the phone.

"How's my favorite news item?" It was Charlie Dumaine.

"Too busy for you," I told her.

"Then you haven't heard."

"Heard what?"

"Oh, this is exciting. Speaking only as a journalist, of course. As a person, it's just one more confirmation of the crappiness of the world."

I didn't say anything, not allowing hope to come out from the rock I'd put it under months ago.

"What is?" I asked, keeping my voice as level as I could.

"Mamie dropped the charges."

"What?" I said stupidly.

"She started wavering about a week ago. Sessums kept putting off trial while he worked her. But, as of thirty minutes ago, Mamie and her mother took off in a chartered jet for Antigua. Do I have an exclusive?"

Roger had gripped my arm so hard his nails were puncturing the skin. "What? What?" From my pole-axed look he must've thought he'd been sentenced to death, the trial phase having been skipped altogether.

I had enough presence of mind to cover the phone. "Mamie dropped the charges." That Charlie was accurate I had no doubt; she would never willingly deliver me good news.

Roger did a bizarre little dance, jumping up and down and then kissing me, jumping again, kissing me again, making strange little cries.

"Do I have an exclusive?" Charlie insisted.

"Hell, yes," I said, half to get her off the phone and half because she deserved it. "Here's your quote: 'My client is, of course, gratified'—Roger was now doing side straddle-hops--'and his father's faith in him has been vindicated. I hope that all parties can blessedly get on with their lives without further recourse to the legal system.'"

"Not you, though, Kyle," she noted.

"No, not me," I said, and hung up.

I was happy for Roger, who continued dropping by the office a couple of times each day, unwilling to wean himself from my relatively steadying influence. As for myself, the place in my heart where celebrations were held had been shut down and boarded up.

I found myself thinking at odd hours about Mamie. I remembered her parents shielding her outside the courtroom—just as I'd tried to shield Jake not two months before—and thought she'd have some long days and longer nights ahead, and wondered, as I had with Laura, whether her lover had been worth the price.

Jake had started physical therapy, but it wasn't going as well as the doctors had expected and they finally told me he'd never walk again without a cane. After a particularly painful rehab session, I sat in the hospital room with Mom while Jake slept.

"How's he doing today?" I asked.

"The same," she said. Then she surprised me.

"What about you, Kyle?"

She looked up at me, the anger in her eyes gone, replaced by the concern that had encompassed and protected me as a child.

"I'll live."

"No matter what you did, or what you do, you're still my son."

I nodded.

"Don't let them take him away," she said.

I nodded again, suddenly unable to speak through the pain in my throat.

"Will you stay with him while I go home to change?"

"Of course."

She left but not without kissing me on the forehead, and the lump in my throat dissolved into tears. When I looked up, Jake was awake.

"Your schedule's gotten slack," he said.

"Got any work for me?" It drew a smile.

"Anything I can do for you? Any way I can help?"

"I'm in good shape," I lied.

"Don't bullshit a bullshitter."

"Good a shape as you."

"I'll give you that."

A nurse came in and changed a drip. One part of me realized she was a good-looking woman, red haired, creamy skin.

But it was just a reflex, and, when I felt her eyes on me for a brief questioning moment, I didn't turn and she walked out.

"I want to ask you something," Jake said, and his eyes were turned away. "Don't answer if you don't want."

"What?"

"You ever think about her?" It was the first time he'd brought up Laura since the stroke.

"Every blessed day."

He nodded, and I didn't need to ask him his thoughts.

Later that day I was in the steam room when Ben opened the door and handed me a message from Myrt. Through the vapors I read, "Come back now," and I knew what it was.

The certified letter from the Office of Disciplinary Counsel was on my desk, neatly placed in the center, with my other mail—all rendered irrelevant if the news were bad—stacked off to the side.

I picked the letter up but was unable to bring myself to open it. As long as it remained sealed, I thought irrationally, I was still a lawyer. In my mind, I'd already bargained the outcome: I was willing to trade total exoneration for a public reprimand. That way I could still represent my father.

But I couldn't. Effective immediately, I was disbarred.

I could petition for reconsideration, I could appeal, but in the meantime the order would remain in place. As April Cahill knew, appeals took a long time, longer than Jake's trial, longer maybe than his life.

I thought I'd better sit down, feeling as I did as if every inner shred of tissue and bone had been in one instant sucked out, leaving only my outer surface, skin, hair, a protuberance here and there—to travel the days and nights. No one but me would know the difference.

There was a hesitant tap at the door, and Myrt looked in. When she saw my face, she closed the door, as if pulling a sheet over a corpse. She knew this went beyond "I'm sorry."

Disbarment seemed extreme. I was, in truth, guilty only of having sex, at least in the Cahill case. But there were other cases, other retributions to be exacted, and the arrow, though misdirected, had found its rightful target. Under that view, this end was begun long ago.

"Tough," said Jake when I told him, masking in that monosyllable the sympathy he knew I wouldn't want. My mother's mouth had tightened at the news, and she'd closed her eyes.

"We'll appeal," Jake vowed from his wheelchair in the study. But as a former Bar president, he knew that initial judgments almost always stood, and we both knew he had to get another lawyer, one who wouldn't reject a doomed case at the eleventh hour. Eight had already turned me down. Two—Jake's friends—had said to call back if Jake could wait for a year.

At work Munger was gracious, telling me to take my time clearing out my office but requesting that I remove my license from the wall. I stored it, not at my apartment but for some reason in my childhood bedroom closet, along with my other artifacts.

I went to check on Dad, and Mom, daily but spent most of my time at my apartment. I didn't really want to go out, and I settled for the sake of simplicity on delivery pizza.

I had some money saved; despite my other excesses I was not utterly profligate. My desires had been fairly easily met before, and now I had no desires, an even less costly proposition. One day I'd have to find a new career, but what? I could try writing but what was there to write about? I could travel but there was nothing to see. With my genes, I had sixty years to go, though heredity can be circumvented.

From Alison, of course, I heard nothing.

I didn't watch TV, knowing how my disbarment would be served up by Charlie Dumaine. Since the national media had already developed a taste for me, I would be franchised throughout the country. On the streets, when I ventured out, I averted my eyes from newspapers, even after reason told me I was good only for wrapping fish.

No amount of bourbon seemed to have any effect.

I went to the F&M to find a girl. I was, I told myself, a free man.

The crowd looked younger than I remembered. No one met my eye, either because they didn't know me, or maybe did. There were girls but none seemed right. When I tried my pirate's smile on one, she hurried away. Catching my reflection in the mirror, teeth bared and eyes dead, I saw why.

It was while I was losing my second game of pool, sighting my cue for a simple bank shot, that I noticed at the bar a lovely pair of legs, lovely and familiar. I made the shot, easily.

"It's yours, friend," I told my opponent, replacing my cue on the wall.

"Game's not over," he protested.

"This one is."

She didn't see when I looked to catch her eye, as I had a hundred years ago that night with Turnage, when Richard Flowers sat shrouded in carbon monoxide and Laura Niles slept unruined.

I slipped into the seat next to her, having enough sense not to attempt my smile. She glanced at me and as quickly turned away. Could she not have recognized me? She had, readily enough, that day in Felix's when she'd invited me to inspect her all-over suntan. I was the same person.

"How's that tan?" I asked, to remind her, just in case.

She turned to look at me.

"Faded," she said. "Got it?" she added for emphasis, just in case.

"Got it," I managed to say. She turned to talk to the guy next to her, some kid not more than twenty-five.

"What'll it be?" asked the bartender, who was maybe fifteen, placing a paper napkin in front of me.

"Absinthe," I said, getting up. My chair was immediately taken. I walked away. "Absinthe."

Fifteen hours was the limit, I found, of how long I could sleep in a day. The remaining nine were a problem. Two at Jake's (including travel time), one-half for pizza, one quarter for hygiene, leaving six and one-quarter hours.

I was sleeping lightly at 7 p.m., having cheated with a 3 p.m. nap, when a hesitant but persistent knock on my door drove me from my fetal bed. I had no idea who it was and an equal amount of interest.

"Are you dead?" Roger asked. "The phone's been busy for two days." I had taken it off the hook some time back. I let him in.

"God, this place looks worse than my room," he said with some alarm. With my Domino's boxes, I had out-Turnaged Turnage.

"Maid's year off," I said. I didn't have to throw on a robe because, to eliminate unnecessary transitions, I slept in my clothes.

"It's freezing," he said, twisting the thermostat dial.

Apparently somehow it had become winter.

"Here," he said, and handed me a can of chicken soup.

"Thanks," I said, tossing it on the sofa.

"Eat it," he insisted.

To humor him, I warmed it up, as he watched sentry-like. I noticed a roach skitter under one of the stack of plates in the sink. I picked up the stack and threw it in the trash. The rest of the roaches in the sink I washed down the drain with the sprayer, then listened as the garbage disposal made pate. A brief crunch then the clean slice of blade on air. Another roach emerged from a Domino's box. He darted along the counter but I corralled him with the sprayer into the sink and down the drain. A tiny chop.

"Jesus, it's boiling over!" Roger cried and elbowed me out of the way. I allowed him to guide me back into the living room.

I ate the soup. Not bad, for canned. Roger watched me with concern.

"Listen, it's going to be all right."

"In the sense that this is all an illusion. Or that it's not." I had, during my six hours of daily consciousness, shallowly explored various philosophies.

"No, really," he said earnestly.

"How so, Roger?" I asked, to be courteous. Roger, though seated right in front of me seemed very distant, as did I.

"I can't say."

I felt the vaguest tickle of curiosity. "Can't say what?"

"What I can't say." Roger no longer seemed distant.

"Have you done something stupid?" I accused, trying my flaccid version of Jake's Medusa-stare on him. God knew what half-brained scheme he'd conceived, something else I'd have to save him from.

"You're one to ask that," he said and I almost had to laugh.

• • •

"Give me a hint." It would be short work getting whatever it was out of him.

"You can't know." I hadn't seen such determination on his face since the day he told Joshua I wasn't fired.

"Eat your soup," he commanded.

To humor him, I did.

Soon I'd gotten up to sixteen hours a day with the phone off. Ginger's secretary reached me at the hospital to say Ginger needed to see me. She didn't know why.

I did. April Cahill. What else could they do to me? Revoke my birth certificate?

"It might be a civil action," Jake said, eyes closed. I'd thought he was asleep. "She could be suing the firm. Or you, individually."

I recalled something about ethical infractions not being covered by legal malpractice insurance. Jake opened his eyes and looked at me.

"What else?" I asked, sensing an undropped shoe.

"A felony charge," Jake said reluctantly. It clicked with horrible certainty. Counseled by Charlie Dumaine, April would obviously seek criminal as well as civil retribution. We'd pass on old Highway 31 to Angola Prison, going opposite directions.

Only my mother's virtually physical restraint kept Jake from going with me. I was totally alert for the first time since my disbarment.

I shambled into the firm in tennis shoes and trench coat, a hoodie obscuring my face. Munger stared at me like I was one of my cockroaches crawling back up out of the drain. Turnage shook his head in wonderment. Ginger firmly escorted me into her office. I searched her face for sympathy but didn't find it.

"You look like a derelict. Not to mention smell." Those daily quarter-hour hygiene sessions had become optional. In

France they bathed weekly and at Angola never if they were smart.

"What happened?" I demanded.

"Who the hell do you know?" She handed me a legal document. The words just swam around on the page, so she translated.

"Our Motion to Reconsider was granted. For the first time in known history. Leland Upshaw changed his vote."

Judge Flowing Mane? "What does that mean?" I asked witlessly.

"That means it's two to one."

"For me?"

I've spent the morning at the Bar. They're scrambling over their rules, and Teresa Levault will appeal, but—"

"I'm undisbarred?"

"So it appears."

"I guess your strategy worked after all," I ventured.

Here she favored me with the most suspicious look I'd yet received from her. "Or something else worked. Any ideas on that, kid?"

Before I could protest that I had none, she stopped me. "I don't want to know. With you, I never want to know."

"This deserves a drink," I proposed, knowing Ginger kept gin in her drawer. It was no more than eight hours to cocktail hour.

"Maybe it does. Not you." She looked at me. "How's Jake doing?" she asked, unable to strip the feeling from her voice.

"It's not over yet."

"That's the spirit," she said and hoisted herself out of the sofa. "Not till the fat lady sings. Speaking of whom." She ungently patted her broadening hip.

"You still look great."

"That's why I never should've put you on the stand. You can't lie worth shit."

"I might surprise you."

"Nothing would at this point."

When the phone rang that night at 4:13, I felt a surge of terror that my father had died.

"Can you meet me somewhere?" Roger whispered.

"Why?"

"It's important."

"Come over here." It was cold out.

"Too suspicious."

I looked at the clock. 4:14. "Why now?"

"Less suspicious."

At that hour only a few tables at the Cafe du Monde were occupied, by hard-core partiers stoking up on caffeine before making another run at Bourbon Street. I ordered coffee and beignets, suddenly hungry and remembering I hadn't eaten that day. Roger appeared at the entrance, wearing a bizarre outfit of pajamas, a Burberry raincoat and flip-flops.

He strolled with deliberate casualness to my table, carrying a paper sack. He placed it on the table midway between us, as if we were Cold War spies. It was definitely plenty cold on the outdoor patio where Roger had insisted we sit.

"Leland Upshaw changed his vote," I said as soon as he sat down. He nodded, unsurprised, though nothing had appeared on the news.

"Why?"

"I don't know."

"You said you couldn't tell me, not 'I don't know.'"

"I can't tell you what you can't know."

"How'd you know everything would be all right?"

He looked at me with mild frustration, as at a dog who can't master an elementary trick, like eating.

"I'll give you a hint. It's not follow the money."

And that was all Roger would ever reveal. It wasn't until the summer that the riddle, by coincidence, unfolded. On July 31—the anniversary of my dinner there with Laura—I drove back to Mosca's. Inside, I recognized two familiar faces at a discreet back booth. One face and one head of hair, actually. The sylph-like Asian hostess from Jezebel's infamous opening night—now equipped with collagen lips and salt-water breasts—sat beside Judge Flowing Mane, feeding His Honor dripping Oysters Mosca with her fingers.

Joshua had made the match, clearly; that was out of Roger's reach. I well knew what Flowing Mane followed. It had been my lodestar all my life.

It was near dawn when I got back from Café du Monde with Roger's package. Inside was a DVD.

She was so young, if I had known her then I could've, what, saved her?

She was with two men. I felt fiercely angry, at the men for touching her, at myself for watching the tape, then when I saw her twine her leg around one of them—at her. Another girl, even younger, stepped into the frame, her eyes hazed with drugs. Joshua was a possessor of child porn, a felony even in Louisiana, and Roger at his mistrial had learned that he who possesses inculpating information may rise up and do what he will.

"Maybe it'll help," Roger had said at the Café du Monde. "Joshua had to have shown it to Munger."

At first I couldn't believe he had the caginess or nerve to out-extort his father. Later, when, like his brothers, he got his own restaurant, I could.

I cut off Laura's tape. In the bathroom I threw up, beignets, then bile, then nothing.

Of course the investigator had found no one, of course no one had come forward with information. Anyone who recognized her would've implicated himself as a child porn buyer.

I stared at the tape, cold and black as my gun. That morning, undisbarred, I'd resumed Jake's representation (I was, he now knew, his only option) and the tape might be evidence, if I could bring myself to use it. But I knew already I would. Laura was dead, Jake was alive. I'd just about made the transition from human being to lawyer.

I examined my end-game strategy. Of course, the end of the game is not the time to originate that strategy. Having seen the tape, Munger would've used it to his advantage. But that would be a motive for Laura to kill him, not the other way around. Still, all I needed was reasonable doubt, and, as I'd shown with Ginger, I didn't care who supplied it.

I had no proof of anything. The only person who might was the woman I'd seen Laura hand an envelope full of cash, the other woman on the tape, Sarah Loretta Lugar.

It was dawn when I pulled up at her old apartment. A mound of old newspapers littered the doorstep, a month's accumulation of cat shit around them. The smell was almost paralyzing. I knocked and knocked. She could've moved five times since my last visit.

I'd given up and was threading my way through the brown minefield when her boyfriend, Wayne, opened the door, wearing nothing but stained jeans that hung, just barely, from his butt. It was probably the first time daylight had struck his face in weeks. Our initial mutual dislike had ripened since my first visit.

"Is Sarah Loretta home?" I asked, like a high school suitor.

He looked at me with, what? jealousy? Finally, he deigned to answer.

"Yeah. She's home. Wherever that is. This ain't it. They moved out last week."

"They?"

"Her and her crazy momma."

"Where'd she go?"

"All she said was, quote, 'Fuck you, I'm gone, I hit the jackpot.'"

When he saw the disappointment on my face, he smiled, suddenly lifted. "You were in way over your head, pal," he said. "So was your daddy."

By this time I was already at my car, and he really wasn't worth the effort of raising my voice, so I just said it to myself. "So was she."

It was later that morning that I found on my doorstop, in an unmarked box left by an unknown demon, another of Laura's movies.

When they finally released Jake from the hospital, it was one of those wet March days with ceaseless sheets of almost horizontal rain, when the bayous overflow their banks, and you realize again why everyone in New Orleans is buried above ground.

Mom waited at the wheel of her sensible Mercedes as the nurse wheeled Jake to the car. Despite the covered entranceway, little lashes of rain attacked us like swarms of insects. The nurse and I helped Jake into the front seat. He was so light.

"How's it feel to be back in the world?" I asked, determinedly upbeat as Mom pulled out in the rainstorm.

He didn't answer. My mother took his thin hand and covered it with hers. "He'll be better once he gets home."

The doctor said that with rehab and diligent work—Jake knew no other kind—he'd be out of the wheelchair in a month, onto a four-pronged cane, then to just a cane. His speech was only slightly impaired and the doctor was uncommitted as to whether that could be remedied. He was similarly uncommitted—I was not meant to hear this but walked into it from the hall—as to the return of Jake's sexual function.

"You gave us a scare, Champ," I said, trying to keep the car from subsiding into funereal silence. "They had you hooked up to everything but the TV cable."

"Sessums call?" he asked unexpectedly. In fact, he had, just as we checked out of the hospital.

"He said he was concerned about you getting out in the weather."

Jake smiled faintly. "Like Death Row. They make sure you stay alive before they make sure otherwise." We listened to the pounding rain the rest of the way home.

I battled Jake's wheelchair for a full five minutes in the garage until I got it to stay open, then held his golf umbrella over him as I pushed him to the porch. My mother had no raincoat, having given half her closet away when the Garden Club called for contributions, so she took over the umbrella. I backed Jake to the bottom step, about to leverage him up, at which time he determined to help me by standing. We were all dripping a steady stream when I finally wheeled him into his old study, converted by Mom to his bedroom. Predictably, he refused to lie down.

"I need work, dammit. I'm no good to anyone without work." He wheeled his chair to his old desk, but after almost two months' absence, there was nothing for him to do.

"I'm going to the office tomorrow. Damn this rain or I'd go today."

"The doctor said at least a month." This was a gentle lie on my mother's part. What the doctor had said was that perhaps Jake could work half days after his trial, but nothing strenuous—and absolutely no courtroom work.

Jake whirled to face me. "Fill me in."

I'd evaded his questions about the firm while he was in the hospital, but now I figured that if I didn't treat him like an invalid, he might recover more quickly. I simply refused to credit the doctor's limitations; the doctor didn't know Tiger.

"Munger hired two new associates. Ginger and Turnage voted with him. They start in the fall."

He nodded and turned his chair back to his empty desk. A minute later he let Mom persuade him to lie down.

As the March rains wore on, I vaguely perceived bits of confetti riding the wind, caught wisps of melodies from saxophones and trombones, and smelled cinders from night paraders' flambeaux. Beads collected on rear view mirrors, drunks collected in archways, beggars collected whatever they could. Rich and poor drank and danced together in the streets and jostled over throws, trinkets and trash.

In years past Jake had maintained a standing reservation at the Royal Orleans for Mardi Gras. With our suite as base camp, we would range out to the various balls and parties that were my mother's birthright. The holiday—exuberant, public, extravagant—was as trying for her as it was invigorating for Jake.

When I was young and Jake paraded on Mardi Gras Day, Mom and I would sit in the Rex Krewe's stands and wave to him to throw us beads and coins from the float. Elevated above us, in white satin and sequins and plumes, he seemed like a Roman god to me when I was small. Once, he tossed Mom a real necklace, gold and amber, to show off her fine blonde hair, and when I was in elementary school he tossed me new silver dollars.

Mardi Gras brought the death of winter, the advent of hope, the sprouting of seeds, a second chance. But the year after Laura's murder, for us, Mardi Gras passed unnoticed and unremarked upon, as Thanksgiving, Christmas and New Year's had done. The Roman god of my childhood had been reduced to hobbling across the den floor as he tried to relearn to walk.

"Your mother is the first priority," he instructed me one day as he forced his traitorous body across the floor. As his trial approached, we were talking less and less of the case and, at his insistence, more of what would happen if he should lose.

"Of course."

"She'll want to stay in the house. It'll be too much for her alone."

"I'll move back in."

"The back hallway has its own entrance. You'll have your privacy."

"This is premature. Even worst case, your appeal will take months, hell, years."

"I won't last years in prison," he said undramatically. He stumbled and edged himself into a chair. "Hell with it," he said, letting the cane clatter to the floor.

"Money shouldn't be an issue," he went on. "Just don't let Munger cheat your mother out of her proceeds from the firm."

"I won't," I said, not bothering to modify my answer with a conditional "if."

"My father," he continued, referring to a list. Jake visited him once a week, sometimes more, though Grandpa no longer recognized him or anyone.

I nodded; I would carry on the visits. We were far beyond the conditional, or even the foreseeable, and into the inevitable. It felt like he was already dead and I was already mourning him.

"Just family at the funeral."

"Alison?"

"She's family."

"St. Alphonsus." He paused. "The family plot, of course." Unuttered was his preference, to be buried next to Laura.

After each item on his list but one had been checked, he asked, "What about you?"

"Law's a jealous mistress."

He nodded. I was glad I could give him a tiny satisfaction. He folded his list then. "I'm tired," he said suddenly. "What time is it?"

"9:00." It was just after 7:00.

"A day's work," he said, and forced himself up. I watched him pummel himself across the room to his bed, taking a full minute to traverse ten feet. Then I picked up his file and stayed there, working at his old desk until after midnight.

I sat with Mom for a few minutes. Lately, I hadn't seen many martinis, and she'd started back cooking to make Jake's salt-free meals.

"We're going to win, aren't we?" she asked.

I couldn't bring myself to tell the truth. "Yes."

"You've just got to."

It was after midnight when I heaved open my garage doors, gun in hand, and started up the stairwell, dark except for a patch of moonlight at the top. Looking up, I saw a flash of thigh. A woman in a short black skirt was sitting on my doorstep. My heart slammed once in my chest. It was Laura, in the black outfit she'd worn to the Demimonde. For a moment all I'd done was rolled away from me, and I felt the longing that had never abated.

I took the stairs two at a time, then slowed at the top. Sarah Loretta, scraped clean and made up, smiled, Laura's smile from the grave.

"Sisters," I realized. What had I needed, a family tree?

"Aren't you the quick one? You're so smart, Kyle."

I let her in. Hadn't I been searching for her, along with three of the best private investigators in the state?

Inside, she looked all around, fingering my clothes, picking up my family photos, avid, like an animal familiarizing itself with a new home. Incongruously, I thought of the mounds of cat shit in front of her house and was suddenly nauseated.

"I've got something I bet you want, Kyle," she said in a parody of coquetry. "Tiny little ole thing. About that big." She held her fingers about two inches apart in the area of her crotch. It took me a full five seconds to realize she meant the tape from Laura's deck of cards.

"Where is it? What's on it?"

"Not so fast, Kyle. I'm in charge here."

"You want money?" I said, suddenly uneasy. "I've got money."

"No, baby. That's not what I want."

She turned, striking what on Laura would be a sexy pose.

"How do I know it has anything I need?"

"You know it does." Like her sister, she seemed to be years ahead of me.

"I saw your movie."

"Lucky you." She smiled and waited. I kissed her. That was what she wanted. Her breath smelled like smoke, corruption and death.

In my bedroom, I performed. The tawdry red neon from the street striped my back like lashes. I'd slipped a long way since that night when I formed my plan to steal Laura, and I could see no end to it. After an eternity, possibly longer, I said, "I'm tired. I've got to stop."

"I know better. You can go all night."

The connection between sex and death—the theme of one of Evan's recommended readings—had never seemed closer, nor the one so preferable to the other. Afterward, as I stared up at the ceiling, Sarah Loretta ran her fingers along my cheek. "Laura always got what she wanted. From day one. I got her hand-me-downs." She stroked my hand-me-down hair.

"Tell me about her," I said, sidetracked and unable to help it, trying to keep the need out of my voice.

And, propped up on one elbow, cigarette lit in a mockery of afterglow, she did: her helpless mother, her dashing daddy, her plan to get him for keeps.

"Backfired," she said and laughed. Apparently it was an old joke, one that Wayne would've found endlessly amusing.

I looked up at her. I knew not to ask but this was my only chance.

"Did she care anything about me?"

She laughed again, another funniest thing.

"Where's the damn tape?" I said, angrier at myself than at her.

"Under the doormat." I put on a robe—Sarah Loretta curled naked in my leather reading chair, watching sardonically—and popped the cassette into my dictaphone. The voices were indistinct, and only after several playings was I able to reconstruct it.

"What do you mean you can't go through with it?" one man yelled. "Trial's tomorrow, goddammit!"

The other man was almost crying. "I can't do it. I'm just no good at lying."

"I'll get you through it. It's what I know how to do."

"I'm confessing. I don't have to say anything about your involvement." Richard Flowers was pleading. "I swear I won't, Tommy."

"You `swear'?" Munger responded. "I'm supposed to believe you when you've been lying about the books for three years?"

"I swear to God."

Then Munger's tone shifted. "Let's work this out over a Scotch, Richard. We've been friends too long. You deserve to fall off the wagon. I'll get you home."

There was a long pause, and the next sound on the tape was Jake, coming into Munger's office to offer his condolences over Flowers' suicide.

The "rogue-employee" strategy that Munger would adopt in the Trust Life trial required that the uncooperative rogue, Flowers, be dead. Voice-activated, likely placed under Munger's desk. Laura must've hacked through dreary miles of tape before uncovering her diamond.

Sarah Loretta snuggled into my chair like her scrawny cat.

"Did Munger know Laura had this tape?" I asked her.

"Consultations cost extra," she said.

It was a windy March night, cold for New Orleans, and we had the lake all to ourselves. I grimly tacked as far from shore as I could get. Sarah Loretta leaned back with a bottle of

Cakebread. As on the first night with Laura, we sailed past the mansion of the Farbers, now solvent.

"I just love to sail, don't you, Kyle? My daddy never took me though." Had Laura told her everything? I imagine they'd shared a good laugh over my little plan.

"Talk," I said.

"Somebody gave Munger our movie. It's a collector's item, you know."

"And?"

"Take off your shoes, sugarpants."

"He was blackmailing her, right?"

She smiled at her apt pupil and pointed to my shoes. I took them off.

"He said he'd tell Jake."

"Unless?"

She pointed to my shirt. I took it off. It had to be fifty degrees out there.

"Unless guess," teased Sarah Loretta.

"Did she?"

No answer. I took off my pants without her asking.

"Of course."

I felt sick. That son of a bitch.

"Did Munger know she had him on tape?" I pressed.

Sarah Loretta pointed to the water.

"It's too cold."

"Do you want to save your daddy?"

I dove in, moving my arms and legs furiously to keep from freezing. In the moonlight, Sarah Loretta slowly stripped off all her clothes and jumped in. She surfaced near me, apparently immune to the cold, either from drugs or garden-variety psychosis.

"Did Munger know?" I stammered in the freezing water.

She smiled and crooked her finger. I had less than a week before trial. I went under.

In that vile lake I began reparations. For each girl I'd never called again, for every Wendy, for Charlie, for Alison—for Laura--part of me was exacted, like Shylock's knife nicking out bits of flesh.

Much later, on the boat, Sarah Loretta, towel wrapped around her, brushed out her stringy hair.

"Course Munger knew," she said, as if nothing had intervened. "She played that tape of him, and his worm shriveled right up."

"So he had motive."

"Seems like there's lots of people with motives." She looked at me, with Laura's illusionless eyes. "But you'd know all about that, wouldn't you, Kyle?"

She was right, of course. The night after our long, silent flight back from Cozumel, Laura had called.

"I'm coming over." That was all she said. I didn't even ask when she'd arrive. Three minutes later, as I was stepping out of an anticipatory shower, she buzzed at the gate, and I threw on clothes and clanged down the stairs. She smiled when she saw my wet hair.

"That was quick," I said.

Another condescending smile, at my nervous banality.

Inside, I offered her the red and white wines I kept on hand for her, or Pellegrino, or cappuccino, or frozen Stoli, or her absinthe.

"Nothing," she said, sitting on the edge of the sofa, her perfect knees, tan from Cozumel, pressed together. "This won't take very long at all."

"What?" I asked but I already knew.

"It's over. And, please, no contact at work." She stood to go. "Understood?"

"Not understood. I won't accept it."

Impatience flickered across her flawless face. "You really have no choice." I could see her mind was elsewhere, that I was just a minor unpleasant errand, like replacing an old hose at the gas station

"But I love you." I'd never told her and knew better now.

"I don't love you. Not that it wasn't enjoyable. In its own way."

God help me, even then I cherished the offhand compliment.

"He'll never divorce my mother. He knows it would kill her. She tried to kill herself before."

"Oh, I know. That's what kept him there. Till you pried him loose."

She held out her left hand; on it shone an antique emerald engagement ring.

"You used me."

That garnered a laugh. She gave me a cool kiss on the lips, and I was powerless to stop her.

"You're not even human."

"I'd watch what you call me, Kyle. Because we're alike. And I don't like myself very much. So you can guess how I feel about you."

She opened the door.

"We'll have you over for a family dinner sometime," she said by way of goodbye.

As the sailboat rocked in the choppy water, I felt Sarah Loretta looking at me. In the clouded moonlight, the resemblance to Laura was striking. No doubt Laura had told her sister about Mexico as well as everything else.

No one knew we were out here. She was thin; I could snap her neck quickly and in one swift movement she'd be overboard, taking with her the knowledge of my humiliation, and any other inconvenient information she might have. I'd lose a potential witness, but everything she had was hearsay anyway. I had the tape, and I knew very well what I was capable of. She started to stroke my cheek again, then stopped when she saw my eyes. I knocked her hand away and made myself tack hard toward shore.

The recording was the first evidence I had against Munger, but it was utterly irrelevant to Laura's murder and, as hearsay, doubly inadmissible in court. I spent the days and nights at the office researching how I could use the tape. I was so frustrated, I was almost tempted to ask Munger, a procedural whiz, for his advice.

The only possible way in was through the back door, by getting Munger to contradict the tape under oath. It might then be admissible to challenge his credibility—and the jury could make whatever it wanted of it, including motive to kill Laura. I'd be relying on Judge Barber's forbearance for what could kindly be called a novel approach.

It was after 2:00 a.m. one night when, as if conjured, Munger appeared outside my office. "Refreshing your recollection on trial procedure, Kyle?"

I immediately clicked off the Louisiana evidence cases on my computer, switched on a moronic computer game and started to play, not bothering to turn around.

"My door was locked," I told him, demolishing one of the rocket invaders.

"I have the key," he replied, and when I did turn, he was gone. I bolted the door. His chilly presence lingered like ectoplasm.

I looked into the parking lot. His hearse was still parked in the shadows. If he was trying to wait me out, I was a marathoner in sleeplessness. A half hour later I looked out the window and he was gone.

Leaving the hallway lights off, I felt my way to the dead files room. I unlocked it with my master key, then stood in the dark for several moments, listening, as if Munger might be coiled down there.

I went down a narrow stairwell and locked the door behind me, turned on a light—a lamp, not the overhead—and pulled down the two cartons marked "Richard Flowers: Notes." They were sealed but I had tape upstairs.

I sat on the floor, slit the seal with my key, and began, glancing back once or twice at the door. Skipping the typed transcriptions, I reviewed Munger's handwritten notes, searching for something admissible that linked him to Flowers' murder and thus to Laura's.

I absorbed page after punctilious page, including a paralyzing discussion of Trust Life's accounting procedures, which I forced myself to decipher. Compelled by terror of defeat, Munger always recorded every detail of every case. That same thoroughness also made it unlikely I'd unearth anything. But then no one had expected Melorette to be wearing the murder weapon around his neck. Immersed in my reading, I didn't hear anything—the key being inserted in the lock, the lock slowly turning, the footsteps moving toward me.

"What exactly are you doing?"

When I turned, Munger's face was white as paper, the same mask of fury Richard Flowers must've witnessed the night before he never testified. I'd guessed that Munger had killed before; I now saw he could again.

"Looking for evidence," I answered.

"Of what?" He took a step toward me, his hand in his overcoat pocket. His expression became calm and somehow much more frightening. I could almost read his mind—a suspicious noise, rifled files, a burglar, a shot, a terrible mistake.

"Evidence of what?" he repeated.

"That you and Richard Flowers were lovers," I said with bold certainty. I watched his face, saw it relax slightly.

"What precisely were you going to do with such evidence?"

"Impugn your credibility, obviously. Jake found out is my guess, wanted you out, so you got him out instead," I explained, extemporizing wildly, my face smug with certitude. "Then," I added to cap my thesis, "when Flowers killed himself, you and Turnage got it on." This last, I feared, might have been too much, but his estimation of my ineptitude was boundless.

"Very devious and intricate," he observed with almost a smile, and he removed his hand from his overcoat pocket. "And did you find any support for your theory?"

"Not yet," I said, easing up the stairs. "Not yet."

"I wish you luck, Kyle," he said as I reached the door.

"You keep it, Tommy," I said, using his first name for the first time in my life.

Wearing my trial suit, I helped Jake, bundled against a spring drizzle, into the Jag, as protective as I'd ever been toward Mom. His voice was weak, the right side of his face partially frozen, but somewhere inside there was Jake, and I thanked God for every vestige of him. After all the months off, I felt as nervous as the first day of his trial when I'd stuttered through my opening argument. Way, way deep, I could feel panic bucking up inside me, trying to break out.

"You know how Munger works," Jake said as soon as I got in the driver's seat. "He'll keep saying he doesn't recall. He'll say it a million different ways. The only way to get the audiotape admitted—

"—is to get him to lie about what he said." We'd been over it a thousand times. And during that thousand times, I'd seen something I'd been able to deny until then: along with everything else, the stroke had taken something of Jake the lawyer. Only I would've noticed the slight hesitation before an idea would coalesce and find voice, the failure to grasp some nuance. As far as the trial went, it didn't matter; all Jake would have to do was sit there. It would be up to me to deal with nuances and everything else.

"The throat," he reminded.

"I've learned that much."

"But first the balls," he added, and I was glad to see that much life in him.

Then we were back in the courtroom. All were in their places, Sessums, Judge Barber, the jury, as if they'd been waiting inanimate all this time.

There'd been some changes. The gardener had grown a beard, making him look Biblically judgmental. The woman interested in "crime in all forms" had lost about thirty pounds, as if, denied her manna, she'd withered away.

Sessums also looked different. Was it anticipation at pocketing two Camerons with one shot? No, it was something more tangible and much more significant. His hair bore no evidence of his wife's shears; the cut was sleek, making him look almost cosmopolitan. Damned if he hadn't grown a well-trimmed goatee. He also wore a new suit, of the four-figure variety favored by the pampered members of Cameron & Munger. Was he dressing for the anticipated media attention once he secured his odds-on victory (40-to-1 was the current betting in the Irish Channel if there were any takers)?

Sessums looked over and nodded pleasantly. His tie was the same color as his shirt, the monochrome look Munger affected as if to camouflage himself. I felt the not unfamiliar feeling of stupidity for failing to see it before. When had it started? After Munger quit as Jake's attorney, or before? No matter. When Charlie Dumaine delivered Ana Lopez, Sessums would've started measuring Persian rugs for his move to Cameron & Munger. Make that Munger & Sessums. I recalled my clever remark on the phone to him about civil servants and imagined his smile as he set down the receiver, took a sip of tap water and gazed upon his wife's artistry. Perhaps he'd want my office, to decorate with her daubings.

I was beyond prepared, closer to paralyzed. I remembered Jake when he had a marathon trial, pushing himself past exhaustion for weeks on end. As a child, I always wondered how he did it. I never thought I could do it. I never thought I would be proud to be like Jake.

My searches and researches were over. Sarah Loretta had disappeared into the underside of New Orleans of which she formed a seamless part. Munger was all we had.

"Did Laura Niles know your client, Richard Flowers, who died in his garage only two months before her murder?" I asked him.

"Not that I recall." A lie, unprovable. Flowers had been in the office at least twice a week for months.

"Where were you the night he died?" He had to be wondering when I was going to suicidally careen off into my affair-with-Richard-Flowers theory.

"We worked on his testimony at the office until around 11:00." He knew, of course, that the firm records showed him leaving at 11:02. "Then I went home," he added gratuitously. Also unprovable, since he lived alone.

"Did you have anything to gain if Laura Niles died?" A softball, to get him to commit.

"Nothing. The law firm lost a good employee."

Now it began, the minefield of answers and objections and responses that I would have to negotiate to hang Tommy Munger.

"No? Didn't Laura Niles try to blackmail you with evidence that you murdered Richard Flowers?" That got the jury's attention.

"Objection!" Sessums called out, outrage and even surprise slipping into his voice. "Irrelevant. Mr. Munger is not on trial."

"It goes to his motive, your honor." I knew—Jake had drilled it into me—that in a murder trial, judges will allow virtually any kind of defense, even, I was banking, Munger's hitherto unmentioned motive to kill Laura.

Judge Barber looked both exasperated and intrigued. "I'll allow a brief expedition down this trail," she said finally. "Brief, Mr. Cameron," she emphasized.

"She did not try to blackmail me," Munger answered, without allowing me to repeat the question.

"Did you ever threaten to tell Jake about her pornographic movies if she didn't have sex with you?" Another two-by-four in the face for the jury.

Munger managed to look offended. "If such exist, I didn't know about them. We wouldn't have hired her." He'd answered as I'd hoped he would, with more than a simple "no." He felt so comfortable that he could afford to refute any slurs on his character.

Now my gambit. My eyes were confident, my nervousness betrayed only by one tapping finger, my Nola gene. I held up a blank sheet of paper.

"What if I told you I had video records to the contrary from Big Easy Videos, which is located precisely one block from your downtown condominium?" Posing as a connoisseur, I'd discovered Big Easy had three videos featuring Laura. Munger would've been thorough before he confronted her; he also would've enjoyed seeing her multiple degradations before degrading her further. Obviously he wouldn't have checked them out under his own name. When I showed his photo to the clerk, he said he couldn't give out customer information. But I saw recognition on his face, and Munger didn't know how much I knew.

He leaned forward and looked right into my eyes. "I'd say introduce them into evidence. If you had them."

"Are you aware of the consequences for perjury?"

"Objection."

"Sustained."

All as expected. The jury now knew about Laura's tapes, Munger's opportunity to see them, and the possibility that he'd blackmailed her. That gave Laura motive to kill him. The reversal would be the trick.

Jake coughed, his signal to ask for a recess. I hesitated. It would look terrible, leaving the jury to mull my apparently failed gambit. Jake had only reluctantly agreed to the porn tape line of questioning, arguing it was too tenuous, but I suspected his real objection lay in sullying Laura's name. He coughed again, a signal I'd promised to honor.

"Your honor, may we have a brief recess?"

As she granted my request—no doubt thinking it was the most sensible thing I'd uttered today—Munger, I noticed, watched Jake's halting steps with imperial pity.

In the witness anteroom, Jake didn't sit, just hobbled to the window and looked out at the rain.

"We didn't need a recess," I argued. "It's under control. Going as planned." And it was. I'd put the idea in the jury's minds. I'd just have to get the momentum going again and hope Judge Barber would give me enough rope.

"We're down to the lick-log, Kyle. We've got to get that tape in. There's no margin for error."

What the hell was he saying?

"I'm taking the wheel, son. I'm going to bring it home."

Nothing had changed, even after all this. Evan had gotten it right. We were who we were, and all that remained was for us to play out our appointed roles.

"Why are you doing this?"

"It's not your fault, it's mine. Your mother and I made things too easy for you. We never made you grow up. A man doesn't overcome that in a few short months. It takes a lifetime."

And that was our script, just with words put on what we'd always felt and known. Jake started toward the door, slowed by his cane.

As I watched him, I felt the old rage pumping malignantly through my blood. All I had to do was not say anything, let it proceed as ordained. I knew with the certainty of clairvoyance what would happen. Jake—if he didn't have a stroke outright—would attack like a wounded bull, unaware how much his strength had waned. Munger would play him, while Sessums pierced him with objections, until Judge Barber cut off the line of questioning. I would watch from the gallery. I remembered once again Charlie Dumaine's observation about my motives.

It was not until he was at the door, many seconds later, that I spoke. "These last few months have been a lifetime. Like war. Except the enemy's been sitting right next to me."

My father turned to face me. "Why was I the enemy, Kyle?" His eyes weren't angry, were something else, and I remembered—or maybe just imagined—how he'd looked, still young and whole, riding the merry-go-round with me at Audubon Park.

"Because you never once thought I could do a damn thing," I told him.

"That's all?"

"That's everything."

"You hated me that much?"

"No. Can't you see that?" And that was as far as I could go.

Jake was silent.

"I'm asking you to reconsider your decision. I've looked at this case from every angle. I've lived it from the night Laura was killed. I know Munger. And he'll underestimate me just like you always have."

He looked at me, weighing me. And then he shook his head and started out the door. "I'm sorry," he said.

He'd done it again. After everything I'd said. Damn him if he hadn't. Not even Evan the pure could fault me now if I let him limp into the ring and be slaughtered. But I had one thing left to say, as long as I was veering off the script, ours and the foreordained.

"Then you leave me no choice."

He stopped. By now he was too aware of what my capabilities were.

"Than to do what?" he said, still not looking at me.

"Confess."

That brought his eyes to me.

"They'll believe it." And they would, as Jake knew. The mountain of my motive put his in shadow.

Now Jake was in a truly impossible position. My death or his. He closed his eyes. When he opened them, I could see I'd won. As I opened the door, he put his hand on my arm and looked at me. How familiar those dark blue eyes were.

"I'm your father," he said. It was a last appeal for mercy in case my motives were twisted.

"I'm your son," I answered.

Munger was sitting just as we'd left him, composed as a corpse. He revealed no surprise at my return, nor any pleasure. Perhaps he didn't care, felt confident he could defeat either of us. None of that mattered to me. All that mattered was making him contradict the audiotape.

"Did you offer to buy Richard Flowers a drink the night he died, a supposed suicide from carbon monoxide in his garage?"

"Objection," Sessums stood. "We are orbiting past Pluto on this, your honor. It's a disservice to this court, and if I may say so, to his own client."

"Your concern is noted, Mr. Sessums. Approach." Judge Barber's normally choleric nature hadn't been improved by the delay. As we stood at the bench, I could see Jake anxiously watching.

"Where are we going, Mr. Cameron?"

"Mr. Munger provided very damaging testimony against my client earlier. We have the right to challenge his credibility."

"He's tried and failed," Sessums interjected, accurately.

"Only inconclusively," I said. "I'm asking you to give me a chance to really fuck it up."

Sessums looked at me, amazed. So did Judge Barber. But I'd guessed she might go for the unorthodox approach. "This is a capital case, your honor," I reminded her, in case the unorthodox approach needed bolstering.

"The rope I'm giving you is so short you couldn't walk a cockroach," Judge Barber informed me.

As I turned, I managed to give Jake a nod imperceptible to anyone else. Instead of returning to the podium, I stood by the witness stand, though proximity was more likely to intimidate me than Munger.

"Did you offer to buy Richard Flowers a drink?" I asked.

"I don't normally recall social chit-chat months after the fact."

"You don't recall? You weren't aware, after representing Mr. Flowers for over a year, that he was an alcoholic?"

"I don't recall being aware of that fact, if it is a fact."

"Did Mr. Flowers want to change his testimony?"

"I believe he voiced some concerns," he said without hesitation, the Mozart of ambiguity.

"Did he say he was confessing about the company books?

"He had some concerns that his figures could be misinterpreted. I don't recall his exact words."

Sessums rose. "Your honor, I renew my objection. This is a fishing expedition."

"Your hook remains empty, Mr. Cameron." She knew as well as I that we could be up here all day as I smashed myself against Munger's impermeable surface. I heard Jake cough.

"One more question, your honor."

"One." I heard a note of finality in her voice.

All or nothing. I put Laura's unlabeled microcassette on the rail between Munger and me. He looked down at it.

"You tried to persuade Richard Flowers to perjure himself, didn't you?"

Munger paused, sensing the trap. "Not that I recall."

"You're saying it's possible you suborned perjury, which as you know is a felony?"

"Your honor!" Sessums cried. "That's two questions."

"It's the same question. I was merely asking for clarification."

"This is it, Mr. Cameron. You may answer, Mr. Munger."

"Possibly he misunderstood my advice."

"Did you pressure him to lie on the stand? Yes or no."

"Objection! That's three. He's out."

"Amplification, your honor," I implored. "He's never answered."

"Mr. Munger will answer the question."

"Not that I—"

"Yes or no," I harried.

"Answer the question," ordered Judge Barber.

Munger looked at the tape, then leaned forward and stared at me, just as he had with the nonexistent porn shop document. It was 99-1 that I, reckless and incompetent, had nothing more than a blank cassette fresh from Best Buy.

"No."

There was a short, ugly session in chambers, after which I introduced Laura's tape into evidence. Judge Barber gave a slight smile, her first, and I pressed "play."

"What do you mean, you can't go through with it? Trial's tomorrow, goddammit!" the tape played for the jury. Professionally amplified, it was quite clear.

"I'm just no good at lying," said dead Richard Flowers.

"I'll get you through it. It's what I know how to do," suborned Munger.

A look of vengeance, angelic in its purity, would've suffused Laura's face as she listened.

"Let's work this out over a Scotch. I'll get you home."

I and, I hoped, the jury could picture Richard Flowers driving home, weaving along his neighborhood street, and beside him, holding his drink in a paper napkin, Tommy Munger.

Munger, on the stand, for once was neither composed nor inscrutable as I clicked off the tape.

"The tape is evidence of the fraud, the perjury, the murder. Three reasons you had to kill Laura Niles."

"This is absurd. Hypothetical. Taking the jury down a lot of winding dead-end roads."

"They're not dead-end, Tommy. They all lead to you."

And, having duly called a forensic expert to authenticate the voices and to testify that Laura's fingerprints were on the cassette, that was what I stressed and pounded and hammered in my closing argument. I'd caught Munger suborning perjury and showed he very possibly murdered Richard Flowers. It was a leap from there to murdering Laura, but he had clear motive and access to Jake's ring and, most importantly, he had lied.

Sessums toured every inch of that leap, stopping to revisit unpleasant attractions along the way, such as Laura's DNA, Jake's fingerprints, his motive. But in the end—and it was a very long end, a three-day deliberation—the image of Munger and that fatal little microcassette was enough to create reasonable doubt, first in three jurors, then seven and finally all twelve.

As Mom clutched Jake, her life and life-support, and well-wishers crowded around, I felt no exuberance, only relief that my ruinous plan had exacted no further toll.

Turnage was the first to reach me, his allegiance shifting like the San Andreas. "Damn, Cameron, you pulled that one out of your ass with a fishing pole."

Charlie Dumaine stood alone, for once not shrieking questions, just watching. Our eyes met by chance and held for a long second that went back ten years. Then she saw Sessums and hurried after him. It had been less than a minute since the verdict, but he was already almost out the door, his face as tightly closed and inexpressive as his new designer briefcase.

I looked at my father. I no longer hated him for winning Laura's love. We daily drew the same barren breath. He looked at me, something new in his eyes. "Blood will tell," he said.

I held out my hand. Instead he hugged me. And I was five years old again, holding onto the carousel horse at Audubon Park with my father right behind me so I'd never fall off. I had a sudden image of him running alongside, tireless, vital, as he yelled, over and over, "Ride 'em, Tiger." Then I was back in the courtroom, as he clapped me on the back, over and over. He was so thin, I hadn't realized how thin.

It's awkward for two men to hug, even father and son, or especially this father and son, and we let our arms drop. Impulsively, I kissed him on the cheek, something I don't ever remember doing, and I saw tears in his eyes.

"Blood will tell," he said. "Blood will tell."

Blood Relations

Edward Cohen and Kathy Cohen

EPILOGUE

ON CHRISTMAS EVE OF THE FOLLOWING year, I sat in Jake and Nola's living room as the family opened gifts by a majestic tree. Alison cuddled next to me on the sofa. She'd taken me back, we were married, and she was six months' pregnant.

Tommy Munger was in Angola Prison for Richard Flowers' murder. Under the spotlight of Munger's testimony, eyewitness evidence placing him at Flowers' murder scene had surfaced. The D.A., reluctantly, hadn't indicted him for killing Laura, though in the court of public opinion he stood convicted of that as well. He'd been sentenced to death, lethal injection, although his well-crafted appeals would, I was certain, keep him alive for quite a while.

Evan went to Hollywood where he died of encouragement. His book, fast-tracked to publication, was on its way to cult though not critical success. He wrote the screenplay, several drafts of it, before it was given to another writer and turned into a teen sex comedy. He then became known as a teen sex comedy writer. He bought one of those shark-faced BMW's and the same night drove it off the Santa Monica cliffs onto Pacific Coast Highway, doing it, with his usual consideration, at 3:00 a.m. to lessen traffic tie-ups. Under Evan's philosophy, his end or one very like it was inescapable, as was Jake's, as was mine. Had he left a note, he might've said that, like his hero John Kennedy Toole, his mistake was trying. But his error was in being my friend. Like a forgotten mine detonating long after the war is over, another of my plans had worked all too well, and this one hadn't even worn the camouflage of good intentions. I'd known what I was doing when I sent that manuscript, not the particulars, perhaps, only that I wished him ill and that ill would find its ingenious way to him.

A few days after his death, I received a postcard depicting a near-naked girl on a beach and his curious final message, "Who laughs last?" Evan now occupied a small crypt in my mind, which I visited late at night when I found myself defenseless.

Per Jake's directive, the firm was now named Cameron & Cameron, though Jake almost never came in, much less tried a case. Business had increased in spite of or due to our notoriety. Ginger had joined another firm, then allowed me to beg her to come back. Somehow Turnage had talked me into letting him be the baby's godfather. I was now quite the successful young lawyer. Though not yet thirty, I looked older and was de facto firm head. I wore wire-rimmed glasses, a reminder of my increased responsibilities.

I almost never drank any more, but this Christmas was a special occasion and I raised a toast to Jake. Contrary to his hopes and daily sessions with a rehab therapist, he hadn't progressed from the four-pronged cane. He'd given me the black Jag, but I left it in his garage, wanting it to serve as his inspiration or at least his fantasy. He toasted my wine with a glass of water. At his feet lay Gumbo, an ancient dog now.

"Like old times, Son," Jake said, almost without irony.

"Like old times," I repeated, as if it would make it so.

Jake swallowed a medication with his water. Mom would be angry, but I said, "Got a new case in this week, Dad. Dead husband, live wife, 9-1-1 calls coming from both."

His eyes quickened with interest. Fiercely protective, Mom shook her head no to me, but I pretended not to see.

"We need you back for this one, Champ. I put you down as counsel of record." I had, as if that too would make it so. His spirit was willing but not the rest.

"You can handle it. You're on a roll."

"Not like the way you can do it. Think about it." I was not going to let it die. Tomorrow he might feel stronger, with something to get out of bed for.

"Here," I said, "open your present from the firm."

I put the wrapped gift near him on the table. Jake pulled at the fine foil wrapping, but he couldn't get the damn ribbon off. Why had they wrapped it so elaborately? We all stood there watching him fumble at it with his stiffened fingers until finally Mom couldn't stand it any more.

"Get some scissors, Kyle. There's a pair in the kitchen drawer."

But they weren't there. Mom had redecorated to make the house more accessible for Jake, and no one could find anything. I remembered the scissors in her sewing box and went to get it from the dining room cabinet. There on top of the buffet was the cloisonné vase I'd bought for her fiftieth birthday, the night I learned about Laura and my father. I opened the sewing box, saw no scissors, so I lifted the top tray.

Raising a gauzy shroud of my mother's delicate work, I stared at a snapshot of Laura. Wonderingly, I picked it up, taking off my glasses to look closer.

Underneath the photo, like a grisly insect collection, was a news story of Laura's murder, a key to her house, a lock of her hair, her emerald engagement ring. And there was a bottle of RTV rubber compound and a copy of Jake's wedding ring. My mother's little museum.

As I picked up the ring—it was identical to the one on Jake's finger—I felt the presence of someone else in the room. I turned to see my mother, watching me. She looked totally self-possessed; more, she looked pleased, even gleeful, like a very clever child.

"I know it seems a bit ghoulish," she said. "I'd meant to throw it away but I just couldn't." She smiled. Look what I did, her imp-like smile seemed to say. And you all thought I was so helpless.

"You killed Laura?"

"She needed to die." No smile now, just the unexpected determination I'd seen the night they arrested my father. He hadn't killed Laura. Until that moment, I hadn't known for sure.

"Sarah Loretta called and told me about the affair," Nola continued, happy to exhibit the handiwork she could show no one else. "She was tired of Laura ruining people's lives." Nola gave a little grimace. "Where do these people come from?"

"Did you want Dad to be convicted? Is that what it was, to punish him?"

"Don't be stupid. You'd have confessed, if it came down to it." She looked at me. "Am I not right?"

I was silent.

"Anyway, your father never loses. I did have to make it seem hopeless though, so he'd know how much he needed me, by his side. The way he does now."

She looked into the living room. I could see Jake walk haltingly with his cane to stand by the fire. His wandering days were over.

"Of course, I thought Tommy would be trying the case. He's very good. Poor Tommy." Here she sighed in what almost seemed genuine sympathy.

I set down my wine glass before I dropped it.

"Yes, your taking over was quite a setback," Nola reflected, and I saw she could still wound me, more even than Jake. Though thin, she looked much stronger, a woman who would undoubtedly live into her nineties with her mind utterly clear and unshaded by doubt. I could cancel my suicide watch, or rather, I could switch it to my other parent.

"I wish I could've testified," she reminisced. "If I could've pulled it off...." She shook her head at the glory that would've been. Her voice suddenly sharpened with remembered impatience. At me.

"After that, Lord, I had to feed you clues. I paid Sarah Loretta half your inheritance for that little tape. She insisted on delivering it. I don't even want to think why."

She spoke so cavalierly, so uncaringly, that it seemed she'd turned into an enemy.

"Sarah Loretta helped you kill Laura."

"Good Lord no. Do you think I'd trust that little drug addict?"

From the living room, I could hear a buoyant Christmas song from the radio. "What's taking you two so long?" Jake called in, querulously. Nola waved cheerily back at him.

"But you're not strong enough to pick Laura up and move her to the bed." The lawyer in me had to keep asking her questions. The son wanted to curl up on my bed in my old room upstairs, except she'd turned it into her office.

"Adrenaline," she said. "Some women lift cars off their babies."

"I loved Laura. Didn't you care? You're my mother."

She looked vexed. Not angry, just irritated to talk about a subject that really didn't engage her.

"Personally, I never wanted children. Or pets. It was always your father. And then came that woman. One more thing you shared."

"But you and I were the ones who were close. Always," I pleaded. "It was us against him. You know that's true."

"Don't ask for what I don't have to give," she said, with that vexed, distracted tone. "No matter what I did, he loved you."

And in that instant, with those last words, the puzzle of my childhood resolved itself into a gruesomely clear picture. All the praise that I'd done nothing to gain, the sheets of warm cookies that rewarded indolence, the understanding heart that forgave every debauchery. She had created, as best she could, someone Jake would be disgusted with, someone who could never compete with her.

Nola held out her hand for the duplicate wedding ring. When I hesitated, she said, "It would kill your father if he knew."

I handed her the ring. She replaced it in the box, closed the lid like a coffin and, walking back to the living room, put the unpleasant little moment behind her.

I saw blood trickling from my fist, opened it, and my shattered glasses fell to the floor.

I followed Nola to the doorway and stood there, watching her and Alison knitting together. Side by side, hunched over their lace, they looked like twin spiders. And it was then that I knew, be it lawyer's intuition, or son's, or lover's—

The night before the firm retreat, Laura would've come out of her bathroom wearing her nightgown. As she pulls down the covers, she hears something and whirls around.

Nola wears gloves and an old raincoat, the one she'll announce later she's donated to the Garden Club benefit.

"You little white trash thief," she says.

Not seeing a weapon, only Nola's slim form, Laura steps toward her threateningly. Then, from behind, the silver candlestick comes crashing down onto Laura's head. She moans and drops to her knees, not ready to give up.

But the candlestick crashes again, and Laura falls to the floor. Alison steps out of the shadows and strikes a final blow.

Swiftly they follow their plan. One grabs Laura's arms—Alison probably, being stronger—and the other, Laura's feet, as they lift her onto the bed.

Which one hides the candlestick under the covers? Nola, more likely, to incriminate Jake. Together they rip the gown off Laura's warm body. Alison arranges Laura's arms. All as planned. Nola spots the engagement ring on Laura's hand and slips it off.

Alison steps close to Laura, drawing back her left fist to strike her, wearing Jake's ring over her plastic glove.

"No," says the other spider. "Let me do it."

Alison hands Nola the ring, and Nola hits Laura's face. At that they stop their work, exultant. Until they hear a key turn in the front door. My key.

My footsteps clatter across her heart of pine floors, nearing. The doorknob twists, and I stand in the dark in Laura's bedroom, only my second time there. My gun is in my hand. That is when I see Laura dead, when I kneel down before her and caress her face. I replace the gun in my pocket, its purpose mooted. My lawyer would've pled insanity and been right.

In Laura's closet, Nola and Alison stare at each other, their chests heaving with panic, their faces and raincoats splattered with her blood. As they hear me leave and close the door, Nola's face relaxes as she smiles in triumph. Alison, her alter ego, smiles back. They take with them Laura's favorite dress, the gold and green, accidentally smeared red.

I looked into the dining room. Jake's gift, a statue of Blind Justice, stood on the mantle. Nola's lace tablecloth, now complete, enshrouded the family table. I watched Nola fuss over Jake, weaving him tight in her web. She tapped her wine glass, summoning me into the room.

"A toast," she smiled.

"Kyle?" In a trance, I realized Alison was talking to me. I blankly held up my wine glass.

"To family," Nola said.

Alison repeated the toast, as innocent-looking as ever. I tried to smile but I was no actor. I looked over at Jake, my only family.

I realized I'd been holding my breath, becoming light-headed, and when I looked back across the table, I saw, not Alison, but Laura Niles in her place.

"You like surprises, don't you, Kyle?" she was asking me.

"No. I like to be in control."

"No, you don't." Laura was smiling, I saw. She was right, and I'd gotten my wish.

Behind Laura, the macabre priest was making the sign of the cross, and his words from her funeral rolled over me again like the curse they had become.

"And dead will stare and sting forever."

• • •

I raised my glass to them all, living and dead, and drank back my bitter blood-red wine.

• • •

Made in the USA
Columbia, SC
22 December 2020

29559790R00231